In Their Blood

In Their Blood

A Novel

Sharon Potts

Oceanview Publishing

IPSWICH, MASSACHUSETTS

ISBN: 978-1-933515-62-5

Published in the United States of America by Oceanview Publishing, Ipswich, Massachusetts
www.oceanviewpub.com

10 9 8 7 6 5 4 3 2 1
PRINTED IN THE UNITED STATES OF AMERICA

For my playful, loving, and beamish dad,
who never doubted I could do anything.

ABRAHAM GEORGE HECHT, 1913–1999

and

In memory of my mentor and dear friend, who
touched so many with her words and wisdom.

BARBARA PARKER, 1947–2009

Acknowledgments

While serving as treasurer of the Florida chapter of the Mystery Writers of America, I was given the nickname "The Countess" for my propensity to count things. And so, here I go, once again trying to count everyone who helped make *In Their Blood* possible:

My kids, who were always there to remind me of what was truly important. Ben, when he logged onto my computer, "deleted" the text from my half-finished novel, and replaced it with an endless scroll of *Priority — Ben or Book*? And Sarah, who once wrote a short story about a demented woman, so obsessed with her writing that she stopped bathing and only sat hunched over her desk wearing a stained, torn bathrobe. Was I really that bad, kids?

Kathleen Gordon, my unofficial creative writing teacher, who taught me how to see life through the loveliest metaphors by introducing me to Vladimir Nabokov's swirling orange-peel goldfish, and so much more.

My friends, critiquers, and mentors at Mystery Writers of America, who showed me how to transform my scribbles into suspenseful, believable fiction.

Delia Foley, Jack and Marilyn Turken, and Maureen O'Connor, my cheerleaders, who never swerved in their optimism and willingly read anything I asked them to, and Mary, Alonda, and Renee, and the campers at Robin Hood Sports Camp, who checked out early drafts.

My amazing mom and mystery aficionada, Anna Hecht, who even in her nineties, can spot a plot weakness, and isn't shy about saying so.

My indefatigable agent, Elizabeth Trupin-Pulli, who read and critiqued how many drafts, Liz?

Everyone at Oceanview Publishing for their enthusiasm and professionalism, and special thanks to Patricia Gussin for leading the charge.

The instructors at the Citizens Police Academy of Miami Beach for the terrific Cuban food, gunhandling instruction, and for explaining the inner workings of a great police department. Please forgive the liberties I took in describing my fictional investigation. Any improprieties were not based on anything I learned or observed about the MBPD.

And of course, my alter ego and dear husband, Joe. Editor and sounding board. And yes, all the great ideas are his. Isn't that right, darling?

Jeez, is that everyone? Probably not, and I'm afraid I've lost count. But thank you all so much. I never would have gotten here without your encouragement, humor, and faith.

In Their Blood

Prologue

Something was off. She had the uneasy feeling of being watched.

Rachel Stroeb stepped away from the darkened portico, leaving her husband fumbling with his keys, their morose teenage daughter surrounded by a pile of winter coats and luggage.

Tall hedges and drooping palms hid their neighbors' houses, a film of dirty clouds blocking the light of the moon. But there was no sign of anyone, or anything amiss.

"Everything okay, Rachel?" D.C. called.

"I thought—" Rachel said. "Never mind. It's probably just the jet lag."

"I don't understand why the sconces aren't lit," her husband said. "I can't see a damn thing."

The darkness—that must be why things seemed out of kilter. Or maybe it was disappointment that their family was still incomplete.

Rachel returned to the stoop, slipping her arm around Elise's narrow shoulders. Her daughter tensed. Rachel understood. It had been an exhausting flight, an unproductive trip. Just the three of them had returned home to Miami Beach from Madrid. Without Jeremy.

"Here we go. Finally." D.C. pushed open the door, depositing their coats, suitcases, and laptops on the white marble floor. "I'll replace those burned-out bulbs in the morning."

Rachel flicked on the foyer light, reassured by the familiar arrangement of photos on the stippled wallpaper, the polished mahogany banister leading to the upstairs bedrooms. But the silence was unsettling. She was accustomed to the radio playing classical music, sounds of healthy family commotion. Their home on Lotus Island, where they'd lived the last twenty years, had mostly been a place of making wonderful memories.

Rachel took a deep breath and held it for a few seconds. Week-old flowers on the foyer table, and dog. No matter how frequently they bathed poor old Geezer, the smell of ripe fur like a dowager's ancient fox wrap hung in the air.

"Geezer." Rachel whistled. After ten o'clock. He was probably asleep for the night in his corner of their bedroom. Some watchdog.

Elise was twirling her long dark braid with one hand as she texted with the other. The smattering of freckles on the bridge of her upturned nose always reminded Rachel of cinnamon on vanilla pudding.

D.C. called from the kitchen. "You wouldn't believe how much junk mail we got in one week. And Flora left a note. She walked Geezer before she left around four."

"Can I go see Carlos?" Elise asked.

"Sorry, honey," Rachel said. "It's late. You have school tomorrow."

"Please, Mom. I won't stay out long. I promise." Her daughter's pretty green eyes were bloodshot, probably from crying on the plane. It hadn't been the winter break any of them had wanted.

"What's that?" D.C. said, coming in from the kitchen. Two days' whiskers covered his chiseled cheeks and chin. Jeremy had grown a beard while in Europe this past year and Rachel was taken aback by the striking resemblance between the father and son.

"I want to go to Carlos's," Elise said. "Just for a little bit."

"Absolutely not," D.C. said. "You're not traipsing over to the Castillos' at this hour."

"Fine," Elise said, eyes overflowing with tears. "I can see why Jeremy didn't want to come home." And she raced up the stairs, the slamming of her bedroom door echoing in the empty house.

"You didn't have to be so harsh, D.C."

"Jeez, Rachel. So now I have to tiptoe around both my kids?"

"You could try being a little less righteous." Rachel slipped off her new boots and stashed them in the closet, noticing blood on them from the nosebleed she'd had on the plane. Her tee shirt was also stained — three drops that looked like splattered tears. She pulled it over her head, hung it from a hook in the closet, and put on one of Elise's sweatshirts.

D.C. was pacing beside their luggage and coats. In a stretched-out tee shirt and worn jeans he looked more like one of his students than a professor of international economics. "Less righteous?" he said. "I've got a twenty-two-year-old son who's wasting his life and a teenage daughter who doesn't like restrictions. What's wrong with asking them to take some responsibility for a change?"

"I'm just saying, maybe you should lighten up. Elise is having a tough time. She's disappointed Jeremy didn't come home with us."

"We're all disappointed."

"Elise is only sixteen. She worships her brother."

"Well, maybe our daughter needs to find a new hero."

Rachel took a deep breath. Why did her husband have to be so damn stubborn?

Geezer had made it down the curving staircase, tail wagging, arthritic hind legs moving stiffly behind him. He licked Rachel's hand as she bent to hug him. "Stinky puppy," she said. "Tomorrow, before I leave, you're getting a bath."

D.C. touched his shirt pocket, perhaps hoping to find a

cigarette, but they'd both quit smoking over a year ago, at least in front of each other and the kids. "Look, honey," he said. "I'm sorry. I'm as upset as you are that he didn't come home."

Rachel picked a wilted chrysanthemum from the vase on the foyer table. "You know, Danny, deep down all Jeremy really wants is for you to be proud of him."

"Hey." Her husband reached for her. He was a foot taller than she, and his chin rested comfortably on her head. "He'll figure it out."

Shortly after eleven o'clock, Rachel and D.C. climbed into their high four-poster bed. The sheets were cool against her cheek. So much nicer than a hotel. Geezer was panting in his sleep in the corner of the room. D.C. slid his arms around her and Rachel pressed against his chest. He smelled like perspiration and smoke. So, he'd found a cigarette after all. She wondered where he kept his stash.

Rachel snuggled closer to her husband. In twenty-five years of marriage, there had been a few bumps and missteps, and this one, too, would pass. He kissed her hair.

Before they went to bed, they had taken Geezer for a walk around the island. When they returned home, Rachel had been surprised to get a text message from Elise. *Please don't be upset with me, Mom. I'm over at Carlos's for a little. He promised to walk me home.*

And Rachel had been furious. But then the anger seeped out with her fatigue. Maybe their restrictiveness was what had pushed Jeremy away from them. Just this once, she'd let it go with Elise.

A key turned in the front door. Rachel glanced at the clock on the night table. Just before midnight. Elise had to get up at six thirty for school. She'd be exhausted. D.C.'s breathing was deep and even. Rachel hadn't told him Elise had gone out, preferring to keep her daughter's secret to starting another altercation. She listened for Elise's light footsteps running up the stairs. Rachel always left the bedroom door open a few inches to hear her kids coming and going. What was Elise doing downstairs? The thin beam that leaked in through the crack in the open door went out. Elise must have turned off the downstairs foyer light. Why would she have done that?

There were footsteps climbing the stairs. Slow, heavy, not Elise's. Had Carlos come back with her? Was Elise trying to sneak him into her room?

Rachel sat up, annoyed. This wasn't like her daughter. She strained to see, but the room was a mass of hulking shadows. The footsteps got louder. But only one set; where was Elise?

Rachel's chest tightened. Could there be an intruder with a key?

She shook her husband. "Danny, wake up. Wake up. I think someone's in the house."

He groaned.

Rachel grabbed her cell phone from the night table and pressed the Contacts button. "G." She scrolled down to "Guardhouse."

The footsteps were just outside the bedroom door. Please God, don't let Elise come home now.

She pressed Send. It rang. Once. Twice. Come on, answer.

The bedroom door opened slowly.

Geezer grunted in his sleep.

There was a shape in the doorway. No face, just a creeping shadow. It was holding something. Pointing it at her.

Rachel heard only the blood pounding in her head. She dug her fingers into D.C.'s arm. Please, take what you want, she thought, but don't hurt us.

The shape moved closer.

Finally, a voice in her ear. "Guardhouse."

"Help," Rachel shouted into her cell phone. "Help us."

Geezer was barking hysterically, wildly.

"Rachel, get down," D.C. hollered.

The weight of her husband's body pressed against hers, protecting her, blocking her. There was a flash of light, then a deafening noise shattered the night. A blow, like a violent wind, threw Rachel against the headboard, taking her breath away.

Something warm and wet spread over her, covering her, drowning her.

"Elise, Jeremy," Rachel whispered as she faded from consciousness. "I promise I'll never leave you."

Chapter 1

Dark, cool, silent. The thick scent in the air reminded him of the fresh flowers his mother always kept in a vase on the foyer table.

His mother. His father.

Jeremy stared at the shiny wooden caskets. Sealed, the man in the black suit had told him. Their ashes inside.

Their ashes inside.

Impossible. Impossible. His parents were back in their house on Lotus Island. Angry with him. They always seemed angry with Jeremy these days. But that's where they were. Not here. Not here in this dark, cool, silent room with a smell that didn't belong. Or maybe they were at work. His dad playing big prof on campus, his mom intense and serious at the accounting firm where she was a partner. And they'd be very busy. Maybe too busy to be thinking about Jeremy. About what an idiot he'd been a week ago. But they definitely weren't here. They couldn't be here.

The room had high ceilings, drapes over the windows, rows and rows of benches. Flowers everywhere. A pulpit at the front. And two caskets. Two. STROEB MEMORIAL SERVICE, the sign outside the room had read.

"Can I help you?" the man in the black suit had said when Jeremy arrived at the funeral home straight from the airport a short while before.

"I'm, I'm Jeremy Stroeb."

"Jeremy," the man had said, his face saddening. "Their son. I'm so sorry for your loss. We held off on the memorial service as long as we could, but your uncle said your flight had been delayed. I'm really sorry, young man. But you're welcome to sit for a while in the chapel with their caskets."

With their caskets.

Jeremy touched the dark mahogany. Their caskets. Impossible. He rested his face against the cool smooth wood. He closed his eyes. When he opened them, everyone would jump from the shadows shouting "surprise!" A stupid, terrible joke. A hoax to get him to come home. But he was ready to forgive them for that.

Please, God, let this be a big terrible joke.

A hand rested on his shoulder. Jeremy jerked up, expectantly.

The man in the black suit. "Your neighbor, Mr. Castillo, has opened his house to anyone wishing to pay their respects. I'm sure your family's waiting for you there. I've asked my limo driver to take you. Whenever you're ready, of course."

The man was being very nice, and it made Jeremy's throat close up. He didn't know what he should say, even if he could speak. Thank you for your kindness, but you've made a mistake?

The limo stopped at the guardhouse at the entrance to Lotus Island. It had been a year since Jeremy had been home and things looked different. Darker and greener, somehow. The flag was flying at half-mast. They did that when one of the island residents died — lowered the flag. His father used to joke that it was a signal to the real estate agents that a fresh property would be coming on the market. He loved irony, his father. Jeremy turned to see if he was smiling. But his father wasn't there. Just the driver waving to the guard.

The car took a right on Lotus Circle and Jeremy was about to correct the driver, until he remembered they weren't going home. Would he ever be able to go home? Jeremy's brain was clogged. So tough to process what was happening. For the last twenty-four hours, he'd refused to think about it. His focus had been on getting home. Getting home. And now here he was.

Mansions, tall hedges, and gated driveways went by in a blur. Something wasn't right. The quiet island had turned into a carnival. Cars were parked along both sides of the street, extending back as far as the guardhouse. Several had pulled onto the grass of the bayfront park. Jeremy and Elise used to play hide-and-seek there, near the huge banyan tree they called "the grotto."

The driver continued just past the park to the Castillo mansion, stopping at the base of the circular brick driveway, which was blocked with cars. The huge ivy-covered house was just visible behind thick hedges and the tall wrought-iron gate. So different from his own house. Jeremy had never been inside this place. Enrique Castillo was a client of Jeremy's mother and Carlos Castillo was Elise's boyfriend, but the Castillos hadn't been close to his parents. So why was the gathering here?

Jeremy thanked the driver and hoisted out his worn backpack and ski jacket. The shirt he'd put on hours ago — the best one he owned — stuck to his perspiring back. The Miami air was so thick, even in January, he could hardly breathe. Or maybe it was something else.

He passed some people his age. The guys, in jeans and sport jackets, were leaning against a car smoking cigarettes. The girls, holding Kleenexes to their eyes, were mostly in short black dresses, though one wore tattered jeans and dilapidated army boots. Probably his dad's students. They eyed Jeremy as he walked up the driveway. The girl with the boots took a step toward him, a confused expression on her face. Jeremy picked up his pace so she wouldn't try to talk to him. He pulled open the heavy front door.

Harsh whiteness struck him like the flash from an atomic bomb. The walls, marble floors, baskets of lilies, columns stretching toward the domed ceiling — everything white, as though life had been sucked out of this place. Mingled voices, sounding like a record played backward, floated toward him from the rooms beyond the entrance hall. The air smelled sickeningly sweet. He dreaded going in there, receiving their condolences, seeing the awkward sympathy in their eyes.

Elise, he thought. He had to find Elise. He stashed his backpack and jacket behind a column, the abrupt movements causing momentary dizziness. How long had it been since he'd slept?

"May I help you?" The voice was deep with a hint of accent. Enrique Castillo, tall and stiff.

Jeremy straightened up.

"My God. Jeremy." Enrique Castillo held him by the shoulders. "I didn't recognize you."

"I just got in. I didn't —"

"I'm so, so sorry, Jeremy. What a shock for all of us. Your uncle said he didn't know how to get in touch with you. No address. No phone. You weren't responding to e-mails."

"I —" Jeremy coughed to clear his throat. "I was in Portugal."

"Yes. Your uncle said you finally checked your e-mail yesterday morning. That you'd be here in time for the services. But then we heard you wouldn't." Enrique stroked his silver beard. "I suggested we have everyone gather here. Your parents' house — well, you understand. It didn't seem suitable."

"I'd like to see my sister," Jeremy said, wincing at the sharpness in his own voice.

"Of course," Enrique Castillo said, "of course."

The living room was an extension of the white. Jeremy blinked from the glare of light bouncing off the bay through the French doors. He reached for the back of a chair to keep from falling. There were people everywhere, but they were backlit and their faces no more than shadows. His friends wouldn't be among them. Chris was with the Peace Corps in Zambia, and Ben was hiking in Machu

Picchu. The others he had grown apart from, and besides, they'd all migrated to New York and the West Coast. Jeremy was alone.

The dark bulk of a woman with flying blonde hair was hurrying toward him. "Jeremy. My God. You're here." Liliam Castillo squeezed his arm. "We're so sorry, Jeremy."

"Thank you." He tried to pull away, but she held fast. "Excuse me, Mrs. Castillo, but I really need to find my sister."

"Elise?" She glanced around the room. Her blonde hair covered one eye. "She was sitting on the sofa with your grandfather a short while ago. But your grandfather went home. He wasn't well. I wonder where she's gone. Perhaps with Carlos." She pressed her fingers deeper into Jeremy's arm. "He was the first one there, you know. My Carlos. He could have been killed himself." She crossed herself with her other hand. "He'd walked Elise home. He knew something was wrong as soon as they stepped into the house. And Carlos pulled Elise outside and ran to get the security guard."

"My uncle said it was a burglary. A surprised burglar who wasn't expecting anyone to be home."

"Is that what Dwight told you?"

Jeremy's heart was racing. "The burglar thought they had a gun, so he shot them. Wasn't that what happened?"

She released Jeremy's arm. "Of course. I'm sorry, Jeremy. I'm not myself. Let me get you a drink and something to eat."

Jeremy sensed a blur of movement around him. Everything surreal. It had been a foiled burglary. What else could it have been? People touched his shoulder, shook his hand, hugged him. And Jeremy nodded as they mumbled things. Told him how great his parents had been, what a tragedy, what a shock.

Right, he thought, grateful for the numbness that had settled over him when he had first learned the news. Wondering how he would survive when the numbness dissipated. Searching the room for his sister.

A stout, ugly man in a wrinkled suit and bow tie was staring at him. He looked familiar. One of his mother's business partners.

Someone was talking to Jeremy. A southern accent. "I know you must be overwhelmed," said the large man. He had a puffy face with small, alert eyes. His mother's other partner. "But I wanted to tell you," he continued, "as well as I knew your mama, I feel like you and your sister are family to me. And if there's anything I can do, you call me, y'hear?"

"Thank you," Jeremy said. "Thank you." The voices in the room got louder, softer, like someone was playing with the volume.

Liliam Castillo was hurrying toward Jeremy with a platter of food and a bottle of beer. "Here you are, Jeremy."

"Excuse me," Jeremy said. "I have to find my sister."

He pushed through the crowd. Where had all these people come from? It seemed as though they were multiplying before his eyes. Their voices bounced off the floors, echoed against the high ceilings, and reverberated in his head. He bumped into a young woman with short black hair and intense blue eyes.

"You're Jeremy, aren't you?" she said. Her eyes and nose were red. "I worked with your mother. She was —"

"I'm sorry," he said. "I really need to go." Air. Beyond the French doors, the sun was setting, covering the sky and bay with bands of pink like smeared blood. A yacht at the end of the dock rocked gently, making Jeremy queasy.

It had happened. It had really happened.

Jeremy hurried toward the water. The smell of fish and brine overwhelmed him. He puked into the bay.

In the distance, a horn bellowed. The sky had turned red.

My mother and father, he thought. My mother and father are dead.

Chapter 2

His house. The house he'd grown up in. The house where his parents had been murdered.

Not his house anymore.

Jeremy stood in the front foyer, his backpack over one shoulder, dropping the new key his uncle had left for him on the foyer table. Breathing caused a physical pain as though his ribs were in a vise. It was the first time he'd been home in a year, since he'd left for Europe. The last time, he'd also stood here, in this very spot. His mother had offered to drive him to the airport, but he told her he'd already called a cab. "I understand why you have to go, Jeremy. But remember, your father and I will always be here for you."

Always?

The house was quiet. Too quiet. "Elise," he called. He didn't think she'd come here alone, but maybe she had. He had borrowed someone's phone at the Castillos' and tried Elise's cell, but it had been turned off. So he'd left word that he was going home if anyone saw her. All he could do now was wait.

Geezer was at the top of the stairwell, tail wagging. The sight of his dog was so unexpected that once again Jeremy thought he'd gotten it wrong somehow. That it had been just a cruel trick.

Geezer hurried down the steps, going as fast as he could with his hind legs dragging behind him. He licked Jeremy's hands and face.

"Hey, boy. What are you doing here? Who's been feeding you? Walking you?"

Geezer seemed to be okay. But now he was sniffing the air, running from room to room, looking for something. For someone.

It was no trick. It had happened. But although Jeremy's brain told him otherwise, he wasn't all that different from the dog, his senses also poised to hear or see his parents in the next moment.

He was drawn to his father's office, adjacent to the foyer. A working office, with bookshelves filled to overflowing and dozens of classical cassette tapes piled high beside the old cassette player he'd had since college. When Jeremy was a kid, his dad would roll back his desk chair to see who had come in when the front door opened. Then he'd smile up at Jeremy. "So, did you beat 'em?" he'd ask, even if Jeremy wasn't coming from a game. Or even if he was, and his dad had no idea who he'd been playing against, or whether it was basketball, soccer, or lacrosse. An inside joke. "So, did you beat 'em?" But now there was no rattle of rolling wheels over the plastic floor protector.

Geezer had returned to the foyer and lain down in front of the entranceway table, his sorrowful eyes fixed on Jeremy. The vase, always filled with fresh flowers, was empty.

Jeremy carried his backpack up the stairs. The door to his parents' bedroom was closed. He couldn't remember it ever being closed. His mother liked to leave it open a few inches so she could hear Jeremy and Elise coming and going. It used to annoy Jeremy, this overprotectiveness of hers. He hesitated, his hand on the doorknob. He couldn't go in there. He might never be able to go in there.

Jeremy went down the hallway, turned on the light in his childhood bedroom, and dropped his backpack on the floor. The room hadn't changed, same deep blue comforter and navy carpet, posters from different phases of his life covering the walls — rock stars, cars, sexy girls. A collection of empty beer bottles from around the world lined the shelf above his desk. He was surprised the room was clean, dusted, but it smelled funny. Like stale cigarette smoke.

He sat down on his desk chair. This was where his parents assumed he did his homework, but mostly he daydreamed and surfed the Net. He'd gotten the big, clumsy computer when he was thirteen — almost ten years ago. It was a 600 MegaHertz Pentium III and Jeremy had thought it was the coolest, fastest machine ever. But today the machine was a dinosaur. He wondered why his parents hadn't gotten rid of it. But they were like that. They kept up with the latest in technology, but never could part with the old.

And then it hit him again like a punch to his abdomen. His parents didn't need to keep up with technology. They were dead. His mother and father were dead.

He rested his head on his folded arms, trying to block it. Trying to breathe despite this unbearable pain. *Don't focus on the negatives, Jeremy,* his mother always said. *Think about something positive.*

Positive? Oh God. Mom, Dad, how could you leave me like this?

He jerked his head up. He must have fallen asleep. Jumbled voices were coming from downstairs.

"Jeremy?"

Jeremy's heart almost ripped through his chest at the sound of his father's voice.

"Jeremy, are you up there?"

And then he collected himself. Not his father. His uncle Dwight.

Jeremy went downstairs and into the kitchen. His aunt Selma was putting platters of food and casserole dishes into the refrigerator.

"Hey, Aunt Selma." He kissed her cheek.

"Jeremy," she said, holding him tight. "Oh Jeremy." She was very skinny with white-blonde hair like cotton candy, and she had always been nice to Jeremy and Elise in the unnatural way some childless people were with kids.

"Ah, Jeremy. Here you are," Dwight said, coming from the direction of the guest bedroom. He gave Jeremy an awkward hug, pulling away quickly. "We're so sorry, Jeremy. What a tragedy for all of us. My big brother. I still can't believe it. Thank God my parents aren't alive to witness —"

"You should have waited, Dwight."

"Waited?" His uncle cocked his head. He looked like a warped version of Jeremy's father.

"The memorial services. I should have been there."

"But we did wait, Jeremy. We waited as long as we could. I had to make a judgment call. I couldn't tell when your flight would finally get in and everyone was already there." He pulled on his thin mustache. "I couldn't very well ask people to leave and come back another time."

"They were my parents. I should have been there."

"Yes, you should have." His uncle's voice rose with the same clipped intonation his father's had. "And maybe if you'd checked your e-mails. Or maybe if you hadn't gone off in the first place —"

"Dwight," Selma rested her hand on his arm. "Please don't."

Dwight pulled his arm away. "You think you're the only one affected by this, Jeremy? The only one that's suffering? He was my brother, damn it. My big brother. He taught me how to ride a bike, for chrissake. How to throw a ball. You don't think that I'm devastated by what's happened?"

"I don't know, Dwight. I honestly don't know."

"Jeremy," Aunt Selma said. "Please, honey. You don't know what you're saying. You're upset."

Jeremy was trembling. "You're right." He took a deep breath. "Where's Elise? Is she okay?"

Dwight shook his head and took a sandwich off a platter on the counter.

"She hasn't been herself," said Aunt Selma.

"She's as unfathomable as you," Dwight said. "Won't talk to us. Won't eat with us. Locks herself in the guest room or goes for long walks."

"Wait," Jeremy said. "Guest room? What are you talking about?"

"She's been staying with your aunt and me at our apartment."

"What?"

"Where did you think she was? The police only released the house from crime scene a couple of days ago. And then we had to get a clean-up crew in here."

Jeremy tried to block that last remark. "I figured she was with my grandfather."

"He can't cope with a teenager."

Damn. Jeremy had assumed Elise and their grandfather had been together. How had they gotten through this past week? "She can stay here with me tonight," Jeremy said.

"That's fine with me." Dwight threw the half-eaten sandwich in the sink.

Geezer had followed Jeremy downstairs. He sniffed Selma and Dwight, then went to lie down in the front foyer. "I wasn't expecting the dog to be here," Dwight said.

"Who's been taking care of him?" Jeremy asked.

"The housekeeper," Selma said. "I forget her name. She had him at her place for a few days, but no pets are allowed there, so she brought him back here after the police left. She's been feeding and walking him twice a day. "

"Flora," Jeremy said. "Her name's Flora."

"Of course," Selma said. There was a smudge of lipstick on her chin. "She seems like a nice person."

His uncle had gone over to the liquor cabinet in the adjacent family room and was pouring himself a glass of Scotch. "Not everyone would be willing to work at a house where there'd been —"

"Have a sandwich, Jeremy," his aunt said. "The Castillos wanted you to have this food. There was a lot more, but I didn't think it would fit in the fridge."

Dwight held up the bottle. "Want some, Jeremy?"

"No thanks."

Dwight took a sip. "Listen, Jeremy. I know you and I never got along well, but in times of crisis, we need to work together."

"What's that supposed to mean?"

"Whatever our past differences, I'm still your uncle. I want what's best for you and Elise."

"That's a bit of a change from when our parents were alive."

"Your father and I had a few issues. But that doesn't mean he and I didn't love each other. And now, I feel responsible for you and Elise."

"I can take care of myself."

"Well, Elise then." His uncle rested his glass on the counter. "We need to think about what's best for her."

Elise. Jeremy's chest tightened at the thought of her. Alone this past week. Without their grandfather. Without Jeremy.

"Tonight you'll be here at the house with her, but what about tomorrow? I need to know your plans, Jeremy. Selma and I have to make arrangements."

"I don't know my plans."

"So you don't know when you'll be going back to Puerto Rico?"

"Portugal. I was in Portugal."

"That's right. It's hard keeping up with you in your virtual world. No wonder your father was so aggravated. You don't call home. You don't respond to e-mails. Don't you think of anyone but yourself?"

"Please, Dwight," Selma said. "There's no reason for this."

"You're right. I'm sorry. I haven't slept much." Dwight ran his fingers through his thinning hair. "I've been trying to hold everything together. The funeral arrangements, your sister, the police."

"What about the police? Have they found anything? Do they have a suspect?"

"I talked to the lead detective for a bit," Dwight said. "Detective Kuzniski. Seems like a good guy. Anyway, Kuzniski says they're homing in on someone."

"Give me Kuzniski's number. I want to talk to him."

Dwight reached into his wallet and handed Jeremy a business card. "Don't take this the wrong way, Jeremy. I know how you feel right now, but there's really no point in your getting involved with the police."

"You don't know anything about how I feel."

"Sure I do. You're angry, frustrated, ineffectual. I feel the same way myself."

"Your parents didn't just get killed, Dwight. You couldn't possibly feel like I do."

"Jeremy, Jeremy, why are you fighting me? I'm not your enemy. I'm just trying to help. You'll be gone soon, then what? You think you can rush through here like a tornado, then leave when you're bored? What about Elise? What happens to her?"

"I'll work things out with my grandfather. Either he'll come live here or Elise will move into his house."

"Your grandfather?" Dwight said. "Why would you do that?"

"Because he's Elise's guardian."

"Maybe you should have a look at your parents' will."

It seemed to Jeremy that Dwight was holding back a smile, but he must have been imagining it.

The front door opened and slammed shut. Jeremy recognized his sister's voice murmuring to the dog.

"What are you talking about, Dwight?"

"Your parents entrusted your aunt Selma and me with Elise's guardianship." Dwight took a sip of his Scotch. "And we have no intention of letting them down."

Chapter 3

Elise rushed into the kitchen and threw herself into Jeremy's arms.

He held her. Just held her. He couldn't speak if he wanted to. His sister. His baby sister. "You must always take care of her," his mother had said, placing the newborn infant in his arms. It had been terrifying holding her. What if he dropped her? He wasn't even seven. How could he take care of his sister?

"Where've you been, Elise?" Dwight asked, assuming an authority that he had no right to. He was full of shit about the guardianship. Jeremy's parents would never have left Elise in Dwight's care.

Elise buried her face deeper against Jeremy's chest.

"We should go, Dwight." Selma tugged on her husband's arm.

Dwight took a quick glance around the room.

"If you kids need anything," Selma said.

"Thank you, Aunt Selma," Jeremy said.

The front door slammed.

They were alone.

"Hey Ellie." Jeremy lifted his sister's face by the chin. She had their mother's pretty green eyes. But now they were red and swollen. How long had she been crying? All week? A week all alone?

He felt a surge of anger. Couldn't his uncle have tried harder to find him? But it wasn't fair to blame Dwight. Jeremy had arranged things so he wouldn't be found.

Elise curled up on the sofa in the family room, letting her shoes drop to the floor. The leather was covered with scratches from where Geezer made his bed when they watched TV. His mother was always rubbing the marks with a rag dipped in oil, but it never seemed to help.

His mother.

Always take care of your sister, she'd said.

"I looked for you at the Castillos'," Jeremy said, sitting beside her.

"They told me. I-I ran right over when I heard you were home. Oh God, Jeremy."

"I'm here now."

"I-I can't stand being around people." The hesitation and slight stutter was something new. "So, so I went. So I went to the park. To the big old banyan tree. You know, where we used to go when I was little. 'The grotto.'"

"I remember. It's a good place to hide."

Her tears soaked through his shirt.

"I called you from Portugal," he said. "After I got the news from Dwight."

"Oh no, you did? I-I turned my phone off. I didn't want to talk to anyone. I-I didn't think you'd call."

"It's okay. I just wanted to let you know I was coming home."

"Dwight told me." She wiped her cheek. "I hate him. He keeps saying he and Selma are responsible for me now. That they're going to move into our house. But he's such a liar."

"Move into our house?"

"He said that's what Mom and Dad wrote in their wills. But, but I don't believe him. Mom and Dad would never do that to me. Never."

"What does Grandpa say?"

"Poor Grandpa."

Jeremy understood. His grandfather wouldn't have been much comfort or help to Elise. He'd be too shattered losing his only child.

"But you're staying with me now," Elise said. "Right?"

"Sure." This wasn't the time to explain that he didn't belong here. That what he'd told his father a week ago hadn't changed.

Geezer rested his head on the sofa and Elise buried her face in his fur. "He smells so bad. Mom needs to give him a bath." She stopped short. "Oh no, Jeremy." And she began to cry hard. "Who's going to give Geezer his bath?"

"It's okay," Jeremy said. "We can do it. We'll give Geezer a bath together."

She took a crumpled Kleenex from her pocket and wiped her eyes.

"Do you want to talk about it, Ellie? If you don't, that's okay."

"I, I'm afraid."

"Of what?"

"I have these dreams," she said.

"What kind of dreams?"

"A dark shadow."

"Does that mean something to you?"

"It's him. The killer. I, I see him."

"His face?"

"Just a shadow. A dark shadow. But then I wake up. And I think, ohmygod, he's coming back."

"But he isn't, Ellie. He isn't coming back."

"But, but I can't stop dreaming it."

"Maybe it would help if you told me what happened that night."

She leaned back against the sofa. One of her bare feet touched his hand. It was ice cold. "That night," she said. "I was really angry with them. Well not them. Dad, mainly."

"Why?"

"Because of the fight he had with you in Madrid. I-I didn't think you'd ever come home."

Jeremy massaged her foot.

"And I just wanted to talk to someone. To Carlos. But they said I-I couldn't go see him. And I ran up to my room and stayed there until —"

"Until what, Ellie?"

"Oh Jeremy, I'm such a terrible person. They told me not to go, but, but I didn't listen. I-I snuck out of the house while they were walking Geezer."

"You were upset. You couldn't have known anything bad would happen."

"But, but I shouldn't have gone after they told me not to. I never disobey them."

"I know, Ellie. You're a good kid. Mom and Dad know that. Tell me what happened next. After you left the house."

"I ran the whole way to Carlos's. We watched a movie, but we fell asleep. Then, when we woke up, it was very late. And I remember thinking. Mom's going to kill me." Tears ran down her cheeks. "Do you believe that? I'm thinking Mom's going to kill me."

"Hey." He pulled her against him.

"But if I hadn't disobeyed them, m-maybe I could have stopped him."

If Elise hadn't disobeyed their parents, he might not be holding her now.

Take care of your sister.

"I-I didn't say good-bye to them," she said.

"I know," he said. "I didn't either."

The house was quiet. Too quiet. There'd always been music. His father's music. How much that used to annoy Jeremy. *Can't you play something besides classical, Dad?* "Then what happened?" Jeremy asked.

"Carlos walked me home. W-we could see something was wrong. The front door was open."

"Open?"

"Unlocked."

"You mean someone used a key to get in?"

"I guess."

Jeremy's mind was racing. A burglar wouldn't have a key.

"It was dark in the house. And I remember thinking, they wouldn't have turned the lights out. They knew I was coming home soon." Elise bit down on her lower lip. "And the smell. It was so strange. Carlos said it smelled like gunpowder, and we should leave." Her eyes flitted around the room. "And then, I don't know. I don't remember."

"Liliam said Carlos pulled you out of the house," Jeremy said softly. "That he ran to get the security guard."

Elise looked at him blankly. "Is that what happened?"

"Isn't it? You were there."

She put the end of her long dark braid in her mouth. "I don't know. I don't remember."

Chapter 4

It bugged Jeremy. The door being unlocked. Either someone had a key or his parents had opened it. And they only would have opened the door at that hour for someone they knew.

But they were shot in their bed. So that had to mean the killer used a key to get in.

Then how could the police believe it was a burglary?

Jeremy had called the number on Detective Kuzniski's business card and arranged to meet him. Elise was still asleep in her room, but Flora was at the house dusting, vacuuming just like she'd always done.

Jeremy parked at a meter outside Starbucks. Several people were sitting at outdoor tables sipping their lattes on the tree-lined street — a couple of gay guys in their jogging shorts, a cute girl with a golden retriever, an old man reading the newspaper. Cars drove by. A motorcyclist revved his engine.

The girl looked up at him, then quickly turned away. It was as though she sensed his freakishness. That he wasn't one of them.

He wasn't one of them. His parents had been murdered.

There was a burst of cold air as Jeremy pulled open the door to the coffee shop. A woman with a toddler in a stroller was waiting for her order. Several people were sitting at tables staring at their laptops and didn't look up at him. At a corner table near the window, two people were watching Jeremy. The man, in his thirties, was wearing a sport jacket and had black hair slicked back. The woman next to him was older, maybe his mother's age, but she had a weathered look about her. She was wearing a poorly fitting pantsuit and was tapping her fingers against the table.

The man stood up and extended his hand. He was as tall as Jeremy, but had a good-sized paunch. "Jeremy Stroeb?"

Jeremy must have looked surprised as he shook the man's hand.

"Photos," the man said. "Almost didn't recognize you with the beard and long hair, though. I'm Detective Kuzniski and this is Detective Lieber." He gestured toward the woman. There were gray streaks in her brown hair.

"We're very sorry for your loss, Jeremy," Detective Lieber said. Her voice was gravelly, as though she'd once been a big-time smoker.

"Thank you."

"Tragic," Kuzniski shook his head. "Really tragic. The last thing we'd expect to happen in a neighborhood like yours. But don't you worry, Jeremy, we'll get whoever did this to your parents. We've got all our resources on this."

"Would you like something to eat or drink, Jeremy?" Lieber asked, putting a stick of gum in her mouth. She had a full cup of black coffee and a pile of gum wrappers near her napkin. The remains of a chocolate chip muffin sat on the table in front of Kuzniski.

"I'm fine, thanks." Jeremy sat down across from them.

"So, how can we help you, Jeremy?" Kuzniski said.

"Actually," Jeremy said. "I would have thought you'd want to talk to me."

"About something in particular?" Kuzniski asked.

"I don't know. Things like did my parents have any enemies? Who do I think may have killed them? You're the detectives. I just watch movies."

Lieber drew her head back, and Jeremy realized he sounded like a jerk.

"Look," Jeremy said. "I'm not trying to be confrontational. This whole thing — it just blows me away. Someone comes to my house and kills my parents?"

"We understand," Lieber said. "And of course we're interested in anything you can tell us that would help the investigation."

"But the good news is," Kuzniski said, "we already have a pretty good idea who did it."

"That's what my uncle said you told him."

"Dwight Stroeb." Kuzniski nodded.

"Would you mind telling me?" Jeremy said.

Kuzniski glanced at his watch, gold with a thick band. "We picked someone up near the island."

"And what makes him a suspect?"

"He had a laptop case in his car. Your father's ID tag was still on it. And he just got out of jail. Has a rap sheet about ten pages long. Armed robbery, assault, drugs."

"Laptop case?" Jeremy said. "What about the laptop?"

Kuzniski shook his head. "Just the case."

"And my mother's?"

"Your mother's what?" Lieber stopped chewing.

"My parents both had laptops. They take them everywhere they go." He paused. "Took them, I mean. They both had their laptops when they came to see me in Madrid."

"We only found the one case," Lieber said, writing something down in a small notebook.

"Was anything else stolen?" Jeremy asked.

"You know, Jeremy," Kuzniski said. "I've already filled your uncle in —"

"It doesn't look like anything else was taken," Lieber said. "He left in a hurry."

"What about the key?" Jeremy said.

"What key?" Lieber said.

"The killer used a key to get into the house."

"We don't know that," Kuzniski said.

"My sister said the door was unlocked when she came home. Did you find any evidence of a break-in?"

"No, but your parents probably left the door unlocked," Kuzniski said.

"Never." Jeremy hit the table, and the coffee in Lieber's cup sloshed over the top. "My parents would never leave the door unlocked when they went to bed."

"They were jetlagged," Kuzniski said. "It may have been an oversight."

"My parents did not have oversights."

Kuzniski glanced at his watch. "Listen, Jeremy —"

"And the weapon?" Jeremy said. "Have you found the weapon?"

"We rarely find the murder weapon," Kuzniski said. "That's just in your movies."

"But I'm still confused. You think this ex-con intended to burglarize our house, but didn't expect anyone to be home. Then he found my parents in their bedroom and he shot them. Why? Why wouldn't he just have run?"

"He must have believed they had a gun," Kuzniski said.

"But he killed them. Both of them." Jeremy felt a rush of heat. "How the hell could he have killed both of them?" The woman with the stroller moved to a table closer to them. "I mean, how many shots did he fire? It's not that easy to shoot someone and kill them. And to kill both of them?"

"One," Lieber said. "That's what Forensics tells us."

"One?"

"It just took one shot," Lieber said.

"It was a shotgun. Double-barreled," Kuzniski said. "With buckshot."

Jeremy felt like he was falling. He had kept the physical image of his parents' murder far, far away. But now, there was no escaping it. A shotgun. His parents had been killed with a shotgun. Once when surfing the Net, he'd seen photos of animals killed by buckshot at close range. Their ravaged bodies. The blood, pieces of flesh torn and thrown everywhere.

Unrecognizable. His parents would have been unrecognizable.

"Can you tell me something, please?" Jeremy could barely hear his own voice. "What kind of burglar uses a key to get into a house and brings a shotgun?"

Kuzniski stood up abruptly, almost knocking over his chair.

"Jesus Christ," Jeremy said. "You pick up some guy who happens to be driving near Lotus Island with a laptop case and a rap sheet and you're done. You've got your killer. The streets of Miami are now safe for its citizens. Children can go back outside to play."

"Mr. Stroeb," Kuzniski said, "this investigation has been given top priority. We're all working hard with the sole task of finding your parents' killer. Where do you get off, barging in here and attacking us?" He ran his fingers through his hair in two rapid movements. "We're busy people, Mr. Stroeb. We don't have time to sit around with some college punk who's watched a few episodes of *CSI* and thinks he knows more than we do. Are you coming, Lieber?"

She shook her head.

"Fine," Kuzniski said and stomped out of the coffee shop.

The woman with the toddler was staring at him. Jeremy caught her eye, and she turned away.

Why had he come here? There was nothing he could do. Everywhere was frustration. His uncle, the detectives. The sense of his own futility. It's why he'd left in the first place.

Tomorrow he'd catch a plane. Maybe he'd go to Greece. The islands. He'd always wanted to go to Santorini.

"I can imagine how difficult this is for you," Detective Lieber said. She'd been watching him. "How's your sister? I saw her at the funeral. She seemed — well, lost."

Her kindness made his throat close up. He shot a muffin crumb across the table with his thumb and middle finger.

"It must be a big relief to her that you're home now."

Jeremy pushed back his chair. It scraped against the floor. "I really appreciate you meeting me," he said, "but I'm sure, like Detective Kuzniski, you have more important things to do."

She was flattening out a gum wrapper against the table and made no move to get up. The skin on her hands was slightly wrinkled and covered with age spots.

"I understand you've been traveling around Europe for the past year," Lieber said after a while. "That your parents and sister had just returned from visiting you."

"I'm sure Uncle Dwight filled you in. Gave you an earful about the wayward son."

"Did your parents seem concerned about anything?"

"Besides me?"

"Yes, Jeremy. Besides you."

He leaned his head back. One of the overhead lights was out. She must think he was one self-centered jerk. "I don't know," Jeremy said. "They were both pretty intense people. They always seemed to have a lot on their minds."

"Tell me about them."

"Why?" he said. "Why do you care? You already have a suspect."

"A suspect is only that, Jeremy."

"So you haven't put the investigation to bed?"

"I don't like loose ends and unanswered questions."

"Thank you." He looked down at his clenched hands. "Thank you."

"So tell me about your parents."

The door to the coffee shop opened and a group of women in sweat suits and oversized designer bags came in, talking loudly as though they owned the place.

"She wasn't like that," Jeremy said, nodding toward the women. "My mother. She was classy and understated and —"

"And what?"

Jeremy's throat had closed up again. He reached for Lieber's black coffee and took a sip. Cold and bitter. "You know she was a partner in a CPA firm. Very smart, respected. Everyone liked her."

"It seems that way from the people I spoke to."

"So you have been asking around?"

"Of course."

Maybe he'd misjudged the detectives.

"Can you think of anyone who may have wanted her dead?"

"My mother? I can't imagine."

"Clients? Partners? Someone on the staff?"

He shook his head.

"She had two partners." Lieber flipped through the pages of her notebook. "Bud McNally and Irving Luria. Did you know them well?"

"Not really. I used to hang out in my mom's office when I was a kid." He thought back to the gathering at the Castillos' yesterday. They had both been there — Irv Luria, the ugly man in a wrinkled suit, and Bud McNally, a large guy with a southern accent.

"How did she get along with them? Any tension you were aware of?"

"I couldn't say. I haven't exactly been around much. But my mom and Bud started at the firm at the same time. I remember they used to tease each other a lot. Like a competition."

"Any animosity?"

He was surprised by her vocabulary. "No. It seemed good-natured."

"And Irving Luria? How'd your mom get along with him?"

"He's much older than my mom. He was like her mentor."

She waited.

"I guess they got along okay."

"And what about your father? Can you think of anyone who may have had a grudge against him?"

"He was a college professor. A harmless college professor. Shit. He even wore a jacket with patches on the elbows."

"And everyone loved him?"

"I guess. I don't know. He used to bitch about the administration. And he was always writing stuff that pissed people off. But you don't get killed for that, do you?"

"You'd be surprised what people get killed for." She turned to another page in her notebook. "Do you know his boss? The dean? Let me see if I can find his name."

"Dr. Winter," Jeremy said. "He's an asshole."

"I see. You know him."

"Not really, but my father hated his guts."

"Why?"

"I don't know. I didn't pay much attention."

She looked back down at her book. "And what about your father's graduate assistant, Marina Champlain?"

He shook his head.

"You've never met her?"

"I don't think so."

"Oh, you'd remember her if you did." She closed her book. "Anyone else we should be talking to? Anyone who came to mind when you heard what had happened?"

"I can't imagine anyone wanting to kill them." He crushed a muffin crumb between his fingers. "They were just ordinary people. A mom and dad with jobs and a family. Who kills a mom and dad with a family?"

"We'll try to figure that out. Right now, all we have is the guy with the laptop case, but we're also checking other possibilities. Lotus Island has a pretty good security system. We've looked at the records and videos of everyone who got on and off the island that night. The suspect drove onto the island around eleven p.m., then off after midnight." She took the stack of wrappers and folded them together in half, then in quarters, in a neat little package. "But the house was pretty clean. No usable fingerprints. It hasn't been easy, Jeremy. And I'm sure you can appreciate how eager everyone is to put the murderer behind bars."

"So what you're saying is it's better to have a suspect, even if he didn't really do it, than to come up empty-handed."

"That's not what I'm saying."

"It seems to be your partner's approach."

"Well, I'm not ready to put it to bed. The problem is, there's just so much information I can get from interviews. Without getting on the inside, it's almost impossible to learn if anyone close to your parents had a motive."

"Plant a mole," Jeremy said. "Someone undercover."

"Nice idea." She half-smiled. "Like in the movies. Anyway, if you think of anything else that might be helpful to us, call me." She handed Jeremy her card. Detective Judy Lieber. "And do you have a cell phone and e-mail address where I can reach you?"

He took her pen and scribbled on a napkin. "I'm not sure I can be much help to you," Jeremy said. "I'm probably heading back to Europe in the next day or so."

"But —" She closed her mouth abruptly. "I see." Then she gathered up the coffee, napkins, gum wrappers, and Kuzniski's crumpled muffin liner and threw them away. She extended her hand. "Well, good luck to you, Jeremy. Rest assured while you're busy seeing the world or whatever you rich kids do out there, we detectives won't rest until we find your parents' murderer and bring him to justice." She scowled and tapped her lips. "I believe that's how they say it in the movies."

Then she looked pointedly at the woman with the stroller and left the coffee shop.

Chapter 5

She was out of line, Jeremy decided as he drove toward his grandfather's house. Lieber had completely misread him. People did that. Assumed they knew him. That he fit some stereotype. Self-centered rich kid. But that wasn't what it was all about. It had never been that. But she figured she'd lay a guilt trip on him. Make him feel lousy about leaving. As though there was something he could do here. Like find his parents' murderer.

He held the wheel tighter. But he had no control, didn't she understand that? He had no control over anything except getting on a plane or train and going to the next place. Then the next one. Being home left him feeling ungrounded. Terrified, even.

So he'd do the one thing he was good at. He'd say good-bye to his grandfather, straighten out the mess with Dwight and Elise, and get the hell out of here.

Jeremy turned left and maneuvered through the labyrinth his grandfather's Coconut Grove neighborhood had become. Palm trees and tangled foliage clogged the streets. Nature was running away with the place. Jeremy imagined one day the houses would be completely inaccessible to humans. Just tiny animals and birds would be able to creep through the thickets.

The house was the only small one left on their street. His grandparents had lived there since before Jeremy's mother was born while neighbors came and went — each new generation building bigger and more garish houses than the ones they replaced.

Jeremy pulled his mother's Lexus up behind his grandfather's old gold Honda Accord.

The last time he'd been here was right after his grandmother had died, over a year ago. That was back last December, halfway into his senior year at NYU. He'd practically grown up in this house, his grandparents watching him when his parents worked late, occasionally with the added treat of a sleepover. So his grandmother's death had been devastating for him, but nothing compared with its effect on his grandfather. Hershel and Mimi Lazar had been like one person, always together. And after she died, Hershel could barely tie his own shoes.

His grandmother had left Jeremy some money in her will and Jeremy believed it was a message to him to get away. "You never know where you'll find your true self, Jeremy," she used to say when he was a little boy. "Never stop looking."

But she was dead. They were all dead.

The screen door creaked open. A frail shape hovered on the porch.

"Grandpa." Jeremy hugged his grandfather, almost dislodging his thick-lensed glasses from the bridge of his nose. This was the man who used to carry him around on his shoulders, throw him up in the air. His grandfather was practically bald except for a few wisps of gray hair, and his cheeks were even more sunken than Jeremy remembered.

"Come in, Jeremy."

The dark living room smelled sour, like used towels. "Would you care for something? A glass of milk?"

"Thanks, Grandpa, but I don't need anything." Jeremy sat down on the worn ottoman near the sofa.

"A glass of milk," his grandfather mumbled. His shirt was stained and misbuttoned. He'd once been a CPA with a successful accounting practice. "How stupid of me. You're a man. You don't drink milk like a little boy."

The coffee table, covered with photos and knickknacks, needed dusting. Jeremy would ask Flora if she could come here one day a week to help out. Do his grandfather's laundry.

"Are you okay, Grandpa? Can I get you anything while I'm here? Groceries?"

"I'm managing. I don't want you worrying about me, Jeremy." He closed his lips together tightly. "I was very angry with your uncle. Not waiting for you at the funeral. But he wouldn't listen to me. I talk and it's like I'm invisible."

"It's okay." Jeremy reached for his grandfather's hand. His fingers were rough and cold and Jeremy massaged them between his own. Last night he'd massaged Elise's foot. How soft it had been.

"How's your sister? Should you be leaving her alone?"

"Flora's with her. The housekeeper."

"I wish I could be more help." His grandfather took his glasses off, absently rubbed them with the bottom of his shirt, then put them back on. They were still smudged. "You're a good boy to come visit me, but you should be with your sister. I'm managing. I told you, I'm managing."

"I know you are, Grandpa. But I wanted to see you. It's been a long time."

"Well that's what happens. You young people don't like to stay in one place very long."

"I need to ask you something, Grandpa. Dwight's making up stories about Elise's guardianship."

His grandfather brought his lips together.

"Do you have copies of the wills?" Jeremy asked. "I checked at the house, but I couldn't find anything."

His grandfather picked up a photo from the table. A graduation picture of Jeremy's mother. "Who could imagine such a thing?" He took his glasses off and covered his eyes. "It's not natural to lose a child."

"I'll go, Grandpa. I shouldn't be bothering you now."

"They're on my desk. The wills are on my desk in my office." His grandfather put his glasses back on. "I'm sorry, Jeremy. I've let you down."

"What do you mean?"

"Your parents redid the wills after Mimi — your grand-mother — passed away. We had always been named guardians in case anything happened to your parents." He licked his lips. "But after Mimi left us, your parents were concerned. I could hardly take care of myself. How could they depend upon me to watch over Elise?"

"What are you saying?"

"They tried to work it out the best they could."

"But they wouldn't have named Dwight. They'd never have done that."

"What choice did they have? There are no other relatives. No close friends they could rely upon."

"But not Dwight. Not to take care of Elise. They would have come up with another option."

"You're right, Jeremy. And so they did."

"Not Dwight?"

"Their wills stipulate that you're Elise's guardian. That Dwight's the alternate only if you're unable or unwilling to serve."

"Me? But that can't be right. You said they wrote new wills after Grandma died. I was in Europe, so how could they name me as guardian?"

"Perhaps they hoped you'd come home."

Jeremy went to the window and pulled the drapes open a few

inches. A piercing light broke through. The small backyard was completely overgrown.

"You're angry," his grandfather said.

"I don't know, Grandpa. I'm not sure how I feel."

"You think they were trying to manipulate you."

A cat had wandered in from a neighbor's yard, poised to jump on something in the bushes.

"So you'll spite them, Jeremy? You'll leave your sister to Dwight because you don't want your father pulling your strings?"

Jeremy let the curtain fall back. The room returned to darkness. "I don't know, Grandpa. I don't know what I'm going to do."

Jeremy was awakened by a noise. He sat up in bed, his heart pounding wildly. It was a little before midnight. Just about the time his parents had been murdered. Was this how his mother had felt that night? Had she heard something? Recognized a threat? Or had she been fast asleep?

He hoped she had been asleep.

The noise was coming from down the hall. Not Elise's room. He got out of bed and grabbed his old baseball bat from the closet. The door to Elise's room was open. The white comforter was thrown back, the bed empty. Was she sleepwalking? Getting something to drink?

The sound was in his mother's office. Like falling papers.

The office was dark. He could make out his mother's desk, the small sofa, bookcases, scattered papers on the Oriental rug. Leaning against the base of the wall was his sister. Her hair covered her shoulders and arms like a cloak. She was bent over a clipboard.

"Hey." He swooped down next to her. "What are you doing?"

Her hand was clenching a pen, making small precise marks on the paper.

"Elise?"

Her eyes were wide open, but she didn't seem to be seeing.

The paper was filled with tight squiggly lines. Up and down, up and down. Not real writing. It was what she used to do when she was four or five while Jeremy would do his homework. She would sit at the table with him and fill up pages with tight squiggly lines. "I'm a big girl," she'd say. "I can write just like you."

"Elise." He put his hand over hers. He could feel the rhythm of her methodical strokes. "It's late, Ellie."

He gently took the pen from her hand and pulled her up. She was wearing a tee shirt and sweatpants like she always slept in. The tee shirt was stained with three brown spots that looked like teardrops. He guided her back to her room and helped her into bed.

"Good night," he said.

"Stop him," she mumbled, her voice sounding strangely similar to their mother's. "I have to stop him."

Jeremy slipped on a pair of gym shorts and tied his sneakers. Geezer had gone into Elise's room and was lying beside the bed. Just in case Elise woke, Jeremy left a note on his pillow. "Went for a run. Back soon."

He double locked the front door behind him, then knotted the key onto the shoelace of his sneaker.

Stop him, she had said. *I have to stop him.*

And what was he doing?

Jeremy jogged past the guardhouse and over the bridge that connected Lotus Island to the mainland of Miami Beach. He ran wide, avoiding the security camera, then glanced over at the guardhouse. No one noticed him. Detective Lieber had said they'd checked the security records and videos of everyone who came and left the island that night. But they wouldn't have a record of a jogger or a bicyclist. Anyone who wanted to get on and off the island without being seen could have done it. But that was for the detectives to figure out, not for Jeremy.

Stop him, she'd said in her sleep.

When he'd returned from his grandfather's house tonight, he hadn't said anything to Elise about the guardianship. He'd wait to tell her in another day or so. Let them be together without the knowledge hanging over her that Jeremy would soon be leaving.

It was unusually humid and muggy, and his shirtless chest began perspiring shortly after he started down North Bay Road. He'd wrapped a red bandanna around his head to keep the sweat from dripping into his eyes. He went from a jog to a run. Occasionally a car would pass him, but otherwise he was alone.

His sneakers pounded against the pavement. Faster and faster. His dad loved to run. Jeremy used to run beside him when he was still in elementary school. His dad would go ahead, come back, then jog alongside him until Jeremy was tired and wanted to stop. The first time Jeremy didn't need to quit was when he was fifteen. He and his father were maybe a hundred yards short of where they normally finished the run. They glanced at each other, then simultaneously sprinted toward the imaginary finish line. Jeremy's heart was pounding in his chest like it might break through, but he had kept going, faster, faster. All his focus on winning. And then he crossed the line at the same moment his father did. His father was laughing as he dropped down in the grass, pulling Jeremy on top of him. Wet, slippery chest against wet, slippery chest. He could feel his father's heart beating in time with his own. "What are you trying to do? Give your old man a heart attack?" And Jeremy remembered feeling angry. Angry that his father hadn't taken him seriously.

Jeremy was sprinting now. He'd passed Mount Sinai Hospital and was racing over the Julia Tuttle Causeway toward downtown

Miami. Cars passed him. Jeremy ran on the path beside the road, trying to catch them. Why couldn't he catch the cars?

The last time he'd seen his parents had been just over a week ago. His parents, sister, and he were sitting at a corner table in a restaurant in Madrid, but they weren't paying attention to the suckling pig specialty they had each ordered. Jeremy's dad had been livid, and Jeremy had felt a familiar frustration growing inside himself.

"We came here to keep you from screwing up your life," his father had said.

"Traveling and seeing the world isn't screwing up my life."

"It's irresponsible."

"Just because my lifestyle doesn't fit with yours and Mom's doesn't make me irresponsible."

"We just want you to come home, Jeremy," his mother said.

His sister watched him with wide, worried eyes.

"You're running away because you're afraid to behave like an adult," his father said. "Afraid to take responsibility."

"Or maybe I'm not inspired by what I see in the adults around me."

"What's that supposed to mean?"

"You've sold out. You and Mom."

"You don't know what you're talking about."

"The CPA and the college professor. You obey your masters and get big fat paychecks, but what are you really contributing to society?"

"And you are? Backpacking in a drunken stupor from one fleabag hostel to the next. That's your idea of contributing?"

"It's better than following in your footsteps."

"Fine." His father slammed the table. "If that's how you see us, stay here and rot. I'm sorry we wasted our time coming out here."

"Danny." His mother rested her hand on his father's.

But his father had pulled away. "I should have known — you'll never grow up, Jeremy. Never."

Jeremy reached the other end of the causeway. The downtown Miami skyline spread before him, but sweat stung his eyes so that he could barely see.

That had been the last time, their last exchange. He'd stormed out of the restaurant, packed his bag, and gone to the train station. He caught the next train out. It was going to Lisbon, Portugal.

He was covered with perspiration when he got back to the house. He grabbed a towel and checked on Elise. She was fast asleep, hugging a pillow. Her hair covered her face. He pushed it aside. She was moving her lips, like a baby bird waiting for food. But no mother would be coming home to feed her.

You'll never grow up, his father had said.

Jeremy went into his bathroom. He squeezed the sweat from the red bandanna and laid it out flat on the counter top. He could almost see his father's face beneath the camouflage of his own long hair and beard as he examined himself in the mirror. He had the same dark deep-set eyes, the same high cheekbones, broad forehead, flat, upturned nose that looked like it had been smashed in a bar brawl. His chest and arms were deeply muscled and defined. Although he had wiped them off, they glistened with perspiration as his body continued to cool down.

Jeremy took a pair of scissors and made the first cut. The sound of sharp metal against metal filled the small room. A lock of brown hair dropped to the counter. Then another, then another. Jeremy took the electric hair trimmer and ran it over the sides and back of his head. The top he left longer, like his father wore his. Then he ran the shaver over his face. And when the beard was gone, he could see it clearly. His father's face. He folded the cut hair into the red bandanna and tied the bandanna in a knot.

Jeremy pushed open the door to his parents' bedroom. The smell of blood and gunpowder, whether imagined or real, made him dizzy and he hesitated as he stood in the doorway.

The bed looked different. The crime scene clean-up team must have disposed of the blood-soaked mattress. Flora had made up the high four-poster bed with just the box spring. The white comforter and pillow shams lay in the dark wood bed frame like the fallen sails of a sinking ship.

Jeremy had always said good night to his parents when he still lived at home, regardless of the hour. That was the rule. He would kiss his mother's forehead and whisper, "I'm home." And she would smile in her sleep. "Good night, honey," she'd say. "I love you."

He slipped the red bandanna under the pillows. He felt her cool hand on his cheek, her warm breath in his hair. And he whispered their names aloud for the first time since he'd learned of their deaths.

"Good night, Mom. Good night, Dad." His voice choked.

"I'm home."

Chapter 6

Jeremy tried to read the newspaper as he sipped his coffee. The words wouldn't stick. He was thinking about all the things he had to do today. The collar of the button-down shirt he'd put on this morning was too tight, so he had left the top button open behind his tie. The suit he had found crammed into the back of his closet, the shoulders covered with dust. His high school graduation suit. Too tight under the arms and the sleeves were too short, but it would have to do.

Light footsteps approached the kitchen. Elise, yawning and rubbing her eyes, stopped abruptly.

"Morning," he said.

"Jeremy. You, you scared me." She touched his cheek. "You look so much like —" Tears filled her eyes.

"I made coffee." He slipped off the counter stool.

She was wearing the stained tee shirt and sweatpants she'd slept in, but had braided her hair. "You shaved. And you're dressed up. Why?"

"I'm going to visit Dwight this morning." He held out the mug of coffee toward her, but she just stared at it.

"Three teaspoons of sugar and plenty of milk," he said.

"Why? Why are you going to Dwight? Is, is it about me? The wills?"

He placed the mug on the counter.

"I figured when you didn't tell me yesterday what the wills said, it meant something bad. That Grandpa isn't my guardian."

"He isn't, but —"

"No, Jeremy. No."

"But I am. And I'm staying right here, in this house, with you."

She stared at him without moving. "You? You're my guardian?"

He wasn't sure how to interpret her reaction, but in the next instant, she threw her arms around him. "Oh, Jeremy. I knew they wouldn't leave me with Dwight. I knew it. But it's you. I know it's wrong to feel happy, but I'm just so —" She hugged him again.

How could he have considered the possibility of leaving his sister to Dwight? Even if his parents hadn't named Jeremy guardian, he should have been prepared to fight for her.

"I never really thought about it before," Elise said, "but they always tried to do what was best for us."

"I suppose they did."

"Dwight's not going to be very happy."

"No, he isn't."

She climbed up on a stool. "He seemed real eager to move into the house."

"Well, he'll have to get over it."

"Yes, he will," she said. "Yes, he will." She reached for the sugar container on the counter and poured more into her coffee.

"Did you sleep okay?" Jeremy asked.

"I guess."

"Do you remember going to Mom's office?"

"What are you talking about?"

"Last night. In your sleep."

"Why would I do that?"

No reason to alarm her about her sleepwalking. She'd get over it once they got back into a routine. He put a couple of pieces of bread in the toaster. Flora had stocked the house with bread, milk, juice, bananas. He was grateful for that. He didn't think he'd be able to eat the leftover platters from the funeral. He'd tell Flora to take them home with her.

It was almost eight. The smell of toast filled the room, reminding him of mornings of coffee, toast, everyone rushing about. "Are you going to school today?" he asked.

Elise seemed surprised by the question.

"You'll have to go sooner or later, Ellie."

"Later. Let it be later then."

"How about tomorrow?"

She stirred her coffee with her finger.

"Well, how about this?" He put the toast and butter on the counter. "Stop by school this afternoon, just for a few minutes. Then it won't be so hard tomorrow. Okay?"

"I guess."

"Flora should be here soon." He took his suit jacket from the chair. "I'll see you later."

"Jeremy?" she called after him.

"Yeah?" He stepped back into the kitchen. She had picked up a piece of toast.

"You look really good without the beard."

Dwight rented office space from a law firm in a shabby North Miami neighborhood. The small, one-story building would have been considered modern in the '70s, when it had probably been built, but now its featureless concrete shell and small windows gave it the appearance of a prison. This was reinforced by the chain-link fence around the parking lot and the uniformed security guard who sat on a folding chair beneath an awning, eating what looked like an oversized Cuban sandwich.

Jeremy rolled down his window. "I'm here to see Dwight

Stroeb." His uncle's black Buick was parked on the far side of the lot. The reserved spots contained a Jaguar and a Mercedes.

"Do you have an appointment?" the guard asked.

"No," Jeremy said.

The guard waved him into the parking lot.

On the side of the building hung a large sign with embossed gold letters naming the law firm. Beneath it, a much smaller plaque read "Law Offices of Dwight C. Stroeb."

"Mr. Stroeb's not in," the receptionist told Jeremy, without looking up from her magazine.

"His car's in the lot."

She shrugged.

"I'm his nephew."

She studied him, a long red fingernail in her mouth.

"If you could just tell me which office is his, I'd really appreciate it."

"All the way back. Next to the bathroom." She buzzed him in.

Dwight was leaning cardboard posters against the wall of his small office, pulling on his mustache absently as he studied the sincere-looking face on the poster. *Judge for Yourself. Elect Dwight C. Stroeb County Court Judge.* His uncle was wearing his suit jacket and his tie was perfectly knotted. Jeremy had left his own jacket in the car.

"Good morning, Dwight."

Dwight glanced up, his face losing color at the sight of Jeremy. "My God. Jeremy. For a moment I thought you were . . . Well, come in. Come in. Big change from a couple of days ago."

"I hope I'm not catching you at a bad time."

Dwight waved at his empty desk top. "I have a lot to do, but I can always make time for you." He held up one of the posters. "How do you like it? I just got them from the printer. Too bad you won't be around much longer; I could have used your help with the campaign."

"Yeah. Sorry I won't be able to help out." There was an absence of photos or other items that might have reflected his uncle's personal interests. Only Dwight's diplomas and certifications hung on the wall. Jeremy remembered his father once remarking that Dwight didn't have time for children of his own — he was too busy admiring himself.

"Why don't you sit down?"

"Thanks." The seat of the guest chair was low. Jeremy found himself looking up at his uncle in his own oversized, padded executive chair.

"I imagine you'll be heading out of here soon," Dwight said. "I envy you, Jeremy. A young man with an opportunity to see the world. But just so you know, your aunt and I wish to make the minimal amount of disruption in Elise's life. She's certainly been through enough without more upheaval. So we'll be moving into the house on Lotus Island."

"I read my parents' wills."

"Yes. And they provide that your aunt and I may live in the house with your sister until she attains majority."

"As well as a generous stipend to take care of all related expenses."

"That's right."

"My parents did a good job of providing for us. Life insurance, wills that tried to consider all contingencies."

"You and Elise are very fortunate. As an attorney, I can't tell you how many stories I hear about unclear or inadequate wills."

"Well, my parents were very clear. Their wills state that I'm to be Elise's guardian. You're only a backup."

Dwight's face reddened. "But, but you're not responsible."

"Well, Dwight, I'm afraid there's nothing about me being responsible in the wills."

"It's implicit. A guardian must be responsible. He can't be gallivanting halfway around the world."

"I'm not leaving. I'm staying here. At home."

Dwight didn't speak for a minute. Was this how his uncle looked before a judge when he realized he was losing his case? "You know, Jeremy." His uncle's voice had softened. "You're a young man. Why would you want to saddle yourself with the burden of taking care of a teenager? And, of course, your aunt and I are far better qualified. Think of your sister. What's best for her."

"That's exactly what I'm doing." Jeremy stood up.

"Do you really believe I'm going to sit back and let you do this?"

"I'm touched by your concern over Elise's well-being, Dwight. Though I'm sure rubbing elbows with your influential new neighbors on Lotus Island would have been nice for your career, too."

"Get out of here, Jeremy." Dwight's chin was trembling. "But I'll be watching you. Any sign that you're not adequately fulfilling your obligations and I'm filing a motion to replace you as guardian."

"My parents would be glad to know that. Glad you're watching out for Elise." Jeremy saluted his uncle from the doorway.

Jeremy drove a couple of blocks away from his uncle's office and pulled the car into a 7-Eleven parking lot. His uncle. His goddamn uncle. But at least that was done. Jeremy was ready for the next part of his plan.

He found the business card at the front of his wallet. Detective Judy Lieber. Should he call her? Let her know he wasn't the slug she'd concluded he was?

No. He put the card back. His dad used to tell him talk was cheap. The only way to impress others was through your actions.

Through your actions.

Chapter 7

The offices of Piedmont Coleridge Miller, known universally as PCM, were located on the thirteenth floor of a downtown Miami office building. Some buildings had done away with the fate-tempting number thirteen, but not the chrome-and-glass one that housed Jeremy's mother's CPA firm. "Superstition is nonsense," she had once said. "Can you imagine what the world would smell like if we all wore cloves of garlic around our necks?"

Maybe that wouldn't have been such a bad idea for her.

"Can I get you something, Jeremy?" Bud McNally's secretary studied him from behind outdated glasses with rhinestones at the corners. After giving Jeremy a powerful hug in the reception area, she had brought him to the partner's office to wait.

"I'm good, Gladys. Thanks."

She hesitated in the doorway. Jeremy had known Gladys since he was little — her hair had been a steely gray even then. Jeremy used to sit in the staff room doing his homework while his mother finished some important project. Gladys would soundlessly appear with a granola bar with chocolate chips. "Don't tell your mother," she would say, then disappear.

"I just want you to know," she said now. "Your mother —" She looked down at her clumsy rubber-soled shoes. "I'm just so sorry, Jeremy."

"Thank you, Gladys."

She wiped her nose with a tissue she pulled out of her pocket. "Well, I guess I'll go and get after Mr. McNally. Make sure he knows you're waiting." She left him alone with the office door open.

Jeremy sat uncomfortably in the modern leather chair, the top button of his shirt closed, tie tightened, and his suit jacket cutting off circulation in his arms. He tried to block the emotion that had built up inside. He needed to keep his head.

An expensive-looking navy pinstriped suit jacket hung from a hanger on a brushed steel coat rack. Framed diplomas and certifications on one of the walls were dwarfed by a red and black banner of the University of Georgia Bulldogs, and the shelves of the credenza housed numerous trophies and plaques. A chessboard near the edge of the desk had what appeared to be a game in progress. The chess pieces looked as though they were made from real ivory. Jeremy picked up a white pawn. Bud liked football and chess. An intellectual jock. Was that an oxymoron?

Jeremy put the pawn back down, noticing as he did a worn leather belt hanging from a hook on the side of the credenza. Its incongruity with the rest of the room caught him by surprise.

"Jeremy, my boy," Bud said in his hearty southern drawl. He strode into the office, dropping some folders on his desk, then turned to shake Jeremy's hand. "Well, look at you." Bud rubbed his own clean-shaven chin. "A bit of a change from a couple of days ago."

Jeremy was able to take in details that had been a blur at Enrique Castillo's house, when Jeremy could hardly tell one person from another. The partner was still a handsome man despite looking as though he'd enjoyed a few too many client lunches and dinners. Beneath his crisp white shirt, Bud's broad football bulk had shifted from his powerful arms and chest down to his stomach. His face looked almost bloated, like a chipmunk's before its winter hibernation, but his graying blond crew cut and the once square jaw gave Bud a marine-like mystique.

"I want to thank you for seeing me, Mr. McNally," Jeremy said.

Bud took a step back as though he'd been slapped. "Mr. McNally? Since when have I become Mr. McNally?" He widened his light gray eyes, set deep into puffy, drooping eyelids. "You've known me since your mama brought you here in your stinky diapers."

"Well, I'm actually here in a professional capacity." It was more difficult than Jeremy expected, presenting himself as an adult to people who still carried associations of him as a child.

Bud raised his eyebrow. "Professional capacity? Well, that's fine, but I still prefer Bud, even in a professional capacity. Maybe I'm kiddin' myself," Bud said, sitting down on his leather chair, "but Mr. McNally makes me feel old."

"You certainly don't look old."

"A charmer. Just like your mama." Bud smiled, but in the next instant he was serious. "If you don't mind, Jeremy." He leaned forward and lowered his voice as though there were people around who might overhear them. "Before we get on with the reason for your visit, I must ask. How's your sister? She seemed terribly upset at the funeral."

"She's doing a little better, thank you."

"I understand she was the first on the scene. That must have been very traumatic for her."

"She doesn't remember much about what happened. It's like she's blocked it out." Jeremy pulled on his collar. "I guess that's a good thing."

"Yes. It's a godsend how our minds protect us from pain." Bud folded his hands. "And you, Jeremy? How are you dealing with everything?"

"I'm just trying to get through one day at a time."

"Of course you are. Of course you are." Bud leaned back in his chair. "So tell me, my boy, what can I do for you today?"

Jeremy was caught by the abruptness of the transition and took a moment to compose himself. "You mentioned at the Castillos' to let you know if there was something you could do to help me and Elise."

"And I meant that, Jeremy."

"Well, I just found out my parents' wills appointed me Elise's guardian."

Bud's facial expression didn't change.

"I guess you know, I haven't exactly been the stay-at-home type. I took some time off from school, and I've been traveling."

"Understandably. Senior year can be a terrifying time. Wondering what you're going to do next. Whether your parents' lives is what you want for yourself."

"Exactly. And honestly, I wasn't ready to make those decisions."

"Sometimes distancing yourself is a good way to see things more clearly."

Jeremy was surprised how well Bud understood him. If only his father had tried a little harder. "Well, it's helped me," Jeremy said. "And, of course, with my parents gone — obviously, there's been a big shift in my priorities."

"Tell me how I can help you, Jeremy."

"I'd like to work here — at PCM," Jeremy said. "I was majoring in accounting at NYU."

"I recall your mama telling me you were an A student." Bud picked up a thick pen and rolled it between his fingers. His shirt cuffs were monogrammed and held closed with gold cufflinks. "I think she was hoping you'd join the firm one day."

"I'd very much like that opportunity now. I feel that if I'm going to be Elise's guardian, I need to start behaving more responsibly."

Bud had the intelligent, understanding demeanor of a clergyman. The desk phone bringed softly. "Hold my calls, please, Gladys," he said into the speaker box. He looked at Jeremy, waiting for him to continue.

"I was hoping you'd consider hiring me as an intern or an assistant auditor. Until I graduate, of course, and can sit for the CPA exam.

Bud put the pen down and brought his fingers to a steeple in front of his face. He had big, strong hands covered with freckles and golden hairs. "And how do you plan on graduating?" Bud said finally.

"I thought I'd take a couple of evening courses at Miami Intercontinental," Jeremy said. "That is, unless you think it might interfere with my work here." His mother had once told him if you want something, give the impression you already have it.

"Of course you know we want to do everything to help out you and Elise." Bud let his chair snap forward, signaling that the meeting was over.

"I'd really appreciate it," Jeremy hesitated a split second, "Bud. My mother often spoke about how much she admired you."

Bud's mouth twitched, as though he was containing a smile. "Did she, now?"

"She once said a gifted salesman could sell ice to Eskimos, but only Bud McNally could turn a company that sells ice to Eskimos into one of the hottest stocks on Wall Street."

Bud let out a full-bodied laugh. "Your mama really said that?"

"She did." Jeremy picked up the pawn he had been holding earlier.

"You play?" Bud said, still smiling.

"Excuse me?"

"Chess."

"Oh, yeah. My dad taught me."

"Take a move."

"I'm sorry?"

"Go ahead. I always have a game in progress, but I'm usually playing both sides. It's nice to deal with a fresh move from time to time." Bud nodded toward the board. "Go ahead."

About half the pieces had already been taken. A black rook was exposed to Jeremy's bishop, but if he took it, he'd lose his bishop to Bud's queen. But that would give him a shot at the black king. Jeremy took the rook.

"Interesting," Bud said. He took Jeremy's bishop, as though he'd been anticipating the move. "Thank you, Jeremy. That changes the direction of the game."

Jeremy wasn't certain whether he had done something right or wrong, or whether Bud expected him to take another move. But Bud leaned back in his chair. He was smiling, fatherly. A bond had been established.

"Tell you what," Bud said. "Go out and buy yourself a few new suits, shirts, and a pair of wingtips. If you want to be an auditor, you'll need to look like an auditor."

"Thank you, sir."

"And get your butt over to Miami Intercontinental. You're going to finish getting your degree, and when the time comes for you to sit for the CPA exam, I expect you to get the highest grades in the state. Y' hear?"

Jeremy nodded.

"We owe that to your mama," Bud said.

Chapter 8

Jeremy stood outside the registrar's building with his class schedule. He had come here directly from Bud's office, changing into jeans and a tee shirt in the car so he wouldn't look out of place among the students.

Miami Intercontinental University. His father's turf.

Jeremy's parents had wanted Jeremy to attend MIU, but he had always known it wasn't an option for him. The professors and students would all have recognized him as D.C.'s son and made comparisons, which Jeremy feared would have found him lacking. It was ironic that circumstances had brought him back here after all.

Imposing oak trees shaded the broad grassy areas and winding paths. Quite different from the urban campus of NYU where classes and dorms were housed in gray and red brick buildings that were indistinguishable from the rest of the city. Here at MIU, the administrative offices were in the original Spanish-style buildings. As though part of a master plan, the subsequent buildings had been constructed with the same red barrel-tiled roofs and beige stucco walls, which made the campus look a lot like a Spanish monastery.

Planning. Jeremy was surprised by how well his own plan was working out. He had a job at PCM and was now enrolled at MIU — giving him opportunities to get on the inside of both his parents' worlds. Plant a mole, he'd suggested to Lieber the day before. He hadn't imagined it would be himself.

Students were walking to class, some in groups, many hurrying along by themselves. Jeremy wondered as they passed him if any had known his father. Professor Stroeb had been very popular amongst his students.

"D.C.," his mother had once said, "you need to turn some of your charm on the administration."

"Why bother?" his father had said. "Their minds have rusted shut. But the youth, Rachel, the youth are hungry and eager to learn. I have an opportunity to shape them, to mold them, to teach them how to think."

"But the students aren't the ones you should be trying to impress. Just because you're tenured, D.C., doesn't mean you're untouchable."

Unpopular with the administration. Could anyone at MIU have had a motive to kill his father? Had his father's outspokenness been a bigger deal than Jeremy had realized? And once again Jeremy was angry with himself — like the time in second grade when he had refused to pay attention to a story his teacher was reading. Only toward the end of her recitation did Jeremy become engaged in the protagonist's plight. And then, he was curious to know what had happened at the beginning. But the story was over, and Jeremy would never know what he had missed.

Jeremy headed across the campus to his father's office. Air-conditioning units stuck out of windows in the three-story building and dripped water onto the hibiscus bushes and croton beneath them. The entrance door stuck as Jeremy pushed it open, layers of chipped paint creating the friction. Terrazzo floors, cracked and in need of polishing, lined the narrow hallways. Bulletin boards covered all available wall space, each buried under layers of announcements.

The air was mildewed, but it was a familiar smell and comforting to Jeremy as he ran up the steps to his father's third-floor office. The door was closed, and it didn't occur to Jeremy to knock. In fact, it hadn't occurred to Jeremy that the office might be in any condition other than the way his father had left it. So when he pushed open the door, he was taken aback by the cartons, piles of papers, and general state of disarray. Then he saw a pair of worn army boots sticking out from behind his father's desk. They were attached to legs in tight, rolled-up jeans. A head popped out next, like a jack-in-the-box, and the expression on the young woman's face was pure horror. What had she been doing that he'd disturbed with his sudden appearance?

The woman's face settled as though in relief. "*Merde.* Do you know how much you resemble him?" She had an accent — probably French — and pale eyes flecked with hazel, like a cat's. Her hair was a mass of copper curls gathered up on top of her head, but dripping over her forehead and shoulders.

She patted off the dirt or dust from the back of her jeans. She was petite and delicate — built a lot like Elise. "You're Jeremy, no?" she asked, extending her hand. She had small hands with bitten-down nails. "I'm Marina Champlain. I worked very closely with your father. I'm his graduate assistant. Was, I mean."

Marina Champlain. *You'd remember her if you'd met her,* Lieber had said.

Jeremy hadn't released her hand. He dropped it, self-conscious.

"I didn't recognize you at first," Marina said. "At the . . . at the Castillos' house, you had a beard — like *Miami Vice,* no? And long hair. I saw you get out of a limo. You missed the funeral. Someone said your flight was delayed. But they should have waited for you. His son. Their son. I'm sorry, I'm rambling, but I want to tell you how much I grieve for you and your sister." Her eyes were watering and her narrow nose had turned red. She opened a booklet that was lying on a pile on the desk, but Jeremy could tell she wasn't seeing it. "He spoke of you and Elise all the time," she said.

How well she seemed to know his father, but Jeremy hadn't even been aware of her existence.

"So you've come to say good-bye to your father's office?"

"Actually, I just registered for a couple of night classes."

"I thought you were traveling. Finding yourself."

"Is that how my father put it?"

Her black bra strap slipped off her shoulder and stuck out of the sleeve of her white tee shirt. She adjusted it. "He was hoping you'd come home. So now it seems you have."

"Yes. I suppose I have."

"To take care of things, yes?"

"Kind of like that."

She waved her hand over the papers and cartons, reminding Jeremy of a conductor cueing an orchestra. "I'm organizing," she said. "It's a lot of work. Your father was a great man. But one thing he wasn't was organized."

"Shouldn't his family have been invited to go through his things first?" Jeremy said.

She covered her mouth, looking genuinely dismayed. "I'm so sorry, but I don't know, Jeremy." She pronounced his name with a soft 'j' as though she was saying it in French. "Dr. Winter asked me to go through your father's papers. But I'll stop if you'd like to do it yourself."

"That's okay," Jeremy said, annoyed by the dean's eagerness to get the office cleared out. "Just keep doing what you were doing."

He flipped through some files behind his father's desk. The corner of the credenza was blackened and the wall behind it was shades of brown.

"You know about the fire, yes?" Marina asked.

Vaguely, Jeremy remembered his mother e-mailing him about a fire in his dad's office a couple of months ago. "Tell me," Jeremy said.

"It was this past November, just after your father's paper against the Cuban embargo came out. It's believed some students — anti-Castro extremists — set the fire. Many Cubans are upset with your father's politics."

"Okay," Jeremy said slowly, thinking, "but why would anyone think extremists set the fire? Maybe my dad just left a cigarette burning."

She shook her head adamantly. Her lips were disproportionately small and round — like a perfect red circle. "They spray painted the door," Marina said. "*Cuba Libre.* The battle cry of the Cuban exiles."

"Was anyone caught?" Jeremy asked.

"It seems not."

"Did my father write anything else after that that might upset them?"

She opened her mouth to answer, then froze.

"Can I help you, sir?" said a tight male voice in the doorway. Jeremy recognized his father's former boss, Dr. Winter. Winter was wearing a navy blazer, pressed gray pants, and a blue shirt. The uniform of the cognitive elite. On his feet, small for such a tall man, were tasseled leather loafers.

"Ah." The dean's face changed in recognition, as he stroked his shiny bald head. "You're D.C.'s son, right?" Winter extended his hand. "You can't miss the resemblance. I'm so sorry for your loss." He paused for a second. "Jeremy, isn't it?"

"That's right. Thank you."

"Your father leaves quite a void."

"Yes," Jeremy said. "Yes, he does."

Marina had backed into the corner, her arms crossed in front of her chest.

Winter seemed to be waiting for Jeremy to say something. He tapped his tasseled loafer against the floor.

"I see you're clearing out my father's office," Jeremy said. "I was wondering why the family wasn't asked to go through my father's things first."

"But of course you were." Winter looked offended.

"No, I wasn't."

"Perhaps you should check with your uncle. He's already been through your father's belongings."

"He had no right to do that."

"I'm sorry? Isn't he responsible for you and your sister?"

"No. He is not."

"Then I apologize. A misunderstanding. But I don't believe your uncle took much. A few pictures, a clock. I'm sure he's planning on giving them to you. No reason to get all worked up. And after Ms. Champlain's finished organizing, you're welcome to come back and go through the papers again." Jeremy felt the pressure of Winter's hand on his shoulder as the dean coaxed him out of the office. "Again, Jeremy. So sorry for your loss. Your father will surely be missed by everyone here."

Jeremy glanced back at Marina. She had picked up some papers, but she looked sad. Terribly sad.

Chapter 9

Elise was floating — weightless, disembodied, connected to the world only by a thin hose, an umbilical cord. Breathing, yet not really breathing. Immersed in darkness. An embryo — that's what she was. And she was terrified of emerging from the protective womb.

She stood beneath a cluster of palm trees at the edge of her high school's campus. Her friends were sitting on benches in the grassy quad between the buildings where they had their classes. They were on break. She could hear their laughter, even in the distance.

Elise had driven here this afternoon, like Jeremy had told her to do. He said it would make it easier for her tomorrow. Would it? Would anything ever be easy again?

She watched her classmates in their school uniforms — khaki pants and navy or green polo shirts. Megan spied her and waved. The others turned toward her, signaling for her to join them. They'd all come to the funeral, then to the Castillos' house. They'd embraced her, cried on her shoulder. "Oh, Elise," they'd said, "we're so, so sorry."

Elise took a step back so that she was blocked from their view by one of the trees. She breathed in the bark. She wasn't ready. Not yet. Maybe never.

"Hey." She was jarred by Carlos's soft voice. Where had he come from? "I didn't think you'd be in today."

"I'm-I'm practicing."

Carlos nodded as though he understood, though she doubted he did. There was a couple of days' growth of shiny facial hair, so faint that he probably wouldn't be sent to the office for not shaving. His blond hair was matted down from the band of a baseball cap. Her boyfriend. He was her boyfriend. She should be happy to see him, right?

"So, you're back at the house," he said. "Is it like weird being there?"

Of course it's weird. It's horrible without them. "It's okay," she said. "Jeremy's home."

He scratched his cheek. "Are you angry with me?"

"Why would I be angry, Carlos?"

"I don't know. I was afraid maybe you felt like I deserted you."

"I haven't exactly wanted to see anyone."

"So you're not angry?"

"I said I'm not."

"Yeah. Okay then." He scraped off a sliver of bark with his fingernail. "So, like, do you want to hang out?"

She shook her head.

"That's cool."

The bell rang signaling the next class. Carlos looked relieved.

"Maybe you'd better go," Elise said.

"Yeah. I've got chemistry." He hesitated, as though he was going to kiss her, then stood back. "So I'll see you around."

"Yeah."

Her friends had left their perches in the quad and were coming toward her.

"And thanks," Carlos said.

"For what?"

"For not ratting me out."

She wanted to ask him what he was talking about, but her

friends were swarming around her. "Poor baby." Megan held out her arms. "Poor, poor baby."

Elise returned home a little after three, and got out of her silver Volvo, not even sure how the car had driven itself from school. Autopilot — she was on autopilot. Flora's car was gone. Elise remembered the housekeeper had said she was leaving early today for a doctor's appointment.

She unlocked the front door. Her uncle had had the locks changed, but as she pushed the door open, her heart made a strange hiccup. Something told her to expect darkness, silence, an unfamiliar smell, a standing shadow. Like in her dream. And for an instant, she wanted to turn and run. But the foyer was brightly lit, classical music playing in the background. Geezer, lying by the entranceway table, wagged his tail but didn't get up.

Elise stepped back out on the front stoop, closing the door, but not locking it. She tried to steady her trembling. Why was she doing this? Why was she making herself relive the worst moment of her life? But that night was a black hole to her. That's all she could see. Blackness. But there was something else. She knew there was something else.

She remembered putting her key in the lock. But it hadn't turned. It was already open. And she'd pushed on the door.

She did it now. Pushing the door, trying to imagine the darkness, the silence, the smell, the shadow. But it didn't work. She saw only the brightly lit foyer, the photos on the wall, the empty vase on the entranceway table, Geezer watching her.

They'd left their luggage on the floor of the foyer that night. In a pile with their laptops and winter coats. The burglar had taken the laptops, her uncle had said.

The burglar. But it hadn't been a burglar. She knew at a gut level it couldn't have been a burglar.

The unlocked door. The laptops. Nothing else taken.

Someone had planned to kill them. A voice in her head kept telling her so. It spoke to her in her sleep.

It was the same voice that accused her. A soft voice, like an echo. Why did you disobey your parents? How could you have left them alone? Alone to be killed?

But what if she'd stayed home instead of sneaking out? She'd be dead herself, wouldn't she? Would that have been better? Sometimes, she wished it were so. At least she wouldn't feel this pain. A pain that wouldn't go away. But she hadn't been home that night. And now she was here, alive, in this world. Could her living have some purpose?

Like to find whoever had done this terrible, terrible thing?

She ran up the stairs to her mother's office. In here. There must be something in here. But what? What was she looking for?

The blinds were partially closed and the outside light cast thin white lines over the desk, the walls, the small area rug. Her mother's scent pulled Elise into the room. The same scent was on her mother's tee shirt. The one Elise had found in the downstairs closet with three teardrops of blood. Her mother had worn it the day they came home from Madrid and Elise slept in it every night.

She sniffed the room hungrily. If she closed her eyes — but no. She wasn't going to do that now. She'd hold the memories for later. She focused instead on the details.

On top of the desk were a Tiffany lamp, desk blotter calendar, paperweight, family photos, crystal clock, printer, and a docking station. No computer. Her mother had used only her laptop and brought it back and forth between home and work. Her dad had done the same. So with their laptops stolen, there was no way of knowing if either of them had anything on their computers that might lead Elise to the murderer.

Unless they'd backed up their laptops.

Elise pulled open drawers. The files, papers, and reports were disarranged, as though someone had already gone through them. At the back of one drawer, she found stacks of floppies and computer CDs. She examined the labels on the CDs, looking for something that might be current.

Nothing. She sank to the floor. A clipboard with a yellow pad was leaning against the side of the desk. The pad was covered with line after line of tight, scribbly writing. Just like Elise's make-believe writing when she was a little girl. She pulled the clipboard against her chest and began to sob. She sobbed until the room became woozy and she was floating again.

Floating. Just floating.

A soft touch on her shoulder. "Elise," the voice said. "Elise."

She opened her eyes.

"Hey, Ellie," Jeremy said. "What are you doing?"

Elise was hugging the clipboard like a pillow. "It, it wasn't a burglar," she said.

"I know."

"You know?"

"A burglar doesn't make sense." Jeremy was in a tee shirt and jeans. Hadn't he been wearing a suit this morning?

"Why didn't you say something?"

"I was planning to," he said. "Tonight, after I got everything arranged."

"Arranged?"

"I got a job at PCM and I'm taking night classes at MIU. I start tomorrow."

"I don't understand."

"I need to get on the inside and try to figure out who might have had a motive."

"A motive?"

"Yeah." He sorted through the CDs. "I see you've been busy."

"I was looking for clues," she said. "The, the murderer took their laptops. So I was thinking that there was something important on them. And maybe Mom had backups."

"These are pretty old," Jeremy said, "but I'll check them out."

"The police left a mess. Mom never made a mess."

"I know."

"And they probably took the newer CDs."

"I'll call the detective and ask her. I see you've found your clipboard."

"My clipboard?"

"I told you at breakfast. You were in here last night. You were scribbling away."

She studied the wavy, regular lines. She must have been holding the pen very tightly because she had practically pushed through the paper. "I wonder what I was trying to write."

Chapter 10

The new-employee packet and company-issue laptop rested on the coffee table in the alcove outside the partners' offices. Jeremy sat back on the hard leather sofa. The inner sanctum waiting area was complete with an areca palm in a brushed steel pot, several newsletters with the PCM logo at the top, a dish of hard candies, and an irritating painting made up of geometric shapes that changed with the angle of view. Was the painting supposed to symbolize the clever ways accountants were known to manipulate the rules?

Bud's secretary, Gladys, had told Jeremy he'd been assigned to Irving Luria and to knock on Irv's door when he was done with his paperwork. Jeremy had done that, but there was no answer. Rather than barge into the office as he'd done yesterday at his father's office, Jeremy had decided to wait here.

He was wearing one of his new suits and a white shirt with thin blue stripes that he'd taken out of its packaging this morning. Wrinkle-free, the salesman had said. But the shirt was covered with packing creases and Jeremy hadn't had time to iron it. Not that he knew how, or even where the iron was. So he had planned to keep his jacket on, though now he was regretting his decision as he felt himself perspiring under the heat of the overhead halogen lights.

He tapped his fingers against the armrest. The alcove was directly across from his mother's office. Its door was shut. He wondered if his mother's things had been packed away in cartons. Had his uncle already been here, posing as the family representative, and taken what interested him?

The hallway was deserted. It really wouldn't be all that difficult to sneak into his mother's office. In fact, could someone have done that before she died? Taken her key, made a copy, returned it without her knowing? Then used the copy to get into the house the night of the murder? It seemed possible.

The door to his mother's office beckoned him. Just a quick look. Just in and out. He leaned forward on the sofa and listened. A phone rang in the distance.

He went quickly to the door. Before he could turn the handle, it opened. A young woman with short, black hair and blue eyes stared at him.

"I'm sorry," he said. "I didn't think anyone was in here." He recognized her from the gathering at the Castillos' house. Hadn't she wanted to talk to him that afternoon?

Low laughter echoed down the hallway. Deep voices were coming toward them.

The woman pushed past him and hurried away through an exit door. What the hell was that all about, and what had she been doing in his mother's office?

The voices were closer. Jeremy stepped back toward the alcove and picked up a magazine just as Bud McNally and Enrique Castillo rounded the corner. He was surprised to see Mr. Castillo until he remembered that Castillo Enterprises was a major client of the firm's.

"Jeremy," Bud said, "good morning."

Jeremy shook their hands. His palm was sweaty.

Bud turned to Enrique, who had a surprised but curious expression on his face. "Jeremy's come to work with us," Bud said.

"In fact?" Enrique raised his eyebrows. "You're not returning to Europe, Jeremy?"

Jeremy shook his head. Although he was in his new clothes,

Jeremy felt awkward next to these two old pros who were so at ease in their surroundings.

"He wants to stay in Miami, to be here for his sister," Bud said.

"Good, very good," Enrique said.

"And he's finishing up his degree over at MIU," Bud said. "Isn't that right, Jeremy?"

"I've already enrolled in a couple of night classes."

"Excellent." Bud squeezed Jeremy's shoulder. "I'm expecting Jeremy to make us all proud when the time comes for him to sit for the CPA exam."

"I'm sure he will. Certainly, if he takes after his mother." Enrique took a deep breath, causing his nostrils to flare. A gold stickpin propped up his silk tie. "Your mother was a brilliant auditor. She'd worked on the Casillo Enterprises audit many years ago. I was delighted when she returned this year to take over for Irv." Enrique turned toward Bud. "Perhaps Jeremy would be interested in learning about the real estate and sugar industries."

Bud retained his congenial expression, but something seemed to be going on behind it. "How about it, Jeremy?" he said. "Would you like to work on the Castillo Enterprises engagement?"

"I'd like that very much.

"I'm sure Rachel would have liked Jeremy following in her footsteps," said Enrique.

Just then Irving Luria sidled up to his office, glancing off the hallway wall with his shoulder. Had he been drinking or did he just have poor balance?

"Morning, Irv," Bud said.

Irv grunted. His seersucker suit and bow tie looked as though he'd slept in them. Jeremy remembered Irv from when he was a child. Irv used to laugh a lot then. A booming laugh that would carry across the room.

"I don't believe I've ever seen you up so early, Irv," Enrique said. "And I see how fortunate I've been. You're quite the bear."

"Nice to see everyone else so bright eyed and bushy tailed." Irv was about to slam his office door behind him.

"Irv," Bud said, "one second. Jeremy's here to help you with that project of yours."

Irv looked at Jeremy like he was a cockroach crawling into his Scotch.

"Whenever he finishes up with you," Bud was saying, "we'll send him out to Castillo Enterprises."

Irv scowled at Bud. Or maybe it was just a permanent expression — anger cast in stone. Then he closed his office door.

"Well, on to your first assignment, my boy." Bud patted Jeremy on the back. "Irv's bark is worse than his bite."

Enrique shook Jeremy's hand. "Come to dinner. Any time. You and Elise are always welcome."

"Thank you. I appreciate that."

Enrique gave a little smile. "You look good without the beard, Jeremy. I wonder if I should shave my own."

Bud laughed. "Don't you dare, Enrique. Your beard defines you. The last of the redoubtable Castillos."

"Not the last, Bud. Don't forget Carlos." And the two men disappeared into Bud's office.

Jeremy knocked on Irv's door, then when he didn't hear any response, knocked again. He knocked one more time, then opened the door. The room was dark: the blinds drawn and the lights off. Jeremy could make out Irv sitting behind his desk, putting something into one of the drawers, then slamming it shut.

"May I come in?" Jeremy asked.

"You're a little late asking. Seems you're already in."

Jeremy stood awkwardly near the door. Irv didn't invite him to sit down.

Years ago, Irv had been a much different person. He was gruff then, sure, but there'd been amusement in the bluish eyes that were now clouded by disinterest. He had always been an ugly man, reminding Jeremy of a gnome with his hunched back and oversized head. He probably would have scared Jeremy, except for the playful way his mother interacted with him. Jeremy couldn't help thinking of Beauty and the Beast.

"What are you doing here?" Irv's voice was jarring.

"I understand you have a project for me."

"I don't mean that. What are you doing working here?"

"Didn't Mr. McNally tell you?"

"Sure. He fed me a line of bullshit that you've decided to become a responsible adult now that you have guardianship obligations. I want to know why you're really here."

Jeremy was glad the room was dark so Irv couldn't see the blood rush to his face.

"Never mind." Irv pushed his chair back, then rose as though the process was painful. "But let me tell you something. If you're on some misguided quest, you're barking up the wrong tree."

Jeremy, his new laptop tucked under his arm, followed Irv to an area two levels below the main offices, on the eleventh floor. Irv hadn't talked on the way. Now he unlocked a door and flicked on the switch. Like battle-weary soldiers, the overhead fluorescent light fixtures responded slowly with quivering, uncertain brightness. They were in a huge file room extending back maybe half the length of the building. There were hundreds of tall gray file cabinets and steel shelving units and papers everywhere. Despite its vastness, the room smelled close.

"This is the old file room," Irv said. "We haven't used it in years. Some of our partners were sentimental about parting with their client workpapers. Now those partners are retired or dead and we need the space for all the new staff people we've been hiring." He nodded his head toward a stack of unassembled cartons. "Box 'em up."

"All of them?" Jeremy said.

"Yeah. And make a detailed list of everything." Irv turned to leave.

"But this could take weeks," Jeremy said.

"At least that," the partner said and closed the door behind him.

Jeremy removed his suit jacket and loosened his tie. He couldn't help wondering if this was supposed to be a test. Like Hercules being assigned to cleaning out the horse manure in the Augean stables.

He sorted through thick binders of dusty working papers, entering their contents into his new laptop, and then sticking them into the cartons he'd assembled himself. The edges of some of the covers were razor sharp and Jeremy stopped from time to time to suck the sting out of a paper cut.

Each binder contained hours of work by a PCM auditor, whose name and initials were clearly indicated on the cover. There were tests the auditors had done, their assessments, and their conclusions. Jeremy couldn't believe the firm was just getting around to disposing of this stuff.

The sorting and boxing was mindless, menial work. It was also frustrating, giving Jeremy no opportunity to mix with any of the other staff. If he couldn't talk to people, how was he going to find out anything about his mother?

His mind wandered back to the woman he'd seen leaving his mother's office. She may have had a legitimate reason for being in there, but then, why had she acted so oddly?

By the late afternoon, he was relieved when he heard the door to the file room open and slam shut. Even Irv would be welcome. But it was Gladys who popped her gray head around the cabinets, sniffing the air like a hunting dog. "I'll bet a person could get cancer inhaling these mites and spores."

"You shouldn't say stuff like that, Gladys. If I do get sick, then I'll sue PCM."

She seemed to think that was funny and sat down on a filled carton. "Just like your mother. Such a kidder." She wore thick stockings with her rubber-soled shoes. Support stockings, Jeremy's grandmother used to call them. Gladys held something out for him. "I noticed you skipped lunch. Trying to get a gold star?"

Jeremy tore the wrapper off a granola bar filled with chocolate chips. He took a big bite. "Thanks, Gladys." She was right about him being hungry, but how did she know he hadn't left for lunch?

"I don't know what Irv's thinking." Gladys shook her head as she peered down the aisle. "He was going to get the archive company to box the files, then when he heard you were coming, he changed his mind." She reached into the pocket of her full skirt and took out two more granola bars. One she handed to Jeremy, the other she opened for herself. "He's become impossible lately."

"Really? Why's that?"

She stopped chewing and frowned at him.

He backpedaled. "I was just wondering if I've done something to offend him. I don't imagine this is the most glamorous job in the firm."

Gladys relaxed. "Irv's a crotchety old man. Not that he's so old — not even sixty-three. But he's angry at the world and that ages a person." She stood up from the carton. Jeremy was surprised by the ease with which she moved. She was several years older than Irv, but except for the deep wrinkles on her face and hands, one would never know it. "And he was so different a few years ago. Such an inspiration."

"What changed him?"

"What happens to people whose lives revolve around their

work? If they don't have a little love, a few interests, they become narrow and bitter. Maybe they even start drinking a little more than is good for them. Because they know once they can't work anymore, they'll have nothing."

Gladys handed Jeremy a third granola bar. How many more did she have hidden away in her pockets? "It's almost five," she said. "Why don't you call it a day?"

He surveyed the endless file cabinets.

"Come on." She patted the crumbs off her skirt and stood up. "It'll all be here tomorrow."

And he was pretty sure she was right about that.

Chapter 11

Jeremy didn't have class until six thirty. He sat in his mother's Lexus in PCM's parking garage, trying to decide what to do for the next hour. Cars were backing out of parking spaces all around him. The five o'clock rush. It was hot in the Lexus. He turned on the ignition to let the air circulate, then took out Judy Lieber's business card. This time, he dialed the number.

"Lieber," she said, rushed or irritated.

"This is Jeremy Stroeb. Sorry to bother you."

"Jeremy. I thought you'd left town."

"No. I'm still here."

"I see."

"I was wondering if you have a few minutes to meet with me. I don't have class until six thirty."

"Class?"

"Yeah. At MIU."

She hesitated for a second, then suggested a McDonald's a few blocks from the campus.

It took Jeremy twenty minutes to get there. The restaurant was brightly lit and surprisingly clean. A party of eight or ten preschoolers were screeching around a clown making balloon animals while their mothers watched. Jeremy didn't see Judy Lieber. The smell of fries made him realize how hungry he was despite the granola bars

Gladys had given him. He went to the counter and ordered a Big Mac, fries, and a coffee. He thought about Lieber. "Make that two coffees."

He brought the food outside where the sound of the kids was replaced by that of heavy rush-hour traffic. There was an enclosed play area with a slide dropping off into a pool of brightly colored plastic balls. Jeremy bit into his hamburger. Chewy, prefabricated meat.

Lieber walked into the restaurant and looked around. Jeremy was relieved she hadn't brought her partner along. She noticed Jeremy waving and came outside, giving him a quick nod as she sat down opposite him. She didn't comment on the absence of his beard or his dress shirt, though she seemed to be taking everything in.

Jeremy handed her a cup of black coffee. "I ordered you this, but if you don't want it, that's fine."

She cocked her head. "Thank you. That was nice of you, Jeremy."

He pushed the packets of sugar and Sweet'N Low toward her.

"I don't need any, thanks." She removed the lid and took a sip.

A truck went by making a thunderous noise.

"My dad used to take me to this McDonald's when I was a kid," he said. "I remember when they put the play area in. I even had a birthday party here once."

Lieber put her coffee down. "What's up, Jeremy? You said you wanted to see me."

"Right." So she wasn't interested in his reminiscences. He held out the French fries. "Want one?"

She shook her head.

"Well, you already know I'm taking classes at MIU," he said. "I wanted to tell you, I also got a job at PCM — my mom's firm."

Jeremy was surprised by the lack of reaction on her part. Disappointed even. What had he been expecting her to say? *Very good, Jeremy. Your parents would be proud of you. I'm proud of you.*

"I figured," Jeremy said, "like we were talking the other day. It could be helpful to have someone on the inside."

"Jesus. I hope you didn't think I was encouraging you to be a mole."

"Why not?" The restaurant door opened. Children rushed into the enclosed play area, shrieking. "It's easy for me," he continued. "I told the partners and registrar I wanted to work and go to school so that I can be a better guardian to Elise. No one suspects I have an ulterior motive."

"How can they not suspect that? Working and studying in your murdered parents' old stomping grounds?"

"I'm not planning on directly asking people if they know who killed my parents."

"But think about it. The average person might not be tuned in to your game plan, but the killer would be hypersensitive to your sudden appearance. He'll be watching you to see if you're getting close. And when you do. Well, let me just say I'm not interested in investigating a third murder."

So much for the pat on the back. "I don't think you have to worry about that. I know how to handle myself."

Lieber shook her head ever so slightly like his mother used to do when she disapproved of something Jeremy was doing but had decided to let him learn from his mistakes.

"I just want to find whoever did this to them," Jeremy said.

A child let out a scream, then began to cry. His mother rushed forward and picked him up — the birthday boy, judging from his hat. "It isn't fair," the little boy sobbed.

"We all want to find whoever killed your parents, Jeremy," Lieber said.

He watched the mother comforting the boy, smoothing his hair, kissing his pink cheek.

"You said you're Elise's guardian," Lieber said. "I thought your uncle was."

"Dwight was just named backup in case I didn't want to do it."

"How does he feel about that?"

"Not happy. I think moving to Lotus Island would have been good for his career."

"I'm sure your sister is relieved you're staying."

He looked away from the play area. "Elise and I have been going through our parents' papers, computer CDs, stuff like that. We figured since the murderer took the laptops, there may have been something important on one of them."

"We looked for computer backups," Lieber said, "but couldn't find anything recent."

"What about the key? If the murderer used a key, then it was most likely someone who knew my mom or dad. You said you checked the security guard's records; did any of my parents' colleagues come on the island that night?"

She shook her head.

"But you do realize it's easy to get on and off the island avoiding both the security cameras and the guards? Joggers, bikers, someone in a small boat."

"We're very aware of that. It's a problem."

"And you've interviewed all the neighbors? Did anyone see anything unusual?"

She half-smiled. Her front teeth overlapped. "Still checking up to make sure I'm doing my job?"

"I don't mean to sound like I'm second-guessing you."

"Jeremy, I appreciate your efforts. But this is a murder investigation. Why don't you concentrate on taking care of your sister and leave it to us to find your parents' killer?"

The clown was carrying a big white square with flickering

lights. "Happy birthday to you," he sang. "Happy birthday to you." Everyone stopped and joined in. "Happy birthday, dear Jamie, happy birthday to you."

Jamie clapped and blew out the candles.

Jeremy remembered his own parents smiling at him. His mother kissing him.

He squeezed his eyes shut. *Happy birthday, Jeremy*.

"Thanks for your time, Detective Lieber." Jeremy stood up. "But I need to get to class."

The professor was talking about mergers and acquisitions. Jeremy had missed the first two lectures and was struggling to follow along. As he listened, Jeremy was reminded of how he'd felt over a year ago sitting in class at NYU. The lack of connection between his future and what he was learning in school. The sense he had of being lost. So he had dropped out before finishing his senior year and left for Europe, hoping that a change of environment would clear the confusion in his mind.

And now he was back, once again sitting in a classroom. How ironic that his future seemed more uncertain than ever.

He was disappointed by Lieber's reaction to his involvement in his parents' investigation. She had to realize there were things he could do that the police couldn't. And he wasn't putting himself at risk. Maybe he was not quite twenty-three, but he had always been an observer of human behavior, and he certainly wasn't about to let himself get caught in anyone's web.

Jeremy's classmates had begun gathering their notebooks and laptops and getting up to leave. Class was over. Most were older students. Some, like Jeremy, were wearing suit pants and dress shirts and had removed their ties. Jeremy's dad had taught during the day, so it was unlikely Jeremy would run into any of his students here, he realized with some discouragement.

The campus was lit by modern overhead lights — anachronistic beside the quaint buildings. Jeremy wondered if Dr. Winter came in at night. Probably not. It seemed like an ideal time to sneak into his father's office and go through his papers.

Jeremy veered in the direction of his father's building, passing a bench where a small figure was stooping to tie the laces on her clunky boot. He doubled back. "Marina?"

Her hair was down in her face, a tangle of shimmering baby copperheads. She pushed it away from her eyes and behind her ear. "Jeremy." She didn't seem surprised to see him, but then she knew he was taking classes here. She gestured toward the notebook under his arm. "Coming or going?"

"Going," he said. "Just finished a class in mergers and acquisitions. I almost forgot what I've been missing."

She didn't smile. She was dressed differently from the day before in a white low-necked sweater that showed a smattering of freckles on her chest. The sweater was loose, but he could tell she wasn't wearing a bra. He tried to keep his eyes from drifting downward.

"You've missed a couple of classes, no? But the son of the brilliant D. C. Stroeb should have no difficulty catching up."

Jeremy felt a jab of annoyance. Even though his father was dead, the references and comparisons were inevitable.

"Of course, academics isn't for everyone," she said as though reading his mind. She took her foot off the bench and hoisted a large canvas satchel filled with papers over her shoulder. It looked like the weight of it might topple her.

"Let me help you with that."

"I got it, thanks. I'm just going to my car."

"I'll walk you." He took the satchel from her. "Damn. Are you grading papers of the entire student body?"

"I'm teaching a lecture, two sessions. Intro to Microeconomics.

A hundred and three students in one class, ninety-four in the other. The survey I gave them was five pages. It adds up to a lot of paper."

"My father enjoyed teaching the intro classes," Jeremy said. "He'd say he liked to get the virgin minds. Then they'd be his forever."

Even in the semidarkness, Jeremy could see Marina's cheeks had flushed. Had he said something to offend her?

"I'm covering your father's intro classes. There was a big scramble for people to take over his schedule at the last minute. None of the other economics professors or instructors had time, so they asked me."

She stopped beside a small yellow car, an old Toyota. It was dirty and when she unlocked the door, Jeremy noticed scattered clothes and crumpled fast-food bags.

"I'm not a very good housekeeper." She took the satchel from Jeremy and threw it in the backseat. "Well, thank you Jeremy, *mon chevalier.*"

"Sure," Jeremy said, wanting to say more, but feeling awkward.

Her lips twitched. A guarded smile as though she was unwilling to give up too much. "Would you like to go for coffee or something to eat?" she asked.

"I guess. If you don't have other plans."

"My laundry and dirty dishes are my other plans. Come. Get in. There's a place not too far from here where I usually have my dinner."

It looked more like a dive than a restaurant, but Jeremy didn't complain as Marina pulled the car into a spot near the Dumpster. A red neon sign flashed "Cerbie's." Inside was a smoky bar with people in collared shirts and loosened ties standing three deep. TVs hanging over either end of the bar were showing boxing matches.

"A lot of business people come here," she shouted over the din. "They like to pretend they're grungy. Like the Sunday Harley-Davidson riders."

He followed her through the crowd, trying not to knock into anyone's beer. The floor was covered with peanut shells that crunched beneath his feet. Even in her heavy boots, Marina moved through the throng with the grace of a dancer. Jeremy's progress was slower. "Excuse me. Pardon me," he said. Coming here was a perfect opportunity for him. He could ask Marina questions about his father. Maybe even, in a roundabout way, ask if his father had any enemies. Lieber was wrong to believe Jeremy might attract the killer's attention this way. And if he did — well, maybe that was what he really wanted.

Marina disappeared through a doorway. It took Jeremy a moment for his eyes to adjust. It was even darker and smokier back here, but at least it was quiet. High wooden booths lined both sides of the room and there were a dozen or so small wooden tables and chairs in the center. Only the booths were occupied. Marina was waving to him from one in the corner.

He slid across the red Naugahyde bench seat opposite her. The fake leather was torn and sticky.

Marina was talking to the waiter, a pimpled young man with spiked hair and a lip ring. He wore a black tee shirt with a three-headed dog and the name of the bar written on it.

"I've ordered cheeseburgers for both of us," Marina said. "Their specialty."

"What are you drinking?" the waiter asked him.

"A beer, I guess."

The waiter looked impatient. We have Corona, Heineken, Bud —"

"Whatever you have on tap is fine."

The waiter disappeared. He'd left behind a basket of peanuts. Marina delicately popped open a shell, examined the nut between her fingers, then placed it on her tongue.

"How old are you?" Jeremy said.

"*Pardon?*"

"I'm sorry. That was rude. It's just you look about sixteen, and you're a graduate assistant."

"Twenty-eight," she said. "Perhaps you think that old for a graduate assistant? But I just seem to have the hardest time with my dissertation." She took a cigarette out of a pack in her satchel — some unfiltered French brand — and lit it with a match from the Cerbie's matchbook in the ashtray. "So today was your first day of work, no?" Marina said, exhaling a cloud of smoke.

Jeremy must have looked surprised.

"I can tell from the shirt. It still has the wrinkles. A virgin shirt, as your father might say." She gave him her muted smile. "So where are you working?"

"My mother's CPA firm."

"That's right. You were studying accounting before you left on your European sojourn, no?"

"That's right." It was cold in this back room, and he had a difficult time keeping his eyes from roaming to her chest.

The waiter put a large martini glass in front of Marina and placed the foaming beer mug down on a coaster with the three-headed dog.

"Cheers," Marina said, raising her glass. Six or eight olives were floating in it.

Jeremy lifted his mug. "Cheers."

They both sipped their drinks. Marina stuck her fingers into her glass and pulled out an olive. She sucked on it, pushed it into her mouth, then licked her fingers. "I love olives. I always order extra."

Jeremy scooped up some peanuts and cracked them open. "So I imagine you worked very closely with my father."

"*Merde!* What happened to your hands?" Marina rested her cigarette in the ashtray, then reached across the table and took his hand in hers.

"It's nothing. Just paper cuts."

"So many? What kind of accounting work makes so many cuts?"

"I was sorting through old papers and boxing them up." He tried to pull his hand away from her, but she held fast.

"You can get infections." She dipped her napkin into her martini glass, then started dabbing each cut with the cold liquid. It stung like hell and his eyes watered, but he no longer tried to take his hand away. She was holding it in her own small one. As she pressed the napkin against his cuts, the sting subsided, and he felt only pressure and the cleansing of his wounds.

"Your hands are like your father's," she said without looking up.

He pulled away.

"I'm sorry. Did I do something to upset you?"

"No." Jeremy wondered himself at his reaction. But perhaps it was shame at feeling something quite the opposite of pain.

The waiter set the cheeseburgers on the table. Jeremy watched her eat — tiny bites, like a mouse. He noticed the way her ears stood away from her head when she pushed her hair behind them and how she licked her fingers when they dripped with grease from her hamburger. He hardly paid attention to what they talked about.

She dropped him off by his car and kissed each of his cheeks, barely touching, but close enough that he could smell the scent of almonds and smoke in her hair. Only then, after she'd driven away, did he realize he hadn't asked her anything more about his father.

Chapter 12

Dwight had chosen a barstool in the elegant lounge at Don Shula's Steakhouse, from which he had a clear view of everyone who came and went. A pianist was playing tunes he recognized from *Chicago*. Classy place. Perfect for making a good impression.

It was a few minutes before eight; Dwight liked to be early. Selma sat beside him sipping a glass of Chardonnay. Her cream-colored suit had long sleeves and a full skirt, so she didn't look as painfully skinny as she often did. She was a good wife. Not the most beautiful maybe, but at least she was no righteous snow queen like his brother's wife.

His brother's wife. She was dead, he reminded himself. They were both dead. A wave of melancholy passed over him — the memory of a time long ago when he was just a scrawny kid and Danny was the big brother he worshipped. Danny, who could ride a bike with no hands, jump off the roof of the house, and had all the best-looking girls hanging around after school hoping for a kiss. And all Dwight lived for was his brother's approval, a ride in his old Corvair. But Danny was always too busy for his kid brother. And when Danny would complain to their mom about Dwight sneaking around after him, whose side did she take? Her firstborn's, naturally. Her golden boy who could do no wrong. Right up until the day she died, she said, "Why can't you be more like your brother, Dwight?"

Well, the competition was over and Dwight was the one left standing. And while on some level Dwight couldn't help but feel redeemed, there was still a deep sadness. After all, his brother had once been his hero. And heroes are tough to forget.

Dwight sipped his Johnny Walker Black and studied the engraving on his thick college ring. *Veritas, Familia, Sapientia* — truth, family, wisdom. How surprised he'd been last year when Danny had asked him if he'd be backup guardian for Elise. And at first, Dwight had adamantly refused. If he'd wanted kids, he told his brother, he would have had his own. But then he thought about it. The house on Lotus Island, the nice stipend. And it wasn't like Elise was a baby. If she turned out to be a pain in the ass, he could always send her to boarding school. So he'd called Danny back and said sure, he and Selma would be happy to help him out. Not that there was any reason to think the contingency would ever become a reality.

But it had. A most advantageous reality. And any guilt Dwight felt over profiting from this terrible event, he justified by reminding himself that this had been Danny's idea — not his.

Several couples came into the restaurant and were taken to their tables by the maître d'.

"You're sure you told Liliam eight?" Dwight said.

Selma was reapplying her red lipstick. "That's what time you told me and that's what I told her." She blotted her lips on a cocktail napkin.

"Maybe Shula's was a bad idea," Dwight said.

"Liliam said Shula's was fine."

Dwight took another sip of his drink. He hated making mistakes. He'd been pretty pleased with himself, coming up with the idea of Selma inviting the Castillos to dinner to thank them for all they'd done. Of course, that was only after he'd left several messages for Enrique and hadn't received any return call. Dwight didn't understand it. He'd thought he and Enrique had gotten on very well at the funeral. "You told her the Shula's in the Alexander Hotel, right? You know there are other Shula's Steakhouses."

"I told her, Dwight. I said eight at Shula's in the Alexander Hotel, just like you told me to."

At precisely eight o'clock, Dwight's dinner guests entered the vestibule. Dwight waved. Enrique gave him an acknowledging nod, then took Liliam's arm and led her into the lounge. What a glamorous couple they made. Funny how you could tell money even from across a room. Enrique was wearing a soft, blue sweater that looked like cashmere, and Dwight immediately felt overdressed in his best navy suit. He had assumed Enrique would be coming straight from work and would still be in business attire.

Enrique reached for Selma's hand and his lips barely grazed it. "How are you this evening, Selma? I must say you look lovely." Then he turned to shake Dwight's hand. "My apologies for not getting back to you, Dwight. I know you left me several messages, but I had a number of crises I needed to deal with. I hope it was nothing urgent."

"No, no problem, Enrique. Thanks so much for joining us for dinner tonight."

Liliam was standing beside her husband dressed in a sleeveless, gold top cut low enough to reveal her magnificent cleavage. Her blonde hair was lightly lacquered and combed so that it fell across one eye. Dwight slid off the barstool and kissed each of her cheeks in the European fashion. "So nice to see you, Liliam. I'm glad you were both able to make it."

"Our pleasure." She gave him a smile that seemed for him alone.

"Shall we go to our table?" Enrique said.

Dwight had expected the four of them to linger over cocktails and then enjoy a leisurely dinner, but Enrique was already leading the two women out of the bar. Dwight fumbled with his wallet and left a twenty. With no time to wait for change, he hurried after his guests.

Enrique felt as though he'd been shanghaied. Liliam had called him at the office and announced the dinner plans. At first, he had told her to cancel — to say he had a previous engagement. But after the fourth phone message came in from Dwight, he realized sooner or later he'd have to submit. He imagined Dwight would be hitting him up for a contribution to his campaign. Enrique would just as soon have mailed him a check and been done with it.

He gave his order for a small filet and a baked potato. Dwight had already ordered one of the more expensive Cabernets on the wine list and sent it back after pronouncing it "too vinegary." Enrique supposed he'd be allowed to pick up the tab even though the wannabe judge had invited him and Liliam to dinner. Enrique didn't really mind. As long as this could soon be over. He'd told Liliam to please not order dessert.

Enrique hadn't been here since twenty years ago when the restaurant was called Dominique's and was renowned for its exotic fare. He and Rachel had sat at a table in a back room, which Enrique could no longer identify. They'd changed the layout when Shula's took over the space, and for that Enrique was grateful. Maybe he wouldn't be reminded of that night. But he was. He couldn't help feeling her presence.

The lights had been dim, dimmer than tonight. It had been late and they'd been practically alone in the restaurant. They'd come directly from the office, where they'd been reviewing the final financial report. Rachel wore a jade-colored suit that brought out her emerald eyes.

Enrique remembered how good he was feeling that night. He had finally gotten his father's approval to begin construction on his own hotel in the Caribbean. He'd call it the Olympus. And although his father had disapproved of his plans, Enrique was confident that once the Olympus was up and running, his father would be so impressed with Enrique's business acumen he would finally have to take him seriously.

Enrique had longed to share his good news with Rachel, but he knew the prospect of success wouldn't be nearly as seductive as the success itself, so he concentrated on the evening and her beauty.

Enrique ordered the rattlesnake salad and Rachel laughed. Called him naïve. "You don't believe they really use rattlesnake?" she said.

"Of course they do."

"It's chicken." And she stuck her fork into the mound of diced meat on his plate and tasted it. "I'm right. Try it yourself." She had smiled at him. "You see? Things aren't always what they seem, Enrique."

"No appetizer?" Dwight said.

"Excuse me?"

"Don't you want an appetizer, Enrique? I understand the stone crabs here are excellent. Of course, if you'd rather not —"

"We love stone crabs," Liliam said. "That would be wonderful."

Enrique's cheeks ached from the polite smile he'd been attempting to maintain. He played the mental game his father had taught him when he was a young boy in Cuba. They'd be hiking through the mountains and little Enrique's feet would be so hot and blistered he could barely walk. "Think about other things," his father would say, "not your distress. *Los pájaros, los árboles, las flores.*" The birds, the trees, the flowers.

"A toast." Dwight held up his wine glass. "To friends and neighbors. I want to thank the two of you for all your help in getting through this very difficult time."

The four of them clinked glasses. Enrique took a sip, then settled his glass on the white tablecloth. "Hopefully things will acquire some semblance of normalcy for Elise now that Jeremy's staying home," he said.

"Yes," Liliam said. "Though I'm very disappointed the two of you won't be our neighbors."

"For the time being," Dwight said.

Liliam raised her eyebrow. "You're still planning on moving to Lotus Island?"

"I would say it's inevitable." Dwight signaled to a waiter. "Could we get some more bread here?"

"Are you buying property?" Enrique asked.

"No," Dwight said, biting into the last roll. "What I meant was, while I'm proud that my nephew has stepped up to the plate, unfortunately, I have my doubts about his follow through."

"Well, he certainly appears to be turning over a new leaf," Enrique said. "I saw him last week at PCM. I understand he's working there and taking night classes at MIU."

Dwight frowned.

"I didn't know Jeremy was getting a job," Selma said. "That's great."

"A job? Taking classes?" Dwight shook his head. "Isn't that just like Jeremy?"

"How do you mean?" Enrique said.

"I believe he really wants to do the right thing," Dwight said. "But he'll never last at the job or school or the guardianship."

"That's a bit harsh," Enrique said.

"I don't mean to be. In fact, I'll do everything I can to ensure his success. But you don't know my nephew the way I do. Jeremy's never been able to commit to anything for very long."

"Perhaps these new circumstances will change things," Enrique said.

"I pray you're right," Dwight said. "I pray you're right." He took a roll from a fresh bread basket before passing the basket to Liliam.

"Thank you, Dwight. Aren't the onion rolls delicious?" Liliam broke off a piece and buttered it. "I still hope you'll get to be our neighbors. It's so hard to find people one has things in common with. Not that I have anything bad to say about Rachel and D.C., may they rest in peace." She crossed herself. "But it's funny how you can be neighbors with people for so many years and not really know them."

The waiter set a huge platter of stone crab claws down on the table.

"My goodness," Selma said. "Don't these look lovely?"

"Were you close with your sister-in-law, Selma?" Liliam asked.

Selma glanced at her husband. "Not really." Her red lipstick was smeared below her lip line. "Rachel was always very busy — her children, her career."

"Oh, I know what you mean," Liliam said. "Some of these career women act like what they're doing's more important than the rest of us."

"I didn't mean to sound like Rachel ever talked down to me," Selma said. "She was always nice and encouraging. In fact, she's the one who suggested I volunteer at the nursing home and it's been very rewarding."

"That's wonderful, Selma." Liliam said. "I find my charity work gratifying, too."

"Aren't you one of the key people at SWEET?" Dwight asked.

"Key people?" Liliam smiled. "You flatter me."

"What's SWEET?" Selma asked.

"We're an organization devoted to helping the sugar workers," Liliam said.

"An organization my brother was quick to denounce as a cover for the sugar lobbyists," Dwight said.

"That's something I never understood," Liliam said. "Why was

D.C. so set on hurting me and Enrique? We always made an effort to be nice to him and his family."

"He wasn't trying to hurt us, Liliam." Enrique said.

"But Liliam's right," Dwight said. "My brother's ravings against the sugar industry could have had a disastrous impact on Castillo Enterprises."

"We're a diversified set of businesses," Enrique said. "We're not dependent on revenue from any one source."

Liliam's brows were knitted. "But Dwight makes an excellent point, doesn't he, *querido?*"

"As I said." Enrique tried to keep his voice even. "Castillo Enterprises is diversified."

"Even your real estate business wasn't immune to my brother's programs," Dwight said. "If his proposal to lift the Cuban embargo was to be enacted, that would damage your hotel business. You'd have all this new competition from Cuba. I'm just saying, Enrique, you're in an awkward position here."

"What do you mean?" Liliam stopped eating her crab claw. There was crabmeat all over her hands.

"Unfortunately, the police investigation hasn't been closed," Dwight said. "Even though the police have a viable suspect, one of the detectives has decided to prolong things. She's digging around, trying to find a suspect with a motive."

"Prolong things?" Liliam said.

"What worries me," Dwight said, "is there's so much pressure to find the murderer that the police may cook up a scapegoat."

"You mean they might think someone from Castillo Enterprises was connected to the murders?" Liliam said.

A slow rage spread over Enrique, a gas leak ready to ignite.

"We're family people, business people," Liliam said. "Not murderers."

"I'm just saying, you can never be too careful," Dwight said.

"But I want you both to know I'm in your court, so to speak." He gave a half-smile. "I have the ear of some very influential people. I'm sure I can persuade my contacts there's no connection between, well let's say, certain people who may have been hurt by D. C. Stroeb's activities and the deaths of my brother and his wife."

Liliam glanced at Enrique.

"And please," Dwight said. "Don't think anything of it. I do this because you're my friends. My friends and one day, I hope, my neighbors."

Enrique gripped the edge of the table, only the greatest effort keeping him from overturning it.

He took a long, deep breath.

Los pájaros, los árboles, las flores.

Chapter 13

The stables. The dungeon. The hellhole. Jeremy had come up with an assortment of names for the place where he now spent a disproportionate amount of his waking hours boxing workpapers. He'd been in the file room for almost two weeks, and each day his frustration grew at having only minimal human interaction. His investigation was going nowhere. Not at PCM. Not on the campus of MIU.

An edge of paper sliced through Jeremy's finger. He brought it up to his mouth to suck out the sting. Marina flashed through his mind. Marina with her martini balm and round red mouth. He hadn't seen her since that night at the bar. At least, not in the flesh — only in his imagination.

He entered the information from the next binder into the laptop. If they're destroying all of these papers, why did he need to keep a list? It didn't make sense to him, but there was no one to ask. Gladys would usually make an appearance once a day and drop off a couple of granola bars accompanied by "tsk tsk" and "I can't believe he's making you do this."

He threw a binder into a carton and picked up another. Many of the papers he'd been discarding were well over twenty years old. They were written in pencil and over the years had smudged or faded. The pages of this one were tattered and its binding coming undone. The disintegrating papers left a powdery film over his hands, jeans, and tee shirt. Dust to dust. He'd stopped wearing his new suits and shirts after the first couple of days when he realized the only contact he'd have with members of his mother's firm would be with its ghosts.

He slammed the drawer shut, then pulled open the top one in the next cabinet. The cabinet teetered and pitched toward him. Jeremy braced himself against it until it settled back into place. Jeez. One of these cabinets could kill someone.

He opened the drawer more cautiously. Castillo Enterprises. Some of the workpapers went back thirty years, though they didn't appear to be in any particular order. Enrique had said Jeremy's mother had been on the audit a while back and then again recently. Jeremy was overcome with a need to see her name, to touch papers written in her own hand. He went through the binders; some were dated fifteen years ago, twenty years ago, eleven years ago. Nothing with his mother's name on it. Then he saw it. Eighteen years ago. His mother's even, confident handwriting. RACHEL STROEB, AUDIT MANAGER, the cover said. And beneath her name, SITE VISITS. He gripped the thick binder tightly and stared at her name, sensing her presence in the room with him. Carefully, so it wouldn't come apart, he opened the binder and flipped through the pages. Hotels and properties owned by Castillo Enterprises, each with photos, description, analyses, and a conclusion. He turned to the thickest section: Olympus, a hotel on some island called St. Mary's in the Grenadines. His mother's crisp Pentel strokes said "total loss." What had she meant by that? There was a photo — the skeleton of a structure, like a forgotten Greek temple. Beyond it, purple cliffs and endless azure waters. A man stood in the corner of the picture, his back to the camera, perhaps to show scale.

The door to the file room slammed. Jeremy, as though he'd been caught with a dirty magazine, threw the binder into one of the cartons. Irv Luria appeared from behind a tall gray file cabinet. "So you're still here." Irv said, thumbs hooked on the pockets of his pants, his round belly protruding beyond his suit jacket. "Well, come on. Let's grab some lunch."

It was not even eleven in the morning, but Jeremy was happy for this reprieve, even if it meant spending time with Irv Luria.

To Jeremy's surprise, Irv took him up to the private club on the penthouse floor that the partners had memberships in. The Osprey Club. Paneled walls, hushed rooms, great views of downtown, Biscayne Bay, and the buzzards that perched on the roofs of nearby buildings. This was the pinnacle his mother had achieved. But Jeremy had told his parents he wanted no part of this world filled with hovering waiters, linen tablecloths, and the clink of expensive crystal. Or had the truth been, he just hadn't believed himself capable of attaining it?

Irv ignored the still unoccupied tables set for lunch. He continued through the restaurant to the dim oak room, its ornate bar covered with hideous gargoyles ready to spring from their perches.

Irv moved slowly, as though his feet had been cut open by glass. In his wrinkled seersucker suit and crooked bow tie, he looked more like a bum you'd see pushing a cart down Lincoln Road than a partner in one of the top CPA firms in the country. What a pair they made with Jeremy in his sneakers and dusty jeans. Jeremy wondered if the scowling men in the portraits on the walls were disturbed by the downward turn their dignified club had taken.

Jeremy had been to the Osprey Club once before with his mom. It had been a special occasion; he'd been accepted to NYU. He remembered being uneasy, waiting for her to suddenly launch into a dozen reasons why it would be better for him to attend college locally, but she had seemed genuinely pleased. She had worn a red suit, pearl earrings, and a matching necklace. He was aware how the businessmen who walked past their table would slow down and look at her. She didn't return their gaze.

She had squeezed his hand. "I'm going to miss you, Jeremy. But

I believe there will always be something connecting us, no matter how far apart we are."

Jeremy felt the sting of the memory. He was relieved Irv had taken a seat at the bar and was engaged with the bartender. Other than the waitstaff and maître d', Jeremy and Irv were the only people in the bar, though no one seemed surprised to see Irv.

The club had the musty feel of another time and place. The stools were padded with tufted leather held in place by brass-headed nails. But the brass had dulled and the leather reminded Jeremy of saddles at ranches where you'd rent horses by the hour. The air smelled stale — lingering cigar smoke and thirty years of expensive cologne and perfumes clinging to the heavy velvet drapes. The bartender put a glass of amber liquid on the rocks in front of Irv.

"Just ice tea for me, please," Jeremy said.

The bartender either didn't hear Jeremy or chose to ignore him and gave him a glass of whatever Irv was having.

"You don't drink ice tea to toast your mother, young man." Irv raised his glass and Jeremy did the same. "To one of the most spectacular meteors I've ever seen." Irv threw his head back, finishing most of the liquid.

Jeremy sipped his drink. It was sweet and unfamiliar.

"Drambouie," Irv said. "Haven't you ever tasted it? Your mother was practically weaned on it." He finished what was in his glass and dropped it down hard on the wood bar. "She'd never order ice tea. At least, not when she was your age." Irv seemed to be searching for something in Jeremy's face. "She was about your age when she started with the firm."

The bartender set a second glass in front of Irv. Irv swirled it around. "I once held court up here in the fading dusk of the sultry Miami days. All the innocent, fresh-faced auditors would gather around, hanging on my every word. Like they were drinking my nectar. You see, Jeremy, I was a god. And they were frightened, awed, obsequious. All of them." He sipped his drink. "All but one. Rachel Lazar. That's right, Jeremy. That was before she and your father were married."

Irv shifted his glass from hand to hand. His thin skin was covered with hundreds of tiny exploded blood vessels, making him appear perpetually red-faced. But the dull blue eyes were shining.

"Sometimes after the others would leave, Rachel would sit with me. Right here, as you're doing. Just the two of us. And she would ask me things." He closed his eyes. "Oh, about everything. She was insatiable. And she'd suck words out of me like a famished leech. I taught her about integrity and honor. I taught her never to compromise." He inhaled deeply and opened his eyes. "Another Drambouie, Pete. Drink up, Jeremy. Make that two more, Pete."

A couple of men in suits walked into the oak room, then catching sight of Irv, turned and walked out.

"One night," Irv said, "we were talking about life. Would you rather live a long, safe life, Rachel, or a brief, magnificent one?" Irv sipped his drink. "What do you think she said?"

"A long one, I suppose." At least that was what he hoped she had wanted, but he wondered just how well he had known his mother.

Irv took another deep breath. "I was disappointed in her for that response. For her lack of total commitment. If you want greatness, you must commit to greatness," I told her. "Your quest must be all-encompassing. You cannot compromise. You must not compromise." Irv was talking to his folded hands now. "I never guessed how deeply my lessons would hit their mark."

Irv waved his empty glass at the bartender. It was noon and Jeremy's stomach growled. The liquor was muddling his brain.

"But I was her mentor. Did you know that, Jeremy? She was

Galatea to my Pygmalion. I shaped her, and she learned my lessons well. Too well, perhaps? Do you think she remembered it was I who taught her everything of value?"

Irv took a long drink from a fresh glass. "And what of her mentor, I'm sure you're wondering? What became of the principled man whose life was ruled by the highest code of integrity?

"I, who held the purest view of an honorable world? Who dreamed of disintegrating in glory as I spun toward the sun? I sit here — a useless old man no one wants to listen to anymore. And your mother, Jeremy. Your mother became the meteor."

Tears the size of giant raindrops ran down Irv's flat cheeks, over the burst red capillaries. "What the fuck are you staring at?" he said. "Why the fuck have you come here?"

Jeremy slid off the barstool. The maître d' and another man were coming toward them.

"Did she send you? Did she?"

The maître d' stepped in between them. A hand squeezed Jeremy's shoulder. "Come on, son," a soft southern voice said.

Jeremy followed Bud McNally out of the bar, into the restaurant. He could still hear Irv shouting. "Did she?"

Bud led Jeremy to a window table some distance from the bar. Jeremy's legs were shaking. He didn't know if it was the alcohol or the unexpected attack by Irv. Bud handed him the bread basket. "Eat this."

Jeremy felt as though he'd done something to unleash Irv. He stared out at the dark, filmed windows of an adjacent office tower.

"I'm sorry about that, Jeremy." Bud tore off a piece of a pumpernickel roll and buttered it. "Irv can get a little emotional." He smiled at the waiter. "You have fried oysters today, Simon?"

"For you, of course, Mr. McNally."

"You like oysters, Jeremy? The chef here makes the best ones

I've ever tasted. And I'm a cracker. I know about such things. Make that two fried oysters, Simon." He slipped the bread into his mouth. "So aside from awkward barroom encounters, what have you been up to, Jeremy?"

"Boxing up old files for Mr. Luria."

"That's right. And how's that going? Almost done?"

Jeremy caught Bud glancing at his cut hands.

"Irv's an unhappy man, Jeremy. I think your mother's death affected him more than he lets on."

"I'd hate to see him when he is letting on."

Bud laughed. "You're all right, son."

"Was he on bad terms with my mother?"

The smile faded. "What do you mean?"

"He seems bitter toward her."

"Irv's a bitter man."

"But was there something going on between him and my mother?"

"Irv's not capable of hurting a fly, if that's what you're thinking."

"I'm just wondering why he seems so angry at her."

Bud signaled to the waiter. "Bring me a Grey Goose, Simon. Thanks." He tapped his thick fingers against the linen tablecloth. "Your mother was concerned Irv's drinking may have been impairing his effectiveness."

"She wanted to fire him?"

"We don't fire partners, Jeremy."

"Retire, then. She wanted him to retire?"

The waiter placed Bud's drink on the table. "Let's just say, she was concerned." Bud sipped his drink. "And Irv was hurt. That's all. Hurt that your mother could even contemplate such a thing."

"Because he'd once been her mentor."

Bud raised his eyebrow. "That's right."

"So is he going to retire?"

"Certainly not. It was just talk. Not anything any of us were seriously considering."

The waiter set two platters of fried oysters on the table. The heavy oil and pungent smell turned Jeremy's stomach.

"Now, don't these look great?" Bud jabbed a big one with his fork. He licked his lips after he'd chewed it. "But perhaps it would be best if you moved on from the filing project, Jeremy. Tomorrow, get back into one of those sharp suits of yours, and we'll get you out on a real audit." He speared another oyster. "Now, how's that sound?"

Chapter 14

Jeremy hadn't returned to the file room after lunch. Bud had shooed him out of the building, telling him to take the rest of the day off, then report to Castillo Enterprises the next morning. So things were looking up. At least Jeremy would have a chance to talk with some of the other auditors, perhaps pick up if anyone besides Irv held a grudge against his mother.

Jeremy had a few hours to kill before his six thirty class. He considered calling Elise, but she was probably in class. It seemed to him she was doing better, though she was still occasionally sleep-walking. They had their late night dinners together, watched TV, then she went to bed while he went for a run.

They talked less frequently about the investigation and per-versely, this had the effect of making Jeremy think about it more. But what could he say to his sister? That he was trying but there just wasn't enough opportunity?

You make your own opportunity, he could hear his father say.

He pulled into the parking lot at MIU, but found no available spaces. The campus in the early afternoon was completely different from when he came here for his evening classes. The paths and grassy areas were teeming with blue-jeaned students carrying backpacks.

Cars were parked along the curb that surrounded the campus. The "No Parking" sign and warning that your car will be towed didn't seem to faze the other drivers, so Jeremy slipped into one of the last remaining illegal spots.

He headed toward his father's building. Maybe Winter wouldn't be around. Maybe Marina would. A group of students in brown tee shirts were milling about like hornets around a damaged nest. One was loping toward him, but Jeremy didn't slow his pace.

"Hey. You're D.C.'s son, right?" The kid was panting. He had greasy hair and sunken cheeks covered with acne. Written on his brown tee shirt in white letters was CAFÉ J. The other eight or ten students gathered around Jeremy, as well.

"You shaved your beard," said a short, plump girl with wild, black curls. She must have seen him after the funeral at the Castillos' house. "Are you here for the meeting?"

"Why would he be here for the meeting, Liddy?" the greasy kid said.

"I don't know, Queso." She looked up at Jeremy. "Are you?" He didn't have a chance to answer. "Well, it doesn't matter. That prick Winter cancelled it," Liddy said. "Locked the door to the room we always use, and when we went to ask the secretary, she said, 'I'm sorry, the economics department facilities are only available for sanctioned clubs.'"

"What club?" Jeremy asked.

"You know." She pointed at her shirt. "CAFÉ J. It stands for Cuban-Americans for Economic Justice. Your father started it."

"Winter's been trying to shut us down for years," someone else said. "He never had the balls while your dad was alive."

"But why would he want to shut you down?" Jeremy said.

Liddy rolled her eyes. "Funding, probably. Some of the rich Cubans who give the school money weren't too happy with your father's politics."

"It wasn't sweet enough for them," Queso said, punching another kid in the arm.

"That's good, Queso. Sweet. Not sweet enough for SWEET."

And everyone laughed as though at an inside joke.

A slight figure weighed down by a satchel was hurrying along the path toward the economics building.

"Excuse me," Jeremy said. "I need to go."

Liddy followed his eyes. "Marina Champlain? You know her?"

"Not really." He didn't know why Liddy made him feel defensive, but he didn't have time to analyze her tone or his reaction. Marina had disappeared behind a crowd of students. "I'll catch you guys later."

When Jeremy reached the door to the building, there was no sign of Marina. He sprinted up the stairs to the third floor, but came to an abrupt stop as he stepped out of the stairwell. At the opposite end of the hallway stood a tall, bald man in a navy blazer. Winter. Jeremy slipped behind a corner and peered out. Winter was talking to a large blonde woman who was dressed in high heels and one of those sheer floral outfits he'd occasionally notice the rich women on Lotus Island wearing. Definitely not a student. In fact, he was pretty sure he recognized the deep, raspy laugh of Mrs. Castillo. But why was she talking to the dean?

A couple of students came up the stairs, giving Jeremy a funny look. When he glanced back down the hall, Winter and the woman were gone.

"You're here early today, Jeremy," said a soft, accented voice near his ear. "Have you quit your job?" Marina asked. Where had she come from? "Too many paper cuts?"

She was wearing a tight, camouflage tee shirt and oversized khaki pants that hung low on her hips. A couple of inches of pale muscled midriff were exposed and a tiny belly-button ring in the shape of a serpent's head with red-jeweled eyes stared up at Jeremy.

"I got the afternoon off," he said.

"Good." She handed him her satchel. "I was hoping to see you. I have something for you."

He felt an inexplicable rush as he followed her out of the building. Her hair was piled high on her head and loose curls surrounded her long, thin neck. He could make out a tattoo at the base of her hairline. Something with wings: a butterfly? a bird? a bat?

They were out in the open now, walking toward the parking lot. His own car was still where he'd left it illegally parked. They passed two of the CAFÉ J students, Liddy and Queso. Jeremy gave them a half-smile. They didn't return it.

"Do you know them?" Jeremy asked after they were beyond earshot.

"The CAFÉ Jers? They were the closest thing your father had to groupies."

Groupies? They seemed more serious than that. "Did you know Winter's closed down their club?"

Marina opened the door to her yellow Toyota, took her satchel from Jeremy, and threw it in the back.

"Winter has closed down all the clubs your father had organized. There were perhaps half a dozen." She held up her small hand and counted her fingers. "Let's see: G-W-E-N — Global Warming Ends Now, S-A-W — Students Against War, F-M-F-W — Free Markets for a Free World. And a couple more." She slid into the driver's seat. "Well, come on. Get in."

Jeremy hesitated. "Where are we going?"

"Are you afraid I'll kidnap you, Jeremy?"

He sat back in the seat. It was too low to the ground, as though the springs had lost their bounce, and his legs felt cramped in the tight floor space. He hadn't noticed this the other night when she'd taken him to the bar.

"I found some papers of your father's." She backed the car out of the spot too quickly. Jeremy turned around to be sure no one was walking behind them. "I didn't think it safe to keep them at the school. I half-expected Winter to burn your father's writings and publications like the church did to the heretics in the Middle Ages."

"Do you think my father was a heretic?"

She pulled out of the campus onto the main road. "I think your father was a genius."

"Why did Winter hate him?"

She patted Jeremy's leg as though he was a child and gave a small laugh. "Let me count the ways."

"I know he wasn't happy about my father's politics."

"Or popularity, or tenure, or the fact that some of the key contributors to the school are representatives of a major sugar growers' organization."

"So they wanted my father shut down?"

"Many people wanted your father shut down."

Marina turned into an old Miami neighborhood. The oak trees were so tall and wide they blocked the sun, and the sparse grass was covered with dead leaves. Several of the houses were two-story and built from coquina, the rock the early settlers had used, Jeremy's dad once told him. But the neighborhood was shabby, with rusted cars up on concrete blocks and plywood on windows that had probably been put up for the last hurricane season. Though judging from the condition of the wood, Jeremy wondered if some of the protective coverings dated back to Hurricane Andrew in '92.

Marina stopped on a gravel driveway next to a turquoise and white Chevrolet that resembled a Checker cab, probably a mid-'50's model. It had a thick blanket of dead leaves on the windshield.

Jeremy was taken aback by the vibrant green lawn. It was a bit jarring beside the two-story gray house that looked like something out of an old black-and-white film. An ancient, hunched woman in a wide-brimmed straw hat and gardening gloves was spraying water from a hose over the front yard.

"My landlady," Marina said to Jeremy under her breath. "Good afternoon, Mrs. Lambert," Marina called as she strode toward the back of the house with her satchel over her back.

The old woman squinted at Jeremy. Her light eyes were so clouded by cataracts Jeremy wondered how she could see. She turned off the hose and tottered toward Jeremy. And then she smiled. A wide toothless grin.

"Come on, Jeremy," Marina said. "I live back here."

But Jeremy was paralyzed by the old woman's smile. "She's waiting for you," she said, her voice quivering as though unaccustomed to speaking.

"Jeremy."

"Did you remember to bring your charger?" Mrs. Lambert asked.

Marina squeezed his wrist. "Come on."

Marina's apartment was in a separate structure behind the house. It consisted of two small rooms and looked as though it had once been a garage.

"What was she talking about?" Jeremy asked. Through a doorway, he could see the bedroom with its unmade bed and a pile of clothes on a side chair. A black bra, pink thong. He turned away. The front room had a futon, a red desk and chair that were chipped and revealing an earlier coat of blue, and a tiny kitchen area with a rust-stained sink filled with unwashed dishes.

"Mrs. Lambert has dementia," Marina said, picking up the newspapers from the gray futon, which appeared to be stained with coffee and red wine. "She never makes any sense." She spread out an old faded blanket with an Indian pattern over the low sofa. "There. That's better, no? You can sit here, Jeremy."

He perched on the edge of the futon.

Marina turned on the ceiling fan to full blast. The force of the swirling air caused her curls to fly out from her face. "It's stuffy in here," she said. "No AC. And I'm not sure the fan helps. It just seems to circulate the same putrid air." She lifted her loose hair and rubbed her neck. There were perspiration stains under her arms and just below the curve of her breasts. He forced himself not to stare at her. His own shirt was sticking to his chest. It was hard to breathe. Why didn't she open the windows? Perhaps they were painted shut. He could just make them out behind the dusty, broken venetian blinds.

"Would you like some wine, Jeremy?"

"I'm fine, thanks."

But she pulled the cork out of a gallon jug and filled two plastic tumblers. Something small and black darted across the dirty terrazzo floor.

She handed him a tumbler. "My wine glasses are all broken. Too fragile for my lifestyle, I suppose." She kicked off her clunky army boots, lit a cigarette, then sat down beside him. He could feel the heat of her body. He could smell her. Smoky musk and almonds. She touched her tumbler against his. "To your father."

To my father. He recalled Irv's earlier toast today to his mother. Marina's knee pressed against his. He had to stay focused. "You said you have some of my father's papers?"

With one small finger, she outlined his cheekbones, his forehead, his nose, his chin, his lips. He needed to get back to school. He had class. His car might be towed away.

She dipped his hand into her wine glass. The red wine dripped on her tee shirt as she took his fingers into her mouth, sucking the wine from each. Chills ran down his spine and his groin tightened.

"My father's papers," he whispered.

She put the cigarette out against the wall and let it drop to the floor. Then she pressed her small, round mouth against his. She tasted like vinegar and tobacco.

Her tongue was rolling around his own. The ceiling fan spun wildly — creaking, screaming. The heat was getting closer.

Don't do this, a voice said. *Stop. Leave*. But the physical need for her was overwhelming.

His hands groped her thin arms, her tight abdomen, her small breasts. He pulled off his shirt, then hers, and his tongue worked its way from her salty neck, down her chest, until he found himself pressed against her stomach, eye to eye with the rubies in the tiny serpent ring.

Then he felt her small warm hand slide deep into his pants.

Chapter 15

Jeremy wondered if it would start. It had been over a month since his dad had driven it. He turned the key in the ignition and listened to the weak sputter, as though the old car were gasping for breath. He tried again. The engine made a valiant effort, like a dying dog staggering the last few inches to its master's feet. Then it was silent and Jeremy knew the battery was dead.

His father's car — the red 1966 Corvair he'd owned since he was a teenager and had maintained lovingly ever since.

Jeremy lifted open the trunk. "Rear-engine, air-cooled," he could hear his father say. The only other cars made like this were the old Porsche and original Volkswagen. And now, even Porsche had sold out. It was liquid cooled and that didn't count. Jeremy hooked up the battery charger cables to the battery, then plugged it in. If he was lucky, he'd be able to jump-start it.

He was already wearing a dress shirt and his suit pants. Stupid. He should have checked first thing this morning before he showered. Now, he'd not only arrive late for his first day at Castillo Enterprises, but he'd smell like a garage mechanic. But the truth was, when he woke up this morning, the last thing he was thinking about was how he'd get to work or get his car out of the tow yard.

Marina had driven him home last night after they'd discovered his mother's Lexus had been towed. It was after midnight. She had kissed him lightly on the cheek as though there had been nothing between them. Good, he had told himself. It had been nothing. And it wouldn't happen again. He wouldn't let it happen again.

He had found Elise sitting on the floor of their mother's office, scribbling in her gibberish writing on a yellow pad. She didn't seem to be aware of him. He had taken her back to her room and tucked her in under her white comforter.

He didn't understand what had happened to him last night with Marina. It was as though he'd been in a trance. And it made him angry. He wasn't some impulsive animal. He had responsibilities — to his sister, to his parents.

He disconnected the charger, remembering a day he'd helped his father work on the engine. How his father had explained each component, every tool. So focused on sharing the experience with Jeremy that he had thrust his pointing finger into the spinning fan, slicing it open. Blood had dripped over the engine compartment, but his father hadn't seemed to care. He'd wrapped his hand in a rag and said to Jeremy, "Well, are you ready to take her for a spin?"

Now Jeremy slid into his father's car, pressed his foot down on the accelerator, and turned the key in the ignition. This time the engine started right up. He patted the dashboard. "Good girl," he said, just like his father used to.

The car felt familiar to him. The vague smell of gasoline, the harshness of the engine, the way you felt all the bumps in the road, reminded Jeremy of riding with his father. Jeremy's hands settled naturally into certain grooves on the steering wheel. And whether it was his imagination or not, Jeremy was almost positive his hands held the wheel exactly where his father's had.

Castillo Enterprises was housed in a recently built glass office tower overlooking the yacht basin in Coconut Grove. It was perched on the Silver Bluff, the largest geological formation in South Florida, and was visible from all directions, the name Castillo shining in blue like a futuristic lighthouse. Everything about the building said money: the lobby's granite floors, the windowed elevators with a view of the bay, and the conference room Jeremy had been directed to with its long, glass table, cushioned chairs, and ceiling-to-floor windows from which he could make out the Miami skyline in the distance.

Jeremy had been told to report to Robbie Ivy, the supervisor on the audit. Robbie had his back to Jeremy. He was hunched over his laptop at the conference table facing the wall of windows. He was a small-boned guy with shiny, straight, black hair, a bit long for a professional, and was wearing a navy suit. Was he working or discreetly admiring the view?

Jeremy let the door close behind him and the auditor spun around. Jeremy did a double-take. Robbie was a female. Jeremy recognized the blue eyes and pale skin of the young woman he'd bumped into coming out of his mother's office two weeks ago. But instead of surprise, she wore an annoyed expression.

"You were supposed to be here at eight thirty." She'd be pretty if she wasn't trying so hard to look pissed.

"I know. I'm sorry. I had car trouble."

"Car trouble." She pronounced 'car' with a flat Boston accent. "I can tell from the smell. Have you worked on fixed assets before?"

"Actually, I'm only —"

"Never mind. You can follow last year's schedules and the audit program."

"Sure. No problem."

She returned to her own laptop. She was definitely irritated by his presence. Was she embarrassed about the incident at his mother's office? He decided to steer clear of it.

"So you're from Boston, aren't you?"

Her head didn't move, but her blue eyes shifted in his direction.

"I can tell from the accent. I had some friends at BU and Tufts. I understand they've got some snow up there now."

She looked back down at her laptop.

He was undeterred. "Since this is my first time involved with Castillo Enterprises — my first audit, in fact — would you mind giving me a little orientation?"

Robbie checked her watch. He was guessing she was only a year or two older than he, but she had the impatient, edgy mannerisms of a grownup. Or maybe it was a remnant of some uptight northeastern prep school. "If you want to come early some morning, say around seven, I can fill you in. But right now we're on billable time and we're wasting it."

So much for fraternizing with the audit staff. Jeremy glanced around the conference room. There were framed photos of properties in amazing settings arranged on one of the walls, evidently the holdings of Castillo Enterprises. He remembered the audit binder he'd found in his mother's handwriting — SITE VISITS. Maybe he should mention his mother's office. Clear the air.

"You know," he said, "we've met before. Twice actually. At the Castillos' house, then in the office. Do you remember?"

She picked her head up slowly. "Look, I realize you're just here to pass the time or whatever, but I'm on a deadline and I really don't have time for chitchat."

"Sure," he said. "And thanks. I appreciate the friendly reception."

At noon, after Robbie had closed her laptop and left the room, Jeremy decided to take his own lunch break. His grandfather lived less than a mile from Castillo Enterprises. Jeremy called ahead to let him know he'd be stopping by. If Robbie was going to be a bitch, at least there was some benefit to working here.

His grandfather was waiting just outside the front door. Jeremy held him tightly. They'd talked a few times over the last couple of weeks on the phone, but suddenly that seemed inadequate. "I'm sorry I haven't been by more often, Grandpa."

"You're a busy young man. Work. School. I want to hear all about it. But come in. You must be hungry."

The bridge table on the enclosed porch was set with plates and silverware and a casserole dish. "I made franks and beans. Is that all right? I'm not much of a chef."

"That's great, Grandpa."

"How about a beer, Jeremy?" His grandfather's cotton shirt hung loosely on his frame, but he seemed a little more solid than when Jeremy had seen him over two weeks ago.

"A beer would be great."

His grandfather shuffled into the house, carefully closing the sliding door behind him. He returned with two open bottles, no glasses, and set them on the table.

"So, you're at Castillo Enterprises. Is that better than the file room?" His grandfather ladled franks and beans onto Jeremy's plate, then onto his own.

"I guess it's better." Actually, another few days with Robbie and he might be begging Irv to let him back into the file room.

His grandfather put a forkful of beans in his mouth and wrinkled his nose. "Cold. I guess I didn't heat them long enough. I'll recook them." He pushed his chair back.

"They're fine, Grandpa."

His grandfather sat back down. "If you say so." He took a swig of beer. "Castillo Enterprises. Funny how things come around. Did you know Carlos Castillo was a client of mine?"

"Carlos? He's seventeen years old."

"His grandfather. Enrique Castillo's father. The man who came to America with little more than the clothes on his back and built an empire."

"And you were his accountant? I didn't know that."

"Over thirty years ago," his grandfather said. "Carlos had saved up and bought some land near Clewiston to grow sugar cane. I did his books. He worked hard, he expanded his business, he started buying real estate. By then, his business was too complex for me to handle. I was just a sole practitioner. So I said, 'Carlos, you need to hire a bigger CPA firm.' And he refused. For two more years he insisted I be his accountant. But finally he realized it wasn't possible."

"So he hired PCM?"

His grandfather took a sip of beer. "He hired PCM, let his son get more involved with running things, and in a few years Castillo Enterprises became one of the most successful businesses in South Florida."

"But that's a good thing, isn't it?"

"You can judge for yourself. I've collected all of Castillo Enterprises's annual reports since the company went public a few years ago. It should make interesting reading for you, a future accountant."

Funny what his grandfather considered interesting. "And Mr. Castillo's dead, isn't he?" Jeremy asked.

"If he were still alive, do you think he'd permit such a grandiose monstrosity to be built in the name of Castillo Enterprises? That new office building is an outrage. All that money spent and for what? Gold fixtures and an impressive view? Carlos Castillo was a humble man. A hardworking man who believed in an honest dollar for an honest day's work."

"Do you think Enrique is dishonest?"

His grandfather studied him for a moment. "You have chocolate on your chin, Jeremy."

Jeremy brought his napkin to his chin.

"I meant that figuratively."

"I don't know what you're talking about."

"You still think you can fool me? Remember when you were five and said you hadn't eaten the brownies your grandmother had baked? But I knew. You had chocolate on your chin. Just like now. You took that job to find out what happened to your mother. Am I right?"

Jeremy stared at the plants on the wheelbarrow carts. Most of them were dead. "I'm sorry, Grandpa, but I just can't sit back and wait for the police."

"I know, Jeremy. I know." His grandfather took a deep breath, then let it out slowly. "If I were a younger man." His voice was softer now, practically whispering. "If I were a younger man, I would find the bastard who did that to my little girl." He removed his glasses and covered his eyes.

"I know you would, Grandpa."

His grandfather took out his handkerchief and blew his nose, then he put his glasses back on. Even behind the thick, filmy lenses, Jeremy could see his eyes were red. "What you're doing would have worried your grandmother. For once, I'm grateful she isn't alive." He looked off in the distance. "That she isn't alive to have witnessed any of this."

Jeremy's chest tightened.

"Promise me, for your grandmother, you'll watch out for yourself."

"Of course I will."

"I know, I know. You young people all believe you're invulnerable. But Jeremy, have you thought ahead? Have you considered what could happen to you?"

And as though the sand churned up by the last wave had settled and he could see clear down to his feet, Jeremy finally understood exactly what Detective Lieber had been trying to warn him about. That if Jeremy got remotely close to figuring out who had killed his parents, the murderer would try to kill Jeremy as well.

Chapter 16

Marina had dozed off. Jeremy watched her pale eyelids flutter and her chest lightly rise and fall. The candles she'd lit were almost burned down and they sputtered an irregular light over the small bedroom. The worn Indian blanket had slipped beneath Marina's breast and her tiny hand opened and closed as though she were trying to reach something.

She was beautiful. The most beautiful woman he'd ever known. Her copper hair spread out over the pillow like wild vines. Her round red lips were moving now, pursed like a fish gasping for air. He wanted to kiss her. To feel her darting tongue against his own. But that would only start the cycle again. And he knew it was time for him to leave. That he shouldn't have come here in the first place.

How had that happened? She had called him when he left work after a frustrating, noncommunicative day with Robbie, and asked him to stop by her house before class. To look over his father's papers. She really wanted to talk to him about the papers. And she was sorry about last night. She got carried away, she said. The emotional stress of everything. Surely he understood.

And so he had driven to her house, understanding perfectly.

"Mmmm," Marina said now, stretching. She touched Jeremy's face. "So serious, *mon amour*." She kissed him. He should leave, but he felt as though he'd fallen into quicksand.

She slipped out of bed before he could say anything. Her naked body was white and perfect. It glowed in the vacillating light. She pulled a stretched-out, ratty tee shirt over her head, combed her fingers through her hair, and walked barefoot across the gritty terrazzo floor toward the other room. "I'm famished. Come, I'll make us something to eat."

Jeremy fumbled for his watch on the wooden crate that served as a night table. He'd missed class — the second night in a row. He had called Elise earlier in the evening, but had gotten only her voicemail. "Sorry," he'd said to the phone. "I'll be home late. I'm . . . I'm studying."

And the papers Marina had promised to show him — his father's papers. Somehow they'd never gotten around to them. Did they even exist?

There was a cracked ceramic lamp with an unraveling straw hat for its shade. Most of the furnishings in Marina's apartment looked as though she'd picked them out of someone's garbage. Jeremy squinted at his watch in the poor light. It was almost two a.m. He needed to be at PCM's main office at eight in the morning for a training meeting. He got dressed quickly.

Marina was leaning over a pot on the small stove. Something smelled amazing. He hadn't imagined Marina being much of a chef. But he had to go home.

She smiled up at him. "Coq au vin. I'm reheating it. Should only take another minute."

She didn't seem to notice he was in his suit. She handed him two mismatched plates, two knives, and two forks. The knives had dried crud on them. "Just clear the papers off the kitchen table and pull up the desk chair."

Jeremy's stomach was grumbling in response to the rich aroma in the air.

"And there should be a couple of cold beers," Marina said. "We finished the wine." She held the spoon up to his mouth for him to taste. "Good, no?"

It was great. The broth reminded him of his grandmother's chicken soup after he'd had a sip of sweet Manischewitz wine.

"I learned to cook when I lived with my father. And he was very particular." She brought the pot over from the stove and ladled the chicken onto their plates. The meat was so well cooked, it was falling off the bones.

He would eat, then go home.

Marina ignored the silverware and picked up a chicken leg with her fingers. "I moved to France when I was twelve." She sucked on the bone. "When my mother decided I was becoming a threat."

"I thought you were from France."

"Peru. I was born in Peru. In Lima. My parents met in the States — both exchange students. Then my mother got pregnant and returned to be near her family. My father was too busy to settle down."

"So you grew up in Peru?"

"Mainly my grandmother raised me. But then the men who came to see my mother became more interested in me than in her. So my mother sent my father a letter, bought me an airline ticket, and I became an international bastard. I never expected my father to show up at the airport. I had no idea what would become of me. I spoke only Spanish."

"But he showed up."

She'd finished everything on her plate and pushed back her chair. It was corroded aluminum from someone's old dinette set. "I was so happy to see him. Such a handsome man. I knew the story of Cinderella and I thought, perhaps he was my prince." She rested her feet on Jeremy's lap. The soles were blackened with dirt and her toenails looked as though she'd torn rather than cut them. In Miami, all the girls Jeremy knew had pedicures.

"And was he your prince?"

"Is life ever a fairy tale?" She ran her index finger over the gravy on her plate. "He treated me like I was his maid. He had me cook and clean for him." She licked her finger. "I wouldn't have minded if only he would have said something kind." She lit a cigarette and rested her head on the back of her chair. "What's wrong, *mon amour*? You look like — how do you say — like someone made your boxers into a wad."

"I need to go."

"Of course you do." She pulled her feet off his lap. They brushed against his crotch. "I'm so sorry. I don't have class until eleven, but you have to go to work, don't you?"

"Yes."

"But you can come back tomorrow, after work, no?" Her tee shirt had risen up on her thigh and a curl of copper hair was visible. The candles in the bedroom were casting pulsing shadows against the wall.

"I can't. I have class after work. And I really need to spend time with my sister."

The faint smile faded. "I don't understand."

"I like you, Marina. You have no idea how much. But when I'm with you I feel as though I'm letting my family down."

"Your family?"

"My sister, my parents."

"Your parents are gone, Jeremy."

He couldn't find the words. "There are things I have to do," he said finally.

"Ahhh. I see." She took a deep puff from her cigarette. "I have become a distraction, no?"

He pushed himself up out of the desk chair.

"We make love, I share my secret world with you, but you won't trust me?"

"That's not it."

"Then why won't you talk to me?"

"I do talk to you."

"Yet I know nothing about your plan."

"What plan?"

"You work at your mother's firm, even though you claim to hate accounting. You sneak around your father's campus ostensibly to take classes, but you don't even show up for them. It seems to me you have some purpose other than advancing your career and edifying your mind." The ashes fell from the tip of her cigarette to the floor.

Lieber had been right. His motives were crystal clear to anyone who was paying the least bit of attention to him. "Okay, fine," he said. "But maybe I can learn things the police can't."

"So why not tell me?" She tilted her head as though to get a better look at him. "Ah. Because you don't trust anyone, is that it? Anyone who was close to your parents may be a suspect, no?"

"Maybe."

"And am I a suspect, Jeremy? You think, perhaps, I killed your parents?"

"Of course not."

"Of course not, he says." She shook her head. "Still, you don't trust me."

"I do trust you."

"Then let me help you." She put the cigarette out in her plate. "I know things about your father. I know the people who resented him. People who may have wanted him dead." Her eyes filled with tears. "Don't you think I want to find the motherfucker who killed your father as much as you do?"

"I've got to go."

He was out the door, standing in the dense stillness of the night, when she came after him. Her arms were wrapped around a large bundle of papers. Her legs were bare and white — carved ivory.

"Take them," she said, so small under the bulk of papers. She pushed the bundle against his chest. "They're your father's. Maybe they can help you."

He kept his arms at his side, unwilling to accept them. "They won't mean much to me."

She took a step back, still clutching the papers. Her body seemed to be communicating directly with his.

"Will you take me through them?" he asked.

She held the papers tighter.

"When I come back," he said, "will you help me go through my father's papers?"

"I don't want you to feel like I'm holding you captive, Jeremy. If there are other things you'd rather be doing—"

"This," he leaned over and kissed her small, round mouth, "is what I'd rather be doing."

It was early morning when he got home. The sky went through its metamorphosis as he stood in front of his house, the weak light turning everything around him into sepia grays. The windows of his sister's Volvo were damp with dew. Jeremy found a rag in the back of his father's car and wiped them off. A car drove slowly by, and a hand flung a plastic-wrapped newspaper onto the driveway.

Jeremy picked up the newspaper, then went inside, quietly closing the front door after him so as not to wake Elise. The smell of coffee drifted toward him from the kitchen.

Elise was sitting at the counter, hunched over a cup. Her bare feet were hooked around the bottom rung of the stool. She didn't look up when he walked in.

"I'm sorry I didn't make it home last night," he said.

Her face was hidden by her loose hair so he couldn't read her expression.

"I won't do it again. Things just got a little out of control."

"Do what you want." She pushed the stool out and stood up. "I'm not your mother."

"You're right." He tried to block her retreat. "But you're my sister." He held her by the shoulders. She wouldn't meet his eyes. "Ellie. I said I'm sorry. I shouldn't stay out so late. It isn't right."

She pulled away. "I, I have to get ready for school."

"But we'll do something later, okay? I don't have class."

"Carlos's mother invited us to dinner."

"Tonight?"

"Yeah."

"Do you want to go? Or we can do something else. Maybe go out for sushi and see a movie."

"I said I'd go. I didn't know about you."

"That's fine," Jeremy said. "We'll have dinner at the Castillos'. Then you and I can go to a movie afterward. Okay?"

"Whatever." She started toward the stairs. "Oh, and Dwight called."

"Last night?"

"Last night. This morning. Basically every hour on the hour until I told him at three a.m. that I was disconnecting the phone. That I had to get some sleep."

"I'm sorry, Ellie. Why didn't you give him my cell number?"

She raised an eyebrow. "Did you really want me to do that?"

"No. Of course not. Thanks for covering for me."

She shrugged.

"Did he say what he wanted?"

"I think he was just excited you weren't home. He got that stupid tone in his voice. 'Your brother still isn't home?'" she mimicked.

"Where did you say I was?"

"Studying. I said you were studying." She pushed her hair out of her eyes. "Isn't that what you told me?"

Chapter 17

The auditorium that served as the firm's training room was filled with young men in dry-cleaned white shirts and women in silky blouses or still wearing their suit jackets. All appeared to Jeremy to be alert and attentive, periodically calling out to ask the trainer a question. The room was carpeted and had acoustical wall coverings that made Jeremy feel as though he were sitting in a sound booth of a high-end audio store.

He tried to pay attention to the balding man with the wide butt who was up at the podium, but the voice was so monotonous Jeremy felt his eyelids close. He could see Marina's face inches from his own. Her hair falling across his chest. He was certain he smelled her scent on his own skin, as though a cat had marked its territory.

He had gotten no sleep. After he'd arrived home from Marina's and tried to right things with Elise, Jeremy had showered, dressed in a fresh shirt and suit, had a cup of coffee, and driven to PCM's downtown headquarters.

The audit manager was discussing some recent changes in accounting practices and how the firm's audit procedures would be affected. He'd been droning on for hours. The idea that people made a living auditing and reporting on the financial condition of businesses made no sense to him. Who really cared? And so what if they capitalized certain expenses instead of writing them off? Did anyone ever die from an improperly recorded leasehold improvement?

People were straightening up in their seats, as though they'd been called to attention. The wide-butted speaker was gone from the podium. Heads turned toward the back of the room. Bud McNally, wearing a white shirt, red tie, and no jacket, was bounding down the carpeted aisle, energy and purpose apparent in every step of his shiny alligator wingtips.

He detached the mike from its stand on the podium and turned toward his audience. "How y'all doing?"

"Fine." "Great."

Bud cupped his ear. "I can't hear you."

"Great," everyone shouted.

"Better. Much better." He smoothed the front of his shirt. The light bounced off his diamond pinkie ring. "What a great group. I feel like a gourd in a cotton field."

Everyone laughed.

"I mean it. This is one of the smartest groups our firm has ever had the privilege to hire. Did you know that? You are the best and the brightest." He made a pained face. "Oh come on, guys. Don't look so coy. Give yourselves a hand."

His claps were amplified by the mike and reverberated in the room over the general applause. "That's better. Much better. Now, take a good look at each other. That's right. Have a look at your neighbors. What do you see? Do you see a mover and shaker sitting next to you? A rainmaker?" He raised his voice. "A future partner with Piedmont Coleridge Miller? A future partner with one of the top regional firms in the country that's on its way to becoming *the* top regional firm in the country?"

Everyone in the room broke into applause.

"Because that's what we're looking for at PCM. We're not one of those dinosaur firms with old-fangled accountants who always have their heads buried in the books. We're not content to say the past is good enough for us. Are we?"

"No," everyone said.

"What was that?"

"No," everyone shouted.

"We want the future, that's what we want. And we're on our way to getting it. This year PCM has moved from the twenty-seventh largest firm in the country to —" he stopped. Everyone in the room leaned in. Bud smiled. "To number twenty. That's right, numero twenty."

Everyone applauded and there were a couple of shrill whistles.

"Is that good enough for you?" He waited while people shifted in their seats. "Because it sure ain't good enough for me. What's to stop us from becoming number fifteen? Or number ten? Or even one of the Big Four?"

The room erupted in applause.

"We're going up and we're never coming down, do you hear me?"

"Yes," the group said.

Bud cupped his ear.

"Yes," everyone shouted.

He smiled with his lips closed. "That's what I like to hear."

People around Jeremy stood up and moved toward the door. Everyone eager to get back to their audit clients. The movers and shakers. Future partners. How easily they were inspired. He noticed Robbie at the front of the room. Their eyes met, but she turned away.

The elevator bank was filled with auditors on their way down and partners on their way up. He'd overheard someone say the partners had a lunch meeting at the Osprey Club. Probably to celebrate the firm's ascension to number twenty while the slugs went back to work trying to make enough rain to get it into the top ten.

The offices would be practically deserted. Jeremy backed away from the elevators and out of sight until the congestion had cleared.

Then he slipped down the hallway where the partners' offices were. There was no sign of anyone. The alcove outside his mother's office was empty. He pushed open the door to her office, then quickly closed it behind him. It had been almost a month since she had been killed. He supposed the room would be empty, or perhaps filled with cartons with her personal belongings. No one had invited him to go through her things, so he assumed Dwight had already made his rounds.

But when Jeremy turned toward his mother's desk, his breath caught in his chest. Everything was exactly as it had been the last time she was here. The plants that hung in front of the windows were green. Her credenza was covered with family photos, a porcelain teapot and a set of delicate matching teacups on a tray. No dust — someone had been caring for her things. There was a computer docking station on the desk. His mother, like his father, hadn't kept a separate desktop computer at the office, just used a laptop and plugged it into docking stations at work and at home. Jeremy opened the desk drawers, then the credenza. There were books, magazines, and company annual reports. No work-related papers. But there wouldn't have been. Someone would have cleared out any papers that belonged to the firm.

Jeremy picked up a stack of directories and brochures held together by a rubber band. *Top 100 Luxury Hotels, World Class Resorts, Small Luxury Hotels — International Series.* A yellow sticky note in her handwriting dropped out. "Not listed?" it said.

His attention was drawn to the framed photos on his mother's credenza. Looking at them still hurt. Regardless of whether his or Elise's baby teeth were missing, if they were wearing braces or had perfect smiles, one thing remained the same. The photos were always of the four of them. The complete family. That had always been the rule.

He picked up one, taken not long before he'd dropped out of school and left for Europe. His father, mother, and Elise huddled together, while Jeremy, arms folded across his chest, stood apart. His confusion and isolation were so apparent to him now, he flinched and put the photo back on the credenza.

Jeremy sat down in her leather chair. It was set too high for him and his knees touched the underside of the desk. A plaid woolen shawl was draped over the back of the chair. He ran it between his fingers. She'd bought it in Edinburgh, and another for Elise with a different pattern. It had been summer, but it was cold. They'd all been underdressed for the weather. "Are you sure you don't want me to buy you a sweater, Jeremy?" she'd asked.

He'd been shivering in his shorts and tee shirt. But no, he didn't want anything. He was fourteen. He didn't like being treated like a child. He walked a distance ahead of his family, hoping no one would think he was with them.

He brought the shawl up to his nose; he could smell her perfume. He wished he had let her buy him a sweater, had let her put her arm around him for warmth.

He didn't hear the door to his mother's office open — only close.

Robbie stood with her back against it. What was she doing here? Was she going to call security? Tell the partners?

"Are you surprised?" she said.

"Surprised?"

"That everything's the way she left it."

"I guess." Jeremy hung the shawl on the back of the chair. Robbie didn't appear to be upset with him. He wondered at the change in her since yesterday. She acted almost human, but he remained on his guard.

Robbie picked up one of the teacups on the credenza. "You

know, I hate when the firm hires people who don't have the skills or inclination to work, just because of some misguided sense of paternalism."

Her tone was nonconfrontational, but Jeremy became defensive. "Is that why you think Mr. McNally hired me — because of my mom?"

"Seems like the logical explanation. I figured someone was putting pressure on you to get a job. Maybe your grandfather, maybe there's some stipulation in the will."

"And you decided I'm a slacker."

"Sure looked that way." She ran her finger around the rim of the teacup. "It really irritated me when you breezed into the conference room late, not interested in working. How should I have reacted? I mean, if Bud wants to play Good Samaritan, that's his business, but I'm afraid I'm not very good with the pity stuff."

"I'm sorry I was late, but I really didn't want your pity. Civility would have been nice."

"Maybe everyone else is bending over backward to be nice to you, Jeremy. And I know it's a terrible thing to have lost your parents. But I hate to say this, your casual attitude made me ashamed for your mother."

His face got hot. "I'm sorry I gave you that impression." He stood up from his mother's chair and took a couple of steps toward the door.

"And then I started thinking about it," Robbie said. "And it didn't make sense."

"What didn't make sense?"

"Your coming to work here. Your chattiness yesterday morning." Jeremy waited.

"So I realized you probably had other reasons for taking a job here."

"And what are my reasons?"

She turned the teacup over in her hands. "She used to invite a few of us to her office for tea," she said as though she hadn't heard Jeremy's question. "Three or four at a time, so it could be intimate. Usually just women. She felt we needed special attention to help break through the glass ceiling."

"You didn't answer me. What are my reasons?"

"Maybe you're hoping to understand your mother a little better. Trying to make sense of what happened to her." Robbie seemed to be studying the teacup, lost in her own thoughts. "You know, it's funny," she said. "There were people who said Rachel just liked being with the men, but it wasn't true. Her partners were all men and most of her clients, so of course, it looked like she was always surrounded by men. I think there was a jealousy thing going on with her. So there always seemed to be rumors about her."

"Like what? That she was involved with someone?"

"They were mean-spirited rumors. Rachel ignored them."

"But there were people who you say were jealous of her. Who?"

"Hard to say where rumors start. Most of the women on the staff seemed to adore her. Rachel really wanted to help us. Not that she was a big-time feminist or anything. She believed individuals should rise on the basis of their own merit. But she also acknowledged there was still a good-ol'-boys network, and if you weren't a member of their special club, you were at a disadvantage."

"So she started her own special club? I guess you don't consider that paternalistic."

"It wasn't a club." Robbie put the cup down and leaned against the credenza. She was wearing a light gray suit with a skirt that showed her legs. She had muscular calves like a runner or dancer. "We'd talk about career issues. But she had no patience for whining or for anyone complaining the guys got privileges the women on the staff didn't." She began playing with an emerald ring on her finger. Her nails were short and even, not torn like Marina's. "Rachel would say, 'If you want a better audit client or a promotion or more money, then go out and do such a spectacular job that you're the one who's calling the shots.'"

"Do you think my mom called the shots?"

"You mean with her partners?" She brought her fingertip up to her mouth. Her blue eyes were unusually large and had thick dark lashes. "Rachel was tremendously respected."

"But was she in charge? I know Bud and Irv and my mom were the three senior partners, but did any of them have more clout than the others?" He was putting her on the spot with his direct questions. Trying to assess if she was his ally. "Like today," he said. "Bud certainly acted like he's the man. Was Irv even there?"

"Irv doesn't go to staff meetings."

"But was Bud that vocal when my mom was alive?"

"Bud's always been gung-ho — like he's leading the troops into battle. He's very . . ." She searched for the right word. "Ambitious, I guess you'd say. Almost obsessive about pushing the firm to greater heights. But your mom was very effective at tempering him. It was a nice balance."

"So you don't buy into Bud's program?" Jeremy said.

"I didn't say that. I just think Bud tends to be a bit aggressive."

"What did my mother think of his program?"

"I don't know, Jeremy." Robbie slipped her hand behind her. "Look. I understand what you're trying to do. And believe me, the first thing I thought of after your parents were murdered was whether anyone here could have had a motive."

"And?"

Robbie shook her head. "I just don't know. I can't believe Bud would have been involved. He and your mom were great pals, as far as I could tell. Competing, sure. But in a collegial way."

"And what about Irv? I get the feeling he and my mother hadn't been getting along very well recently."

"Irv adored your mother."

"Even after what happened at Castillo Enterprises?" He was remembering the comment Enrique Castillo had made on Jeremy's first day of work. That Jeremy's mother had replaced Irv on the Castillo audit. "How come Irv was taken off the audit and my mother put on in his place? Could he have resented her for that?"

"Rotating partners is firm policy." She didn't seem to be the least defensive about Jeremy's line of questioning. She responded like a good student who had done her homework. "Irv was on the Castillo audit for more years than he was supposed to be. Finally, National said that Rachel needed to be rotated on. She had more real estate background than the other partners, so she was a natural fit."

"And that's why they took him off the audit? You're sure? Firm policy? Not something else?"

"I'm positive. There was a big fuss about it. The managing partner from National had to come down here to lay down the law."

"Okay," Jeremy said, slowly, "maybe Irv was upset with my mother about something else."

"Like?"

"Would he have kept adoring her if she was trying to get him fired?"

"Rachel would never have done that. She had too much respect for him."

"That's not what I heard."

"What did you hear?"

So, he'd finally gotten a rise out of her. "Bud told me my mom was concerned about Irv's drinking. She didn't think Irv should remain on as a partner — something like that." He was stretching what he'd heard, fishing for more.

"I'd never heard that."

"But does it sound possible to you? Possible that Irv would have been upset with her for trying to get him fired? His whole world revolves around PCM. How would he have reacted to someone try-ing to take it away from him?"

Robbie looked disturbed. "It doesn't make sense." She ran a fin-ger over the dustless credenza. "If Irv was so bitter toward your mom, why did he insist no one touch a thing in her office?"

Chapter 18

Carlos's arms tightened around her. Elise liked that. The close sensation made her feel safe. She once read how an autistic woman had designed a confining chute for cattle on their way to be slaughtered. How because of it, the cattle went contentedly to their deaths. Carlos's tongue found hers. He tasted like smoke. He lightly kissed her nose, then pulled away. So much for intimacy.

Carlos began rolling another joint. He had taken off his school uniform shirt and wore only khaki pants and a wife-beater undershirt that exposed his long, thin, defined arms. Carlos wasn't muscular like Jeremy, but he was still in good shape.

The rec room in the back of his parents' house was dim, although Elise could make out the last glow of daylight from behind the drawn shades. It was a beautiful room with an L-shaped suede sofa, several wide chairs that could comfortably seat two, and a built-in entertainment center that housed a large plasma TV and Carlos's many video game systems.

She and Carlos had been here the night her parents had been murdered. They'd been curled up on the sofa watching a sci-fi movie. She remembered being startled by Carlos's mother, who was standing over them, holding a tray. "I brought you darlings some hot chocolate," Mrs. Castillo had said.

Carlos had jumped up. "Don't you believe in knocking?"

And Mrs. Castillo had let out a deep chuckle that sounded

like a tiger purring. "You look exhausted, Elise. Have some hot chocolate."

Elise had taken a cup and thanked her. "It's probably jet lag. I'll be going home soon."

"No rush," Mrs. Castillo had said.

When Elise next woke up, the movie was over and Carlos was asleep against her shoulder. Elise had been horrified; her mother would be furious. It was bad enough Elise had snuck out, add coming home late on top of that. But when they got to the house, everything spiraled out of control. Darkness, shadows, strange smells, Carlos shouting at her.

But there was something else. Something she couldn't remember. She had been trying hard to dredge it up, but the effort exhausted her. She just wanted to be done with it. To forget. To forget everything.

Elise pulled the shade away from the window. The sun was setting over the bay. A speedboat bounced across the waves, leaving a large wake. The rec room had a spectacular view, but Carlos always kept the windows covered. She had assumed it was because he didn't want anyone boating by to see in, but now it occurred to her perhaps Carlos didn't like looking out. She let the shade fall back. Maybe Carlos had the right idea — not looking out.

"Wanna smoke?" Carlos held up the freshly rolled joint.

"I don't know."

"Come on, Elise. Believe me, it's much easier to get through dinner with my parents if you're stoned."

Elise didn't even smoke regular cigarettes, as many of her friends had started doing. And marijuana and alcohol were just a copout for not being willing to deal with things head on. That had always been her philosophy.

Carlos lit the joint and its tip brightened as he inhaled. The slow stream of smoke was pungent.

Why should she keep trying so hard? No one cared. Even Jeremy had slipped away from her, busy with other things. More important things. And the pain of losing her parents wasn't lessening as people said it would. It was spreading. She could feel it growing inside her like a fungus. If she died tomorrow and someone cut her open, all they'd find would be her shriveled, blackened heart.

Carlos held the joint out. "Come on, Elise. It really helps."

She took a toke and coughed on the thick smoke.

"Hey, not all at once."

She tried again. More slowly she brought the sting deep into her lungs and held it. She could feel it numbing her. Slowly, she released the smoke through her mouth.

"Better," Carlos said.

She did it again. Imaginary arms wrapped around her. Yes, it was better.

A melodious voice filled the room. "Carlos, Elise," Mrs. Castillo sang over the intercom. "Dinner is served."

Elise giggled. She didn't know why that seemed so funny. "Big Mother is watching you." And she burst into peals of laughter. "Big Mother, you know, like Big Brother in *1984*."

Carlos took her hand. "I know."

The long, glass dining room table was set for five. The room had a high, domed ceiling with a huge crystal chandelier that reminded her of the *Phantom of the Opera*. She tugged on Carlos's arm and giggled. "Do you think the Phantom's going to send that crashing down on us?"

Jeremy was talking to Mr. Castillo and they were both holding drinks. Her brother was still wearing his suit, so he had probably come directly from work.

Elise was angry with Jeremy. Very angry. But even more than that, she was hurt. He'd deserted her. In the middle of her worst nightmare, he'd come riding in on his white horse to rescue her. Then, just as abruptly, he was gone. She wondered where he'd spent the last couple of nights. With a girl. She was certain of that. Someone to hide away in. Kind of like Elise was doing with Carlos since she didn't have Jeremy anymore.

Mrs. Castillo was coming toward her, arms extended, stiff blonde hair covering one eye. She was wearing a white outfit with a low-cut neckline that showed off a diamond necklace that dripped into her cleavage.

Elise almost choked on her strong perfume as Mrs. Castillo embraced her, but hopefully it masked the smell of marijuana in Elise's clothes.

"Don't you look sweet tonight?" Mrs. Castillo had a husky voice and Elise liked the sound of it. "And what beautiful long hair you have, like an Arabian princess."

Mr. Castillo crossed the room toward them. His pants and shirt had no wrinkles and fit him as though they'd been made for him, which they probably were. Elise's dad never wore clothes like that. Even his "good" clothes looked like he'd pulled them out of the bottom of a drawer. But Elise loved that about her father. How he didn't seem to care about stuff like that.

Mr. Castillo was scowling at Carlos, who was still only wearing his wife-beater tee shirt. "Go put on a proper shirt," he said in a low voice, though everyone could hear him. "You're being rude to our guests and your mother."

Carlos left the room, returning a couple of minutes later. He had put on a shirt but wore it inside out, most likely to piss off his father. Mr. Castillo didn't comment.

Elise was glad she'd smoked the marijuana. It took the edge off what she imagined would have been a tense meal. A woman in a black-and-white uniform was pouring wine. She glanced at Mrs. Castillo when she came to Elise's glass.

"Yes, of course," Mrs. Castillo said. "A little wine won't hurt anything." The server filled Elise's glass, then Carlos's.

Elise picked up the cut crystal wine glass; the light glinted off the edges. She took a sip of wine. Ummm, nice. Everything was feeling much nicer than usual. Jeremy was looking at her curiously. Maybe she'd forgive him, after all. They'd go to a movie tonight and then, after they got home, they'd talk about things. That's what she missed most. The talking.

"These wine glasses belonged to my great-grandmother," Mrs. Castillo said. "She brought them from Spain. My family was from the Basque region. Aristocracy. We go back many, many generations."

"Your family moved to Cuba?" Jeremy asked. Her brother was far more alert than Elise was.

"Yes," Mrs. Castillo said. "But we're of Spanish descent."

"You were born in Cuba," Carlos said. "So anyway you cut it, you're Cuban."

Mr. Castillo gave Carlos a silencing look.

"The wine glasses are beautiful," Elise said.

Mrs. Castillo smiled. She had very small teeth.

"I'm glad you were able to join us for dinner, Elise and Jeremy." Mr. Castillo's facial expression had returned to amiable host. That's probably why he was so successful — he didn't show his real feelings. Elise's dad had been the opposite. If he was angry about something, he couldn't hide it. "I know how busy you both are," Mr. Castillo was saying, "with school and work. In fact, Jeremy, I understand you're at Castillo Enterprises this week. How are you enjoying it?"

"It's pretty interesting."

He was lying, Elise knew. He looked you straight in the eye without blinking when he was lying. She knew that about Jeremy, but no one else did.

"My grandfather said he was your father's accountant many years ago," Jeremy said.

"My father had the greatest respect for your grandfather, as do I." Mr. Castillo sipped his wine. "As I did for your mother."

"Have some more wild rice," Mrs. Castillo said. She pushed the serving platter in Jeremy's direction. "And another Cornish hen. Aren't they wonderful?"

"Very good," Jeremy said.

"I'm sorry I can't show you around the offices personally, Jeremy," Mr. Castillo said. "I'm flying out to visit some of our properties for a few days."

Mrs. Castillo widened her eyes. "You've rescheduled your trip to the Olympus Grande? Why didn't you tell me? I'd like to come."

Mr. Castillo was cutting his Cornish hen and didn't look up. "You'd be bored, Liliam. I'll just be in meetings."

"I could go to the meetings with you." She turned toward Elise. "He thinks I'm just a housewife and I'm not capable of running anything but my home, but I'm very involved with my volunteer organizations. I don't need a fancy career —"

"Liliam, you're boring our guests."

"You always say that when you don't like what I'm saying. But you talk about how much you respected Rachel just because —"

"Liliam, that's not appropriate."

"Mom, why can't you just be quiet?" Carlos's face was pale.

"*Ay, dios mio.*" Mrs. Castillo raised her hands to her cheeks. "I'm so sorry. I didn't mean to upset everyone. And certainly, I meant nothing against your mother. She was a wonderful woman." She crossed herself and glanced over at her husband. "It's just, I've always wanted to see the Olympus, and my husband never finds the time to take me."

"It's a business trip, Liliam, not a vacation."

"You know, Jeremy and Elise," Mrs. Castillo said, "Olympus Grande is one of the most exclusive hotels in the world. It's on its own private island called St. Mary's. Can you imagine, only villas and executive and junior suites? Regular people don't even know about it. Just the very wealthiest. That's right, isn't it, *querido?*" She smiled at her husband.

"Perhaps next time I'll take you. When I won't be so busy. Would you care for some coffee, Jeremy?"

Chapter 19

The boy was like his mother — a natural-born auditor. He had a sixth sense for sniffing out trouble, Irv Luria decided. The skeletons everyone else wanted to keep buried.

Irv knotted his bow tie in the mirror, trying to ignore the reflection of the grotesque face that couldn't possibly be his. But the blotched red cheeks, the flattened nose, the dead eyes, kept entering his peripheral vision. Fuck this. He stepped out of the bathroom, his bow tie hanging crooked.

Jeremy Lazar Stroeb, youthful avenger, quixotic hero. Just like his mother.

Irv had seen him after the staff meeting, hovering suspiciously behind the elevator bank. He'd probably gone snooping around his mother's office while the partners were at lunch. The teacup and shawl had been out of place.

But what could Irv do? He'd tried to keep Jeremy hidden in the file room, but Bud had killed that plan. And now the boy was out. And with his charm, how long before people would warm to him and spill their guts — tell Jeremy everything they knew, or thought they knew? Because the fact was, no one knew shit about the truth.

And no one knew Rachel like Irv knew Rachel.

He shuffled across the stone-tiled floor of his penthouse toward the kitchen. The path was clear — thanks to the absence of furniture. When Candace had announced she couldn't stand living with a self-centered, egomaniacal prick, he'd told her to get the hell out. To take her things and get the hell out. He'd returned from work that night and found the apartment completely empty.

At first he'd been furious. That little bitch. Good thing he hadn't married her like she'd been pressuring him to do. Then, he had sat down on the cold floor, which she'd had installed when she'd moved in a couple of years before. He began to laugh and laugh until tears ran down his cheeks. Candace was an interior designer and she'd furnished the place in some weird Buddhist-Louis XIV eclectic style all the home design magazines wanted to photograph. So naturally, when he'd said to take her things, she'd included the quarter of a million in furnishings she'd selected. Too bad she couldn't have taken the stone floors, as well.

He'd made do with a mattress on the bedroom floor and a couple of plastic chairs he'd picked up at the drugstore. And it turned out he liked that better. A hell of a lot better.

His feet were throbbing in his tight shoes. He was tempted to believe the shoes had shrunk in his closet, but he knew they were a full size larger than he used to wear. Water retention, his doctor had said. And try to lay off the drinking, Irv. Your liver's gotten so big, there's practically no room left for it in your gut.

Irv opened the refrigerator door. The shelves were stacked with cans of Budweiser and Coke. No food. He rarely ate at home. For an emergency he had a loaf of bread and a couple of steaks in the freezer. He took out a can of Coke and popped off the lid. See — he didn't have a drinking problem. It wasn't as if he needed to grab a beer first thing in the morning.

Rachel had been completely mistaken about him. But even though she'd made a stink about it, he knew it wasn't his drinking that disturbed her. Maybe she'd decided it was time to bury her fallen god. But he was kidding himself. In Rachel's eyes, Irving Luria had lost his luster a long, long time ago.

Irv pulled open the sliding glass door to the balcony. There was still a splendid view of Biscayne Bay and the Rickenbacker Causeway. He'd bought the condo over thirty years back, when it was one of the first high-rises on Brickell Avenue and most of the surrounding lots were verdant estates. Since then, building after building — one taller than the next — had sprung up along the bay. He leaned his elbows against the railing and sipped his Coke. He remembered the one time he brought Rachel here.

He and Rachel had taken a prospective client, a major bank, out to dinner. Rachel had been with the firm less than three years, but Irv had insisted she team with him on closing the deal. And what a team they made. Witty, charming, dazzling, and above all, professionally credible. The bankers shook hands with them after dinner and announced they were delighted to have PCM as their new auditors.

Irv invited Rachel back to his place to celebrate. He'd occasionally brought other young women back to his apartment — usually to fuck them — but never Rachel Lazar. She wasn't like the others — giggling, painted creatures who would do anything to please him to get a promotion. Rachel was pure, like Mary, Mother Mary. And he remembered thinking as he handed her a glass of Drambouie, Rachel would be the crowning glory of his life's work. He would teach her, guide her, help her become the mother of all accountants. The most highly respected and admired woman in the accounting profession. One who never compromised.

God and Mary. It was perfect. She was perfect.

As they stood on the balcony, watching the lights of the cars going over the causeway, he had decided to tell her his plan. The breeze blew her hair across her face and into her mouth. She laughed as she pulled it away. "This has been such a wonderful night, Irv. I feel like I'm flying."

God and his Mary. "As do I, my dear."

"You mean so much to me, Irv. You've taught me so much. I want to tell you something. Something wonderful I haven't shared with anyone yet."

He took her hand. "Yes?"

"I'm getting married. His name is Daniel Stroeb."

She had continued talking. At first Irv hadn't heard anything else she'd said. The lights on the causeway had become a blur and the bay had grown dark and bottomless. And then he realized she was walking away, pulling the sliding glass door closed after her.

"Rachel, wait. Please listen to me."

She hesitated and extended her head through the gap of the sliding door. He thought of Marie Antoinette at that moment — the potential sliced off in a split second.

"You can do great things with your life. But if you marry and have children, you compromise. You dilute your essence."

"I don't see it that way."

"Ah, Rachel. That's because there are stars in your eyes. Because a handsome young man is telling you he loves you. Think of what you're giving up. And think of what you'll be left with when he stops telling you how pretty you are, how wonderful, how much he loves you."

"He won't stop."

And he had realized he could let her go. That it would just be a matter of time before she'd return to him.

He glanced down at the crushed Coke can in his fist. What a fucking fool he'd been. How could he not have seen the inevitable?

He went back to the kitchen and got a Budweiser. It was after nine a.m. No longer first thing in the morning.

Irv arrived at the office a little before eleven. Not great, but there'd been days he'd gotten in even later. Someone in a dark suit was sitting in the alcove, stiff as a mortician. Irv didn't really care. He had limited client responsibilities these days and certainly wasn't taking on any new ones.

Bud stepped out of his office, noticed Irv, and signaled to him to wait, then went to shake the mortician's hand — a bland man with thinning hair and a moustache. Irv recognized him. Something Stroeb — Rachel's brother-in-law. A lawyer running for judge or some such shit. A total asshole. Irv pushed open the door to his office, hoping to escape any contact with him.

"Irv," Bud called after him.

Shit.

"You remember Dwight Stroeb." Bud rested his large hand on the man's shoulder. Dwight looked disoriented, like someone who just sat down and realized there was no chair. "Dwight tells me he needs to speak with us about something of great urgency."

"That's right," Dwight said. "Just a minute of your time."

"Unfortunately, I have to run off to a prior engagement." Bud patted Dwight's back. "But Irv will take good care of you. And I promise, Dwight, you and I will get together real soon." Bud was halfway down the hallway moving at a brisk pace when he turned. "Take care now, y'all."

Dwight was filling the air with his vapid noise as he stepped into Irv's office. "A real pleasure. And I believe my friend, Enrique Castillo, is a client of yours. He's been very receptive —"

Irv regretted he'd only had a couple of beers and a small glass of Drambouie before he came to work. He remained standing, hoping the man would follow suit, but Dwight parked himself in one of the guest chairs. Irv looked longingly at his bottom drawer. Dwight had stopped talking and seemed to be sizing Irv up.

"What do you want?" Irv said, sitting down in his own chair.

"You've had a difficult time," Dwight said.

"What the hell's that supposed to mean?"

"I remember years ago, you were a bit of a legend. The tough businessman — fair but demanding. A maverick. You used to get written up all the time in the business journals." Dwight pulled on his mustache. "This must be difficult for you."

Irv narrowed his eyes.

"No one hears your name much anymore."

"This meeting is over, Mr. Stroeb." Irv pushed his chair back.

"I'm sorry," Dwight said. "You're a busy man. Let me get to the point."

"I've heard enough of your point." Irv started to stand.

"I'm here about the murder investigation."

Irv froze.

"I'm concerned," Dwight said.

"About?"

"You."

Irv sat down.

"You're vulnerable, Irv. I'm sorry, may I call you Irv?" Dwight smoothed his moustache. "In any event, I'm sure you're aware the police are continuing to dig deeper, looking for a viable suspect. My nephew wasn't satisfied with the way things were going."

"Jeremy?"

Dwight nodded. "He's stirred up the lady detective on the case, asking questions. And unfortunately, the police don't have a lot to go on. That means their focus is very limited."

"Which means what exactly?"

"That they're concentrating on people who were closest to my brother and sister-in-law."

"What are you suggesting?"

"I'm only saying you're in a particularly bad position. The police know all about your fall from grace, your drinking problems, the fact that Rachel was taking over your key accounts."

"How dare you come in here and accuse me? Get out. Get the hell out of here."

Dwight didn't move. "You misunderstand me, Irv. I'm not here to accuse. I'm here to help protect you."

The veins were pulsing in Irv's temples, ready to explode.

"As it happens," Dwight said, "I have a close relationship with a key person on the investigation. I know he'd be willing to listen to reason. After all, no one wants PCM or its partners embroiled in embarrassing attention from the police."

"You come here to blackmail me?"

"Blackmail? What do you think I am? I came here to offer you protection. To save you and your firm from needless expense, wasted time, and unwelcome publicity."

"Get the fuck out of my office, you scumbag." Irv slammed his hands on the desk. "Before I throw you out."

Dwight stood up tentatively, decided against saying whatever he'd been about to, then left the office looking more like a blowfly than a mortician. But then, there wasn't much of a difference, really. They both subsisted on the dead.

Chapter 20

The bedroom resembled a war room, Jeremy speculated, or a class-room with a maniacal professor. Scotch-taped to all available wall surfaces were pages from a flipchart Marina had taken from MIU. On each, written in red marker in all capital letters were the following headings: THESIS/PREMISE, WHO IT OFFENDS, MOTIVE FOR MURDER, then SUSPECTS. Piled helter-skelter on the floor, like un-matched pieces of a jigsaw puzzle, were his father's papers and polemics. The theses, which Marina had arrived at after sorting through all of Jeremy's father's work, included rants about govern-ment welfare, free-trade hypocrisy, agricultural subsidies, the Cuban embargo, and many other themes that meant little to Jeremy.

But even without fully grasping the issues, Jeremy could see one thing. D. C. Stroeb had offended many people. His father may have been brilliant, but he had also been reckless.

Marina was scribbling something on the page headed, ECO-LOGICAL FALLACIES. A cigarette quivered from the side of her mouth. She hadn't adhered to their customary routine. Usually they ate right after they'd made love, then they'd study the papers.

She was wearing a black thong and a torn-off tee shirt that left her midriff exposed. This was her best effort at "dressing" so as not to distract Jeremy as they explored motives and suspects in his par-ents' murders.

Right — no distraction. Jeremy watched her small, muscular

butt jiggle ever so slightly as she wrote. It had deep dimples and was almost perfectly white, with no tan lines. Marina had probably never even been to the beach. And if she had, it would have been to spray-paint political messages on the pier pilings, not work on a Copper-tone tan.

Jeremy had been coming here every night for almost two weeks. He hadn't seen his sister in more than a week. After dinner at the Castillos', he and Elise had gone to the movies, but that had been the last time they'd done anything together. Jeremy would arrive home long after she'd already gone to sleep. If she was still having nightmares, he saw no evidence of them. And she seemed to have a thing going with Carlos. Maybe Jeremy was rationalizing that she was doing okay, but he couldn't help it. The pressure of needing to be there for his sister, of not letting her down, was getting to him.

So he had concentrated on Marina, hoping she would help him find his parents' murderer. He would drive directly to Marina's apartment after work, skipping class. They'd pull off each other's clothes and pounce on each other like he'd seen sharks attack a meal of entrails at the Seaquarium. Marina wasn't a big fan of her bed. So they'd screwed on the futon, on the old Indian blanket covering the filthy kitchen floor, in the tiny bathtub — with or without water — and occasionally, mainly just for variety, in her bed with its sagging mattress.

Then she'd feed him. And Jeremy had come to crave this part of the evening ritual almost as much as the sex. There was always something amazing. And not just French cooking. Marina was accomplished in Peruvian cuisine as well. One night she'd made *cebiche de pescado* — she'd called it. Cubes of mahi mahi cooked in crushed garlic and a hot pepper sauce that burned his throat and brought tears to his eyes. But then she handfed him pieces of cooked sweet potatoes that balanced the harshness, which he devoured like a starving dog. And another night, *lomo saltado*, thin steak sautéed in garlic with onions, peppers, and chopped tomatoes. They ate it with fried potatoes out of the blackened, crusted iron skillet, which she'd rested on a pile of newspapers on the tiny kitchen table.

And just when he believed Peruvian food was the most tantalizing in the world, Marina reverted to French with *rabbit sauté chasseur*. They'd eaten that in bed. Marina had poured it steaming from the pot into a chipped ceramic mixing bowl and set it on a pillow between them. They sat cross-legged on crumpled sheets, naked, and picked the rabbit bits, which had been sautéed in butter with tarragon and mushrooms, out of the bowl with their fingers. Brown sauce had dripped down Marina's chin onto her white breasts. He'd leaned over to lick it off. In the next moment, she was smearing the rabbit gravy all over him — on his arms, chest, abdomen, lower still. Rubbing it on, lapping it up with a powerful, purposeful rhythm. Causing such intense sensation he had to bite down to keep from screaming out. Feeling like a helpless rabbit himself.

Faraway thoughts would peck at his consciousness. Was Elise really okay? Shouldn't he at least go to class, maybe talk to some other people at the school? Were he and Marina really getting any closer to finding his parents' murderer? And the guilt would overtake the ecstasy. His head would clear. He couldn't keep doing this. He had other responsibilities.

But then Marina would wipe her chin and climb out of bed, her hair wild and tangled as though she'd just emerged from months in the jungle. She'd put on a few small items of clothes, then would turn to the pages hanging from the wall. Her manner would change. She became the teacher and he the student, and the guilt would dissolve. This was why he came here night after night. And they were making progress. Good progress. So how could there be anything wrong with it?

"There," she said. Each word was written in bold caps as though everything had special significance. The room smelled like magic marker and her hand was smeared with red ink. "SFWPA. The South Florida Water Protection Agency. Today's suspect and today's lesson." She sat down in front of him, Indian-style, and took a puff on her cigarette.

He tried to focus on the paper on the wall, not on her tight thong. "But they're an environmental protection group. Why would my father attack them?"

"Jeremy, Jeremy. You disappoint me."

His father used to say that and it made him feel stupid and defensive.

"Fine. Tell me how they're corrupt. Tell me what he found."

"It's back to the sugar growers, I'm afraid." Marina pulled the cord to the ceiling fan, then fell back against the mattress, leaning on her elbows. The fan spun above them, shifting the stagnant air. "The sugar growers have a vested interest in the Everglades. If they had to keep the runoff of fertilizer and pesticides from their fields out of the Everglades, their business wouldn't be nearly as profitable. So they use their money to influence the watchdogs."

"Like the water protection agency."

"That's right."

"Jesus, Marina. It seems everyone's bribing everyone else just to keep making money."

"Corruption. It's what makes the world go round, your father liked to say."

"So he attacked the water protection agency for allowing the Everglades to be polluted."

"And the sugar growers for doing it."

"And pissed off lots of people in the process."

"You're starting to get the feel of things." She climbed off the bed. "Fillet of veal with Cointreau tonight. The veal's been soaking in liqueur for over two hours. It'll take a few minutes to fry. Are you hungry?"

Jeremy followed her into the kitchen as he flipped through some of his father's papers. His father had named several organizations as being fronts. One was SWEET — Sugar Workers' Ecological Enterprise Trust. The CAFÉ jers had made a joke about SWEET. Could there be a connection? Jeremy scanned the names his father had listed of its key members not expecting to recognize any, but there, in black and white, was the name Liliam Castillo. Jeremy felt a rush. "Who is SWEET?"

"You are, *mon amour*."

"The organization."

"I know. I was making a little joke." She moved a pat of butter around the skillet with her finger. "Smells good, no?"

"Yes. Tell me about SWEET."

"What's caught your interest?"

"I recognize one of the names, Liliam Castillo."

"Ah. Your neighbor and gracious hostess to your parents' funeral services. You think she murdered your parents?"

"I just want to understand her connection to this organization."

"It's a bit complicated. You see, SWEET purports to be a benevolent group, interested in the welfare of the migrant workers. Many of the people on the board are society women. They throw parties, raise money — it makes them feel important and altruistic. I wouldn't be caught dead at one of their benefits, but I doubt the charity ladies are murderers."

Jeremy wasn't amused by her humor. "But why would my father have a problem with a group of fund-raisers?"

"Because the charitable operations are a front. SWEET is actually a lobbyist group for the sugar growers. Yes, I'm sorry — them again. SWEET is one of the organizations your father maintained bribes the water protection agency and other influential groups."

"So they would have hated my father's positions."

"That's an understatement. They're also one of the largest

benefactors of MIU's business school. You can imagine the embarrassment to Dean Winter every time one of your father's pieces came out."

The rich scent of melting butter hung in the air. "So SWEET and Winter both had a strong motive for wanting my father out of the picture." He was feeling encouraged, optimistic. Maybe not Liliam Castillo, but certainly one of the other names on the list could be the murderer.

But this was no different from the way he'd felt last night, and the night before. Every thesis he'd reviewed with Marina had revealed a new set of suspects. Everything his father wrote about pointed to a villain. But by now, they had four or five lists of people who had pretty good reasons for wanting D. C. Stroeb stopped. And Jeremy was wondering whether he was in fact getting closer to the truth, or just being led on a wild goose chase. But why would Marina want to do that?

The butter sizzled. Marina had dropped the Cointreau-soaked veal into the skillet. She slipped one leg on either side of him, as though she were mounting a horse, and settled herself on his lap. "You look sad, my Jeremy."

"I just don't see us getting any closer."

She tensed on his lap. "Did you think we'd come up with a solution overnight? That we just do a little research and zap, we're done? Instant gratification? This isn't like one of your video games, Jeremy."

"And what if my mother had been the target? I'm spending all my time here."

Like a cat's, the pupils of her eyes seemed to expand and contract. "After all we've uncovered about your father, do you really think your mother was the target? Because if you do, leave now. I don't want to keep you any longer from finding the murderer."

She was right. His father had left a wide wake of outraged people. And whom could his careful mother have alienated?

"We're almost ready to narrow it down, Jeremy." She rested her warm hand on his shoulder. "I just want to be sure we haven't missed anyone."

"So many people." He shook his head. "He made so many people angry."

" 'If what you say doesn't piss someone off, it's not worth saying.' I'm quoting your father. He enjoyed being the rabbit all the dogs chased around the track."

But didn't his father consider what happens to the rabbit when it gets caught?

Marina's thighs tightened around his own. With a flick of her finger, she shifted aside the crotch of her panties. "We have ten minutes," she breathed into his ear. "Ten minutes until the veal is done."

Chapter 21

Elise held her mother's hand tightly as they walked through the mall. Her mother wore white pants and a yellow shirt the color of a happy face button. Her hair was held up in a ponytail with a red ribbon. She smiled at Elise. Elise felt so happy she wanted to laugh out loud. She and her mother, together, forever.

But there were hundreds of people at the mall, all zipping past them. Why couldn't she and her mother keep up? Her feet were heavy; she could barely lift them. And the black-and-white tile floor that looked like a giant chessboard was moving backwards, carrying them farther away from their destination. The sound of carnival music became louder. Over the edge of a railing, she could see a carousel.

That's where they were going—to the carousel. Elise heard screeches of delight as the horses rose and fell in time to the music. The children's black wings lifted them higher and higher, far above the painted ponies.

The children's black wings.

All the children and all the people had wings, like bats. That's why they could move so quickly. They could fly. Elise felt her back with her free hand. Yes, she had wings too.

She began rising high into the air. She squeezed her mother's hand. "We're flying, Mommy. We're flying."

"I'm not your mother," said a thick shadow with a black mask.

"But she's calling you," the shadow said in its deep distorted voice. "Your mama's calling you."

Elise touched her back. The wings were gone. And she began falling, falling into a deep, dark hole.

Elise awoke with a start. The tee shirt she slept in was soaked with sweat. The shadow. The dark shadow was in her dreams every night. But she could never see its face.

How she wanted her mother back! Her mother in the yellow blouse with her hair held up by a red ribbon. Her mother smiling at her. Elise closed her eyes, trying to reconnect with the happy part of her dream. Mommy, she whispered. Mommy, come back.

But only black bats flew across her mind, blocking out the sweetness as they flapped their dank wings.

Elise reached for the water glass on her nightstand. She was thirsty, so thirsty. The glass was empty. It was after two in the morning. Dwight had called around midnight asking for Jeremy, as he did most nights, and she had unplugged the phone.

She turned on the faucet in her bathroom and held her mouth under it to catch the cold stream of water. She couldn't seem to get enough.

Her mother smiling. So happy, so real, Elise was certain she had touched her. Elise's heart ached with unbearable emptiness. It had been a dream. Her mother was dead. Her mother was dead. Tears ran down Elise's cheeks mingling with the tap water. Was that why she was so thirsty? So she had something to make more tears with?

Her legs were heavy, like in the dream, as she went to Jeremy's room. She was frightened. She was always frightened being alone in the house. She would lock all the doors as soon as she was inside, but it didn't seem to help. The murderer had gotten in with a key last time. Why would locked doors stop him now?

Jeremy was stretched out across his bed. Elise felt a wave of relief. She wasn't alone. Then she realized it was only a couple of piles of laundered clothes. Jeremy wasn't asleep in his bed. Jeremy never slept in his bed anymore.

A terrible sadness pulled Elise down to the floor. Carlos had given her a pill tonight. It had a tiny black Batman insignia. Ecstasy. "Take this," he'd said. "It'll really make you fly."

And perhaps because she was already high from the pot, she'd washed it down with a glass of water.

"You have to drink plenty of water," he'd said. "This shit makes you real thirsty."

And she was. So thirsty. She went back to her bathroom and drank from the faucet. The water splashed her tee shirt. Her mother's shirt. The one she'd found hanging in the hallway closet. It had three brown teardrops. Her mother's blood from the nosebleed she'd had the night they'd come home from visiting Jeremy. Elise could still smell her mother's perfume on it. She wore the shirt every night, refusing to wash it. Unwilling to lose any more of her mother than she already had.

Moonlight was seeping in through the partially open blinds in her mother's office. Elise sat down at the desk and rested her head on her arms. A sharp point poked her. The clipboard with its yellow pad and squiggly writing was lying on top of the desk. She had only scribbled on the top page the last time she'd noticed the clipboard. Now, she found every page filled with her tight, intense pen strokes. Had she done this? In her sleep?

She flipped through the pages. The letters became almost legible as she got to the end of the pad. She could make out *m, g, e*. And there were breaks in the scribbles, almost like she'd been writing words.

Elise studied the last few pages. It seemed as though she'd been making columns. *Geezer.* That was one of the words. She was sure of it. Then, *Elise, Jeremy*, something that looked like *May 2*, Elise's birthday, and *February 20*, Jeremy's birthday. In a few days, he'd be twenty-three.

But what had her subconscious been doing? She turned to the next page and tried to decipher the words. *Corvair, freedom, Mozart.*

"Corvair, freedom, Mozart," she said aloud. Her father's favorite things. And the names and birthdays were important to her mother. Passwords. Could she have been making a list of possible passwords in her sleep? Trying to break into her parents' e-mail accounts?

Elise got her laptop from her room. She set it on top of her mother's desk blotter.

Passwords. She logged onto her parents' mail server to input each one. *Geezer, Jeremy, Elise, May 2, February 20.*

Invalid password. Please try again, the computer said.

She tried her father's account. *Corvair, freedom, Mozart.*

Please try again.

Each time she input a new word, she felt a stab of pain. Just like in the Kafka story she'd read in school called "In the Penal Colony," where a torture machine wrote the name of the crime into the culprit's body with a sharp needle. With each word came a memory, which stabbed her like the needle in the story. But Elise couldn't stop. She threw the clipboard on the floor and started typing in her own memories.

Bicycle. She remembered her father pushing her on her little pink bike after he'd taken the training wheels off, shouting, "Go on Elise. You've got it. Go on, pumpkin."

Pumpkin. One Halloween when she was four or five, her father had taken her outside in the dark. On the step sat two large heads with fire growing out of their eyes and mouth. Elise had screamed in terror. "They're only pumpkins," her father had said, pulling her close. "Come on, baby. Don't cry."

Baby, she typed in now. *Don't cry.* But she couldn't stop herself. With each word, her loss spread wider and wider, like a drop of blood in a bowl of water. Mommy, Daddy, how could you leave me?

It was the Ecstasy, she knew. The depression was a symptom of coming down from the high. She needed to stop this self-pity. She had to do something to find her parents' murderer.

To close the dark hole within herself.

She focused her attention on the desk blotter. Her mother had used it as a reminder calendar. Each word, each letter was written in her mother's graceful handwriting. So different from the scribbles Elise had made. So different, yet so much the same. Her mother's notes were as cryptic as the words Elise had written on the yellow pad.

Elise looked at the entry her mother had made for the day after they returned from visiting Jeremy in Madrid. *Geezer — bath; drycleaners; Opa Locka — St. M, 1PM, Passport.*

Her mother had been planning on traveling, that was clear. But where? She was often flying off on business trips, and Elise had stopped paying attention to her mother's destinations or even to how long she was going away for. She would find herself pleasantly surprised when she returned from school and her father would say, "Well, looks like it's just you and me tonight, babe. Can you stand it?" And Elise could more than stand it. She'd loved those evenings when it was just her and her dad. So, probably out of guilt, she'd block out her mother's travel talk.

Elise flipped through her mother's file drawer looking for a travel itinerary, but the only ones she found were from before Madrid. Maybe she'd left the tickets or itinerary out on her desk and, hopefully, the police hadn't taken them. She searched the desk blotter, under the coin paperweight, behind the calculator. Nothing.

She focused again on the words. *Opa Locka — St. M.*

Opa Locka was a small neighborhood just outside of Miami. St.

M. Was that a street in Opa Locka? No, then it would have been M St. Elise pressed her hands against her head. She had a dull headache and she was thirsty. So thirsty. And this was too difficult. She couldn't figure it out. But she had to. St. M, St. M. St. Mary's? Where had she heard of St. Mary's? Mrs. Castillo had said the Olympus Grande resort was located on St. Mary's. Could her mother have been planning a trip there?

Opa Locka was also the name of an airport for private planes. Was her mother supposed to fly from Opa Locka to St. Mary's at 1 p.m. the day after she was murdered? It made sense. She would have needed the passport.

But what did it all mean?

Geezer licked her hand. She wished Jeremy was home so she could ask him. There were so many things she wanted to talk to him about. Was he feeling as lost as she was? Did he also get angry at their parents for leaving them? Did he know how to make the pain go away?

But she couldn't ask Jeremy anything. Jeremy didn't come home anymore, nor answer his phone.

Elise lay down on the Oriental rug in her mother's office. She closed her eyes and concentrated as hard as she could until she saw the smiling woman in the yellow blouse with her hair held high by a red ribbon.

Chapter 22

Jeremy awakened with a throbbing headache as if someone was hitting him with a rubber hammer. He went down to the kitchen and took three Motrins. The sun was pouring through the kitchen windows, and Jeremy had to squint to keep the pain from flaring up. He closed the blinds.

"Another rough night?" Elise asked, walking into the kitchen. She was dressed in her school khakis and polo shirt, but looked like crap with dark circles under her eyes, her hair messily braided.

"I got to bed pretty late."

"That's an understatement."

"Look, Ellie. I don't want you thinking I'm wasting my time when I'm not here with you."

She took a glass from the cupboard.

"I'm making progress. I'm pretty sure the murderer targeted Dad."

"Why?" Elise filled the glass with water and drank it down.

"Because Dad made a lot of people angry. I just have to narrow it down."

"Sounds like you have everything under control." She refilled the water glass, drank it, and started toward the door.

"Aren't you going to eat anything?" he asked.

She gestured toward the countertop, empty except for the bottle of Motrin. "Aren't you?"

"Touché, I guess."

"Gotta go." She waved without meeting his eye.

"Ellie, wait a sec."

She leaned against the refrigerator, her arms folded across her chest. "What?"

"I want to make sure you're okay. You were asleep on the rug in Mom's office when I got home last night."

"Was I?" Her tone said she couldn't care less.

"You were holding the pad — the one you'd been writing in the night you were sleepwalking."

"So?"

"Every page was filled with scribbles."

"Is, is that a crime?" She'd pushed off the refrigerator with her foot. Her lower lip was trembling. "At least I come home at night."

"I'm sorry. I wasn't criticizing. I just want to make sure you're all right."

"Thanks. You win the good brother award. I'll make sure Dwight knows."

"What does Dwight have to do with anything?"

"Nothing. He, he calls. That's all."

"When?"

"Most nights. Usually he starts at ten or eleven and keeps calling until I unplug the phone."

"What does he want?"

"You, I guess. He keeps asking for you."

"Shit."

"Yeah, well. We all have problems. I'm going to school."

"He's not going to take the guardianship away from me, Elise. You don't have to worry about that."

"You know something, Jeremy. I don't care anymore. M-maybe it would be nice to have someone in the house to talk to." She flung her braid over her shoulder. "Even if it's Dwight."

Jeremy walked Geezer to the park where he used to take Elise when she was little. She loved climbing the huge banyan tree they'd named "the grotto," or hiding in its thick roots. But taking his sister to the park was very different from having complete responsibility for her. Flora did the shopping and cooking, but late at night Elise was all alone. And even if she spent time with Carlos, it wasn't the same as being with family. So maybe Dwight and Selma moving in with Elise wouldn't be the worst thing in the world.

It seemed to be what Elise wanted.

He rested his hand against a low smooth branch protruding from the banyan tree.

Take care of your sister.

"But I'm no good at it, Mom. That's why I went away in the first place. Because I wasn't ready for commitments or responsibility."

Geezer looked up at him and wagged his tail.

Of course, if Elise wanted him to stay, it would be different. But she'd said herself that she didn't care. So he'd finish working with Marina to find the murderer, then get the hell out of here.

Back where he belonged. Where there were no mothers, fathers, or sisters.

Where there was no one to worry about but himself.

He left the park and pushed his sunglasses up on his nose. The sun was already strong. He lit a cigarette. A bicyclist whizzed by. Jeremy resisted the impulse to run after him. His father used to do that — run after speeders and shout, "Slow down."

A slouching woman in a dark pantsuit was walking toward him. He took another puff on the cigarette. It was after eight. Time to leave for work, not that it served much purpose for him to be there anymore.

"I thought you might be walking the dog," the woman called out as she got closer. "There's a car in the driveway, but no one answered the door."

"How are you, Detective Lieber? I've been meaning to call you."

"But you haven't. You must be pretty busy." In the harsh sunlight, the gray in her hair gleamed.

"I figured you'd let me know if anything was happening." He dropped the cigarette on the ground and stubbed it out with his shoe.

Lieber leaned over to pet the dog. "Geezer's looking well," she said, pulling herself back up.

"Our housekeeper usually walks him."

"But you wanted some fresh air this morning?"

He checked his watch. He remembered Detective Kuzniski doing that the first time they'd met, as though he didn't have time to be bothered by Jeremy.

The bicyclist zoomed by, causing Jeremy to pull Geezer out of the road.

"I won't keep you long." Lieber gestured toward a stone bench at the edge of the bay. "Why don't we sit there so we don't get run over?"

The reflection from the water hurt his eyes, even with sunglasses on. Jeremy twisted around on the bench so that the direct glare didn't hit him.

Lieber took a small bottle from her handbag. She held out the Advil. "Need one of these?"

"Thanks, I've already taken three Motrin."

"You're keeping up a heck of a pace — work, school, taking care of your sister. How's it working out?"

"Great."

She popped a piece of gum in her mouth. "That's a beautiful car you're driving. I remember someone telling me your father really cherished it."

"Yeah, well. I wish he would have cherished his family as much."

"I was under the impression he did."

Jeremy rubbed his temples. How much did he want to tell the detective about his relationship with Marina and what he was discovering about his father?

"I thought you and I were on the same side, Jeremy. What's going on?"

Geezer pulled on the leash, straining to chase a squirrel. "I think I'm onto something," Jeremy said, "but I don't want to be premature."

"I'm just here to listen."

"I've been looking over my father's papers. He was a pretty outspoken guy. Seemed to get a kick out of pissing everyone off."

"You think he was rash? That he didn't consider the repercussions?"

"Well, he sure gave a lot of people a motive to kill him."

"Is that what his graduate assistant believes?"

"What are you talking about?"

"Marina Champlain smokes those unfiltered cigarettes, too."

"She's helping me. Is that a problem?" He was sounding as defensive as his sister had earlier.

"Not at all. As long as you remember one source isn't very objective. I assume you've been talking to other people at the school. Confirming what Marina tells you."

"Look," Jeremy said. "Marina's been great. She's explained my father's theories to me and who they may have offended."

"It's obvious she wants to help you."

"That's right."

"Why?"

"Why? Why wouldn't she? Marina cared about my father and she wants to find his murderer. I think it's pretty clear something my father said provoked the murderer. You know about the fire in his office?"

"I do."

"My father was brilliant. He knew just what buttons to push. How to enrage the opposition."

"It sounds like you're very angry with him. Do you want to believe he was the target?"

"What the hell's that supposed to mean?"

"I'm just curious why you stopped considering your mother's business associates."

"My father got a lot of people to hate him."

"And that's your basis for believing him to be the target?"

"My father didn't care who he offended. He wanted to be sure everyone understood exactly how he felt. Even if he knew he was making people angry enough to want to kill him."

"So free speech is a crime, Jeremy?"

His throat tightened. "It is when you value it above your family."

Chapter 23

Just after nine a.m., Jeremy turned the Corvair onto the MIU campus. It was congested with slow-moving cars cruising the full parking lot. Several were parked up against the curbs with the "No Parking" signs. It had been almost two weeks since his mother's car had been towed away. He'd made no effort to reclaim it. It just hadn't been a priority.

A car was pulling out of a legitimate parking spot. Jeremy zipped around a curve to get to it before another car cut him off.

He was annoyed after seeing Lieber this morning. He could tell the detective didn't trust Marina. And why was Lieber making it seem as though Jeremy wanted his father to be the reason for the murders? If his father had incited the killer with his glib talk, then he was responsible. Jeremy was merely telling it like it was.

He cut the engine.

Some kid was staring into the car. "Nice car. What is it, a Corvette?"

"Corvair," Jeremy said, slamming the car door. He headed toward the campus. He didn't care that Lieber doubted him; Jeremy was sure he was on the right track. And he'd find another source to prove it.

Students were swarming over the quad, congregating under the trees. He debated going over to the economics building, but didn't want to risk running into Winter. Marina didn't have a class until eleven, so there was no chance he'd bump into her.

On the path toward the cafeteria, Jeremy spotted two people in brown tee shirts, Queso and Liddy, the CAFÉ Jers. He called after them. They waited for him to catch up. Liddy's curly black hair was tucked under a baseball cap and they were both wearing sunglasses as though hoping not to be recognized. They would have done better wearing different shirts.

"How's it going?" Queso asked. "Anything new about —" He rubbed his neck like he had an itch. "You know, your dad."

"Not really," Jeremy said. "Hey, you guys have time for coffee?"

Queso and Liddy exchanged a look. "Sure," Liddy said.

They sat at a table a distance from the other students. The outdoor eating area bordered the edge of a man-made lake with a fountain at its center. A running path went around the lake's circumference. Several joggers, the wires from their iPods dangling from their ears, ran by.

Jeremy used to go jogging every day, but hadn't run in weeks. Jeremy had stopped doing many of the things that once seemed so important to him.

"CAFÉ J meeting today?" he asked Queso and Liddy.

They looked confused. "Oh, you mean this?" Queso said, pulling on his tee shirt. "No. No meeting. A few of us have been wearing our CAFÉ J shirts since your father — you know."

"To keep his memory and the movement alive," Liddy said.

"Have you been allowed to hold meetings?"

"Winter doesn't exactly know about them." Queso scowled over his sunglasses at Liddy. "What? You think I shouldn't say anything? You think he's going to squeal to Winter? Come on, Liddy. Get real."

"Fine." Liddy dipped a pastry into the *café con leche* she'd ordered at the La Carreta kiosk in the food court.

"You don't trust me?" Jeremy said.

"Not you," Liddy said, "the administration. We already have a reputation as troublemakers."

"Are you afraid SWEET might try to do something to you?" Jeremy said, deliberately dropping the name. "Maybe get you all expelled?"

"They can't touch us," Queso said.

"How do you know about SWEET?" Liddy said.

"Everyone knows SWEET's one of the biggest donors to the school. That they hated my father." Jeremy sipped his coffee. He'd ordered it American-style, but it tasted like diluted espresso. "I can't imagine they'd be happy knowing his legacy lives on."

"That's an understatement," Queso said.

Flakes from Liddy's pastry had settled on her brown tee shirt and she brushed them off. "Your father said he'd be damned if he'd let anyone compromise his academic freedom, no matter how much money they gave to the school."

Sure. His father would have said that.

"And after they threatened to cut off funding," Queso said, "your father got like really upset."

SWEET had threatened to cut off funding?

Liddy licked her fingers. "So your father sent articles and letters to the editors of all the major newspapers and really pissed Winter off."

"Yeah," Queso said. "Remember when Winter interrupted one of our meetings and asked D.C. to come to his office? We stood in the hallway and could hear them yelling, even with the door closed."

"Winter said," Liddy changed her voice in a parody of the dean's affected one, " 'If you don't stop of your own volition, Dr. Stroeb, I'll have no option but to curtail your partisan activities myself.' " She changed her voice back to normal. "But Winter knew he couldn't do much — D.C.'s a tenured professor."

"And then there was the fire in D.C.'s office," Queso said.

"What do you know about the fire?" Jeremy said.

"Nothing," Liddy said, gathering up her books.

"There's a story going around that a bunch of anti-Castro extremists did it," Queso said. "But that's bullshit."

"Bullshit?" Jeremy said.

"I've got class," Liddy said.

Queso looked over at her. "We know all those rich Cuban guys — Juan Lopez, Fernando Calderon, Luisito Padron. Those assholes are too busy color coordinating their Ralph Lauren shirts and sweaters. You think one of them would take a chance setting a fire and messing up their clothes?"

"Then who do you think did it?" Jeremy asked.

"I've got to go." Liddy adjusted her sunglasses.

"Do you think it was someone from SWEET?" Jeremy's mind was racing. The connection seemed so obvious.

"Are you kidding?" Queso said. "Those guys swipe their Amex cards — not matches."

"Then who?" Jeremy's coffee had turned lukewarm. "Winter?" Jeremy said suddenly.

"Shhh," Liddy said, glancing around.

"So Winter did it, then started the rumor about the anti-Castro extremists." Jeremy had lowered his voice. "As a warning, right?" He could feel his heart pumping. "He certainly had a motive. Winter was the one who cared the most about SWEET's funding." That's where Marina had been leading him. Winter had killed his parents. Jeremy felt a surge of relief or redemption, he wasn't sure which.

"Winter didn't set the fire," Liddy said.

Jeremy took a second to regain his bearings. "But he must have."

"You know who did it, Liddy?" Queso said. "Why didn't you say something to me?"

Liddy glanced around. "Keep your voice down."

Queso leaned across the table. "So who was it?"

She mumbled something.

"You're kidding," Queso said.

"Who?" Jeremy said. "Who set the fire?"

"His graduate assistant," Liddy whispered.

"What? You mean Marina?"

Liddy nodded.

"That's the stupidest thing I ever heard," Jeremy said. "Marina doesn't care about the funding. She's not involved with any Cuban extremist movements."

"I saw her."

"You couldn't have," Jeremy said.

"Are you calling me a liar?" Liddy's full cheeks flushed. "I saw her come out of the office, then spray paint the door — *Cuba Libre*."

"That's impossible. She admired my father. She's helping me find his murderer. Why would she set fire to his office?"

"Don't believe me. That's the problem with everyone. Why believe a troublemaking student about anything?" She gathered up her trash and stood up. Queso did the same.

"Why?" Jeremy asked. "I asked you why?"

"Maybe you'd better ask Marina," Liddy said. "Given that she's clearly so interested in helping you."

Chapter 24

Marina's beat-up yellow Toyota was parked next to Mrs. Lambert's old Chevy. The green lawn glistened in the morning sunlight as though the old landlady had just watered it, but there was no sign of her. Hanging from rusted chains, a wooden swing swayed back and forth despite the lack of breeze.

Jeremy stood outside Marina's backyard apartment for a good ten minutes without moving. Through the dirty windows, he could see the blinds were closed and there were no lights on inside.

What was he going to say to her? If he confronted her about the fire, what did he expect her to do? Fess up? Tell him it was an accident, a misunderstanding? More likely, she'd just deny it. Then where did that leave him?

Not knowing. Not knowing if she set the fire. Not knowing if the past couple of weeks with her had been some kind of game on her part.

And if she had set the fire, why? Was she hiding some personal vendetta against his father? And if she was, what did that imply?

But she couldn't have done it. The idea that Marina may have killed his parents was beyond his threshold of acceptance.

He raised his fist to knock on the door. No, she couldn't have done it.

The door opened. Marina was trying to stop the smile that

tugged at the corners of her mouth. She wore a too-large white terry robe with a partially torn-off sleeve and her hair was in damp ringlets, as though she'd just come out of the shower. Her face had a glow, like a child's after some exertion. How could he even have considered Marina had deceived him?

"I thought I heard someone outside." She stood on her toes and pulled his face toward hers, dizzying him with a kiss. "I imagined, perhaps, it was a peeping Tom or the neighborhood rapist," she breathed into his mouth, "but I'm relieved it's only you." She licked his lips. "Playing hooky today, *mon amour*? Couldn't wait, could you? I'm glad. I'll play hooky, too." She closed the door behind him and placed his hands inside her robe. "*Mon dieu*. So cold. And I'm like an overheated engine, no? Because all I could think about is being with you. And here you are. Right out of my dreams." She unbuttoned his shirt, then looked at him quizzically. "Is something wrong? Has something happened?"

Using all his willpower, he took his hands off her breasts. "Can we talk?"

"Oh my God. Something's happened. They've found the murderer, haven't they?"

Jeremy picked up a pile of students' tests that were lying on the futon and threw them on the floor. He sat down, his legs stretched out awkwardly in front of him. Marina slid next to him and massaged the back of his neck. Her robe had fallen open exposing a hard, brown nipple. He turned away and stared at the thin white lines in his pin-striped pants.

"Tell me about the fire in my father's office."

"The fire?" She stopped rubbing his neck then resumed after a pause. "Yes, of course. Didn't I tell you? It happened a few months ago. Some Cuban expatriates did it. Exiled Cubans who hate Castro. They were angry about your father's stand against the embargo.

What's happened? Did they catch someone? Is that why you're be-having so strangely?"

Jeremy's mouth was dry. "Did you do it, Marina?"

"Do it? What do you mean, did I do it?"

"Did you set the fire in my father's office? Did you spray paint his door? Did you —" But he couldn't ask any more questions.

"How could you ask me such a thing?" She plucked angrily at her wet curls. "You think I set the fire? You can possibly believe that of me?"

"I just need to hear you say it. That you didn't do it."

"I don't understand you, Jeremy. What have we been doing night after night? All the papers, all the work, trying to find your father's murderer."

"My parents' murderer."

"Yes, your parents' murderer. Trying to find your parents' mur-derer. And do you imagine I could have ever wanted to hurt your fa-ther? Have you not seen how I admired him? Adored him? How could you accuse me?" She reached over for a cigarette from the pack on the table and lit it.

He wanted to believe her. He needed to believe her. "Someone saw you, Marina."

The round red lips disappeared into her mouth like a deflating toy. She was staring him straight in the eye. He did that when he was lying. He'd look the other person straight in the eye. But she wasn't lying. She hadn't deceived him.

"Impossible." The ashes from her cigarette fell onto the futon. "It's impossible. Either I'm being mixed up with another person or someone's lying." She took a quick puff on the cigarette. "Who told you this story?"

"It's not important."

"It's important to me to know who my accuser is. Why won't

he come forward if he's telling the truth? Why hasn't he reported me to the police? If I set the fire in your father's office, I'd be a likely suspect in the murder, no?"

Why hadn't Liddy told anyone? Marina had a point. If Liddy had really seen Marina, she certainly would have told someone. Especially after the murder.

"So you have no answers for me, my Jeremy. Just accusations. You hear a rumor, a lie, and you're quick to believe it. Ready to believe a stranger over me. I don't understand, Jeremy. Has nothing I've done or said meant anything to you?" A single tear raced down her cheek. She wiped it away.

He wanted to reach for her, but he couldn't. He just couldn't.

She picked up the papers Jeremy had thrown on the floor. Her robe fell open; she quickly closed it and tightened the belt.

Let it go. Let it go. But the words slipped out of him. "The person said she saw you spray painting my father's door."

Marina stopped what she was doing and straightened up. "Who is she, Jeremy? A student at the school? I have many students." She held up the stack of papers. "Many of them don't like me very much; did you know that? I'm a tough grader, they say. Some call me unfair. You don't suppose this person — this trustworthy eyewitness of yours — may be one of my students, do you? Perhaps a student I gave a poor grade to? A troublemaker?"

Of course. That had to be it. Liddy was being vindictive. A troublemaker. She'd even called herself a troublemaker, hadn't she?

"Oh, my Jeremy, come here." Marina opened her arms. "Someone is playing with your head, *mon amour*. Someone who is perhaps jealous of our relationship."

Her robe slid to the floor. She pressed her naked body against him. He could feel himself respond to her touch. Regardless of the disorder in his head, his body had its own agenda. "Don't you know how I felt about your father, Jeremy? I could no sooner hurt him than I could you." She touched herself between her legs, then rubbed her moist finger over his mouth, leaving behind her powerful scent. "You believe me, don't you?" Her flecked cat's eyes penetrated his. "Because if you didn't, *mon amour*, I don't know what I would do."

Chapter 25

Marina heard the growl of the old Corvair's engine as it pulled out of the driveway. How ironic he'd chosen to drive his father's car. The car she'd come to identify with the man — unconventional, contrarian, uniquely beautiful.

She turned on the burner to boil water for a cup of tea and tightened the terrycloth robe around her. She was cold despite the stagnant heat in the apartment and the smell of sweat and sex that hung over her like a heavy drape.

She hadn't cooked tonight. He had come over too early and upset her schedule. Then she had become disoriented by his disturbing confrontation, and all she could think about was trying to set things right with him.

She had been planning on making *papas a la huancaina* — a favorite of hers from her childhood. She'd thought about her grandmother early this morning when she'd gone to the Peruvian market to buy potatoes, cheese from Mayobamba, hot peppers, and black olives. The last time she'd seen her grandmother was the day her own mother had dragged Marina off and put her on a plane for France. Her grandmother wore an apron and smelled like garlic and spices. Marina had clung to her, mixing her own tears with the perspiration on her grandmother's neck. "Don't let her send me away," Marina had begged.

"*No llores, preciosa*," her grandmother said. Don't cry, precious. "You come back soon. I'll be waiting."

But her grandmother hadn't waited. Six months later, Marina received a cursory note from her mother that her grandmother had died.

After that, Marina wanted no memory, no association with that earlier life. She spoke only French. Cooked only French. Was only French. Until the day D.C. had reawakened something in her.

Her car wouldn't start. She'd been standing beside it in the school parking lot, kicking the door.

"That's not likely to be effective," D.C. had said. He was carrying his laptop and a load of papers to his own car. She had been his graduate assistant for the past three months, but he'd always been reserved and formal with her. She had craved more of this brilliant, contentious man, but had been reluctant to approach him — knew it would be futile. His gold wedding band was too shiny, too conspicuous. So she had settled for being a dazzling protégée, a worthy student, reading every word he wrote, and becoming his most vocal advocate. "I can try jumping it," he said.

"Do what you like," she said.

The car had miraculously started up, but kicked and coughed like a convulsing old man, and D.C. said he'd better follow her home in case the car quit.

He worked on it behind her house. With his own tools. What kind of college professor is this, she marveled, who carries around a set of tools? And her neighbor, Mrs. Lambert, had seen him and asked if he'd fix her old Chevy. And he said sure, that it probably just needed a charge.

It had been hot and his light blue tee shirt turned dark with sweat. He pulled it off and wrapped it around his head like a turban. His body was lean and golden. And she wasn't sure why, but she had the urge to cook. To make one of her grandmother's comfort dishes. *Huevos con salchichas y papas.*

She left the front door open as she fried the sausage and potatoes, remembering the smell from her childhood. Remembering her grandmother smiling at her. "*Come, mi tesora. Come.*" Eat, my treasure.

He had been watching her from the doorway. He was still shirtless. "Well, it's fixed. You should get another five thousand miles out of it without much trouble."

She pushed the hair off her perspiring forehead. "Thank you. Have a beer." She gestured to the refrigerator. "Sorry it's not very cold. Nothing keeps cold in that old thing."

He popped off the top of a beer, then stood behind her at the stove. "That smells good. I never pictured you being remotely domestic."

"No? How did you picture me?" Her heart was racing.

"I don't know. Sitting on your bed grading papers, eating cereal from a box, biting your nails."

She scraped the eggs, sausage, and potatoes onto a chipped plate and handed it to him with a spoon. "I don't have any clean forks."

He put the plate on the pile of newspapers on the kitchen table and unwound his shirt from his head.

"You can leave it off. It's not a restaurant. Shoes and shirts aren't required here."

He hesitated, then left the shirt hanging on the back of the kitchen chair.

She had watched him eat, barely able to breathe. Wanting to touch him, but afraid.

"This is great, Marina," he said, finishing the last bite. "Really great." He smiled at her like her father had never done.

"I can make some more."

"I need to get going." He reached for his shirt and put it on.

"Are you sure?" She was close enough to smell him. "I can make coffee. Or you can have another beer."

"I'd better not." He paused at the refrigerator. "But would you mind if I take a quick look at this? I'm a sucker for a broken machine." And he pushed the refrigerator away from the wall revealing a thick mat of dust. Black bugs scurried for cover, but D.C. didn't seem to notice. He unscrewed the back with something he'd taken from his pants pocket, then touched and poked and prodded. Finally, he wiped his hands on his shirt and pushed the refrigerator back into place. "It needs a new fan."

"*Bien*. I'll pick one up. Then I can install it. It will be very simple for me, no?"

He studied her. "I can do it, if you'd like."

"No, please. Don't be absurd. I'm resigned to warm beer and no ice cream."

"I'll come by after class tomorrow or the next day," he said.

And Marina knew she shouldn't get her hopes up; he was a married man. He was just being paternal and kind. But after he fixed the refrigerator, he returned a few days later and fixed the ceiling fan, then the leaky faucet, then the shower nozzle. He'd even left a small red toolbox beside the kitchen sink. And she had gotten into the habit of cooking for him. She'd prepare glorious, seductive meals, then serve them wearing her shortest shorts, her sexiest tops. She'd never met a man with so much self-control.

She would watch him eat, sensing he desired her as much as she wanted him, but held back by his fake morality. Then one day, she exploded at him as he lit one of her cigarettes for himself.

"What's the matter with you?" she asked.

"What are you talking about? What's wrong?"

"How can you ask me that? You come here week after week. You say it's to fix things, but that makes no sense. Why do you care if my milk goes sour or my toilet overflows?"

"I'm just trying to help."

"That's a lie. You come here to watch me. To stare at my ass when you think I don't see. To fantasize about fucking me."

He stood up suddenly and the chair crashed down. "I'm leaving now."

"Why? Because you can't stand hearing the truth? You're a hypocrite, D.C. How many times have you fucked me in your mind? If you were a good Catholic, you'd go to confession for it, wouldn't you? Lusting in your heart is as evil as lusting in the flesh. Right? Isn't that right? You're going to hell either way, D.C."

And he grabbed her and pressed her against the wall. His eyes were glassy and unnatural. She felt his heart pounding against her chest. Then his mouth closed over hers. He clawed at her clothes, pulled her hair, sucked her flesh. She didn't want him to stop. Not ever.

The tea kettle was squealing. Marina turned the burner off. She poured the boiling water into a chipped mug and swished the teabag around.

She had lost him. The love of her life. But he had come back.

Younger and better than ever.

Chapter 26

Carlos was acting weird. "I don't want to hang out here," he'd said when they got to the rec room, and he brought Elise to the yacht instead.

Elise had never been on the large boat before, and she wasn't even sure the Castillos ever used it. The gleaming white yacht was always gently rocking at the end of the dock. So she was surprised to find it completely furnished with four cabins, two and a half baths — heads, Carlos called them — a modern kitchen and living room area with a large flat-screen TV.

"This is nice." She fingered the soft leather sofa as Carlos rolled a joint on the coffee table. He sat on the floor wearing the black tank top he'd had on under his school shirt. The room was dimly lit by the late afternoon sun, which peeked through the portholes despite the drawn shades.

"At least there are no cameras here that I know about," Carlos said.

"Cameras?"

"Yeah. So my mother can't watch us." He licked the rolling paper, then lit the end of the joint with his cigarette lighter and took a hit.

"What makes you think she's watching us?"

"Just a feeling."

Elise took the joint from him and sucked the smoke down into her lungs.

"Do you ever get feelings?" Carlos said.

"What do you mean?"

"You know. Like about that night?"

"Sometimes."

Carlos seemed to tense. "Like what?"

"I don't know." On the paneled wall were pictures of hotels with beautiful views of water and mountains. "It's crazy," she said. She'd never told Carlos about the nightmares. "I keep thinking he's coming back. That, that he wants to hurt me."

"The murderer?"

She nodded.

"Why do you think that?" Carlos was biting on the skin around his fingernails. Over the last few weeks he'd ravaged his fingers.

"I, I don't know. Look, do we have to talk about this?"

Carlos went over to a porthole. He held the shade out, blew on the glass, then smeared it with his finger. "I'm just curious why you think the murderer's coming back. I mean, you don't remember seeing him, do you?"

The tiny butt of the joint burned her. She threw it in the bar sink and ran cold water over her fingers. "Why are we talking about this? I thought we came here to get high."

"Right." He let the shade fall back against the porthole, then reached into his pants pocket and took out a couple of little pills.

Did she really want to take one of those again? Last night's depression still clung to her. Or maybe it was the sadness from her fight with Jeremy this morning. Why had she said she didn't care if Dwight was her guardian? Well, of course she knew why. She'd wanted to hurt Jeremy. To make him pay for not coming home when she so desperately needed him. But now, she was afraid after this morning, he'd never want to come home again.

Carlos handed her a pill and a glass of water.

She took it. Why not?

He turned on the CD player and lay down next to her on the leather sofa. John Mayer was singing. She liked that, soft and easy. She kicked off her boots — her mother's leather boots that she'd found in the downstairs closet. Her mother had bought them in Madrid. They were stained, but Elise didn't care. Wearing them made her feel closer to her mother. Like she was somehow with her.

Elise closed her eyes. Shadows darted across the room. She tried to sit up, but she was bound. A scream caught in her throat.

"Hey," Carlos whispered in her ear. "You were having a bad dream." It was his arms around her, but her heart was still racing. Was it fear or the Ecstasy? "It's okay," Carlos said. He wasn't wearing a shirt. Or pants. She wasn't either.

He pulled off the clip that held her braid together and ran his fingers from the base of her scalp all the way down to the ends. Tingly, magical. He handed her a glass of water. She drank it down. It dripped on Carlos's chest. She lapped it up and they laughed. Then they started kissing. Cold, wet mouths. And it was so good, she just wanted to suck on his tongue and lips forever while John Mayer sang to her about fathers and daughters and mothers and lovers.

She was being caressed by silk scarves. Slipping and sliding on satin and velvet. Everything felt so good. She was happy, like her heart was chirping.

Something hard pressed against her belly. Hard, yet gentle. Carlos took her hand and wrapped it around his penis.

He touched her special place with his fingers. "You want to?"

And she did. She snuggled against him as his tongue went deeper into her mouth.

Mothers, fathers, daughters, lovers. Mayer's words swirled around her brain.

Her mother would be upset; her father, too. But they weren't here to stop her. No one was here to stop her.

Oh Jeremy. Tears stung her eyes. Why have you deserted me?

Her hand swept over her mother's boot.

"What's wrong?" Carlos said.

She pulled away from him. "I, I can't."

"Sure you can. I've got protection."

"I'm sorry, Carlos." Elise slid off the sofa and found her clothes in a pile on the floor. "But I've got to protect myself."

It was only a little after seven when Elise got home to an empty house. The radio was playing. Elise was relieved. Flora often forgot to leave the music on like Elise asked her to. Garlicky roast chicken and acrid dog smell mingled in the air.

Her senses were heightened from the Ecstasy. The lights were brighter, the smells stronger, her sadness deeper, and her fear more intense.

Elise went from room to room, testing the windows, making sure the French doors and the door to the garage were locked. Geezer followed her. Jeremy had promised to fix the house alarm when they discovered it didn't work, but he'd never gotten around to it. Maybe she'd call the alarm people herself since she didn't know if Jeremy was ever coming home again.

She poured herself a glass of water, went upstairs to her mother's office and sat down at the desk. Her mother had a thick fountain pen that made beautiful calligraphy. "Mom," Elise wrote on a piece of stationery that had her mother's name at the top. The ink blotted on the "M". "I miss you, Mommy," she wrote. The pen felt heavy and smooth in her hand, like Carlos's penis.

Had she been leading Carlos on? Of course she had. It was her fault. She put the cap back on the pen and laid it back down on the desk. It didn't matter that she didn't love him or that she was scared or that she knew it was wrong. What mattered was she had tricked him. She hated girls like that and she'd always promised herself she wouldn't be one.

Maybe she should go back to the boat. Back to Carlos. Let him do it. What was the big deal? It was only sex.

She picked up a photo that had been taken on a family ski trip a couple of years ago. Her dad and Jeremy were holding snowballs, making like they were going to throw them at Elise and her mom. They were all grinning, but Elise's mother had a Mona Lisa smile, with her lips closed as though she knew something the rest of them didn't.

"Mommy, what should I do?" she asked the picture. "I don't know what to do." And she cried for a while until she was spent. Then she blew her nose in a Kleenex her mother kept on the desk and took a drink of water. She felt a little better. As though her mother was there with her.

Elise picked up the heavy gold coin her mother used as a paperweight and turned it over between her fingers. Her father had given it to her mother as a birthday present. It was called a sovereign. "It means excellent or superlative in quality," Elise remembered her father telling the family. "It also means autonomous and independent." He had winked at his wife. "Just like your mother."

She turned the coin over and over. Sovereign. "Oh my God." She banged her knee against the desk as she jumped up and ran to the computer in her room. Geezer, disturbed by her movement, began to bark.

"It's okay, Geezer." Her knee throbbed, but she barely felt it. "I think I've figured it out." She typed her mother's screen name in the Internet e-mail account, then for password, typed in "sovereign."

She held her breath.

Invalid password. Please try again.

Her eyes refilled with tears. She'd been so certain.

Someone unlocked the front door and slammed it shut. Geezer began to bark.

"Elise?"

For an instant, her heart stopped. Jeremy sounded so much like her father. Then it hit her.

She typed in her father's user name. Then she typed "sovereign."

A new screen flashed. "Welcome, D. C. Stroeb. You've got mail."

"Jeremy," Elise shrieked as she raced down the stairs. "Jeremy, I did it."

Chapter 27

Jeremy brought in an extra chair from his bedroom. He and Elise stared at the hundreds of e-mail entries on her computer screen. It was only eight in the evening, but Jeremy felt drained after confronting Marina about the fire and then their hours of carnal reconciliation. He hadn't stayed for dinner. He'd been eager to come home, anxious after his fight with Elise this morning. But she no longer seemed upset, caught up in the thrill of having unlocked their father's e-mail account.

"There has to be an easier way than opening every single one," Elise said, her hair loose on her shoulders. She scrolled down the e-mails. "Dad merged his MIU and his personal e-mail accounts. At least everything's in one place."

There were dozens of e-mails from university employees. Jeremy recognized them from the miu.edu addresses. He opened a few from wintert@miu.edu. All the e-mails from the dean were broadcast messages to the staff. There was nothing of a personal nature to his father. Well, that figured. Winter was the quintessential bureaucrat. He knew better than to put anything remotely controversial in an e-mail.

Jeremy searched on champlainm@miu.edu. He still couldn't block Liddy's accusations from his mind. There were only four entries, way fewer than he would have expected. He hesitated before opening them.

"Who's that?" Elise asked.

"Dad's graduate assistant. Marina Champlain."

"Oh. Marina."

It hadn't occurred to Jeremy that his sister might be aware of Marina. "He mentioned her?"

"Yeah." She sipped her water. "I don't think he was very happy with her."

"Sure he was."

"Why would you say so? Have you been speaking to her?"

"She's been going through Dad's papers with me."

"I see."

"Don't be upset, Ellie."

"I'm not upset. I don't care who you hook up with. I'm just surprised she'd help you. I remember Dad saying he was interviewing for a new graduate assistant."

"That doesn't make sense. Marina never said a word about that."

"Maybe she didn't know."

Jeremy opened one of Marina's e-mails, surprised by how anxious he felt. The e-mail was about the syllabus for an introductory economics class. The other e-mails were equally businesslike. But what if Marina had also communicated with his father from a personal e-mail account? He remembered his father once saying the MIU system was right out of Orwell's *1984* and he'd never use the university e-mail for confidential communication.

Jeremy scrolled down the entries looking for anything that didn't say .edu or .org. and for those that sounded as though they may have been pseudonyms for Marina. No French words, no combinations of the letters from her first or last names. Was it possible his father had deleted all nonbusiness correspondence to and from Marina? But why would he have done that?

His attention was caught by an e-mail with the subject line,

"Need to meet with you!!!!!" Five exclamation marks — probably a student. The address was underlid@msn.net. He opened it. It had been sent to his father's personal account. His father would have done that — given his personal e-mail address out to certain students, especially the ones in his clubs like CAFÉ J.

"Dear Professor Stroeb," the e-mail began. "Can we please meet somewhere off campus? I have to talk to you about something very, very important!!!!! Just let me know where and when. Liddy Debajo." The e-mail was dated in November, which was when the fire had taken place. So maybe Liddy had contacted someone in authority after all. But that didn't prove anything. She still could have been trying to set Marina up.

"Do you know who Liddy Debajo is?" Elise said.

"A student. She's active in one of the clubs Dad ran." Best not to mention Liddy's accusations against Marina. Not unless he found something more substantive.

He checked his father's outgoing mail. There was an answer to Liddy the same day telling her he'd meet her at a particular Starbucks that afternoon at four.

He searched on other entries for incoming messages from underlid@msn.net. There was just the one. So she hadn't put anything about the fire and Marina in writing. It was looking like a dead end.

"Maybe we should look at the e-mails Dad sent out in the last week," Elise said. "See if he was concerned about anything."

Jeremy re-sorted the sent e-mails by date. His father had done a bit of e-mailing primarily to professors and students at MIU the week he'd gone to see Jeremy in Spain. There was nothing to Winter, nothing to Marina.

"spenserp@mcgillu.edu," Elise said. "That's Dad's old frat brother, Pete, right? Dad sent him three e-mails in the last two weeks."

The subject line was: "Special consideration." Jeremy opened the latest one. It contained a lengthy thread of correspondence. The last entry was:

> Dear Pete,
>
> I was disappointed to receive your e-mail, though I must admit, I'm not surprised. I will speak with Ms. Champlain when I get back into town on Monday. I hope this doesn't present an inconvenience to you with your scheduling. Thanks again for your help and patience.
>
> D.C.

The previous message from Pete was short.

> Sorry to bother you, D.C., but I just received a phone call from Ms. Champlain telling me she's changed her mind and won't be coming to McGill this semester, after all. What's up with her?

"I told you he wasn't happy with her," Elise said.

The blood had rushed to Jeremy's head. His father had been trying to get Marina to transfer to McGill University in Canada? Marina had never let on there had been a problem with his father.

Jeremy scrolled down through the e-mail thread to the original email, which his father had sent to Pete in November. It was dated the day after his father had been scheduled to have coffee with Liddy.

> Hi Pete,
>
> Hope all is well with you, Kari, and the kids. I have a situation on my hands and wondered if you could help me out. My graduate assistant, Marina Champlain, is a bright, capable young woman, who has unfortunately developed

what I'll call an unhealthy attachment to a married faculty member. You know how that is. I suggested she continue pursuing her doctorate at another institution, but she refused at first. Then yesterday, I was finally able to persuade her that her interests would be better served elsewhere.

That brings me to my favor of you. Sorry for the short notice, but would you entertain Ms. Champlain's application to your program for the upcoming semester? I feel fairly confident once she's left this environment, she can return to being the productive, energetic graduate assistant I once knew her to be.

I'm attaching her C.V. She is, by the way, fluent in French, which I know appeals to you Francophone-loving Canucks. ☺ Thanks for your help, buddy. I owe you one.

D.C.

Jeremy felt icy, like he'd fallen into a glacial crevasse.

Elise drew her knees up to her chest. "Do you think he was talking about himself? That she'd had a crush on Daddy?"

"I don't know, Elise."

"I wonder why she finally agreed to go to McGill. What could Daddy have said to persuade her? Jeremy? Are you okay?"

"Sure." His voice was as flat as the rest of him felt.

"Dad had a problem with this woman and she was supposed to have left MIU. Then she didn't." Elise sucked on the end of her braid. "Jeremy," she said quietly, then stopped as though reluctant to go on. "You don't think —"

Chapter 28

When Jeremy was a freshman at NYU, he'd fallen for this girl. She had reminded him of an injured sparrow. Her jaw and cheek were scarred and slightly askew, which he had supposed made her self-conscious and aloof. But he had pursued her: waiting for her after class, walking with her, trying to make her laugh. He wasn't sure if he had befriended her out of pity or if something about her apparent needfulness made him feel vital.

One night they were at a bar and a group of drunken upperclassmen began teasing the girl. Jeremy, who'd had a few too many beers himself, took a swipe at the biggest, loudest one. Moments later, they had dragged Jeremy outside and beaten the crap out of him. Jeremy couldn't get out of bed for three days. He had a broken rib and every time he took a deep breath, the pain just about caused him to pass out.

But when a week later he was walking on campus and saw the girl kissing the bigmouthed jerk who'd started the whole thing, the rage he felt at that moment far exceeded the physical pain he'd borne when he had believed himself to be her heroic protector.

Why had that memory come to him now? Perhaps the heaviness in his chest reminded him of that moment. Or maybe he was once again feeling betrayed.

He turned over the hot, damp pillow as he tried to sort through what he and Elise had discovered. It was difficult to be objective.

Difficult to even consider without feeling as though he was smothering. Each time he tried, a louder voice said, she lied to me. She lied to me. But the extent of the deception went far deeper.

He saw her in his mind — the reluctant smile, the untamed hair, the feral eyes. Marina, you couldn't have done this. But after a tormented night of reworking what he had learned in his father's e-mails, he could only come to one conclusion. The one he didn't want to accept. He'd found his parents' murderer. It was what he had set out to do. But there was no elation in the discovery. No satisfaction. How could there be when the murderer was the woman he had fallen in love with?

"Doesn't look like you slept either," Elise said, coming into the kitchen in her school uniform. She rotated her head as though her neck was stiff.

He handed her a couple of pieces of buttered toast.

"What's this? You made me breakfast?"

"Sure. Why not?"

"Everything seems strange this morning, doesn't it?" She sat down on one of the counter stools. "I mean, we should be feeling pretty good, right? It's like we had a breakthrough."

"I guess."

Elise broke off a corner of her toast. "Do you think once it's over, things will be easier for us?"

"Easier?"

"You know. Having closure."

"Closure would be good," he said, knowing that's what she wanted to hear, recognizing that if it was Marina, he would never know closure. "Do you want some eggs?"

She shook her head. "So what are you going to do?"

He cracked a couple of eggs into the frying pan and they sizzled. Geezer sidled up to the stove and watched. Jeremy wasn't hungry, but he had to be doing something. Unfortunately, the sound and smell reminded him of the other night when Marina was making dinner.

"You're not thinking of talking to her alone, are you?" Elise said. "Jeremy, you can't. You need to call the police and show them these e-mails."

"I'm not worried about being alone with her."

"Right. Because a murderer couldn't possibly hurt you."

"I said I'm not worried."

She slid off the stool and fed Geezer the rest of her toast. "I guess you know what you're doing." She gathered up her backpack and car keys. Her eyes were shiny. "So I'll see you later, right?"

"Absolutely."

"You know, I didn't mean what I said yesterday," she said. "About not caring if Dwight was my guardian."

"I know you didn't."

"I, I don't know what I'd do without you, Jeremy. You're the only one I have. You and Grandpa."

"I know, Ellie."

"So you won't do anything stupid? You'll come home, right?"

"Hey." Jeremy slid his fingers beneath her chin and lifted her head. She closed her eyes. "Look at me," he said. Tears were running out from between her lashes. "Look at me, Elise." She opened her eyes and bit down on her lip. "I won't leave you alone again, Ellie. Do you hear me?" She averted her eyes from him. "I promise. Okay?"

"Okay," she said softly.

"Okay then." And he hugged her—longer than usual.

He drove to Marina's house with the radio turned up. A couple of talk show hosts were making jokes. Jeremy tried to listen, but couldn't concentrate.

The morning was overcast with no sign the sun might be breaking through. Even Mrs. Lambert's green grass was covered by a purplish shadow like a creeping mold. The swing hung motionless on the porch.

Marina, satchel weighing down her shoulder, was walking toward her car as he pulled in behind it. "Jeremy." She looked surprised.

He opened the passenger door of the Corvair. "I need you to come with me, please."

"Now? I'm sorry, but I have a faculty meeting this morning. I'm already late."

Jeremy held the door open. "Please, Marina. It's important."

"But where are we going? You aren't still upset about what that girl said about the fire? You seemed okay with everything last night, no?"

"Would you please come?"

She touched his cheek. He tried not to wince. "What is it, *mon amour*? You seem so — *je n'sais pas* — so unlike yourself." When he didn't answer, she got into the Corvair.

Her eyes were on him as he drove. A heavy metal song on the radio and the throbbing of the engine made Jeremy feel as though he'd been chained to a speaker in a club, but he wouldn't turn the volume down. At least it was drowning out the turmoil inside him. Marina was chewing on her fingernails. They didn't talk until he got to the gatehouse on Lotus Island.

"We're going to your house?" she said.

Of course, she'd have known that. She'd been on the island for his parents' funeral and to drive him home the night his car had been towed. And how many times before?

When he opened the front door, Geezer began barking wildly. "What is it, boy?" Jeremy bent down to calm the dog.

Marina took a step back, away from the dog. Geezer was growling now, a deep guttural sound. "I'm not an animal person," she said. "I think they can sense that, no?"

Jeremy stood up. "So, this is the place. Have you ever been inside before?"

She shook her head. She was wearing a loose white blouse and looked more like a nervous little girl than a murderess.

"I thought maybe my father had invited you and a few of his colleagues over some time. You know, for an intellectual powwow or something like that. "

"Why have you brought me here, Jeremy?" Her hair was wild on her shoulders. She gathered it up in her hands, then released it.

"Didn't you want to see where I live? Our housekeeper has the day off, so it's just you and me." The rage he had been holding back rushed to the surface. "Would you like to see where my parents were murdered?"

She turned pale. "I think I'd better leave."

"Not yet, Marina. Come on. Let me show you." He pulled her toward the stairs. He had loved and trusted her. She had killed his parents.

"You're hurting me. Why are you doing this, Jeremy?"

Geezer growled as he followed them up the stairs, periodically letting out a sharp bark. Jeremy pushed open the door to his parents' bedroom. "Here it is. The crime scene. Did you think it would still be bloody and all torn up?"

The room was stale, and the gray morning light that seeped through the closed shades and drapes did little to lessen the crypt-like atmosphere.

Marina was crying. "What do you want, Jeremy? What are you doing?"

"You tell me, Marina. You tell me why I brought you here."

"I don't know. I don't know what you want from me."

"Maybe this will help." He pushed a printout of the e-mails between his father and the McGill professor toward her.

Her expression changed from fear to comprehension as she read. "Oh God." She wiped her cheeks. "It's not what you think. Believe me, Jeremy."

"It's not what I think? Tell me then, Marina. What's going on here? You never told me my father wanted you out of MIU. That he was trying to dump you on his friend. And how do you explain that he was able to persuade you to leave all of a sudden? Could he have found out about you setting the fire?"

"You don't understand."

"I think I do, Marina. You were chasing after him, making his life miserable, and he was going to get rid of you. But you didn't want to leave. You said you would, but then you changed your mind. Why did you change your mind? Because you had a better idea? Because you figured out a way to punish my father and still keep your position? Because you figured once D. C. Stroeb was dead, no one would ever know the truth about your sickness?"

"You think I killed him?"

"You killed my father, you killed my mother. And now you've been playing with my head so I'd never suspect you. You feed me, you fuck me, you act like we're going to find the murderer — but it's all a big game to you, isn't it Marina?" His voice cracked. "Damn you, Marina. I trusted you. I —" But he couldn't say loved. That he had loved her.

"Jeremy, no. You've got it all wrong. I didn't kill anyone. I couldn't kill anyone. Especially not your father." She leaned against the wall as though she'd lost her balance. "Please, let me tell you what happened."

"I know what happened."

"Not all of it." She took a ragged breath. "It's true. I fell in love with him. And I believed he had fallen in love with me."

She was lying. Trying to trick him again.

"He would come to my apartment and fix things for me: my car, the refrigerator, the leaky faucet."

His father would fix things for her. Jeremy sat down on the edge of the bed and put his hands over his ears, but he could still hear her.

"And I would cook for him."

She would cook for him.

"And I knew he was married, but then why did he keep coming back? Then, one day, we made love."

"Oh, Jesus."

"And I was so happy. But he became upset and said he'd made a mistake."

"My father slept with you?" It wasn't possible. His father loved his mother. He never would have cheated on her.

"Once, Jeremy. Once. But then he couldn't bear to be around me and he asked me to go away, but I said no; I wouldn't go. Even if I couldn't have him, being away from him was impossible. Impossible. And he started avoiding me. So I set the fire. I thought he'd believe the world was against him and he'd need me. But it didn't work. Someone told him I'd done it. But I knew if I could just talk to him one more time and tell him how much I loved him, he wouldn't send me away."

Jeremy could hear her talk; it sounded garbled as though he had cotton in his ears. His father had fixed things for her; she had cooked for him. And he had slept with her. His father, perfect husband, exemplary family man, had fucked Marina.

Forgive me, Jeremy.

Jeremy held his hands tighter over his ears. He didn't want to hear this. He didn't want to hear any of this.

"I never got to speak with him. Someone killed him first. Believe me, Jeremy. I didn't kill him." She was speaking in short bursts and it seemed he could see her heart fluttering in her chest beneath the gauzy blouse, like a bird with a broken wing. That's what she was — another injured sparrow. And somehow he knew Marina couldn't have done it. She may have lied and manipulated and deceived, but she hadn't killed. But there was no relief in that knowledge either.

"I was devastated beyond words when I heard your father had been killed. I barely wanted to live myself. Then you showed up that day. And you were so much like him."

He went over to the covered, closed window. He needed air, but he made no move to open it. He had idolized his father. All he had really wanted had been to one day hear him say, "Good job, son. I'm proud of you." Who was this man he had thought he'd known? Not a hero. Just a shattered memory. "Go away, Marina. Go away, please."

Forgive me.

"Don't be angry with me, Jeremy. At first when I was with you, all I could think about was your father. But then, I realized I wasn't thinking of him at all."

"Go away, Marina."

She was beside him, grabbing his hand, bringing his fingers up to her lips. "Jeremy, no. I can't lose you, too."

Her tears dripped on his hand. He didn't move; he didn't have the strength to fight anymore. She opened his hand and kissed each finger.

"They've healed," she said in a whisper. "Your cuts have healed." She rubbed his fingers against her cheek. "You see, my tears don't sting. You don't feel anything."

She was right. Scar tissue had grown over his wounds. And that's where he'd leave things. Covered with scar tissue.

So he wouldn't have to feel anymore.

Chapter 29

He still wasn't home. Elise pulled the Volvo into the empty driveway. She wondered if Jeremy had been by while she was at school, but she doubted it.

Yesterday had been one of the most anxious days of her life. When she'd left Jeremy in the morning, she'd had this bad feeling. It didn't matter that Marina was a woman. If she had killed their parents, she could kill her brother, too. And Elise had sat in class, her cell phone on vibrate squeezed in her hand, waiting for him to call. Then finally, a text message from him. "It's not Marina."

That was all. "It's not Marina."

He didn't call or text her again. That was yesterday around noon — twenty-eight hours ago. How could Jeremy be so sure it wasn't their father's graduate assistant? What proof had she given him? If Jeremy had been sleeping with her — which Elise was almost positive he had been — wasn't he gullible enough to be pulled into her trap? So Elise was still worried. If Marina wasn't the murderer, then why hadn't Jeremy come home?

She put her key in the lock. This had become her pattern. She'd hold her breath as she turned the key, half expecting the door to be unlocked and something evil to be waiting for her on the other side. But the lock turned over with a small click and Elise released her breath. Safe, she thought, remembering a game she played with

Jeremy when they were little. If you touched the base, you were safe.

She prepared to step over Geezer, but he wasn't lying in the front foyer as usual. She locked the door, dropped her backpack on the entranceway table, and looked up the stairs expecting to see the dog shaking sleepily as he roused himself to greet her. "Geezer?" she called.

She checked the family room sofa where Geezer would occasionally nap, even though he wasn't allowed. She wished Flora had left the radio on, but she must have forgotten. Elise hated hearing only the sound of her sneakers padding over the marble floors. There was an indentation in one of the seat cushions and swirl marks from Geezer's claws in the leather fabric that would have infuriated their mother. His scent hung in the air. "Geezer?" she called again.

The house was eerily still. Elise trotted up the steps. She went from her bedroom to Jeremy's bedroom to their mother's office, checking every corner, every closet. Sometimes if Geezer wasn't feeling well, he'd hide in a small, dark space. "Hey, Geezer. Here, boy." The beds were made and fresh towels were hanging in her and Jeremy's bathrooms, but there was no sign of Geezer.

She stood in the hallway wondering where else to look for him. Then her breath caught in her chest. The door to her parent's bedroom was open a few inches. She hadn't been in their room since the murders. Elise trembled as she pushed open the door. The drapes were drawn and the room felt stale.

"Geezer?" she whispered. "Are you in here?"

Geezer's dog tag clinked lightly against his collar. He was under the oversized skirted chair in the corner of the room. Elise used to hide there when she was a little girl and she and Jeremy played hide-and-seek.

"Come here, boy." Elise slid to the floor and gently pulled him out by his front paws. He was panting, but her own heart was racing. She needed to get out of this room. She could feel her parents in here, but it was too intense, like staring directly into the sun. "Let's go, Geezer." She pulled on his collar, but he lay down on the floor, making himself into deadweight.

A key turned in the front door. Jeremy. She could hear him climbing the stairs. But something was wrong. The footsteps were wrong. Geezer began to bark.

The room was spinning. The murderer. She'd known he would be coming back for her.

A shadow stood in the doorway. Elise squeezed her eyes shut and began to scream and scream and scream. Geezer barked uncontrollably.

"Stop that," the murderer said, shaking her. "Stop that screaming."

"No," she shouted. "No. No. No."

"Elise." He smacked her face hard. Back and forth. The pain took her breath away.

Stunned, she opened her eyes. Crouched in front of her was her uncle Dwight.

"What the hell's the matter with you?" he said, massaging his hand. A thick college ring protruded from his finger like a brass knuckle.

She wanted to cry, but something held her back. She pushed her hair out of her face. Her cheek was hot beneath her hand. It throbbed painfully and she could feel a lump rising. "You, you didn't have to do that."

"You were hysterical."

"I would have stopped when I saw it was you."

"I'm sorry. Maybe I overreacted."

"How did you get in here?"

"With my key."

"You have a key?" She stood up, uncomfortable about being alone in her parents' room with him.

"Of course. I kept one when they changed the locks in case of an emergency."

"But this wasn't an emergency. Why didn't you ring the door-bell?"

"I was worried about you." He followed her out of the bedroom. Geezer sniffed Dwight's leg, a low rumble coming from deep in his chest. "Can we put this damn dog outside?"

"Why were you worried?"

Dwight stepped back against the hallway wall, but Geezer continued growling.

"Because your brother didn't come home last night. I wanted to make sure you were okay."

"That doesn't explain why you didn't ring the doorbell. Were you trying to frighten me?"

"Of course not." He moved a few inches along the wall toward the stairs. Geezer had him boxed in. "Can you get this damn dog away from me?"

"Geezer. It's okay, boy. Let's get a treat."

The dog went down the stairs after her, looking back now and then at Dwight.

Elise found the dog biscuits in the pantry and gave one to Geezer. He circled the corner of the room and lay down, his eyes remaining fixed on Dwight.

"I see the housekeeper's already gone," Dwight said. "What's the deal? Is she on banker's hours?"

"Flora takes perfectly good care of us," Elise said, opening the freezer door.

"Maybe she does a good job keeping the house clean, but a housekeeper's no substitute for parental guidance. And, apparently, an older brother isn't either."

"What's that supposed to mean?" Elise held a bag of frozen peas against her cheek, which was still smarting.

"Jeremy is completely irresponsible as a guardian. He doesn't come home until early in the morning most nights, and last night he didn't come home at all."

"So? What business is it of yours?"

"Young lady, your parents expected me to take care of you if your brother wasn't willing or able to. It's clear to me he's neither of those things."

"Well I'm fine with how he's taken care of me."

"But I'm not. And a court of law would never permit this abuse of his guardianship."

"I'll call him," she said. "Please, Dwight. I know he'll be home soon. And I'll make sure he comes home at night."

"It's too late for that. I've already filed papers to assume your guardianship. Selma and I will be moving in here with you."

"No." She threw the bag of peas on the floor.

"Behaving like a three-year-old won't change things."

"Show me the papers. Show me the court order or whatever papers you have. Because I don't believe you can just come in here and do this."

"You cocky girl. You should be grateful."

"I don't want you to be my guardian. And I'll tell the judge that. I'll tell the judge how you frightened me and hit me."

"How dare you twist things?"

She took her cell phone from her pocket and snapped a picture of her cheek. "I'll show him this."

"You're a stupid girl. You have a lot of your parents in you, Elise."

She didn't want to cry, but she couldn't control herself. "Well good. I can't think of anyone I'd rather be like. Certainly not you."

Geezer dropped the biscuit and snarled at Dwight. Dwight pressed against the refrigerator. "Get this damn dog away from me."

"No. You get away from me." She was crying hard. "You get out of my house."

Geezer growled. Dwight held his back against the wall as he inched his way out of the room. "Have your tantrum, Elise. But I'll be back with the court order and then we'll see about your tantrums and your disrespect."

Chapter 30

The late afternoon sun scorched his face and chest as he lay on the coarse sand at the edge of the surf. Jeremy imagined it was a branding iron, searing his flesh, obliterating healthy skin tissue, permanently altering the person he had once been.

He reached like a blind man into the brown paper bag for another beer. He'd bought a six-pack and was on his fourth or fifth, he couldn't remember which. This one was warm as piss, but he guzzled it anyway, not bothering to lift his head or open his eyes. It spilled out the side of his mouth and dripped down his neck.

He heard tittering laughter and smelled coconut oil. A couple of teenage girls walked past, too close, trying to be annoying as they kicked sand over him. The tide was rising. Cold, spreading waves lapped at his feet. Only a few hours before, he had been quite isolated on the vast expanse of beach. But now the world was closing in around him, and even the boozy blur couldn't protect him from this feeling of claustrophobia.

After Marina had left his house yesterday, Jeremy had been desperate for a confrontation. Anything to keep him from thinking about the betrayals. A bottle of Jack Daniels had loosened his natural restraint. He had driven to the MIU campus. It was sick, perverse, but he needed to see her again.

He had raced around the parking lots looking for her beat-up car, honking crazily as students and professors watched with expressions of curiosity or fear. But after circling several times, he realized she wasn't there. That he was never going to see her again. That it was over.

Exhaustion overcame him and all he wanted to do was sleep. But he couldn't go home. Home had become the place where bad things happened. He checked into one of the fleabag hotels off Washington Avenue and passed out on sheets that stank of sweat and liquor. He awoke to the squealing of brakes and clanking of a delivery truck and realized he'd slept through the night and the morning. He had a dozen voice mails and text messages — a few from Robbie, but most from Elise.

His sister was worried, but he didn't know what to say to her. How could he explain what their father had done? What Marina had done? So he bought a six-pack of Corona, walked down to the beach, stripped down to his boxers, and lay down on the sand to let the sun burn him out.

His cell phone was vibrating against his leg. He shielded the brightness from his eyes as he read the caller ID. Elise. It was time he spoke with her.

"Jeremy?" She was crying.

"Are you okay, Ellie?" The blurriness in his head cleared. He sat up.

"Dwight. Dwight came to the house. He said he was filing papers against you for the guardianship. Please, Jeremy. Don't let him do this."

A flock of small black birds hovered in the air surrounding him like bats.

"Jeremy, do something. Stop him."

"Do what?"

"Come home."

"I can't. I'm no good for you. Maybe it would be better if —"

"No. I won't live with Dwight. I hate him."

The wind shifted and the black birds settled around him in the sand.

"I'm no good, Elise. Don't you understand? I'm all broken."

"Come home and we'll talk about it. Please, Jeremy. I'm so frightened staying here without you."

He drank the dregs of the last warm beer. "Go to Grandpa's. Take Geezer with you."

She was crying hard. "But I want you. Please, Jeremy. Don't leave me."

The birds rose in the air, making a terrible squawk. He turned off the phone and lay back down in the searing sun.

Chapter 31

Robbie drove slowly up and down each street on South Beach looking for a red car. Jeremy's father's car. She'd seen it in the garage a couple of times and knew the beautiful old classic would be easy to spot.

After getting to Jeremy's house and finding no cars in the driveway, she had driven to the beach to check out her hunch. After all, wasn't South Beach a likely place for a twenty-something to play hooky?

Jeremy hadn't shown up for work yesterday or today. Hadn't called and hadn't answered his phone. She didn't know why she just couldn't let it go. She pictured him leaning back on a conference room chair, running his fingers through his hair. So distracted. So in tense. It wasn't that she was attracted to him. No. Nothing like that. It was more that his presence comforted her. Almost like having Rachel back.

And then today, she was going through the Castillo Enterprise reports and she remembered something Rachel had said. But there was no one to talk to about it. No one she could trust. So she called Jeremy over and over, until finally she got in her car and came here.

She turned off Washington Avenue onto Seventh Street. A group of adolescent girls wearing bikinis with towels wrapped around their waists were laughing and pushing each other. Just ahead, a red car was poorly parked, its rear sticking into the street. Jeremy's car. There were several papers shoved under the windshield wiper.

Robbie scooted her car around the block to a small parking lot, then hurried back to Jeremy's car. He had gotten two parking tickets, one from yesterday and one from today. This was disturbing. Why had he left his car here?

She went down to the beach, looking at every tall, athletic man she passed. Most were shirtless, their bathing suits low on their hips. Robbie was wearing a blue silk dress and pearls. They must have thought she was crazy. And maybe she was. She took off her heels and walked barefoot in the sand.

The surf was in, narrowing the beach and creating a smaller area for her to search.

At Fifth Street, she saw him. He was lying directly on the sand in only his boxers. His clothes were crumpled up in a pile. There was a brown bag next to him and an empty beer bottle beside his outstretched hand. He was asleep — or dead.

How dare he do this? His mother's murderer was free and he was lying here in a drunken stupor?

She rammed her foot against his leg.

"Hey," he shouted, sitting up suddenly. "What the fu —" Then he recognized her.

"What are you doing, Jeremy?"

"Jesus. Did you honestly come out here to kick and yell at me?"

"You deserve a lot worse."

He lay back down on the sand and closed his eyes. He was badly sunburned.

"I'm taking you home," she said.

"No thanks, Mom." He didn't open his eyes.

"I'm not your mother. If you recall, your mother's dead. You were trying to find her murderer."

He opened his eyes and slowly sat up. "That was harsh."

"I'm sorry. I don't know how else to be. I can't understand why you're doing this to yourself."

"Maybe it's none of your business."

"Please, Jeremy. I need to talk to you about something your mother told me. It's important."

"I've had my fill of good-looking women trying to help me find my parents' murderer."

Robbie sat down in the sand next to him. A breaking wave spread over the sand, wetting Jeremy's feet. He didn't move.

"I can see that something bad's happened," she said finally. "And I understand that you don't want to talk about it. But even if you've given up, I want you to know I haven't." Robbie got up and wiped the sand from the back of her dress.

He let her pull him up. The hair on his legs and arms was golden against the reddish brown of his skin. She handed him his clothes. They stank of booze and sweat.

He dressed and followed her to her car without speaking. What could have happened to him in the last couple of days to bring him down so low?

Robbie drove up Washington Avenue.

"Where are you going?" he said, as though awakening from a stupor.

"To your house, so you can shower and change."

"No," he said.

"No?"

"Not my house. Anywhere but my house."

Chapter 32

He hadn't wanted to leave the beach, but now that he was here, Jeremy felt a sense of peace — a brief reprieve. Robbie lived on the other side of Coconut Grove from his grandfather, but he couldn't recall ever being in this part of the Grove, nestled within a thick hammock. The inside of Robbie's townhouse was mainly white. Not the stark, overwhelming white of the Castillos' mansion, but a soft, floating whiteness like pillows and clouds.

He wanted to sink down into her sofa and go to sleep.

"The shower's in here." She held a door open. "There's soap and clean towels. Let me know if you need anything else."

The bathroom was mirrored and Jeremy's reflection bounced around the room like a nightmare — the sunburnt nose, red eyes, the stubble on his chin and cheeks.

There was a light knock on the door. "Are you all right, Jeremy?"

"Yeah."

The door opened a few inches and Robbie's hand appeared. "Give me your clothes and I'll run them through the washer on the quick cycle."

He stripped down and passed her his shirt, pants, and boxers. His eyes caught hers. "Thanks," she said, and slammed the door closed.

Jeremy showered, then wrapped a towel around his waist and

stepped into the living room. Everything was carefully arranged: magazines in a neat stack, a collection of blue vases in size order, unused red decorative candles on top of the glass coffee table. Stagnant. It felt stagnant.

He backed away into a small office. Unlike the living room, this room seemed alive in its disorder. There were more books than shelf space and they were stacked unevenly by subject, rather than size. He took a book off a shelf. Homer's *Odyssey*. The pages were yellowed from age. He tried to remember, had Odysseus ever made it home after his odyssey? He put the book back.

On Robbie's desk, which was covered with piles of papers, was a photo of a pretty dark-haired woman. "Your mom?" he asked, aware that Robbie had just come in the room.

"Yes." Robbie was still wearing the blue dress and pearls she'd had on at the beach.

"You resemble her. Does she live down here or in Boston?"

She let him study the photo for a few seconds, then she put it back on her desk. "She doesn't live anywhere. She died a few years ago."

"Gee, Robbie. I'm sorry." How little he knew about her — her family, friends, interests. And yet she had decided to help him.

"Let's go out to the patio." Clearly she didn't want to talk about her mother. "I don't actually cook, but I made you a cheese sandwich and some coffee. I figured that might absorb some of the alcohol in your system."

Sometime between leaving the beach and now, it had gotten dark. A fat candle sputtered on the wrought iron table in the hedged-in patio.

The pattern of light triggered an unwelcome memory. Marina. "Would you mind putting that out?" He gestured toward the candle.

Robbie looked momentarily confused. "No problem." She blew out the candle. It was still bright enough to see, the sky lightened by the downtown glow and a moon that appeared between the drifting clouds.

He ate the sandwich in four bites and washed it down with the coffee.

"I guess my cooking's better than I realized. I'll make you another."

"You don't have to."

"It's no big deal."

A white cat rubbed up against his bare leg. How long could he stay like this? Numb and swaddled. Not having to think.

Robbie put a platter with two more cheese sandwiches in front of him, refilled his coffee mug, and sat down. Her slender neck and pearls reminded him of his mother. "Do you mind if I talk to you?" she said. "I didn't know who else to go to."

"Sure," Jeremy said.

"It has to do with Castillo Enterprises. I keep thinking there's some connection between the Olympus Grande — one of its hotels — and your mother's death."

Another connection. Jeremy had been down this road enough times with Marina to know not to take this seriously.

"Last year, I noticed the revenues coming from the Olympus looked odd," Robbie said. "I told Bud about it, but he brushed me off. Then I mentioned it to Irv and he told me to stick to the audit program." She scratched the cat's head. "This year, when Rachel took over, I brought it up to her. She hadn't been involved with the Castillo audit in years, but she still remembered every detail."

"And she agreed with you?"

"Rachel looked over the reports and said the numbers couldn't be right. They were way too good."

Jeremy picked up some crumbs on his plate with his finger. He was getting that surge of optimism he'd experienced with Marina. But how many false theories had she led him through?

"What's wrong, Jeremy?"

"I'm not sure I see the point of this."

"The point is that maybe your mother figured out something she was murdered for. She was killed the day before she was planning to go to the Olympus."

"But visiting major assets is a standard audit procedure, isn't it?"

"Sure," Robbie said. "Standard for someone on the staff to do the site visits. Not the partners."

Site visit. He could envision his mother's handwriting on the workpaper binder from eighteen years ago.

"But only the partners went to the Olympus," Robbie said. "Bud or Irv — never a staff auditor."

"Maybe they liked the golf, the beaches, the fun in the sun."

"Maybe they did," she said. "But what if it was something else?"

He was getting sucked in. "So the only auditors who have ever been out to the Olympus have been Bud and Irv and, years ago, my mother? No one else from PCM?"

"That's right." She seemed disturbed. "We need to talk to them — Bud, Irv, Enrique Castillo."

He felt a cold panic. He wasn't going to do this again. "What do you mean we? I don't work there any more."

"Sure you do. You can bop into Bud's office, apologize for disappearing for a couple of days, and maybe ask him a couple of questions."

"I'm sorry, but I'm finished playing amateur detective." As he stood up, his towel loosened. He grabbed it around himself.

"Your clothes are almost dry."

"I don't care if they're wet. I'm leaving."

"What's the matter with you?" She shook her head in disgust. "Fine." She went inside. A moment later, she threw his damp clothes at him. They fell to the floor.

"I don't see what you're getting so huffy about," Jeremy said.

"And I don't get all this new drama in your life, Jeremy. First you're looking for your parents' murderer, then you're not. You're too busy getting wasted. And when I have something of substance that I think we can go on, you're not interested. You're out of here." She picked up the empty platter and the coffee mug.

"Jesus, Robbie. Stop twisting things."

"I'm not twisting."

"Did it ever occur to you my life's pretty screwed up right now? That I'm not mentally or emotionally ready to deal with my parents' murders?"

"Why not? You were charging forward a few weeks ago."

"That was a long time ago."

"I'm sorry, but I don't get it. What could possibly have happened that's remotely as horrible as the deaths of your parents?"

"You're right." He sat back down. "You're right."

The white cat jumped into his lap. "These last few weeks," he said, "I'd convinced myself if I did everything I could to find their murderer, they would have been proud of me."

"And they would have, Jeremy."

"I was deceived."

"By whoever was trying to help you?"

"By my father." A cloud passed in front of the moon, dulling its light. "My father wasn't the person I believed he was."

The cat raked the towel with her claws. "There was a woman," Jeremy said. "His graduate assistant. I don't really need to get into the details, but I realized there's nothing I can do. I'm impotent."

Robbie reached across the table and covered his hand with hers. "But you're not."

"Or worse than impotent. Everything I touch turns to shit."

"Jeremy."

"I'm supposed to be taking care of my sister. But I've blown that, too."

"What do you mean?"

"My uncle filed papers to take the guardianship away from me. He says I'm irresponsible, and he's right."

"You're not going to fight him?"

"I can't fight anymore."

"Because you're angry with your father? Because he let you down somehow?"

"This isn't about my father."

"Isn't it? Isn't that why you left for Europe in the first place? Because of your father?"

"What the hell do you know about it?"

"Your mother said something once. About fathers and sons being so busy competing that they don't realize they're the same."

Jeremy picked up his damp shirt from the floor and pulled it over his head.

"Listen. I'm not trying to talk you out of being angry with him. I never met your father, and I certainly couldn't begin to understand your relationship. But I did know your mother. And you were her touchstone. You wouldn't believe how she'd light up when she spoke about you."

His mother would light up when she spoke about him?

Robbie's fingers closed over her pearl necklace. "She loved you, Jeremy. Are you really willing to walk out on her?"

Chapter 33

He told himself he was doing it to humor her. Because she was a nice person. So he directed Robbie to his grandfather's house, explaining about the annual reports for Castillo Enterprises that his grandfather had collected over the years. But it wasn't the reports Jeremy was interested in seeing. It was his sister. He needed to put things right with her.

At least in this respect, he would try not to let his mother down.

His grandfather looked relieved to see Jeremy.

"This is my grandfather, Hershel Lazar," Jeremy said to Robbie. "Grandpa, this is Robbie Ivy. She's an auditor at PCM."

"A pleasure, Robbie." His grandfather took Robbie's hand. "My daughter spoke of you."

"She did?"

"She did indeed. She said you reminded her of herself when she first started out."

Robbie bit down on her lower lip.

"And how are you doing, Jeremy?" His grandfather had his hand on Jeremy's shoulder as they walked into the living room. "Elise told me you were unhappy about something."

"Better," Jeremy said. "Mostly better." He glanced around the room. "Where is she?"

"Your sister's watching a movie in the guest room. She said she didn't want to see you just yet."

"I'll go talk to her," Jeremy said.

His grandfather restrained him by his arm. "You needed some time, Jeremy — well perhaps your sister does, too."

"But —"

"Come, Robbie," said his grandfather. "Let's sit. Jeremy tells me you're interested in seeing the annual reports for Castillo Enterprises."

"Very much," Robbie said. She perched on the edge of the sofa and crossed her legs. The hem of her blue dress was stained, probably from sitting in the damp sand.

"Here they are." His grandfather moved several photos, a nutcracker, and a cut-glass candy dish filled with walnuts out of the way and set a pile of glossy-covered booklets on the marble-topped coffee table. "Castillo Enterprises went public over ten years ago," his grandfather said. "I have all the reports dating back to the initial public offering. Would you like a little history?"

"Please," Robbie said.

He moistened his lips like a professor getting ready to launch into his seminar. "Carlos Castillo, Enrique's father, was a conservative man. He talked to me many times about the pressure on him to take his company public, particularly from his son, but told me he didn't have the heart. He believed once you go public, you're at the mercy of Wall Street. Short-term profits and ever-rising earnings per share, central to a publicly held company, aren't necessarily the best things for its long-term growth."

Jeremy noted how sharp his grandfather appeared, how much better than he'd been a month ago and just after Jeremy's grandmother had died. Perhaps if his parents had seen Hershel Lazar as he was now, they'd have left Elise's guardianship in his hands. Jeremy felt hopeful. Maybe a judge would recognize his grandfather as the best possible choice for Elise.

"But Carlos senior realized he was getting older," Jeremy's grandfather continued, "and it was time to turn the reins over to the next generation. To his son."

"And once Enrique was in charge, he decided to take the company public?" Robbie asked.

"It's the way of the young to believe they can do things better than their elders," his grandfather said.

"And many times they do," Jeremy said.

His grandfather smiled, though Jeremy couldn't imagine at what. "That's very true, Jeremy." His grandfather picked up another booklet and flipped to a page as though he knew exactly where to find what he was looking for. "Enrique took a good portion of the funds from the IPO and invested them in rebuilding the Olympus."

"What do you mean rebuilding?" Jeremy asked.

"The original Olympus was destroyed by a hurricane eighteen years ago."

"That's when my mother went out to see it. I found her work-papers in the file room."

"You found her audit papers from eighteen years ago?" Robbie leaned forward, alert.

"I remember when she came home from that trip," his grandfather said. "She told me she didn't believe anyone could make a success out of the Olympus. Too many obstacles."

"But Enrique Castillo decided to try?" Jeremy said.

"Was the senior Mr. Castillo upset?" Robbie asked.

"That would be an understatement. Carlos senior had reluctantly agreed to let Enrique build the original Olympus and that had turned into a failure." His grandfather picked up a walnut and cracked it open. "I never saw the old resort, but I understand it was relatively low-key. Carlos had kept Enrique on a tight leash and limited budget. But when Enrique took over the company ten years ago, the first thing he announced was his plan to build the Olympus Grande. His father told me he wanted no part of his son's delusions of grandeur, and he retired from the business." His grandfather rolled another walnut between his thumb and forefinger. "It took years to rebuild, you know. Enrique wanted everything perfect. The extravagance infuriated his father right up until he died."

"But it seems the senior Mr. Castillo was wrong," Robbie said. "The Olympus Grande is a tremendous success. Look." She pointed at a graph in one of the reports. "Profits are up every year."

"I suppose an old man can be mistaken," his grandfather said.

Light, hurried patter and rapid panting entered the room along with a distinctive dog odor. Geezer rushed to Jeremy. "Hey, boy." Jeremy gently tugged his ears. "This is Geezer," he said to Robbie. The dog sniffed her, wagged his tail, and returned to lick Jeremy.

Just beyond the entrance to the living room, Jeremy could see Elise holding back. So she'd decided to come out after all. "And this is my sister, Elise. Ellie, this is Robbie Ivy. She worked with Mom."

Elise remained just outside the room. "Nice to meet you."

"You too," Robbie said.

Something was wrong with Elise's face. First Jeremy thought it was the way a shadow hit her, but now he was certain there was a bluish green bruise on her cheekbone. He started toward her. "What happened to you?"

Her hand rose to cover her cheek. "It, it looks worse than it is."

"And what exactly is it?" He reached to touch her, but she backed away.

"A misunderstanding, that's all."

"What kind of misunderstanding?"

"This, this afternoon." She took a breath and started again. "I was at the house. Someone unlocked the front door. I thought it was you, but it wasn't."

"Unlocked? Someone used a key?"

"Yeah. And I got frightened. But it was just a giant misunderstanding."

"Who, Ellie? Who came into the house?"

She looked down at her sneakers.

It took Jeremy a second before he remembered what Elise had told him earlier on the phone. "Dwight? Dwight has a key?" He pulled her hand away from her cheek. Besides the bruise, there was redness and swelling. It almost looked like a handprint.

"It, it really isn't a big deal, Jeremy."

"Jesus. Did Dwight do this? Did he hit you?"

"I thought the murderer had come back. I wouldn't stop screaming."

"So he hit you?" Jeremy said. "That bastard hit you?" His grandfather squeezed Jeremy's shoulder, but Jeremy jerked away. "I'll kill him. I'll kill him for touching you."

"No," Elise said. "No, Jeremy."

"He can't do this to you. He can't touch you." He smashed his hand into the wall. The pain traveled all the way down his arm.

"Jeremy, calm down," his grandfather said. "This isn't a rational way of behaving."

"I already told Dwight I'd report him. I stuck up for myself." Elise started to cry. "I don't want you to do anything to him."

Robbie held Elise in her arms as she continued to sob.

"I hate this," Elise said. "I hate all of this."

Jeremy was pacing. That bastard hit his sister. And he was planning to get custody of her? "Over my dead body," he mumbled.

"What was that?" his grandfather said.

Jeremy took a deep breath. His family had been violated when his parents had been killed. And Jeremy hadn't been able to do anything about it. Well he'd be damned if he permitted anyone, anyone at all, to touch or hurt or break anything in his family again.

"Robbie, can you give me a lift to my car?"

"You can't go to Dwight," Elise said. "Please don't go to Dwight."

Robbie whispered something to Elise, but Elise didn't seem to hear her.

"Jeremy," Elise said, "you'll just make things worse."

Chapter 34

Robbie was thrumming her fingers against the steering wheel. "So what exactly is your plan? You're going to barge into your uncle's house and do what? Beat him up? Shoot him?"

"I don't know."

"Good. That should guarantee a positive outcome."

"I don't appreciate your sarcasm."

"You're right. Sorry. It's none of my business." She stopped at a traffic light. The headlights from the oncoming cars flashed on her face. Her long, thick lashes made a pattern on her cheeks like a painted doll's. "It's just," she said, "you've been through a lot of intense shit in the past forty-eight hours. Dwight will still be there in the morning—as evil as ever. I just think you'd be more effective after you get some sleep."

"Still playing Mommy."

"Fine. Call it Mommy. But you know what I'm saying is simply good common sense." The light turned green. The car behind them honked.

"What are you waiting for?"

She pulled over to the side of the road. The traffic streamed by next to them. "I have an idea how you can channel all this anger more productively tonight."

"What do you have in mind? Maybe a little sparring practice?"

"That or the file room at PCM."

"What are you talking about?"

"You said you found the workpapers from your mother's visit to the Olympus eighteen years ago. Maybe there's something in the papers that will make sense to me."

"So you want to go to the file room tonight?"

"No one will be there. We can get in and out. Maybe actually find something tangible that will lead to your parents' murderer. Of course, the alternative is going to your uncle's house, threatening him until he calls the cops, and maybe lands you in jail." She pressed her finger against her lip. "Hmmm. Tough choice."

"Okay. We'll check out the file room. I'll deal with my uncle in the morning."

She gave him a thumbs up and pulled the car back into traffic.

Jeremy and Robbie stood in the deserted hallway outside the PCM file room. It had been over two weeks since the last time Jeremy had been here and he was sure Irv had called the archive company to come in and finish the job. There was almost no chance the files would still be there, but Robbie was optimistic that no one had come to take them away yet.

The hallway was dark except for the lighted exit signs and widely spaced night lights. "What's that?" Robbie pointed to an object protruding from the ceiling opposite the door. "I never noticed it before."

"Looks like a night light."

"But that one's a little different. See how it's tilted? Like it's aimed at the door."

"You think someone installed a surveillance camera to watch a room full of files that no one cares about?"

"I was just asking." She scowled up at the light, then stuck out her tongue. So Robbie wasn't quite the grownup she made herself out to be.

Jeremy tried the key Irv had given him. He had forgotten to turn it back in. It turned easily in the lock. That made him even more certain they'd find the room empty, but the familiar smell of decaying paper and stale air filled his nostrils and lungs. He flipped on the wall switch. The overhead lights flickered as they struggled to come awake.

"I told you," Robbie said, pushing the door closed behind her. "Everything's still here."

She wandered down an aisle between rows of cabinets and metal shelving units filled with binders. "I don't see how anyone could find anything in here."

Jeremy tried to remember where he'd been standing when Irv had surprised him and he'd thrown down his mother's workpapers. There were dozens and dozens of cartons lining the numerous aisles. It was like trying to find your car at Disney World when you forgot if you'd parked in Goofy or Pluto.

He bent down beside a likely carton and went through the top binders. Every time he lifted a binder out, a searing pain went through his arm. His knuckles were bruised from punching the wall at his grandfather's house.

Was he doing the right thing coming here, or should he have confronted Dwight? But what Robbie had said made sense. Tonight, with no one around, had been a perfect opportunity to do this.

Robbie fanned herself with a folder. The room was hot and a thin layer of perspiration had settled on her upper lip. "Tell me where to look. I don't want to just stand around."

"I threw the Olympus binder into a carton in either this aisle or possibly the next one. I can't remember."

She disappeared, but he could hear her dropping rejected binders on the floor. They hit with a hard thump. This was probably pointless. What connection could his mother's observations of eighteen years ago possibly have to the Olympus today?

"I found them," Robbie called. "Your mother's workpapers."

She was sitting on the gray linoleum floor. Her blue dress had ridden up to the middle of her thighs. She caught his glance and pulled the hem down. "Here's the section on the Olympus site visit." She flipped through and scanned the pages. He slid down next to her.

"This was a couple of years after they'd begun developing the original Olympus," she said.

Jeremy peered over her shoulder.

"So, according to your mother," Robbie said, "they'd finally finished building the Olympus, despite all kinds of labor problems, but it was wiped out by a hurricane before it opened, like your grandfather said." She scanned the rest of the papers. "Nothing else jumps out at me."

He took the binder from her and found the page with the photo. A ruin of what looked like a Greek temple, purple cliffs and blue-green seas, the back of a man standing in the foreground.

Robbie pushed herself up and straightened out her dress. "Do you know where the other Castillo audit papers are?"

"The filing system sucks, but some are in here." Jeremy pulled out the top drawer of another file cabinet. The cabinet teetered forward. Jeremy quickly pushed the drawer in a few inches so it wouldn't topple. "You need to be careful with these cabinets. They're unstable."

Robbie lifted out a stack of binders and thumbed through them. "Okay. Here's something interesting. Looks like they spent a ton of money when they starting rebuilding the Olympus Grande ten years ago." She looked frustrated. "But this doesn't help. We need the binders that came after this."

They both froze at a sound. A hollow clunk. Had someone followed them to the file room?

They waited, but heard nothing more. Jeremy remembered the

creepy feeling he'd had when he had worked in here. That Gladys seemed to know when he came and left. Maybe that was a camera in the hallway. "I think we should get out of here," Jeremy whispered.

"But we haven't found what we need."

Jeremy took her elbow.

Robbie looked startled when they got to the door, but she continued to the elevator and didn't talk until they'd driven out of the garage.

"What?" Jeremy said. "You're acting like you saw a ghost."

"It was probably nothing," she said. "But I could have sworn I'd closed it when we got there."

"Closed what?"

"The door. To the file room. It was open just now."

Chapter 35

Jeremy leaned against his mother's Lexus. His hands were tucked into the pockets of his suit pants as he waited in the parking lot where Dwight worked. The uniformed security guard had inquired of Jeremy's business, then returned to his folding chair beneath the awning to consume his café Cubano and guava-filled pastry. Jeremy's was the only car in the lot, but Jeremy knew his uncle's obsession with punctuality and expected him to arrive in a few minutes, at eight a.m.

After leaving the file room last night, Robbie had first taken Jeremy to pick up the Corvair on South Beach, then to retrieve his mother's car, which had accumulated a small fortune in charges at the tow yard. Jeremy decided he'd had enough of his father and his car and had left the Corvair at the house.

It was blustery this morning and the wind blew several loose pieces of newspaper against the chain-link fence. The rapidly shifting clouds formed a slushy gray ripple. Just yesterday, Jeremy had been lying in the heat, feeling spiritless. His face still ached from the sunburn, but his internal mood had changed. Even the discouragement last night of not finding anything useful in the file room hadn't dampened his drive. If anything, the possibility that someone may have observed him and Robbie heightened his purpose. But first he had to take care of things here.

A black Buick turned into the lot. It stopped, then quickly

began to back out. His uncle had seen him. Jeremy ran to the rear of the car and banged on the trunk. As crazy as his uncle was, Jeremy doubted he would run his nephew over — at least not while a security guard was watching.

Jeremy gestured for his uncle to roll down the window.

"What do you want, Jeremy?" Dwight said.

"Just to talk."

"You've had plenty of opportunity. I've been trying to reach you for weeks."

"Yeah. Sorry. Elise told me."

"And I'm afraid I'm too busy this morning to listen to your excuses and apologies."

"Come on, Dwight. Just a few minutes. We can talk out here."

Dwight rolled up his window, shaking his head with annoyance. He pulled into a parking spot and got out of the car, taking his suit jacket from a hanger over the backseat. He made a show of putting it on, straightening his tie, smoothing down his thin hair. "Good morning, Mario." Dwight smiled at the guard, who didn't respond.

"I understand you've been busy," Jeremy said to his uncle.

"I do what I have to, unlike some people who shirk their responsibilities."

"Well, I have to agree with you there, Dwight. I'm afraid I haven't been keeping up with mine."

Dwight's shoulders relaxed. "I don't know what your parents were thinking. They never should have left you in charge. You can cut your hair and put on a suit, but that doesn't change what you are."

"Thanks for that vote of confidence. But you know, you've actually done a lot to help me see the error of my ways."

"So you're a transformed man."

Jeremy smiled.

"Unfortunately, it's too late for that, Jeremy. I've filed papers."

"I heard."

"So you might as well buy yourself an airline ticket to wherever the hell you go. Maybe one of your little doped-out bimbos will still be waiting for you."

"You're a thoughtful guy, Dwight."

A gust of wind blew Dwight's necktie up in the air. He held it down as he took a couple of steps toward the office building. "I'm afraid I have a busy morning."

"I'd like the key."

"Key?" Dwight stopped in his tracks.

"To my house. Legally, I believe you were trespassing yesterday."

"I have a right to check up on my niece."

"Really? Show me where it says that."

"I'm not getting involved in a legal discourse with you. I know my rights."

"So you have the right to enter your niece's house, terrify her by not announcing your presence, then hit her after she becomes hysterical with fear. I wonder how a judge would react to that. But wait, you're running for judge, so you should know exactly what one would think."

The guard stopped pouring coffee from a thermos into his small cup. He scowled at Dwight.

Dwight reached into his pocket and took out his key case. As he tried to release the key, the hook jammed under his fingernail. He put his thumb in his mouth and sucked on it, looking like an obscene caricature of a baby. "Damn, that hurt."

"As much as your hand hurt when you hit my sister?"

Dwight got the key off its hook and held it out on the palm of his hand. "Take the damn key. This conversation's over."

"You think?" Jeremy's hand clamped over Dwight's. He held fast, feeling the bones and spongy flesh shifting as he tightened his grip.

Dwight tried to pull away. "What the hell are you doing? You'll break my hand."

"I want to make sure we understand each other, Dwight." Jeremy squeezed harder, as he jerked Dwight's arm behind his back.

"Do something," Dwight shouted to the guard. "This is assault."

"Are you listening to me, Dwight?"

"Yes. Yes." He writhed like a suffocating fish. "Let go. Please let go."

"Withdraw the papers you filed against me for Elise's guardianship. If not, Elise and I will file charges against you for illegal entry and — what is this you say I'm doing to you?" He squeezed tighter as he twisted Dwight's arm behind his back. "Assault? And we'll file charges against you for assaulting Elise. Am I clear?"

"Let go."

"Am I clear, Dwight?"

"Yes." His eyes were squeezed shut. "Just let go."

"Good." Jeremy released his grip.

Dwight opened his hand slowly. "Look what you've done. The key's practically embedded."

Jeremy pulled it out of Dwight's palm. It left a mark as if he'd been branded. "You won't need this again."

Dwight backed away from Jeremy. "You and your sister. Just like your self-righteous parents. More trouble than you're worth. If you think I'm going to withdraw my claim against your guardianship, you're sadly mistaken." He kneaded his hand. His bulky college ring protruded above his knuckle.

Had that lying bastard hit his sister with his ring?

"You're lucky you didn't break anything."

"Didn't I?" Jeremy brought his fist back and punched Dwight hard in the face. "I hope I did better this time."

Blood spurted out of Dwight's nose. "Do something," he screamed at the guard. "Arrest him."

But the guard leaned back on his folding chair and sipped his café, a look of deep satisfaction on his face.

The throbbing ache in Jeremy's fist was a sweet one. Much more satisfying than hitting the wall at his grandfather's house. Sweet revenge, Jeremy thought, as he drove away from his uncle. So that's where it came from.

Over the last few weeks, he'd almost lost his taste for it. He'd been so blinded by Marina that, like Odysseus on the island of the lotus-eaters, he had forgotten his true purpose. He'd only been going through the motions and had lost his taste for sweet revenge. All he could taste was Marina.

"Marina." He said the name out loud. It sounded harsh against the purring engine and muted highway noises.

"Marina," he said again. He waited for the contraction in his chest, the momentary sense of suffocating. It had lessened. He was getting over her.

"Marina and my father." His chest convulsed as though someone had punched him. In his mind he could see his father touching her, kissing her fingers, licking her small round mouth.

Shit. He had to stop doing this to himself.

"Let it go," he said, but he couldn't. Talk about irony. His mother had told Robbie that Jeremy and his father were so busy competing they didn't realize they were the same. Well, that was an understatement. They were so much the same that Marina couldn't seem to tell him from his father.

Jeremy squeezed the steering wheel. He wanted so much to confront him — scream at him, shout at him. How dare his father do that? He was a husband, father, responsible adult, role model. Why was he running around fucking young graduate assistants?

The traffic slowed to a halt. A fender bender over to the side of the road. People shouting and flailing their arms. Jeremy drove past.

His dad would never know how much he had hurt Jeremy. Someone had killed him. Murdered both his parents and taken away Jeremy's right to a father and a mother with whom he could be angry. And in doing so, taken away Jeremy's ability to forgive.

And be forgiven.

Chapter 36

There was a minor commotion outside Bud's office. A man with several cameras slung over his chest was fumbling with a tripod. Then Jeremy noticed the endless slender legs, the short skirt, the waves of blonde hair of the woman standing in the doorway smiling. "It's been a real privilege," she said.

Bud, in a crisp white shirt, sleeves rolled up to forearm, stepped out of his office. "The privilege has been mine, Jessica. You're a most astute interviewer."

"You're embarrassing me." Her guttural laugh sounded like sexual foreplay. "But I must tell you, Bud, I'm very excited about this piece. It's important that someone with a story as powerful as yours gets to be heard. You're truly an inspiration."

"Now, Jessica. I'm just a little ole country mouse that's made good in the big city."

"Some mouse," she said, looking like she was about to pounce on him. Then she noticed Jeremy and pulled back.

"Jeremy." Bud didn't seem the least put out by his presence. "Have you come to see me?"

"If this is a bad time —"

"Not at all." Bud turned to Jessica. "Jeremy Stroeb's one of our auditors." He put his hand on Jeremy's shoulder. "Jessica and I were just finishing up. Jessica's with *Your Business* magazine."

"Stroeb?" She checked out Jeremy, as though she was trying to connect him to the name. "We're doing the cover story on Mr. McNally and how he's transformed PCM into one of the top firms in the country."

"That's great," Jeremy said.

Jessica extended her hand and shook Bud's firmly. "Again, thank you, Bud. It's been a true adventure."

Bud winked and led Jeremy into his office, closing the door behind them. The partner didn't sit down. He seemed wired as he paced the room. "Damn," he said. "Cover of *Your Business*. Talk about product placement."

Jeremy wondered what product he had in mind.

"That's the kind of exposure we need," Bud continued. "Did you know that *Your Business* is the number one magazine among CEOs? They've left *Forbes* and *BusinessWeek* in the dust."

"That should definitely increase PCM's exposure to prospective clients," Jeremy said.

"But it's more than that." Bud had taken the worn strap that hung behind his desk and wound it around his fist. "The rags-to-riches stories have universal appeal. Even ordinary people read the magazine."

"Is that what she's writing?" Jeremy asked. "A rags-to-riches story on you?"

"The masses have always gobbled up stories of the poor boy who makes good. The magazine is simply trying to capitalize on what sells." Bud hung the strap back on its hook. "Of course, the article is first and foremost about the growth of PCM. And Rachel Stroeb was an instrumental part of that growth. I made certain Jessica was aware of that. I don't want you thinking I'm trying to take anything away from your mama."

"I didn't mean to come across like I was questioning you."

"No, no." Bud rubbed his chin. "Of course not. Of course not.

Well, sit down, Jeremy. Here I'm squawking like a flock of blue jays when you've come to talk to me."

Jeremy sat down in the guest chair across from Bud's.

The partner took in Jeremy's hand, bruised and swollen from his encounter with his uncle this morning. "I'd hate to see the other guy's face," he said, smiling at his little joke.

Jeremy returned the smile.

"So how can I help you, Jeremy? I understand you've taken a couple of days off. Is everything okay at home?"

"It's been a tough adjustment."

"I'm sure. How's Elise doing?"

"Hanging in there."

"You have a lot on your plate, but remember, your sister is your priority."

"I know that."

"Good. Good." Bud seemed distracted, his attention shifting to the chessboard on the corner of his desk.

Jeremy was starting to lose his cool. What had he hoped to accomplish coming here? Asking Bud questions about Castillo Enterprises would raise its own questions about Jeremy's intentions. So would any reference to the audit papers in the file room. What Jeremy needed to do was eliminate suspicion of his ulterior motives, not create it.

Bud moved the black rook.

"I don't mean to keep you," Jeremy said. "I just wanted to apologize."

Bud's eyes moved from the chessboard to Jeremy. "Apologize?"

"For disappearing for a few days. It was unprofessional. I should have let you know what was happening."

"I certainly don't want to intrude in your personal business, but if you need a sounding board, I'm always here for you."

"Thank you, Bud." Jeremy rubbed his fist. He needed to play this carefully. "I did something pretty stupid." He had Bud's interest now. "I got involved with someone at MIU who promised to lead me to my parents' murderer."

Bud leaned back in his chair.

"I know. It was dumb. There are detectives working to find the killer. I don't know what made me think I could be any more effective."

"It's a natural impulse, Jeremy. Don't beat yourself up over trying to do what you believed was the best thing."

"I guess I'm beating myself up because I failed."

"How so?"

"I got in over my head. I can't run my own crime-scene investigation."

"You're giving up?"

"Not giving up, but I'm going to let the police do their job while I try to do mine." Jeremy covered his red knuckles with his other hand. "I've been so busy playing sleuth that I've neglected my sister."

"I see."

"And well, as you said, Elise is my priority. I'm going to try to be a better guardian and keep my focus on doing a responsible job here."

Bud was staring at something in the distance. "Sometimes I think it's harder for you kids who come from affluent, supportive parents to make your mark in the world."

"What do you mean?"

"You don't have the natural instincts. You start out having everything, and as long and your mama and daddy are there to back you up, you've got it made. But if they're gone, God help you. You're like fledglings cast from your nests. You'll starve or be eaten without your mamas and daddies."

Jeremy felt a wave of anger. "That's right. You're the poster boy for the self-made man. You think you would have been better at coping if your parents had been murdered?"

Bud let out a sharp laugh. "I would have jumped through hoops if someone had shot my daddy." He sobered suddenly. "I didn't mean to sound critical of you, Jeremy. I'm sympathetic, if anything. Nothing in your life prepared you for this."

Jeremy's throat tightened. Now wasn't the time to get emotional.

"But you say you're back on track and I'm glad to hear it. I've told you before, but I'll say it again, if you need me for anything, don't hesitate to ask."

"Thanks, Bud. Thanks for understanding."

Jeremy shifted in his chair, ready to leave. What else was there to say? But Bud had made no move to dismiss him, so Jeremy waited. The partner had returned his attention to the chessboard. "I wonder if you could do one thing for me, Jeremy."

"Sure."

"What's your next move?"

Next move? Could Bud read him so well? Then Jeremy realized the partner was talking about the chess game. "You want me to take a move?"

"Would you? I don't suppose you recognize it, but the board is set just like in the 1972 tournament between Bobby Fischer and Boris Spassky. This was the point when Fischer made the move that determined the outcome of the game and made Fischer the first American world champion.

Jeremy wasn't sure why he'd begun to sweat. It was just a chess game, just a bunch of ivory pieces. He studied the configuration on the board. Bud was waiting. Why did this feel so significant? Jeremy made his move. He glanced up at Bud, who had an odd look on his face.

"What?" Jeremy said. "Is that what Fischer did?"

Bud shook his head. "No. But it's the precise move your mama made."

Chapter 37

Jeremy and Robbie sat in the reception area outside Enrique Castillo's office. Robbie had arranged the meeting while Jeremy had been back at PCM talking with Bud. This was the first time Jeremy had been to the penthouse office. The floor was a highly polished marble that looked blue or green depending on the light. There were floor-to-ceiling windows with an unobstructed view of the bay, which created the illusion that the reception area flowed right into the expanse of water. This afternoon, with the thick cloud cover, the bay was a deep blue and the effect on the room seemed almost sinister.

Robbie, dressed in a dark suit and white blouse, was turning her emerald ring around and around on her finger.

"I thought you did this client-auditor stuff all the time," Jeremy said in a low voice.

"This is a little different, wouldn't you agree?"

"What? Trying to figure out if a murderer's lurking behind your most prestigious client's books?"

"You're awfully cavalier suddenly."

"I had a satisfying morning with my uncle Dwight."

"But not so great with Bud."

"It would have been weird asking questions about Castillo Enterprises. He would have suspected I was up to something."

"Well, maybe that's why I'm nervous. You don't think Mr. Castillo will wonder what's up?"

"You said it's not unusual to have an end-of-audit conference with him."

"He still may find it strange for me to show up at his doorstep with you."

"I'm sure you'll make it smooth."

"Right." She turned her ring around. Her straight, dark hair had fallen forward across one eye.

"So why are you doing it?" Jeremy said. "If you're worried, why put yourself on the firing line?"

She studied her ring for a few moments. "This may sound corny, but I feel I owe it to Rachel."

A secretary opened the door into the reception area. "Mr. Castillo will see you now."

The office of the president and CEO of Castillo Enterprises had windows on two sides and a marble floor. Jeremy almost reeled at the expanse of open space and the optical illusion that continued from the reception area. The desk and conference table were glass and the chairs made of a clear Plexiglas, the effect of which was of waves, or breaks in the otherwise straight lines of the room.

Enrique stepped forward to greet them. He wore a light gray suit and a shirt and tie of almost the same shade. "Robbie, Jeremy, how nice of you to stop by." He shook their hands, then gestured toward a round glass table close to the window.

"Thank you for agreeing to have this impromptu meeting, Mr. Castillo," Robbie said. "I wanted to make sure I have all my questions answered before I give the reports to the partners for their final review. I also thought it would be a good experience for Jeremy."

"Certainly," Enrique said. "I'm glad to see you so involved with the audit, Jeremy. Your mother would have been very pleased, I'm sure. Has the audit gone well this year, Robbie?"

"Very smoothly, as always."

"Well then." Enrique folded his hands on the table. He wore no rings, not even a wedding band. "What can I do for you?"

Robbie opened a leather folder with a legal pad written over with questions. It reminded Jeremy of his mother's clipboard, the one Elise had scribbled in. He wondered how his sister was doing today after spending the night at their grandfather's house. She was probably still in school. He'd call her later and tell her what happened with Dwight this morning.

"Just a few questions," Robbie said. "About the audit."

"Naturally," Enrique said.

She took a moment to compose herself. Could Enrique pick up on her nervousness? "First, Mr. Castillo, I'd like to mention that although the revenues from sugar operations and most of the Caribbean hotel businesses remain down, Castillo Enterprises ended the year with a sizeable profit due to the success of the Olympus Grande."

"Yes, the Grande has been a godsend."

"Ninety percent occupancy rate throughout most of the year. That's well above the industry average. It's pretty amazing given you do no advertising and how inaccessible St. Mary's is."

"That's an excellent observation, but the Grande's business is so unique, it's not quite appropriate to evaluate it in terms of what other hotels are doing."

"Does that explain why its performance is so different from your other Caribbean hotels?"

"The clientele at the Grande is more specialized than most." Enrique stroked his perfectly trimmed silver beard. Jeremy noted that he was giving a politician's answer — not quite responding to the question. "Very wealthy individuals, many with private planes or yachts—these are the people who are attracted to the Grande because of its inaccessibility."

"But how do you attract them without advertising?" Jeremy asked.

Enrique reclined his chair back toward the window. A steely gray screen covered the sky. It had begun to rain. "Ironically," Enrique said, "glossy ads in *Conde Nast* and other high-end publications would put off our particular clientele. Our clients think of the Olympus Grande as their own private club. And they're willing to pay premium prices for that exclusivity."

Jeremy remembered something in his mother's office. A stack of luxury hotel directories and his mother's yellow sticky: Not listed? "Keep it off the radar of the little people," Jeremy said.

Enrique laughed. "In fact, many of our clients do feel that way. I, personally, am not an elitist, but my vice presidents and the partners from your firm assure me we have a unique product and should try to keep it that way."

He was so confident, so self-assured. How many times had Enrique made this speech to Wall Street analysts and investors? Tout the Olympus Grande, ignore the underperforming assets.

Robbie chewed on the top of her pen as she looked back at her pad. "Bad hurricane season this year. Did you have much damage?"

Enrique glanced down at his watch—a thin gold one with an oyster face that probably cost thousands. "Again, Robbie, we were fortunate. The Olympus Grande is built like a fortress. It's able to withstand even the most severe weather conditions." He pushed back his chair and stood up. "I hope I've been able to answer your questions satisfactorily."

"Yes. Thank you so much." Robbie closed her leather folder. The interview was over, at least as far as Mr. Castillo was concerned.

"I'm delighted to see you doing such a thorough job. Rachel would have been pleased." He took Robbie's hand. "She spoke very highly of you, Robbie. Said you were one of the firm's rising stars."

Robbie's cheeks reddened.

He walked them toward the door. "If you have any other questions, don't hesitate to stop by."

A series of pictures hanging in the alcove beside the entranceway caught Jeremy's eye. Photos of the properties, like the ones that hung in the conference room. One looked particularly familiar, but Jeremy didn't recognize it from the conference room. Purple cliffs, azure seas, ruins of what looked like a Greek temple. Just like the photo in Jeremy's mother's workpaper binder from eighteen years ago. But something was missing. The man in the corner of the photo with his back to the photographer had been cropped out.

"That's the Olympus," Jeremy said.

Enrique's even, calm demeanor gave way to something like surprise or confusion. "It is, in fact," he said, recovering his composure. "Magnificent view, isn't it?"

"Yes," Jeremy said. "It certainly is." But as he walked across the gleaming marble floors through the reception area, he wondered why that particular photo hung on the wall rather than a more recent one of the splendid resort that Castillo Enterprises was so proud of.

Enrique took the photo off the wall and brought it over to his desk. His heart was racing. How could Jeremy have known it was the Olympus? It was as though he'd recognized it.

Funny how you could obscure, obfuscate, even obliterate, and like relentless weeds, truth always found its way out into the light. Enrique rested his head on the back of his chair. How much had her son discerned of the truth?

Eighteen years ago. A business trip. But despite the bad news he expected, Enrique had been filled with anticipation. He and

Rachel. Just the two of them. Since they had discovered their love, it had been difficult for them to see each other alone. A clandestine rendezvous in a shabby hotel; a late night in his deserted office. So little to slake his insatiable need for her. There were rumors; people guessed. But he and Rachel had been discreet. They were, after all, still married to others.

That's why he had been so eager to get to the Olympus with her. Time alone together; a new beginning. Eighteen years ago. It seemed like yesterday. They had flown out to see the ruins of his first effort at showing his father his business savvy. Millions of dollars invested in thatched guest cottages, a casual outdoor restaurant and bar, free-form pool and cabanas, all laid waste by the hurricane that had swept over St. Mary's.

His father had told him it was impossible to make a go of a resort on a remote island, particularly in the Grenadines. But his father never understood Enrique. Never realized how much pressure was on the son to equal his father's accomplishments. Everyone admired Carlos Castillo, self-made businessman. A man who had pulled himself up by his bootstraps. And here was Enrique. What could he do to trump his father? He'd excelled at school, attending the most prestigious universities in the world. But what good were academic credentials? He had to show his father that he could take the company he had built and make it even greater.

He studied the photo, remembering the moment. Eighteen years ago. He had been staring out at the sea, already planning the Olympus Grande. He had been unaware of Rachel taking the photo until he turned. She still had the camera up against her eye.

"Sorry," she said, putting the camera in her bag. "I know it may seem insensitive, but I need to document this for the audit."

"I understand." He stepped up to the rise where she was standing. He was feeling optimistic, despite the devastation around them. He saw the hotel as a metaphor for his life. An opportunity to start anew. He had made his decision. His future lay with this woman. "Don't be discouraged," he said. "The foundation is still intact. Next time, I'll do it right."

"Right?" she said.

"Last time, my father made me cut corners, but I know that perfection can't be put on a budget. And for you, my darling, I will only build that which is perfect. That which shall last forever."

"Enrique," she said.

"I will create a legacy that will sustain the Castillos for generations to come. Greater than anything my father ever dreamed of. A temple that even the gods will envy. A legacy for our children."

Rachel looked at him — her emerald eyes reflecting the sea and their future. He held her against him and pressed his lips against hers. He could hear the waves breaking, the seagulls screeching.

She pulled away. "I'm sorry, Enrique. I'm so sorry."

Chapter 38

Elise heard chimes. Church bells. The notes broke through her dream.

Church bells? She shook the sleep from her head. There it was again. Ding-dong.

The doorbell.

Someone was ringing the doorbell. Why didn't her grandfather answer? Then she remembered. He'd gone to the grocery store.

She sat up on the sofa and adjusted her tee shirt and sweatpants. She touched the three teardrops of her mother's blood, instantly soothed by her mother's presence.

Ding-dong.

Maybe it was a delivery or a neighbor. The quilt her grandmother had crocheted fell to the floor as Elise stood to answer the door. Through the peephole, she recognized the polo shirt and khakis of her school's uniform. A navy blue hooded sweatshirt hung over Carlos's shoulders like a cape. Elise unlocked both locks. She was surprised by how dark the sky was and the coolness in the air. Wasn't it still afternoon? Then she heard distant thunder.

"Hey," Carlos said.

Elise held the door open. "You can come in."

"Holy shit. I can see why you didn't go to school today. What happened to your face?"

"My uncle mistook me for a punching bag."

"Oh man. He hit you? Did you call the cops? What did Jeremy do? He must have gone apeshit."

"He was pretty angry." She ran her fingers through her tangled hair and plaited it in a single braid. She'd been so worried last night and most of today. But then Jeremy called and told her he'd taken care of things with Dwight. He sounded almost happy. Their uncle wouldn't be bothering her anymore. And she wondered, but didn't ask, what Jeremy had done to Dwight that would make her brother so certain.

Carlos followed her into the darkened living room.

"So what happened? I mean, like why did he hit you?"

"It was just a giant misunderstanding."

"Are you living here with your grandfather now?"

"I-I don't know. I'm not sure what I want to do."

"Right." He pulled on the loose sleeves of his sweatshirt and hung his head. He looked like he wanted to say something, but couldn't get it out. Elise had been avoiding him since the night he'd wanted to have sex with her. "Well, I didn't mean to bother you," he said finally.

"It's fine. I'm glad you came."

"Really?" He straightened up. "Do you want to go for a ride or something?"

Elise glanced around the living room. She'd closed all the drapes, and her grandfather had let her stretch out in here on the sofa.

"We don't have to talk," Carlos said. "You know, just hang out."

How close the room felt suddenly. How much she needed to smell fresh air.

Her grandfather came in with several plastic grocery bags draped over his arms. His forehead and glasses were covered with droplets of water.

"Hi Grandpa. I'm going for a ride with Carlos."

"Hello, Carlos."

"Hello, Mr. Lazar."

Her grandfather placed the bags on the table, took off his glasses, and dried them with the bottom of his shirt. "It just started raining. Be careful."

"I will." She kissed his cheek. His sweet, scratchy cheek.

Elise stepped off the front porch of her grandfather's house. The rain was coming down with force. She opened her arms and turned her face upward. She tried to catch the drops in her mouth. How good the rain felt. How good everything smelled. The damp dirt, the grass, the flowers. Dwight wasn't going to bother her any-more, and Jeremy sounded almost happy.

"You're getting soaked," Carlos said, grabbing her arm. "I'm parked just over there." He ran and she ran with him. She climbed into the car. The rainwater was streaming down her face and neck. Her tee shirt was soaked through and the teardrops had spread. They felt warm against her skin.

Carlos got in the driver's side and slammed the door after him. "Here, Elise. Put this on." He took his hooded sweatshirt off his shoulders. "I don't want you getting sick on me."

She slipped it over her head. It smelled vaguely of Carlos's cologne. Nice.

The rain pounded against the windshield.

"Not a great day for a walk in the park," he said.

She laughed.

He smiled, then sucked in his lip. "Look, I know things turned kind of shitty last time we were together."

She looked away. The rainwater had created a puddle along the side of the road.

"I feel like a real jerk. You've been going through this terrible time and instead of helping, all I'm doing is trying to get you stoned and, well, whatever." He touched her shoulder so lightly that her nerve endings tingled. "I miss you, Elise."

She leaned against the side window. It felt cold against her forehead. A child's faded blue ball was floating on the stream of rainwater.

"I'm getting heavy on you," Carlos said. "I didn't mean to do that. I just... Well, never mind."

She couldn't speak. She wanted to tell him it was okay. That just him being here and caring about her made it okay.

"You want to go to the yacht?" he asked. "My parents aren't around. No one will bother us. We can watch a movie."

Elise turned toward him.

"Just a movie," he said. "Nothing more. I promise."

"Do you have *The Sound of Music*?"

"*The Sound of Music*?" Carlos's face broke into a wide grin. "I'm sure my parents have that on DVD somewhere."

Elise reclined against half a dozen blue and green silk pillows on the king-size bed in the yacht's master suite as Carlos removed stacks of cassettes and DVDs from the cabinet beside the large-screen TV. "My dad keeps the old movies in here," Carlos said.

This was the first time Carlos had brought her to the master cabin. The walls were paneled in polished wood and fitted with built-in cabinets and mirrored display shelves. The crystal vases and sculptures looked expensive. How dumb — expensive crystal. It was obvious the Castillos didn't use the yacht for boating.

She and Carlos had driven directly to Lotus Island and sneaked through the park and around the back to avoid being seen. She was grateful that Carlos hadn't asked if she wanted to stop by her house. Her uncle had contaminated it for her. Maybe she'd be able to talk Jeremy into moving in with their grandfather. She brightened at the idea. Why not? The three of them and Geezer. Then no one would be lonely.

She raised the hood of Carlos's sweatshirt over her damp hair as she tunneled deeper into the pillows. It was windy outside and the yacht rocked ever so slightly, like a cradle. Coming here was a good idea. She took off her sneakers and ran her feet against the silky comforter. If Mrs. Castillo caught them in here on her expensive bedding, she'd kill them.

Carlos dumped an armful of tapes on the bed. "Doesn't look like they have the DVD. Maybe there's an old cassette of the movie."

Elise sat up and sorted through the tapes on the bed. There was one of *The Wizard of Oz*. "We can watch this, Carlos." She held it up. "It's one of my favorites."

"I'm sure we have *The Sound of Music*." He'd completely emptied out the cabinet. From her perch on the bed, she could see the wooden dividers and open drawers. Carlos was tapping on the backing. "I bet this drops down. My dad probably keeps a secret stash of porno in here."

"Then I doubt you'll find *The Sound of Music*."

Carlos pulled on something and the backing flipped open like a door. "Told you." He reached into the cabinet and dropped a stack of files on the bed, then stuck his head into the empty space. "Man. I was sure they were in here."

Elise's foot touched the pile of folders and they spilled over. "Sorry," she said, sitting up to gather them back up.

They were accounting reports with endless columns of numbers like her mother used to review. But why would Mr. Castillo keep them hidden?

"Wow," Carlos said. He slid down to the floor with a pile of cassettes. "Would you believe my dad has the complete collection of *The Three Stooges*?"

Elise flipped through the spreadsheets. They went back at least four or five years. Dates, numbers, initials, a column headed Transfers to Corporate, and columns labeled EX, JR, VL. Strange.

"Hey, look at this," Carlos said, turning his head to show her a cassette box. He frowned. "What are you doing?"

"N-nothing. These papers fell all over the place. I'm trying to put them back where they belong."

"Oh, okay. My parents would kill —" He stopped at the sound of something slamming. Voices were approaching, low and garbled. "Shit," Carlos said. "We need to put this stuff away."

Elise shoved the accounting reports into their folders. The voices were directly above. She couldn't make out what they were saying, but could hear their timbre and pitch. There was laughter, then an uncannily familiar voice. A pattern of words that she'd heard once before. Elise's breath caught in her chest. She was hot, then cold; her insides pulverized, ready to explode out of her.

"Elise, give me those folders." Carlos tried to pull them out of her hands, but she held them with a death grip. "Shit, Elise. Let go."

The voices were closer. And again, she heard the familiar pattern. A pattern that absolutely terrified her. She couldn't catch her breath or speak.

He's coming, she wanted to tell Carlos. The murderer's coming. But nothing came out. Like Lot's wife, she'd turned into a pillar of salt.

"And this is the larger master cabin," Mrs. Castillo said as she stepped inside. Just behind her were Elise's mother's two partners, Bud McNally and Irv Luria, and Mr. Castillo. They all looked at Elise and Carlos with confusion. Then, Mr. Castillo spoke.

"What the hell are you doing in here, Carlos?"

"We were looking for a tape," Carlos stuttered. "*The Sound of Music.*"

"Don't get so worked up, Enrique," Bud McNally said, "They're just kids." He glanced at a file and frowned.

Mr. Castillo swooped down and gathered up the files.

It felt like insects were crawling around in Elise's stomach. The voice. She needed to match up the voice. But whose was it? All four of the adults had low voices. And why did she only recognize it through the hatch?

"Don't you have your own room, Carlos?" his father said. "Didn't we spend fifty thousand refurbishing the rec room for your entertainment?"

"Enrique, you're frightening Elise," Liliam said. "What's wrong, honey? You look ill. My goodness, what happened to your face?"

"I said I was sorry," Carlos said.

Irv Luria was staring at Elise, his fists in two fat balls. He'd always frightened her when she was little, but he seemed even scarier than she remembered him. Scary and angry. But why would he be angry?

The cabin was shrinking, the four adults hovered around the bed like circling wolves. They sucked up all the air in the room. Elise tugged down the hood of the sweatshirt.

"I'm sorry if I upset you, Elise," Mr. Castillo said.

"Do you want some water, honey?" Liliam said.

"What's wrong, Elise?" Bud said.

"Maybe you should get some fresh air," Irv said.

Elise jumped up, pulled on her sneakers, and brushed past the four adults. She hurried out of the cabin and up the ladder. Don't pass out, she told herself. You can make it. She heaved herself up by the handrails and pushed open the door.

Only when the breeze hit her was she able to catch her breath. The rain whipped against her face, but the pain in her gut was almost too much to bear.

The murderer had been in that room. She was certain. She had heard the murderer's voice. And recognized it. But how? How could she possibly recognize something she had never heard before?

Chapter 39

He found her hidden in a crevice between the roots of the banyan tree. Jeremy had walked past twice, not noticing her behind the curtain of rain that streamed down as from a broken gutter. Even as he stared directly at her, she seemed to blend in with the tree in her dark, hooded sweatshirt.

He darted through the sheet of rain and pushed into the nook beside her. Elise's arms were crossed tightly in front of her chest and the cascading rainwater made a pattern on her face.

"Hey, Ellie," he said softly. There was barely enough room for the two of them and his suit pants and shirt were soaked through. "Can I take you home?"

She shook her head.

"What about Grandpa's house?"

"N-no." Her lower lip was trembling. He had been back at PCM's offices with Robbie when he'd received her call. She was hiding in the park, Elise had said, sounding terrified.

"Do you want to tell me what happened?" Jeremy asked now.

"I'm so scared."

"I know, Ellie." He slipped his arm around her. Her entire body was shaking. "You're all wet. Let's at least get you some dry clothes, or sit in my car."

"No. Not yet." She burrowed her face against his neck. He could smell the baby shampoo she still used to wash her hair. "The, the murderer. I'm not safe."

"You are safe. The murderer has no reason to hurt you."

"He knows."

"Knows what?"

"I-I heard his voice."

Jeremy's stomach dropped. "What are you saying? You heard his voice? When?"

"On the yacht. I was there with Carlos. And we heard voices above us. And one of them — when I heard it, I thought I was going to pass out. It was the murderer."

"But, Ellie. You never saw the murderer or heard him speak."

"I know it was his voice," she said. "I know it."

"Okay, I believe you." He needed to keep her from becoming hysterical. He'd calm her down, then get her some dry clothes. "You heard voices. Then what happened?"

"Then they came down below. They were very angry when they saw us."

"Who? Who saw you?"

"Carlos's parents and Mom's partners — Irv and Bud."

"The four of them were on the yacht?"

She nodded against his chest.

"Which one sounded like the murderer?"

She shook her head. "I-I don't know. They sounded different when they came down below."

"What exactly did you hear that made you think it was the murderer?"

"I don't know exactly what it's called. Do you remember Daddy used to say every voice is like a musical instrument with its own special sound?"

"But had you ever heard the murderer speak before?"

"I don't know." She started to cry. "This is so frustrating."

"I know it is, Ellie."

"I-I hear the voice in my nightmares."

"The murderer's voice?"

She wiped her nose. "And it was the same as the one I heard on the yacht."

How could this be? Was his sister psychic or was this a repressed memory? "Tell me again what happened that night — the night you came home."

"I hate trying to remember."

"Just this one time."

She was quiet for a moment, then made a soft squeaking sound. She was sucking on the end of her braid. "Okay." She took a deep breath. "I got to the house with Carlos, and it was late and I thought Mom was going to be mad. And the door, it just opened. And I re-member thinking Mom and Dad had gone out looking for me and left the door unlocked. But something was wrong. It was dark and the house smelled funny. And Carlos said maybe we should leave."

"And did you leave?"

"Carlos said, 'Come on, Elise. Let's get out of here.' He pulled on my arm."

"Why was he pulling? Didn't you want to go with him?"

Her closed eyelids fluttered ever so slightly. "There was a shadow."

"In your nightmares, you see a shadow."

"Not in my nightmare." She opened her eyes. "That night I saw a shadow in the foyer." Her fingers gripped Jeremy's wrist. "A large, dark shadow. It was perfectly still, but I knew it was wrong. It didn't belong in our house. I took a step toward it. It still didn't move. But I could hear it. I could hear it breathing."

Jeremy was holding his own breath. "What about Carlos?"

"I don't know. I guess he left."

"Go on. Go on, Ellie."

Elise trembled against him. "I smelled something weird. And I thought, there's someone in our house. But I couldn't move. I just stared and stared at the shadow. And then I could see it wasn't a shadow, but his face was all dark. No nose, no mouth, no hair, just eyes. Bug eyes, like goggles. And he was staring at me. And I wanted to scream, but nothing came out."

Jeremy's pulse was racing. "He must have been wearing a ski mask and night goggles."

"And then he said something."

"Jesus. What? What did he say?"

She closed her eyes again. "It was hard to understand, like the voice I heard on the yacht."

"He was probably covering his mouth. That's why it sounded garbled."

"Covering his mouth."

"What happened next?"

She shook her head.

"Did he touch you?"

She seemed to be studying the dripping rainwater. "I I don't think so."

"Then what? Do you remember him leaving?"

She started to cry. "I don't know. Stop asking me. I can't remember anything else."

"Okay, Ellie." Jeremy hugged her tightly. "I'll take you to Grandpa's."

They drove in silence most of the way. He had made Elise take off her wet sweatshirt and wrapped her in a blanket his mother had kept in the trunk of her car.

Elise seemed hypnotized by the windshield wipers. She had seen the killer. No wonder she had been freaked out being back in the house. And all those nights he'd left her alone. Well, that wouldn't happen anymore.

"You did really well remembering all that stuff," Jeremy said. "I think it will help the nightmares go away."

Elise kept staring at the wipers, her head gently rocking from side to side.

"I know you're worried that the murderer's coming back for you, but he has no reason to think you recognized his voice."

"He . . . he thinks I figured it out," Elise said very quietly.

"Figured what out?"

"The papers. He saw me looking at the papers."

"What are you talking about?"

"On the yacht, Carlos found these files. And I wondered why they'd been hidden, so I started going through them."

"You found files?"

"Accounting stuff, like Mom used to work on. But nothing made sense to me. And then they all came down to the cabin and started yelling at us."

"You mean the Castillos and Mom's partners? They saw you going through the papers?"

She nodded. "And I got this feeling there was something important in them. Something I wasn't supposed to see."

"They might just be Enrique's personal files. They don't necessarily have anything to do with what happened to Mom and Dad."

"But you weren't there. You didn't see them. How they looked at me." She started to cry again. "Don't you understand, Jeremy? The murderer was in that cabin with me."

"It's okay." He reached for her hand. "I believe you. You don't have to be frightened."

She rested her head against the side window and stared again at the windshield wipers.

Chapter 40

Jeremy believed she was being paranoid, but as soon as he'd gotten his sister settled at his grandfather's house, he called Judy Lieber on his cell phone.

"What's up?" Lieber asked.

"I want to make you aware of some recent developments," Jeremy said, hoping he wouldn't come across like the boy who cried wolf. It had been only a few days since he'd spoken to her at the park. At the time, he had been certain that the murderer had targeted his father and that Marina was only interested in helping him.

"I've been wondering about all those leads on who was out to get your father," Lieber said.

He couldn't tell if she was being sarcastic. It didn't matter. He stood in the corner of the living room pulling on the venetian blind strings. He could hear his grandfather in the kitchen, clanking pots, running water. "My sister may have seen the murderer that night."

There was a long pause. "I'm listening," Lieber said.

"I think she's been blocking it out, but tonight she remembered something."

"That can happen. What does she remember?"

"When Elise and Carlos got to the house that night, they went inside."

"Carlos Castillo said they could tell something was wrong — the house smelled funny — and they ran out."

"Not they," Jeremy said. "Just Carlos. Elise thought she saw something in the foyer; she was paralyzed with fear."

"So Carlos left her?" Lieber said. "That's not his story."

"Maybe he was ashamed of leaving her behind."

There was silence. "Where are you now?" Lieber said finally. "Where's your sister?"

"We're both at my grandfather's house."

"Good. I'll be there in a half hour. I need to talk to her."

"Wait. Please. Elise is very upset. Something happened tonight and she's spooked. Can you talk to her in the morning?"

"What happened?"

"She was on the Castillos' yacht with Carlos. She found some papers, which she believes may be connected to our parents' murders."

"What kind of papers?"

"Accounting reports. She couldn't figure out what they meant, but they'd been hidden."

"Jeremy." There was a tinge of impatience in Lieber's voice. "Many people keep personal papers hidden on their private property. Why does Elise think they have anything to do with your parents? Were their names on them?"

"No. Nothing like that. It's just, Mr. and Mrs. Castillo, Bud Mc-Nally, and Irv Luria surprised her while she was going through the papers. They seemed very angry."

"Well, wouldn't they be?"

How foolish Jeremy must sound to her. "But she heard their voices," he said. "When they got on the yacht, she recognized the murderer's voice."

"Back up," Lieber said. "Had the murderer spoken to her at the scene of the crime?"

"She says he had."

"And what did he say?"

"She doesn't remember. His voice was muffled."

"So she saw the murderer and he spoke to her."

"That's right. And from what she described, I'm guessing he wore a ski mask and maybe night goggles, so he could see in the dark. And now she's afraid he believes she recognized him on the yacht. That he wants to hurt her."

Lieber was silent. In the background he could hear phones ringing, people talking. Was she still at her office? "Then who is it?" she said finally. "Who's the murderer?"

"Well, it's one of them. Mr. or Mrs. Castillo, McNally, or Luria. She's positive. She recognized the voice, but she couldn't tell whose it was."

He was pretty sure he heard Lieber sigh. "Jeremy," she said. "This may not be my business, but has your sister been getting enough psychological support — from you, your grandfather, her friends? Is it possible she's just very lonely?"

"That's not it."

"She's only sixteen. She's experienced a tremendous shock. She really should be speaking to a professional — someone who can help her sort this out."

"She found suspicious files on the Castillos' yacht."

"We don't know that they have anything to do with your parents."

"Well, can't you get a warrant to search the yacht and look at them?"

"Do you honestly believe if someone saw Elise going through papers that might connect them to the murders they'd leave them lying around for the police?"

"You're right," Jeremy said. "The papers are probably gone."

Elise came into the living room. Her hair was wrapped in a towel and she wore an old bathrobe that used to belong to their mother. Her face was flushed as though she'd taken a hot bath or shower and the blue-green bruise on her face was more vivid than ever. "Who's that?" she whispered.

He covered his cell phone with his hand. "Detective Lieber. She wants to talk to you."

"Oh Jeremy." Elise's eyes filled with tears. "I don't want to have to do it again."

Lieber was talking into his ear. "Tell her I'll come by tomorrow morning. Early. Before school."

"She'll come by in the morning," Jeremy told his sister. Then into the phone in a low voice so his grandfather couldn't hear him in the next room. "But what about the threat to my sister? What if she's right about the murderer? That he believes she can identify him?"

"I'll send someone over to watch your grandfather's house tonight."

"Thank you," Jeremy said.

"Make sure she stays in."

"Right. I don't think we have to worry about that," he said, but she'd already hung up.

Lieber had made him feel foolish. True, Elise's story didn't quite make sense. To someone who didn't know her, she sounded like a hysterical child seeking attention. But Jeremy knew his sister never made up stories or embellished.

His grandfather came into the living room carrying a tray with cups, a steaming teapot, a couple of packages of cupcakes and a jar of honey. His arms were trembling under the strain.

"Let me help you with that, Grandpa." Jeremy took the tray and set it down on the coffee table.

"Tea and honey," his grandfather said, sitting down next to Elise on the sofa. "Your grandmother used to say it's the best remedy in the world. A panacea for whatever ails you." He poured the tea into the three cups. He hadn't asked what had happened tonight — why Elise had been sopping wet and so upset. That had always been his way. Just to be there for them.

Jeremy went to his grandfather's desk. He found a pen and an old-fashioned columnar pad that this grandfather used long after electronic spreadsheets had been invented. He put the pad down on the coffee table near Elise. She was holding the hot cup in her hands, inhaling the heat.

"Can you write down what you remember?" he said. Elise's practically photographic memory had been a source of delight to the family. They used to play a game with her. She'd look at a page in a book, then recite it from memory.

Elise studied him through the steam. "So you believe me?"

His grandfather raised his eyebrow.

"I never said I didn't," Jeremy said.

Elise put the cup down and picked up the pen. She filled in a few of the columns — deposits, dates, initials, totals, EX, JR, VL. "The totals from these columns were broken down into these columns," she said. "The ones that say EX, JR, VL."

Their grandfather examined the paper. "'Transfers to Corporate?' What's this?"

"I found some accounting papers on the Castillos' yacht."

He frowned. "You've been going through someone else's property, Elise?"

"No Grandpa. It wasn't like that." Her eyes overflowed again. "Why is everyone trying to make me feel like I've done something wrong?" She pushed herself up off the sofa and ran from the room.

"Elise," his grandfather called after her. "I'm sorry, sweetheart."

Jeremy put his hand on his grandfather's. "Just let her be." It was the advice his grandfather had given him only the day before.

"But I've upset her. I didn't mean to upset her. I was simply worried she might get herself into some trouble."

"She'll be okay. She wasn't looking for them, but she found these papers. I'm not even sure they have anything to do with Mom and Dad. But does any of this make sense to you?"

His grandfather studied the columns. "EX, JR, VL." He shook his head. "Execute? Junior, or maybe Journal? Volume? Volunteer? I don't know, Jeremy." He looked toward the hallway. "I didn't mean to upset her."

"I'm going back to the house," Jeremy said. "Maybe this will match up with something in Mom's office that we hadn't noticed before."

His grandfather opened the package of Twinkies and stood up. "I'll bring her these. They were always her favorite when she was a little girl. And maybe a glass of milk. Warm milk." And he shuffled off.

Chapter 41

It still didn't make sense. Robbie rubbed her eyes. She'd been staring at the same numbers and bits of information for over three hours.
It was nine at night and everyone else at PCM had gone home. About
a half hour ago, one of the junior partners had passed Robbie's office
and popped his head in. "Looks like you're the last one here, Robbie.
Shall I wait for you?"

"No thanks."

"I'll lock you in, then. A minute later, she heard the echo of the
heavy front door thumping shut down the hall.

Her small, standard-issue office was eerily quiet. A photo of her
mother holding a pink-cheeked Robbie in a snowsuit sat on the credenza. Beside it was a snapshot she'd framed of herself and Rachel
at a firm picnic, toasting the camera. The two most important
women in her life. Both gone.

She returned to her papers. Trying to come up with a theory of
why someone would have wanted Rachel Stroeb dead. She studied
the notes from her and Jeremy's meeting with Enrique Castillo, the
financial statements of Castillo Enterprises, the annual reports that
Jeremy's grandfather had loaned her. It had to do with the Olympus; she felt certain of that. There was some connection to Rachel
being on the audit eighteen years ago. But what? If only they hadn't
been frightened out of the file room last night, they might have found
more audit papers containing the answer. She checked her watch.

9:05. Should she try the file room again? But this was a futile mental exercise; what was the likelihood the door would be unlocked? And if it was, would it be safe for her to be alone in there? What if they hadn't imagined the camera, the strange noises, the open door that she thought she had closed?

She picked up the photo of herself with Rachel. When Robbie had first met her, she found Rachel almost intimidating in her self-confidence. A partner and so smart, so pretty. Robbie had kept her distance. But Rachel had sensed the emptiness in Robbie. And gently, like a wave closing up a hole in the sand, Rachel had filled her void. They had been close for almost two years. Friends, yes, but something more. In Rachel, Robbie had found her mother again.

She put the photo down. She hadn't heard from Jeremy since he'd gone after his sister earlier this evening. Maybe he'd be willing to hit the file room with her. This time, one of them would stand guard at the door.

He picked up on the fourth ring. "Hey." He sounded tired or distracted.

"How's Elise? Is everything okay?"

"Yeah."

"Well, you said she sounded very upset when she called." Why was Jeremy talking in monosyllables?

"She's better now." He obviously didn't want to share whatever was going on with her. "So," he said finally, "what are you up to?"

"I'm at the office, going through some stuff."

"Alone?"

"I'm usually the last one out."

Jeremy was silent for a moment. "You should leave, Robbie."

"Why?"

"Just to be safe. After last night in the file room."

"We were probably imagining things."

"Maybe. I still don't think you should be there by yourself."

She definitely couldn't ask him to meet her, not with his paranoid attitude. "Okay," she said. "I'll leave in a few minutes."

She gathered up her papers and laptop. She'd stop at the file room. It was most likely locked anyway. Then she'd go home.

A noise in the hallway, quiet and shuffling, made her jump. The hair on her arms stood up. She poked her head around her doorway. "Hello?" she called.

It was probably the A/C unit shutting down. Her conversation with Jeremy was making her jumpy. She turned out the light in her office, then went to wait for the elevator. Her stomach grumbled. She hadn't eaten since grabbing a yogurt around lunchtime. The elevator binged softly and the door opened. Her finger hovered by the "L" for lobby. Maybe she should just go home. But as the elevator door slid closed, she quickly pressed a different button.

The door opened on the eleventh floor. The elevator bank was dark except for the lighted exit signs. She hesitated, then jumped out as the door closed behind her.

She went down the darkened hallway and tested the door to the file room. It opened easily. That was what she'd been hoping for, but now she felt uncertain. Why was it unlocked? And why had it been open the other night when she left with Jeremy? She was sure she was overreacting. That her mind was playing games with her as it had been all evening. But she wasn't going to be a fool about this. She dialed Jeremy's number and waited as it rang several times. "Hey —" his voice said.

"Jeremy?"

"Leave a message," his voice mail continued.

"Damn," she said softly. Well, she was already here. The phone beeped. "Jeremy. I'm on the eleventh floor. Just wanted you to know. Don't worry. I'll be in and out." She closed her phone and dropped it in her handbag.

Robbie flipped on the light in the file room and leaned against the closed door, this time making certain she locked it behind her. Everything appeared just as she and Jeremy had left it the other night. She took a deep breath to settle her nerves. Why was she feeling so shaky? She went directly to the aisle of cabinets that she knew held at least some of the old Castillo binders. The tapping of her heels echoed against the linoleum floors in the cavernous room.

She stopped abruptly. It was completely silent. Okay. Get the right binders and get out of here.

The gray cabinets stretched out in a perfect line like tombstones in a military cemetery. She went to the end of the row to the cabinet where she had found the other Castillo binders.

She pulled out the top drawer, too quickly. Oh my God. It was off balance. The cabinet was moving of its own momentum, falling toward her. She tried to brace her weight against it, but she was no match for it. Jump. Get out of the way, her brain said. But her body couldn't respond in time.

Something hit her head hard. Then a flash of unbearable pain. And she realized in that split second there was nothing she could do to stop the cabinet from toppling and crushing her.

Chapter 42

Jeremy lay on his bed in the darkness. The wind outside was blowing in gusts, flinging raindrops like pebbles against the windows. He had spent the last hour rummaging through his mother's office hoping to find papers, reports, anything that might connect to the abbreviations Elise had picked up on the accounting report on the Castillos' yacht. He'd found nothing.

The house was lonely without Elise. All the times he'd been here over the last month, she had been home as well. Elise and Geezer both. Now, Jeremy was alone with the silence of the rooms, the wind and rain pounding against the windows. How scared Elise must have been sleeping in the house by herself, while he was busy screwing Marina and deceiving himself into believing he was doing something virtuous. The thought made him very angry with himself. How ashamed his parents would be if they knew.

But they would never know how he'd let them down, would they?

He took a deep breath, dragging a smoky smell into his lungs. Stale cigarette smoke. He sat up and focused, alert to every sound, every detail in his surroundings. It reminded him of one time during exams he hadn't slept for thirty-six hours straight. How his sensory perception had become magnified. Why hadn't he noticed the smell before? Geezer. Of course. Geezer's rank fur had masked the odor.

Jeremy turned on the lamp on his nightstand. He was remembering the lingering reek of cigarettes in his room the day he'd returned home after his parents' funerals. It had been fresh, recent.

He pushed his laptop out of the way and pulled his old computer forward on the desk. It blinked to life as he pressed the on switch. It made sense, suddenly. His parents using this room as their private haven. They'd sneak in here to smoke, to think, maybe even to use the old computer to back up their laptops.

The Desktop displayed on the screen. Jeremy clicked "My Documents." There were his old high school papers, his music files, his college application essays. And there were two folders he hadn't made. One was labeled, "DC" the other, "RLS."

His cell phone rang. Robbie again, probably to let him know she'd left the office. But his adrenaline was pumping; he'd get back to her.

He clicked on his father's initials. The folder opened to ranks of other folders. How easy it was. If only he had realized weeks ago that his parents had been using his long-abandoned computer, would he have been able to get to the truth that much sooner? Would it have saved him from Marina? The cell phone beeped, letting him know he had a voice mail. He ignored it.

He found the papers he had gone over with Marina at her apartment, but there probably wasn't anything new here to shed light on the murders. It was his mother's files that were important.

He clicked on RLS. The folder flew open revealing dozens and dozens of folders.

"Yes," Jeremy said, hitting the desk with the palm of his hand.

Jeremy clicked on a folder called "Olympus." There were spreadsheet files containing calculations of revenue, analyses of reserve accounts, dozens of papers with numbers and formulas. He looked for the abbreviations: EX, JR, VL. Nothing. He let the computer search for them. No matches.

Whatever was in the papers Elise had found on the yacht didn't seem to have a connection to his mother's work or observations.

Jeremy opened a recent text file. A memo addressed to Bud McNally with a copy to Irving Luria. He read it through twice, trying to absorb its significance. A few days before she left to visit Jeremy in Madrid, she had sent the memo to her partners. It was fairly straightforward. She would be visiting the Olympus Grande the day after she returned from Spain to review the on-site records. That she'd notified Enrique Castillo and he planned to be there as well.

He remembered Liliam mentioning the trip at dinner. So, the Castillos and his mother's two partners all knew his mother had been planning a visit to the Olympus. But Elise had already said that one of those four was the murderer. This new memo didn't narrow anything down.

He typed in the word "Olympus" to do a computer-wide word search and waited as the old computer processed. It seemed to take forever. Jeremy had forgotten how slow the old technology was. Finally, the computer spit out the dozen or so files he'd already found for his mother. But there was a new document he hadn't seen before, a letter addressed to his mother within their father's folders. Jeremy clicked on it.

Dear Rachel,

In accordance with our attorneys' instructions, I have put together a list of our assets divided as I think is fair. Please review them and make whatever changes you determine to be appropriate.

That's the business part of this letter. Now let me tell you what's in my heart. I know I haven't been the best husband and that we've drifted apart this past year. But the thought of losing you dismays me beyond what words can express. We have a family,

Rachel, the beginning of a future. Can't we give it one more chance?

His parents were on the verge of getting divorced over Marina? He read on.

I know you love another. I understand that.

Jeremy stopped. What? What was his father saying? His mother loved another?

But please, Rachel. Don't throw our lives away. When you return from the Olympus, let's talk. Please.

And then he took in the date. The letter had been written eighteen years ago. His mother had been in love with another man eighteen years ago — the first time she had visited the Olympus.

"Jesus," he said. First his father, then his mother. Jeremy had lived his entire life with people he hardly knew. They had shown him a veneer — the caring mother, the demanding father, the happily married husband and wife. And Jeremy had never much concerned himself about it. After all, they didn't yell or throw things at each other, so it followed that they had a good marriage, right?

And maybe they did. Maybe this stuff he was learning went far deeper than he'd ever imagined his parents' lives were. Here he'd been angry with them all these years because they failed to understand what was going on inside him, and he had been clueless about them.

The cell phone beeped again, reminding him of the voice mail.

He had to focus. Getting emotionally sucked into these revelations wouldn't help him find his parents' murderer. He needed to put this letter together with what he already knew.

He lay back down on the bed. The wind had let up and the rain was coming down evenly now.

Elise had said that all four — the Castillos, Bud, and Irv — seemed upset over her finding the files. But the accounting reports had been hidden on Enrique Castillo's yacht. So didn't that narrow it down to Enrique and Liliam Castillo?

But what if Elise was mistaken about the files? Maybe they had nothing to do with his mother.

That brought him to his father's letter. His mother was in love with someone. Could it have been Enrique? He was going to be at the Olympus with her at the time his father wrote the letter. Had Enrique loved her? Did he still? Had she spurned him?

Did Liliam know about their relationship? Had she been crazed by jealousy when she learned her husband and Rachel Stroeb were going to the Olympus together?

Did Enrique kill his parents? Did Liliam?

Or was he once again going in the wrong direction?

His cell phone beeped again. Jeremy stared at it. Maybe Robbie had found something. And if not, maybe she could help him sort this out. Jeremy dialed his voice mail.

"Jeremy. I'm on the eleventh floor. Just wanted you to know. Don't worry. I'll be in and out."

"Shit." He dialed her number, but she didn't pick up. He dialed again. It rang through to her voice mail.

She'd gone to the file room. Why had she been so stupid? And why wasn't she answering her phone?

He spoke to her voice mail as he ran down the steps and out the front door.

"Robbie, call me back. Please call me back."

Chapter 43

Marina saw the Lexus on its way out as she drove onto Lotus Island. She hadn't been able to make out the driver, but she was pretty sure it was Jeremy in his mother's car, driving fast and wildly. Where was he going?

But no matter. Now she could do what she came to do without accidentally bumping into him. She should have been relieved, but instead she felt the heaviness of loss. Stop it, she told herself. Seeing him again can't possibly change things. It's much better this way. Much better.

The security guard came out of the guardhouse holding a clipboard and looked at her questioningly. She smiled as though she belonged. He raised the gate arm without asking where she was going or taking down her license number. *C'est incroyable*. Two people are murdered, and security is still lax.

She drove slowly past Jeremy's house. The red Corvair was parked in the far corner of the driveway, partially hidden by tall hedges. The lighting around the house was poor and the Corvair was almost completely in shadows. That was good. It was unlikely that anyone would see her. But she still didn't want to take any chances.

She remembered a small bayfront park next to the mansion where the gathering after the funeral had been held. That's where she had parked last time. Now, there were a couple of cars pulled up next to the park and a group of teenagers were standing around smoking despite the nasty weather. Marina drove beyond them, stopping her car a distance from the Castillos' imposing house.

She walked through the park, pulling the hood of her dark sweatshirt over her hair, as much to ward off the sporadic drizzle as to hide her identity, then hung her satchel over her shoulder. It was heavy. As heavy as when she carted papers around in it. But soon it would be much lighter.

It was a couple of blocks back to Jeremy's house, and the rain sprayed her face like water from a distant garden hose. The teenagers had gotten into their cars and driven away, and the streets were deserted.

Marina walked more quickly. Soon she would be finished here; then she would be able to leave. She had already bought a one-way ticket to Lima. She would find a place to live in her grandmother's old neighborhood, where she had grown up. She hadn't heard anything about what had become of the house or her grandmother's things. She only knew that her mother had moved to Germany with a rich tourist.

Maybe her grandmother's very house would be available. She could still remember the smell of cooking and baking floating through the open windows as she sat on the front stoop. Where she'd watch her grandmother returning from the market, her arms weighed down with bundles. Her dear, sweet grandmother. *Preciosa,* her grandmother had called her when the rest of the world had convinced her she had little worth.

Marina turned down Jeremy's street. She sensed a presence stepping out from behind a copse of trees on the corner. She glanced over her shoulder. Nothing.

She pressed her satchel closer to her chest. Her good-bye to Jeremy.

Jeremy. She could hardly think his name without overwhelming sadness. She had lost the father; now she had lost the son. Two beautiful, beautiful men. Both lost to her forever.

Hot tears mixed with the cold rain on her face. She had no choice. She had to say good-bye. The Stroeb house was dark and silent. She didn't want to think about the morning Jeremy had brought her here. Brought her and accused her. *Je t'accuse.*

Headlights brightened the street. Marina jumped behind the bushes so she wouldn't be seen. Was Jeremy back so soon? But the flashing light told her the car was the security guard's. She waited until it passed, then crept along the hedges to the Corvair.

His car. The father's, whom she had loved with a passion she hadn't known she possessed. But he hadn't returned her love. And then he had died, and Marina had been bereft. Until she saw the son. And she was so certain she could make him love her forever. But the shadow of his father had come between them. And now she was left with no one. With nothing.

She slipped around to the driver's door. It was unlocked. She opened it, relieved when the interior light didn't come on, and dropped the satchel on the driver's seat. She could smell them. Their scents had merged into one. The father, the son. It was time to say good-bye. She ran her hand over the seat their backs had touched, the steering wheel their hands had held. "Oh my love, my love," she whispered.

He was standing just behind her. She could feel his warm breath through the hood of her sweatshirt on the back of her neck. D.C. had returned to her. But no, it must be the son. Alive and real. Jeremy. He had forgiven her. He caressed her cheek. "Jeremy," she whispered as his fingers grazed her lips.

"Jeremy, my —" but his hand pressed tightly over her mouth. She couldn't speak. She couldn't breathe.

A powerful arm wrapped around her chest, immobilizing her. Her head was jerked back. Something cold on her neck. Slicing across her neck quickly like a feather.

Like the feather her grandmother used to tickle her with.

Chapter 44

The security guard didn't look up from what he was reading when Jeremy stopped at his desk in the main lobby. Jeremy flashed his PCM ID card, then wrote his name on the sign-in sheet and the time. 9:48. The last person to leave PCM had left around 8:30. No one had checked in or out since. Robbie's voice mail had come at 9:15.

The elevator bank on the eleventh floor was deserted and lit only by exit signs. Jeremy tried the door to the file room, cursing himself for being so unprepared. How could he have rushed over here without bringing a weapon of any kind?

The door was locked. He used his key.

The lights were on, but there was otherwise no sign of anyone. He started down an aisle listening for noises, footsteps, breathing, the click of a gun. It was absolutely still except for the sound of his sneakers padding on the linoleum floor. Robbie would have gone straight for the Castillo binders.

He came to an abrupt stop at the head of the aisle and inhaled sharply, trying to process what he was seeing. Praying it wasn't as bad as it looked.

A file cabinet had toppled over. From its position, he could tell it was the one that held the Castillo audit papers. It had fallen against another cabinet across the aisle and was leaning against it like a felled tree that had been propped up against its neighbor. There was a gap of about a foot between the fallen cabinet and the floor. And in that space was a motionless body.

Robbie's.

Her eyes were closed, her arm extended and motionless.

A contracting pain twisted his abdomen. No. Not Robbie, too.

He leaned toward her.

Her chest was rising and falling ever so slightly. She was alive. She was alive.

"Robbie," he said.

She opened her eyes, startled.

"Don't move," he said.

"What —" her voice was barely audible.

"The cabinet fell on you. It must have knocked you unconscious. I'll try to move it without hurting you."

The cabinet's weight was being borne by the other cabinet and Robbie was free of its main impact, but the cabinet was perched precariously and the slightest movement could upset its balance. Robbie's ankle was pinned beneath the bottom drawer so it was impossible to slide her out.

Jeremy evaluated the weighting and balancing of the cabinet. The lower drawers were practically empty and the top one filled to capacity. If he removed the binders from the top one, that would upset its equilibrium. It would be like playing a child's game of Pick-Up Stiks and he wasn't willing to risk that with Robbie. He needed to try something else.

Jeremy tried to get under the cabinet so that he could lift it with both his arms, but the angle was impossible. There wasn't enough space between it and the cabinet it was leaning against. He would have to do it from a side angle that wouldn't give him the best leverage. He had no choice.

"Robbie. The bottom drawers may fly out and hit you, but

there's nothing in them, so it shouldn't be too bad. I wish there was another way."

"Do it," she said.

"Okay, Robbie. Now." He slammed the top drawer in with all his strength and heaved the cabinet, but was unable to propel it upright. He couldn't believe how heavy it was. There had to be more than papers weighing it down. It felt like there were bricks of lead in the top drawer. And now the cabinet was slipping backward against the linoleum. Quickly, he needed to lift it straight before it crushed Robbie. He slid his hands down lower and gave another shove. Sweat dripped into his eyes. "Robbie, try to slide out." He could see movement in his peripheral vision.

"I can't," she said. "I'm sorry."

He pushed and pushed, feeling as though the blood vessels in his brain might explode. Just when it seemed as though his arms would give out, the cabinet moved. Up, up, up, until it swung back into place with a lurch.

He helped Robbie sit upright. There was a bruise and large bump on her head and her ankle was swollen to about twice its normal size.

"Tell me where you're hurt," Jeremy said.

"I think just my ankle." She took a deep breath and stretched her body in different directions checking for other injuries. The collar of her white blouse stuck out above her navy jacket and was covered with brownish red stains. Blood from her head injury had coagulated on her cheek. She let out a gasp of pain and reached for her leg. "Oh my God. My ankle."

Jeremy studied the bruise on Robbie's forehead.

"The cabinet was falling toward me. I tried to get out of the way."

"Did someone push it, Robbie? Was there someone in here with you?"

"I don't think so. It just fell when I pulled out the top drawer."

Jeremy opened the lower drawers. "I don't know why these are empty," Jeremy said. "It's almost like someone cleared them out knowing that would upset the balance of the cabinet."

"You'd warned me not to pull the top drawer out too quickly," Robbie said. "It was just a stupid accident."

Jeremy opened the top drawer slowly and as he did, he could feel the cabinet tilt. It hadn't been so off balance before. Something besides audit papers was in it. He tried pushing binders away, but they were packed in too tightly.

Robbie shifted her position and let out a gasp of pain.

"I'd better take you to the hospital." He didn't need further confirmation that someone had intended for the file cabinet to fall.

"Stupid accident," Robbie mumbled.

The rain had let up when Jeremy got to Robbie's townhouse. They'd been in the emergency room for over three hours. Robbie had been thoroughly X-rayed. Although her ankle had been broken in several places, they were clean breaks and wouldn't require surgery. She was put in a cast that extended to her knee and given a pair of crutches. The bump on her head had turned purplish and her eyelid was swollen and partially closed.

Although Robbie didn't complain, Jeremy could tell she was in excruciating pain. He had stopped to fill the prescription for painkillers on the way home, and Robbie took one before they left the pharmacy.

Now, he helped her out of the car. The wet driveway and grass glistened under the overhead light. Robbie seemed a little woozy. He found her house keys in her handbag and unlocked the door.

She was breathing hard as she hoisted herself forward on her crutches.

"You doing okay?" he asked.

"Yeah, but can you just light the candles on the coffee table? I can't deal with bright light."

He lit the three large red candles and turned off the foyer light. The scents of burning wax and smoke filled the room. As it had the other night, the smell reminded him of Marina. But this time, he would deal with it. "Do you want tea or something?"

"Something, I think." She hopped toward the white sofa and collapsed on it, letting the crutches clatter against the tile floor. "There's brandy in that cabinet."

"You sure that's okay? You've just taken a Percocet."

"I'll just have a little." She put her legs up on the glass coffee table; one in the knee-high cast, the other barefoot. She'd kicked her navy pump off under the table. In the pulsing candlelight, her bare leg looked like it had been carved from white marble.

Jeremy opened a pull-down door on the white shelving unit. There were several bottles of liquor, none of them open. He found Courvoisier and poured some into two brandy snifters.

"Thank you." She took the glass from him. "I don't generally drink much."

"I noticed. Unless you like to finish the bottle once it's open."

She tried to smile, but she winced with pain.

"Hey," Jeremy said, putting a sofa pillow under her leg cast. "No smiling."

She sipped the brandy. She'd taken off her jacket at the hospital. They must have forgotten it there. Her white blouse was damp from perspiration and the bloodstain on her collar looked like a giant ladybug. "You were sweet to take me to the hospital and bring me home."

"Right." He sat down next to her. "Was I also sweet to get you mixed up in something that almost got you killed?"

"I was stupid. I shouldn't have gone down there alone."

"I won't argue with that." Now didn't seem like the right time to tell her the falling file cabinet hadn't been an accident. With the painkiller, she probably wouldn't remember much of their conversation. He'd talk it over with her in a couple of days and warn her. There was no chance she'd go back to work anytime soon in her current condition.

She leaned back against the sofa. "You don't look like your mother at all."

"Nope. I'm practically a carbon copy of my dad. At least physically."

"But you're a lot like your mom. Did you know that?"

He sipped his brandy. The rain had started back up and was pattering against the skylight just above them. The white cat jumped up on the sofa and made a nest in his lap.

"It takes a while, Jeremy."

"What does?"

"Getting over the pain of loss." Robbie closed her eyes. Her head rested against his shoulder. "I still haven't gotten over losing my own mother."

Jeremy slid his arm around her. She snuggled against him. In her hair, he could smell the day's exertion mixed with violets.

"I miss her so much. And now I've lost Rachel, too."

The rain picked up force and pounded against the skylight in rhythmic waves.

"I'm here," Jeremy said.

"Yes, you are." She touched his cheek.

Her eye was practically swollen shut, but she was still beautiful. Gently, he took her hand away from his face. They were friends — just friends.

"Sometimes the hurt gets so bad, I don't know what to do," she said.

"I know, Robbie."

She pressed closer to him. "The rain," she said sleepily. "Do you like the rain?"

"Sometimes."

"I like the way it sounds when I'm inside. It makes me feel safe." She burrowed her face into shirt. "I feel safe with you, Jeremy. Did you know that?"

He took the glass out of her hand and put it on the coffee table next to his. "You should get some sleep now."

"Stay with me tonight." She took his hands between hers.

Her hands were warm. So warm. "It's late, Robbie. You've had a rough night."

She pulled his face toward her. Her lips rooted against his. Warm and soft. "Please," she said.

"Oh God, Robbie." The candle guttered and the shadows against the wall grew. "You don't know how much I want to."

"Then stay with me."

He kissed her fingertips.

"Please, Jeremy."

He drew her against him and stroked her hair. The cat jumped out of his lap.

"Close your eyes," he whispered.

"Make love to me," she said.

"Shhh," he said, stroking her hair. "Shhh."

It was still raining when Jeremy pulled onto Lotus Island. A drizzle that barely justified the windshield wipers, but enough to make the roads hazardous. He'd passed two accidents on the way home from Robbie's house. As Jeremy had driven by the flashing emergency lights, he had slowed down more than he might have a few months ago when he still smugly believed he and everyone else who populated his little world were invincible.

Robbie had fallen asleep after two, but he'd sat with her for another hour or so. He had shifted her position so she was stretched out on the sofa and left a second pillow under her leg to keep it elevated. He kissed her forehead before he left. He yearned for her, but it wasn't right. Tomorrow she would be devastated. How ironic. If he hadn't cared about her so much, he would gladly have made love to her. But he couldn't risk losing her friendship. He'd already lost so much else.

He pulled the Lexus into the driveway. His attention was caught by a strange configuration of shadows near the Corvair.

The driver's door was open. The dome light wasn't on, but that made sense. The battery often lost its charge. But why was the door open?

Something dark and substantial was hanging out of the open car door like a rolled carpet.

He turned over the inert form. A cry of shock roared out of him. "Noooo."

Marina's head fell backward from where her throat had been slit. Her eyes were open as though she'd been startled and her small round mouth was pursed in surprise.

Marina. No, not Marina.

He rested her head on his lap. Her dark sweatshirt was soaked through with blood. The hood was pulled up over her hair, but a few bronze strands had escaped. "Marina, who did this to you?"

Marina's cheek was cold. Blood no longer flowed from the gaping slit in her neck. Her body was rigid. She must have been killed hours ago.

The police. He had to call the police. Someone had murdered Marina.

He gently lowered Marina to the ground. He took off his jacket, rolled it up, and placed it under her head like a pillow. Why had she come here tonight?

Vaguely, he was aware of a car stopping, someone's horrified voice, a door slamming, then the car screeching off.

Jeremy stroked Marina's hair under the hooded sweatshirt. He held her hand. So stiff. So unlike his Marina. Blood from her cut artery had sprayed over her chin and cheeks.

The car door. The door of the Corvair was open. Had she put something in the car?

Jeremy tentatively peered inside. The mess of fabrics didn't make any sense to him. Then he recognized her canvas satchel. It had been sliced open, its contents strewn over the driver's seat.

The blanket. The Peruvian blanket she'd brought from her childhood home. That they had made love on so many times. It had been folded, but now was crumpled and stained with blood. She'd brought him the blanket? Why?

On the seat was a small, red metal box. A toolbox. He felt its weight in his hands. He'd bought the Father's Day present when he was thirteen. "This is great, Jeremy," his father had said. "Tools-to-go."

So his dad had left the toolbox at Marina's place. He expected to feel a surge of anger, but the knowledge of his father's love affair with Marina no longer seemed important. Marina was dead. They were both dead.

He put the toolbox down and shook out the blanket. The damp wool released a smell that brought him back to another time and place. Damp wool and sweat and cooking grease and Marina's fluttering tongue.

Why would someone have wanted to kill her?

A white envelope fell from the folds, landing in a pool of blood. "JEREMY" it said in all capital letters. He wiped it off against his jeans and shoved it in his pocket just as he heard the sound of sirens. Flashing lights appeared on his street.

The rain was coming down hard now. He thought of Elise hiding behind the curtain of rain when he'd found her at the park hours earlier, the hood of her sweatshirt up over her hair.

He looked back down at Marina, the dark hood framing her face like a nun's habit. And with a jolt of recognition, he realized Marina hadn't been the intended victim.

Elise was.

Chapter 45

The next few hours were a jumble for Jeremy. People coming, going, asking questions, taking photos. He remembered perversely the family photos of the four of them. "Okay, everyone. On the count of three," his father would shout, the timer blinking as he raced back to his family throwing his arms around his wife and daughter while Jeremy stood off by himself, "everyone smile."

But these pictures of Marina wouldn't make it into anyone's photo album.

Judy Lieber touched his arm. "Sorry I got here so late. I was at my son's house in the Keys when I got the call."

She had a son? Somehow he'd pictured her working 24/7, no family, no outside commitments. Just being a detective. But that's exactly what he'd done with his own parents, imagining their lives revolved around him alone.

"Why don't we go somewhere quieter?" She led him away from the crowd of curious neighbors and the crime-scene crew out to the back patio.

The sky was lightening to the east, a pale crisp blue that seemed incongruous with the blur in Jeremy's own head. The rain had stopped. When had that happened?

"I know Detective Kuzniski has already asked you questions," Lieber was saying, "but I prefer speaking to you myself." She was wearing old jeans and a sweatshirt, as though she'd been too rushed to change into her customary detective clothes.

He was suddenly itching for a cigarette. The unfiltered kind Marina had introduced him to — that he'd stopped smoking when he'd discovered her deception.

"What do you think she was doing here?" Lieber asked. "The blanket, the toolbox — do they mean anything to you?"

"I think." His voice caught in his throat. "I think she meant to say good-bye to me."

Lieber glanced at the brownish smudge on his pants. "Did you see her? Talk to her?"

"I wasn't home when she got here."

"Where were you?"

"With Robbie Ivy, one of the auditors at my mom's firm."

"I know who Robbie is."

"Someone tried to kill her."

"Robbie?" Lieber widened her eyes. "That's a pretty extreme statement."

"She was in the PCM file room. A cabinet toppled over — the one with the Castillo Enterprises audit papers. It crushed her."

"Crushed her?"

"Well almost. It hit her head and broke her ankle. I took her to the hospital, then back to her house."

"So she's okay."

"Pretty much. She's on painkillers. She'll probably sleep through most of today."

"And what makes you think the falling cabinet was deliberate? Did she see someone push it?"

"No, but it was weighted to fall. When I pulled it up off her, it felt like the top drawer had been loaded down with lead."

"You confirmed this?" She was taking notes copiously. "Did you see the lead?"

"No." He was annoyed with himself for not following through. "I needed to get Robbie to the hospital."

"That was the right thing to do, Jeremy." She kept writing. "Can you give me the exact location of the file cabinet?"

"Not exact. It was about halfway back into the file room. You'll see it out of line. And Robbie was bleeding, so there should be blood on the floor."

She glanced again at his pants pocket. "And you believe your parents' murder is somehow connected to the incident in the file room?"

"I'm sure of it."

"Why?"

"Because Robbie was getting closer to the answer. We'd been in the file room the other night. Someone booby-trapped the file cabinet knowing either Robbie or I would be back to look through the old Castillo audit papers."

"Then what about Marina? Did the murderer also believe Marina was onto him? And how could he possibly know Marina would be coming here tonight?"

"It wasn't Marina he intended to kill."

"What do you mean?"

"He thought Marina was Elise."

Lieber stopped writing. She pushed her hair away from her eye. "I know you believe the murderer has targeted Elise, but you need to help me out here, Jeremy. How could he have made that mistake?"

"The sweatshirt. Elise was wearing a dark hooded sweatshirt, just like the one Marina had on. And they all saw her wearing it."

"Who are 'they'?"

"On the yacht, when she found the papers, Elise was wearing a hooded sweatshirt. Enrique and Liliam Castillo and Bud and Irv all saw her."

Lieber finished writing something on her pad and closed it. She seemed to be in a rush. "You've been a big help. Why don't you go to your grandfather's house and get some rest? I'll try to get some more cars over there to keep an eye on things."

"I think I'll just stay here."

She shook her head in that disapproving way his mother had, put the pad into her handbag, and made her way through the backyard to the front of the house. He heard her car pull out and speed away.

He was dizzy when he stood up. Dizzy, sick, disoriented. A lot like he'd felt when he'd come home after his parents had been killed. He stumbled past the crowd of neighbors who stood behind the yellow crime-scene tape. They were staring at him, but he didn't turn to meet their eyes. What were they thinking? A cursed house? A cursed family? Three deaths — murders — in less than two months.

Why weren't they stoning him? "Get out of our neighborhood! Leave us alone with your blood, violence, and drama."

He tripped as he walked. Drunk. They must think he's drunk.

"Jeremy." Out of the corner of his eye, he could make out Liliam and Enrique Castillo. He quickened his pace.

There was a crime-scene group gathered around an old yellow Toyota a short distance from the park. Marina's car. She'd left it here. Had the murderer seen her walking from the park and thought it was Elise leaving her hiding place in the banyan tree?

Jeremy stepped through the soggy park ground, wet leaves sticking to his sneakers. Dizzy. He was so dizzy. He crawled into the "grotto" where he and Elise had huddled together the evening before. It was damp and smelled too fresh, like someone had tilled dirt and thick red worms, exposing what should have been kept buried.

He rested his head against a protruding root. A ray of morning light pushed past the dense trees and found its way into his hiding place.

Marina's letter seemed to be throbbing against his leg like the telltale heart in the Edgar Allen Poe story.

The folded envelope was stuck together. He pulled the two corners apart. Marina's blood had spread from the crease outward creating a symmetrical pattern, like a Rorschach test. It reminded Jeremy of butterfly wings.

And he thought about the butterfly tattoo at the base of her neck. How he would lick it and taste her salty sweat. He tore open the sealed envelope. Sealed with her own saliva just hours before. He pictured her small round mouth, the tiny crease between her eyebrows, her wild, wonderful hair.

Oh Marina. Oh God.

The letter was written on yellow legal paper in her all-caps handwriting. How familiar it was to him. All those charts listing suspects and motives. Had she really intended to help him or had it simply been the spider's way of keeping the fly in her web?

Mon amour:

I'm going away. That will be a big relief to you. Perhaps I should have left sooner. When your father had wanted me to go. At least I would have spared you the pain I've caused you.

I cannot leave without telling you some things about your father. Yes, he was a man, like most men, who didn't have the strength to resist a woman's seduction. But ultimately, he did. And not because of your mother or his marriage. No, Jeremy. Your father was no saint, but he couldn't bear the thought of disappointing you. Of losing your respect should you ever learn of his human weakness.

He cared about you more than you realize. It was you he was always talking about. Yes, sometimes in frustration, but mainly with pride. He once said. "My son has the character to become the man I've been too weak to be."

He loved you, Jeremy.
Marina

Jeremy squeezed his eyes shut. His father hadn't really said that. Marina had just been trying to fix what she had destroyed between him and his father.

He loved you, Jeremy.

But he knew the letter was the truth. His father had loved him. But that still wasn't enough to numb the hurt.

Chapter 46

Liliam had decided on a black St. John's knit suit with gold buttons after rejecting a low-cut cashmere sweater set and a pastel silk dress. Neither the sex kitten nor the ingénue seemed the right choice under the circumstances. Batting her eyelashes and faking tears wouldn't achieve her purpose. She was playing for keeps this time.

She waited with Dwight in the alcove outside the PCM partners' offices. He was picking at the bandage over his nose like a nervous child. Had she made a mistake involving him? Certainly not. People tended to underestimate her, but Liliam always had things well in hand.

That's why she'd asked Dwight to draw up the papers weeks ago. She didn't know when she'd have the opportunity to set her plan in motion, but she had wanted to be ready when the time came. And now, it had.

"They'll be with you in just a moment," Bud's secretary said, appearing noiselessly from around the corner. "Can I get you anything, Mrs. Castillo?" Gladys, in her outdated glasses, looked straight through Dwight as though he were invisible. "Coffee? A soft drink?"

"How kind of you to offer, Gladys, but I'm fine. And again, thank you. I know I'm intruding without an appointment."

"Mr. McNally and Mr. Luria are always happy to make time for you, Mrs. Castillo."

The door to Bud's office opened and the firm's managing partner, looking crisp and energetic, filled the hallway with his presence. "Liliam, what an unexpected pleasure." Bud took her hand in both of his. "Dwight, nice to see you, too. Why don't you both come into my office? Irv's already here." Bud glanced at his assistant. "Thank you, Gladys. Hold our calls, please."

Irv, looking sullen and gray as though he'd binged on prunes, had the good grace to stand and acknowledge Liliam's presence when she entered the room.

"Nice shiner," Bud said to Dwight. "I'd hate to see the other guy's fist."

"My nephew," Dwight said, settling himself into a chair.

"Jeremy hit you?"

"I was worried about his sister and went to check on her. My nephew attacked me because I let myself in."

"You have a key to the Stroeb's house?"

"Several, actually, from when I had the locks changed. And now I'll probably have this damn tattoo the rest of my life. " He opened his hand, revealing the outline of a key branded into his palm. "Look at this." He covered the outline precisely with a silver key he'd taken from his pocket. Liliam had seen his little performance before, but Bud seemed fascinated.

"He practically broke my hand."

"How terrible." Bud leaned forward and picked the key up out of Dwight's hand. He examined it, placed it back over its outline, then picked it up again and twirled it through his fingers.

"What a mistake his parents made naming him as guardian."

Liliam cleared her throat.

"I'm sorry," Dwight said. "These are my problems."

"Well," said Bud. "I'm sure you'll work things out." He turned his attention to her. "So Liliam, I understand you're here on urgent business."

"Enrique's left," she said.

Bud cocked his head and scowled slightly. "What do you mean?"

"Packed his bags and left. And not just an overnight bag. Two large suitcases."

"When was this?" Bud's voice was even. She couldn't tell if he was concerned.

"Some time this morning. After they found that dead girl at the Stroebs' house."

"Fuck," Irv said.

"Did he say anything?" Bud said, ignoring his loutish partner. "Where he was going? Why?"

"Not a word. I didn't even realize he was gone until I returned home from the gym. Then I went up to our bedroom and sensed something was wrong. I opened his closets and found his clothes and the luggage missing."

"No note?" Bud asked. "Anything to indicate where he went?"

"I'm sure he's gone to the Olympus Grande. It's always been his obsession."

Irv looked over at Bud, who ignored the glance.

"Ordinarily," Liliam said, "I wouldn't be concerned. Except this time, I don't think he's coming back."

"What makes you say that?" Bud asked.

"He hasn't been himself since the murders. I think he's had a breakdown and I'm worried. Not just for me and Carlos — we can take care of ourselves — but for the company. I'm worried about Castillo Enterprises."

"That's very selfless of you, Liliam," Bud said.

"Castillo Enterprises is important to me. I don't know if you realize this, Bud, Irv, but I've been the wind beneath Enrique's wings. I'm the reason Castillo Enterprises is what it is today."

"I've never minimized your role in the success of the company, Liliam," Bud said. "I know about your tireless work at SWEET, your zealousness in encouraging your husband's endeavors."

Liliam wasn't sure whether he was bullshitting her, but she smiled. "Thank you, Bud. In any event, what was Enrique thinking? That the company will run itself in his absence?"

Bud looked disturbed. "So you believe Castillo Enterprises is at risk?"

"Very much so," Liliam said. "It's apparent that Enrique doesn't care about the survival of Castillo Enterprises. I think if it were up to him, he'd be happy to see the company his father built ruined. I can't let that happen."

Bud was sitting up straight. "What do you have in mind?"

"I'd like you to support me as president and CEO of Castillo Enterprises."

Irv shook his head almost imperceptibly.

"I've taken the liberty of asking Dwight to prepare the relevant papers." Dwight handed her a blue-sheathed packet, which she placed in her lap beneath her folded hands, acting a composure she certainly didn't feel.

Bud rubbed his chin, as though considering something. He glanced down at the chess set on the corner of the desk. "Y'all play?" he asked.

Instinctively, she smiled.

"Chess," he said.

"Oh. I'm afraid chess was never my game."

Bud gave a little half smile. "Well then, how about letting me have a look see at those papers?"

He was expressionless as he read, turning each page slowly.

"What we're trying to do here —" Dwight said.

Bud held up his hand to silence him and continued reading. "These documents transfer majority ownership of Castillo Enterprises from Enrique to you, Liliam."

"That's correct."

"Now Liliam, don't get me wrong — I'd like to help if I

could — but it seems to me this is something between you and your husband."

"You're the only one he'll listen to, Bud. You and Irv," she said, trying to be polite. "Please, won't you go to St. Mary's and talk to him? Persuade him that it's the best solution for everyone?"

"These papers would give you complete control of the company," Bud said. "Are you sure that's what you want? My mama always said, 'Don't go eatin' little brown nuggets thinkin' they be chocolate.'"

"I'm prepared for the bad as well as the good. It's my son's future."

Bud closed the packet of papers. "Irv and I need to discuss this."

"Of course," she said, trying to hide her disappointment.

Bud patted Dwight on the back and shook Liliam's hand at the door. "I'll be in touch with you very soon."

She lifted her chin, as she imagined her forebears would have done under the circumstances. "You know you and PCM will have my undying loyalty."

Bud turned a hand-carved chess piece over in his hands. Mammoth ivory. The finest. The ivory was hard, yet fragile. If he dropped it, it would shatter irreparably. But he wouldn't drop it. Bud hadn't gotten where he was by dropping things.

And now, as often happened when he laid out the pieces strategically on the board, a solution had presented itself. Who would have imagined — Liliam Castillo, a knight in shining armor? A knight with no interest in protecting her king.

"So what do you think, Irv? Time for a changing of the guard?"

Irv's hands were palsied, a sign that he was long overdue for a drink. "You do what you want. I'm finished with this business."

Bud put down the chess piece. "Care for some, Irv?" Bud said, opening his credenza and holding out a bottle of Drambouie like a cube of sugar for a horse.

Irv stood up. "I'm going back to my office."

Bud left the bottle on the far corner of his desk. "Come on, Irv. Come with me to St. Mary's. Help me persuade Enrique to turn over his company to Liliam."

"I said I was finished. I'm not going anywhere."

"Sit down, Irv." Bud scrutinized his partner. There'd been a time Irv could have put Bud in checkmate, but that was many years ago. Now, Irv was simply a blight on the firm's image. Rachel had been right about that. "So I suppose you're willing to let Enrique prevail? Willing to let him get away with murder?"

"What are you talking about?"

Bud took the strap off its hook and slid it through his fingers. The strap his daddy had used to teach him that there were certain things in life he needed to avoid at all costs. "I spoke with the detectives this afternoon. They called after Enrique fled the country in his private jet. It's apparent to them that Enrique left because of that girl's murder."

"They think he killed her? What business could he have had with Danny Stroeb's graduate assistant?"

"That's the thing. They believe she was killed in error. That Elise was his intended victim."

"Impossible."

"She found the transfer files on his yacht. Easy to imagine that he believed Elise connected them and him to her parents' murders."

"What are you saying? That Enrique killed the Stroebs?" Irv shook his head. "Impossible."

"Impossible? You know what Rachel would have discovered when she got to the Olympus. And so did Enrique."

Irv stood back up, teetering. "I'm leaving."

"He was once in love with her. Come on, Irv, don't give me that look. Everyone knew how they felt about each other. And with his macho Latin ego, do you think he could have handled Rachel seeing him for the failure he really was?"

"It's not possible."

"Think about it, Irv. Are you willing to let the man who murdered Rachel enjoy his memories on his private island?"

Irv brushed past him, picking up the bottle of Drambouie. "I want nothing more to do with this."

Bud laid the strap down flat on his desk. "And here, I always thought Rachel meant more to you than that."

Chapter 47

Jeremy awoke with a start. He was lying fully dressed on his bed. He checked his watch. 7:45. The brightness coming through the closed shades told him it was a.m., not p.m. He'd slept straight through since early yesterday.

His body was sore as though he'd been in a fight. He sat up, resting his elbows on his knees as he hung his head. Dried mud and leaves were stuck onto his sneakers.

The park. He'd gone to the park and read Marina's letter. Then he had just sat there. In the grotto. It had to have been for hours. He remembered coming home, passing the tow truck with his father's Corvair, going up to his room.

Jeremy heard voices downstairs. Tired footsteps climbed the staircase. A soft knock on the open bedroom door. "Jeremy?"

"Hi, Grandpa."

"Elise was worried." His grandfather leaned against the door jamb, as though needing the support. "Detective Lieber told us she'd seen you. That you were spending the night here at the house. But your sister was worried."

Jeremy hugged his grandfather. "I'm okay, Grandpa."

"I told Elise we'd stop by to see you on the way to school."

"That's good. Where is she?"

His grandfather looked around him, seemingly surprised that

Elise wasn't standing beside him. "Elise?" he called out. "That's strange. She was so anxious to see you."

He and Jeremy hurried down the steps.

Elise was in the front foyer, standing perfectly still.

"Hey," Jeremy said softly. "Are you all right, Ellie?"

She seemed to be unaware of her surroundings.

"Elise?"

She blinked her eyes, as though coming awake. "Oh God, Jeremy."

"What is it?"

"I-I remembered."

"What? Remembered what?"

"Just now. I was standing here and the house was so quiet and I heard his voice."

"He's not here, Ellie," Jeremy said. "The murderer's not here."

His grandfather was shaking his head. "We never should have come."

Jeremy took Elise by the arm, but she pushed him away. "You don't understand. I know he's not here now. But I remembered. I remembered what he said."

"You remember his words?"

She nodded. She was trembling, an excited trembling, like when a kid's had too much soda or chocolate. "Your-your mama's calling you."

"What?"

"That's what he said. 'Your mama's calling you.'"

"What on earth?" his grandfather said. "Who would say such a thing?"

Elise's eyes were glassy.

"We'd better go, Elise," his grandfather said. "I'm not as fast a driver as you, and you don't want to be late for school."

"That's a good idea, Grandpa," Jeremy said.

"I need to stay here," said Elise.

"Why in the world?" his grandfather said.

"There's something I'm almost remembering, but I only feel it here. In the house." She tightened her arms around her as though chilled. "I know it's connected to my nightmares."

"Why would you want to awaken your nightmares?" his grandfather asked.

"Because I can't stand the feeling of almost remembering. It's so close to the surface. I, I keep touching it, but then I lose it. Please, Grandpa. Please let me stay."

His grandfather's eyes begged Jeremy for help.

"You have to get to school, Ellie," Jeremy said. "Why don't you come back later?"

"That's a good idea," his grandfather said, herding Elise from the room. He glanced back at Jeremy, his expression so distraught that Jeremy turned away.

The house was silent once again, but Jeremy felt as though conch shells were up against his ears and the sound of crashing waves filled his head.

Your mama's calling you.

It was one of them — Enrique, Liliam, Bud, or Irv. He just needed to figure out which one. Should he call Detective Lieber? Maybe she could put it all together. But Jeremy couldn't do that. He had to see this through himself.

Jeremy needed to make him bleed. To writhe in pain. To suffer like an animal at the bottom of a pit as his flesh was consumed by scavengers.

Suffer. He had to make their murderer suffer.

He opened the door to his parents' bedroom. The smell was

still wrong. No matter how thoroughly the room had been cleaned, their splattered blood would have seeped through the porous walls and into the wooden floorboards.

Jeremy sat on the edge of their bed and slid his hand under the pillow. It was where he had left it, soft and small, like a child's stuffed animal. He held up the red bandanna in the weak light, knowing it contained his hair — his promise to his parents.

They were watching him, trying to tell him something. What was it? He understood Elise's need to be in the house. Because here, they still existed. If Jeremy could only listen hard enough, he could hear them.

Your mama's calling you.

He slipped the bandanna into his pocket and went to his father's closet. The Smith & Wesson 9-millimeter automatic was still in the place his father had shown him when he was fifteen.

He remembered the thrill. His father taking the gun from a hard plastic case hidden between some blankets and handing it to Jeremy. He had never imagined there had been a gun in his parents' bedroom closet.

"I'm going to teach you how to shoot and reload this thing, Jeremy. But I don't want you saying a word about it to your mother."

No chance of that. A secret between Jeremy and his father was far more powerful than any guilt about not telling his mother.

His father had squeezed his shoulder. "You may be young, but I know you're responsible. I trust you, Jeremy. I trust you to take care of your family."

Jeremy ran his hands over the gun. He'd forgotten that scene until this moment. His father had once trusted him. Believed in him. How much he wanted to forgive his father for all that had happened. How much he wanted him back — alive and well, with all his flaws.

My son has the character to become the man I've been too weak to be.

Jeremy took the cartridges from their box on the shelf and loaded the gun.

Chapter 48

Robbie rested against her crutches, waiting for a taxi outside her townhouse. It was seven forty-five a.m. and her entire body ached. She felt as though she'd been bounced around in a clothes dryer for hours. But the fact was, she had slept most of the day yesterday. The Percocet had dulled her senses, but unfortunately not her memory.

How could she have come on to Jeremy like that?

There had been no calls in the almost thirty hours of her deep sleep. PCM, she understood. They often lost track of their auditors, not knowing which client engagement the auditor might be working at on any particular day. So they had no reason to wonder where she was or be concerned by her absence. But she'd been hoping Jeremy would call. Hoping he'd make light of the other night. But he hadn't, and that could mean only one thing. That she'd stepped over a boundary and irrevocably damaged their friendship.

She studied her cell phone. Should she call him? But what would she say? That she was sorry about the other night? Wouldn't Jeremy already know that? But if he did, why hadn't he come by to see her or at least call?

Two newspapers still in their yellow plastic wrappers were lying on the lawn. She threw them behind some bushes, wondering if anything important had happened in the outside world while she had slept.

No. She wouldn't call. It would be too awkward. And then he might ask what she was doing now. And she couldn't tell him she'd decided to go to the office despite her condition. He'd surely be disgusted with her then, if he wasn't already.

There was honking in the street. The taxi had come.

The PCM offices were quiet when she arrived ten minutes later. Although she lived close by, she couldn't drive with her broken right ankle. She could smell coffee brewing and hear joking voices coming from down the hall. She propelled herself toward the partners' offices on her crutches, sweating and breathing hard as she went. She couldn't believe how much work it was to thrust her body weight forward.

She passed Gladys's desk, relieved to see she wasn't there. Although it was early, she was hoping Bud would be in and she could speak with him without his assistant running interference.

The accident had brought Robbie an epiphany. What was she doing chasing paper? The answer wasn't going to be hidden in a pile of old reports. Rachel had already gone that route and had concluded the only way to find the truth was to go to the Olympus Grande.

But the other night had also changed Robbie. There had been a sense of release when she'd asked Jeremy to make love to her. She was following her instincts and not overanalyzing things the way she usually did. While the lack of control disturbed her, there was also something thrilling about it. And, like a junkie, she craved another fix.

Robbie caught her breath as she stopped outside Bud's office. She knocked. There was no answer. "Damn," she muttered.

"Jesus, Robbie." Bud's voice surprised her from behind. "What the hell happened to you?"

She touched the bruise on her forehead. What a mess she must look like. But at least Bud gave no indication he knew about the file room accident. "I fell down some stairs," she said. "At a friend's house."

"You look like hell. What are you doing at the office? Shouldn't you be in bed?"

"I'm okay. Just a broken ankle. I can work."

He shook his head and opened the door to his office. He was less formally dressed than usual, in a casual shirt and sports jacket.

"Do you mind if I speak with you for a few minutes?" she said, hopping after him.

He glanced down at his watch. "I wasn't even planning on coming in this morning."

"It's kind of important."

Bud looked impatient. "Then why don't we set up an appointment for tomorrow late afternoon? I wouldn't want to rush you."

"Actually." Robbie struggled to hoist herself forward, closer to his desk.

Bud was thumbing through some papers, found the ones he was looking for, and slipped them into his briefcase. The worn leather strap that usually hung on the hook behind his desk was missing. Robbie had always found its presence disturbing.

"It's about the Olympus."

Bud gave her an odd look. "What about the Olympus?"

"The site visits."

He waited for her to continue.

"I was thinking now that Rachel's gone, National may be concerned with the independence issue, again."

"Meaning?" He remained standing.

"They may want to bring in another partner. To replace Rachel. You know, so there's no perception of impropriety."

"And let me understand this, Robbie. Were you going to remind National of their obligation?"

"No, of course not. I'm just concerned they may realize this on their own. Bringing in someone new would be a terrible inconvenience to Castillo Enterprises. I thought there may be a way to placate National, at least for now."

"And your suggestion is?" He glanced again at his watch.

"Well, the biggest area of exposure is the Olympus Grande. It's Castillo Enterprises's major source of profits. The problem is, no one other than you and Irv has done a physical review of the property in years." Her upper lip was perspiring, but she didn't dare wipe it. "I think if someone else visits the property, that would eliminate National's concern."

Bud sat down in his chair, carefully adjusting his jacket so it wouldn't wrinkle. "Why don't you have a seat, Robbie?"

She hobbled over to the guest chair and awkwardly rested her crutches against it. The chess game that was always in progress on his desk was in its final stages with only a few pieces still standing.

"You bring up some interesting points." He folded his fingers, no longer in a rush. "Did you have someone in mind to do this independent site visit?"

"I was thinking I should." There was a nervous palpitation in her chest. The controlling side of her brain was battling with the newly ascendant impulsive side.

"You think you should," Bud said flatly.

"I'm most familiar with the client. I'm senior on the job, under you and Irv."

"It's hilly with rustic paths; how would you get around?"

"I'd manage." The two feuding sides of her brain had worked a compromise. First, she'd get Bud to agree. Then, she'd insist on bringing a couple of staff people along with her. She certainly wasn't reckless enough to go to the Olympus Grande by herself.

He turned his Mont Blanc pen around in his thick fingers. "Your concern about National is valid, Robbie. And I'm impressed with your offer, but I can't let you go in your condition. You might hurt yourself."

"You don't have to worry." Her voice was stronger. She'd almost worn him down. "I can take care of myself."

He closed his briefcase. "I'm sorry, Robbie. I can't let you do it." He stood up slowly, as though weighing something. "I have a meeting this morning, then I'm flying out to St. Mary's. Enrique's already there and Irv will be joining us."

Robbie's stomach did a flip-flop. Today, Bud and Irv were meeting Mr. Castillo at the Olympus. It was too tempting an opportunity. And no one would dare pull any hanky-panky with the others present.

"Let me go with you. Please, Bud."

"That's impossible. We have private business to attend to. In fact, I shouldn't have mentioned the meeting to you. I'd appreciate it if you wouldn't discuss it with anyone."

"Please, Bud. I'll stay out of the way."

He glanced down at the chessboard. Something seemed to have captivated him. He moved the black bishop and removed the white queen from the board. He laid the queen down carefully, then looked up at Robbie with a smile.

Chapter 49

Jeremy checked the time as he pressed down on the accelerator, edging between cars, trying to outrun the rush hour traffic. eight twenty-five.

I-95 southbound was moving at twenty miles an hour. He should have called her yesterday. Regardless of how messed up his own life was, he should have called her. He picked up his cell phone and dialed Robbie's number. Still no answer. Maybe she was asleep. At least, that's what he hoped.

He turned off the highway and navigated through the street traffic. Not much faster, but at least he had a sense of progress. At eight forty-five, he turned onto her block.

Her car was there. Okay. Good. She was home. He knocked on the front door. Could she hear it in her bedroom? He doubted she was still sleeping on the sofa. He rang the doorbell and waited. He tried again. Nothing.

He walked through the overgrown plants on the side of the house and tapped on her bedroom window. The blinds were closed so he couldn't see in. "Robbie," he shouted. "Robbie? Wake up."

He listened for any sound. A white cat sidled up to him, rubbing against his leg. Robbie's cat. He tried to remember. Was the cat inside or out when he left her the other night? In. Definitely in. Which meant sometime since he'd left her sleeping, over twenty-four hours ago, Robbie had gotten up and at least opened the door to let the cat out.

Something yellow was lying between the bushes and the house. Newspapers. A strange place for the newsboy to throw them. He pulled off the plastic wrappers and checked the dates. Today's and yesterday's. Had Robbie already seen them? Why were they in the bushes? Unless she'd thrown them there on her way out.

He banged on the front door again. She couldn't have gone to the office. Not after what had happened in the file room. How could he not have called and warned her?

And then, a taxi pulled up. Robbie got out. She hopped a few feet, balanced on her crutches. She gave Jeremy a tentative smile.

"Jesus, Robbie. Where've you been?"

"Excuse me?" Her face changed at his tone of voice. She brushed past him and fumbled to unlock the door.

"I asked where you've been."

"I heard you. And I'd like to know where the hell you've been and why you're showing up now like a raving lunatic on my doorstep."

"I need to talk to you."

"No, you don't. Apparently, you need to shout at me. And you know something, Jeremy? I don't need to be shouted at." She got the door open.

He tried to follow her in, but she pushed the door closed catching him in the doorway. "Please, Robbie. A lot's happened since your accident. You may be in danger. Let me in."

Robbie looked skeptical, but she took her weight off the door. She hopped into the living room, dropped her crutches on the tile floor, and collapsed on the sofa. The bump on her forehead had receded and her eyelid was normal size, but a bluish bruise covered the upper side of her face. Robbie and Elise, both injured. How come he couldn't take better care of the women he cared about? Then he thought about Marina.

"Did you watch the news?" he asked.

A look of alarm replaced the one of annoyance. "Something happened?"

"He killed again."

"What? What are you talking about?"

It was still difficult for him to say it aloud. "He killed my father's graduate assistant. In the driveway. At my house. He slashed her throat."

"My God. No."

"She was lying there dead when I got home. After I brought you here from the hospital."

"Oh Jeremy. But why? Why would he have killed her?"

"He thought she was Elise."

Robbie covered her mouth to stifle a cry. "Is she okay? Is Elise okay?"

"Yeah. But I was worried you might not be. That the killer might go after you again."

"Again? What do you mean again?"

He felt drained suddenly, like coming down off a high. He sat on the sofa next to her. Just like the other night.

Robbie took his hand. Warm, just like the other night.

"The file cabinet was weighted so it would fall on you or me if we went back to look for the Castillo reports."

Her face became pale. "It wasn't an accident?"

"No. That's why I needed to get to you. To warn you."

"To warn me." She seemed to be having difficulty processing this.

"He wants to stop us. He knew we were getting close."

The red candle he'd lit the other night had burned down and the coffee table was splattered with red wax. "Were we, Jeremy? Were we getting close?"

"Yes."

"You know something?" She straightened up. "You figured it out?"

"I know a little more. I just can't put it together."

"Tell me. Tell me what you know."

Robbie was back. She'd help him. Together, they'd figure it out.

"Elise was hanging out with Carlos on his parents' yacht," he said. "She found these hidden accounting papers."

"Accounting papers?"

"Yeah. Elise has this incredible memory. She described the way they were set up. There were columns with amounts, dates, and the column heading, 'Transfers to Corporate.' Then there were columns labeled EX, JR, VL."

Robbie shook her head. "That doesn't mean anything to me."

"But I'm sure there's a connection. Mr. and Mrs. Castillo, Bud, and Irv saw her with the papers. There was a scene, and Elise got frightened."

"The killer must think Elise put something together from the accounting records."

"That's why he tried to kill her." Jeremy looked down at his muddy sneakers. "But he got Marina by mistake."

The room was quiet except for the humming of the air conditioning. The cat meowed outside the front door. Robbie didn't seem to hear it.

"Why would legitimate accounting records be hidden?" she said. "They must be a second set of books."

"What do you mean?"

"I'm not sure. But it sounds like money laundering records where deposits from illegal operations were transferred to make them look legitimate. But EX, JR, VL?" She scraped the red wax off the glass tabletop with her fingernail. "I don't know what that means. EX? Exclusive?"

Somewhere in the back of his mind, Jeremy could hear Liliam Castillo's voice. *One of the most exclusive hotels in the world. Only villas and executive and junior suites. Regular people don't even know about it.*

Jeremy felt a rush. "It's the Olympus. That's it. But EX isn't for exclusive. It's for executive. Executive suites. EX, JR, VL — executive suites, junior suites, and villas." He shook his head, frustrated. "But why would Castillo Enterprises need to run a laundering operation when they were making so much money legally?"

"Were they? Most of Castillo Enterprises was losing money; only the Olympus was a major success. Successful enough to keep the entire company profitable and the stock price rising. "

"But what if there wasn't an Olympus?" Jeremy said, feeling a surge of excitement. "What if the hotel had been destroyed by hurricanes, like my mother had predicted?"

"Then the entire company would have collapsed," Robbie said. "Someone must have come up with an illegal business that was run through the Olympus's books as legitimate earnings."

"Something my mother would have discovered if she'd ever made it out there. That's why she was stopped."

"But by whom?" Robbie said. "Who killed them?" She chewed on her lip. "Enrique? Could it have been Enrique? He had the most to lose. So did his wife."

"They had a lot to lose," Jeremy said. It was finally coming together for him. "But so did someone else."

"Irv?"

"The only thing Irv was afraid of losing was his job. PCM was his life. So he'd be willing to play along with any scheme."

"So who was behind it?"

"Who masterminds everything?" Jeremy said. "The grand master."

"Bud?"

Jeremy nodded. "It makes sense that he would have come up with the laundering scheme."

"But why would Bud have done that?"

"Because Castillo Enterprises was his biggest client, generating huge audit fees, not to mention prestige for him and the firm. He couldn't afford to lose them."

She twisted her ring around her finger. "Bud's certainly smart enough; I just don't see the motivation for him to kill anyone."

"Really? If Castillo Enterprises came down, Bud would be discovered as being behind their illegal operations. Bud would be ruined along with PCM. Imagine the negative national publicity. You think Bud's ego could have handled that?"

"But you're still speculating. You have no proof. No witnesses."

"My sister saw the killer the night of the murders. She couldn't recognize him, but she remembered him saying, 'Your mama's calling you.'"

Robbie shook her head. "Anyone might have said that — Enrique, Irv."

"True, but Enrique or Irv say, 'your mom' or 'your mother.' I've heard them. Bud's the only one who says, 'your mama.'"

She took her ring off, put it back on, took it off. Why was she so nervous?

"Hey." He covered her hand with his own.

"Bud." She mumbled something, but he didn't understand her. "What?"

"That's where I was. This morning. I went to see him."

"Bud?"

"I tried to talk him into letting me go to the Olympus. I figured the only way we'd know what was really going on, was to fly out there."

"Jesus, Robbie."

"I thought he was going to say yes, but then he changed his mind. He told me he was going to St. Mary's today. He and Irv. Enrique's already there. He said not to tell anyone."

Jeremy's adrenaline was pumping.

"What, Jeremy?" Robbie looked alarmed.

"It's perfect."

"What? What are you thinking?"

"I'm going to St. Mary's."

"God, Jeremy. No. He knew I'd tell you. He wants you to follow him out there."

"Maybe."

"No, Jeremy. Don't do this. It's a trap."

Jeremy felt the weight of the gun against his thigh. "Don't worry, Robbie. It's only a trap when the prey doesn't know one's been set."

Chapter 50

Jeremy sat on the torn leather seat at the front of the shabby fishing boat, gasoline fumes mingling with the stench of old fish guts and salt water. The boat bobbed in the pristine green-blue water. The captain, whose leathery face was shaded by a dirty baseball cap, counted the American bills Jeremy had given him. Jeremy had brought plenty of cash, knowing credit cards wouldn't be the best medium of exchange for what he needed here in the Grenadines.

He'd flown from Miami to Grenada, the southernmost of the Grenadine Islands. In compliance with regulations, he had declared and checked the small bag, which contained his father's Smith & Wesson and a box of ammunition.

After his initial burst of purpose when he left Robbie's house and headed for the airport, he'd become jittery. Why was he going off to the ends of the earth to confront his parents' murderer? Was it that he needed to be absolutely certain that Bud had killed his parents? Robbie had been skeptical. And he'd already jumped to the wrong conclusion once before, believing Enrique had done it. Was the word "mama" enough to justify pulling the trigger? And what if Jeremy arrived on St. Mary's, and discovered a magnificent five-star hotel?

The captain had one hip on his chair, a dirty white sneaker planted against the helm. His triceps rose and fell beneath the loose skin on his arm as he languidly turned the wheel. He throttled up the engine. The mountain peaks of Grenada grew smaller and smaller as the boat continued into the broad expanse of the Caribbean. The water was a darker blue out here, with just a hint of green. In another hour or so, the sun would be setting. An hour. Just an hour.

In the distance, he could make out the shapes of islands rising from the sea — mounds of volcanic lava now covered with thick vegetation. St. Mary's hadn't been on any maps he had found back home, but the boat captain seemed to know exactly where it was.

"Is it much farther?" Jeremy asked.

"Eh?"

"Much farther. Is St. Mary's much farther?"

"Not much." The captain had a thick accent or maybe he just naturally slurred his words.

"Can you bring the boat in a back way?" Jeremy asked.

"Eh?"

"The back. I don't want to be seen."

The captain shook his head in annoyance. Jeremy wished he was better prepared, with more than the memory of the photo from his mother's workpapers to rely on. He didn't know how he would sneak onto St. Mary's, what time Bud was arriving, or what he would do when he finally came face-to-face with him. If Bud was, in fact, his parents' murderer.

He wondered if his uneasiness was some form of procrastination, the lack of willingness to accept responsibility his father had always accused him of.

The sound of piston airplane engines filled his ears. An old, battered DC-3 cargo plane rose from one of the hilly islands just in front of them.

The boat slowed. Purple, jutting cliffs loomed out of the clear water along the uneven coastline. White sandy beaches bordered the mound of green shrubs like a halo. The captain brought the boat into a cove and left the engine idling.

"St. Mary's?" Jeremy asked.

The captain nodded.

Jeremy's stomach knotted with apprehension. The gun was now in a pocket of his cargo pants.

He put on his backpack, climbed over the gunwale, and landed in a couple of feet of water. He sloshed through until he reached the sandy shore. A thin dirt path wound upward through the under-brush. The engine of the boat picked up speed. Jeremy turned to see the captain guide it out of the cove and into the open sea. Jeremy had told the captain to return the next day to pick him up. Would he think anything of it if Jeremy wasn't here? Would he bother report-ing it? Probably not.

After the first eight or ten feet in from the beach, Jeremy was surprised by how steep the path had become. The trail was rocky and uneven and wound back and forth across the south slope of the island. He could see the crest, but didn't seem to be getting any closer. He hadn't imagined from the photo in his mother's workpa-pers that the hills would be as steep and high as they were.

In the distance, the sound of engines grew louder. The high-pitched whine was no tramp cargo plane. A graceful white jet, prob-ably a private one, approached the island. Jeremy ducked so he couldn't be seen. From the sound, the plane was landing just ahead. Could Bud be on that plane?

Jeremy was almost at the ridge that ran across the top of the is-land. He pushed past the shrubs and stopped to catch his breath. The scene opened up before him. On either side were seemingly end-less fields of tall, delicate, dark green stalks. They wafted ever so slightly in the breeze. A man's deep laugh floated toward him. Two dark-skinned men stood together, talking in some unfamiliar dialect, rifles hanging from their shoulders. Guards. And the plants were familiar — marijuana. So the money laundering theory had been correct, but he still had a strange need to see what had become of the Olympus Grande.

Crouching until he got past the guards, Jeremy followed the ridge up a farther rise, hoping to gain a view of the entire island. Another ten minutes brought him to the summit. He climbed to the highest rock and surveyed the paradise that was St. Mary's.

The sight was dizzying. The endless blue sky blending with the blue-green sea. A lot like the sensation he'd experienced in Enrique's office.

To the east, he could make out an airstrip, a straight, level strip of grass. Several plain low buildings that looked like bunkers were nestled under a canopy of trees. Near them was a pallet of crates, probably dropped off by the cargo plane he'd seen leaving the island. So St. Mary's was probably also a transshipment point for drugs. Their operations were more extensive than he'd imagined. From his cover behind the bushes, Jeremy could see two white Lear jets. Bud's and Enrique's? Where were the two men now? Would Jeremy be able to confirm that Bud was the murderer and pull the trigger?

Beyond, built almost into the side of the steep hill, were more than a dozen run-down huts. From their prime location surrounding a sandy cove and overlooking the Caribbean, these could have once been posh villas. The Olympus. This was the Olympus! The collapsing, overgrown ruins were mostly uninhabitable. Thick leafy branches obscured his view. He parted them. And then he saw it. White columns rising toward the blue sky like reaching fingers. The temple from his mother's photograph. He pushed through the bushes to get a better view. Half a dozen pillars formed a semicircle on the ledge, which jutted out from the top of a cliff and overlooked the azure sea and purple rocks of the photo.

Something moved. A man rose from a stone bench in the center of the columns. A tall man with a silver beard. He was squinting at something and took a step back.

"Enrique, my amigo," Bud McNally called out. "I believe you and I have some things to talk about."

Chapter 51

Irv Luria struggled up the dirt path on the east side of St. Mary's. This was the shortest route up, but also the steepest. He kept losing his footing as his smooth-soled shoes slid on the loose pebbles. Stupid. He hadn't thought to bring a more sensible pair of shoes. He ignored the sting of cuts on his hands, his bruised knees and elbows, and the constricting pain in his ever-tightening shoes.

Sawtoothed and prickly plants spurred him on like a whip does a horse. With each slash, he moved a little faster. A little closer.

A short while ago, he had heard a jet overhead. That was how Irv had always traveled to the Olympus in the past, but this time, he had to arrive undetected. He'd flown to St. Vincent, found a derelict boat at the dock, then paid the captain a small fortune for transportation and a gun — the captain's own shotgun, a rusty thing that Irv questioned would even work. Now it banged against his back, suspended from a makeshift sling Irv had created from his belt. Every time he fell or slipped, it pounded against him, practically knocking the wind out of him. But on some level, the pain was reassuring, almost comforting. His own cross to bear.

Heat and dehydration slowed him down. He stopped for a sip of Drambouie from the hip flask he had filled back at St. Vincent. He knew it aggravated his thirst, but it also kept him numb.

Numb so he wouldn't have to think about Enrique Castillo. The man who had taken Rachel from him forever.

Irv was short of breath and sweating like a pig as he neared the summit. The path led over a flat gray rock that lay in the hill like a giant slide. He climbed up a few feet, but lost his footing and found himself rolling back down, the shotgun jabbing him in the ribs like an angry bayonet. His fall was broken by a large bush. A weight lifted from his back. The belt had come loose and the shotgun flew down the side of the mountain, out of Irv's sight.

He lay with his face in the dirt, almost lacking the will to get back up. He had gotten to the point that he believed nothing would ever matter to him again. Rachel, his protégée, his Mary, had risen within the firm, succeeding without him. And maybe that's when he sensed his uselessness. That his protestations about integrity and honor were nothing more than self-aggrandizing ravings. And that's when he had stopped caring. When he decided that nothing he said or did meant shit to anyone.

But now he knew that bastard had killed her. Killed her because she was the one with true integrity. Killed his Rachel. Irv tasted the dirt in his mouth and spit it out.

He eased himself up, brushing off his hands. He had one last chance to do something that mattered. And perhaps then he could leave life the way he'd always imagined. Like a meteor speeding toward the sun.

He opened the cap on his flask and poured the Drambouie onto the dry dirt. It left a dark stain, like a puddle of muddy piss. Then he threw the flask down the hill. It clanked against the rocks until it came to rest, and everything was silent.

Chapter 52

Jeremy watched from behind the thick bushes. He'd dropped his backpack in the undergrowth, taken his gun from the pocket of his cargo pants, and released the safety. Bud was a bit more than twenty feet away, talking to Enrique. A clear shot. Well, maybe for someone with more experience with firearms than Jeremy. His arms were shaking and he lowered the gun.

Even if he could hit him, was this what he wanted? To kill his parents' murderer without making him suffer? And what if he was mistaken? What if Bud wasn't the killer?

He'd wait. He'd wait until he was sure.

The wind was blowing from the west, carrying their voices toward him.

"So what are you planning to do, Enrique? Call the SEC? The police? Tell them you've been fronting a major drug route for the past few years?"

Enrique had his back to Bud and stared off toward the edge of the cliff. The sky had a pinkish cast; the sun had begun to set.

"I understand you might could run away from everything, Enrique," Bud was saying, "but have you given any thought to what happens to your son?"

"My son is none of your damn business."

Bud held up his hands. "Of course. Of course. But he's your

business. Do you really want him to go through life the son of a felon? His father a disgrace to his family and the community?"

"Why are you here, Bud? What do you want from me?"

"I have a solution."

"The last time you had a solution, I ended up turning my father's company into an opium den."

"This may suit your purposes somewhat better." Bud reached into his briefcase and pulled out a sheaf of papers with a blue cover. "These papers transfer your interest in Castillo Enterprises to your wife."

"You believe I'd give Liliam anything?"

"You can wash your hands of the whole dirty business."

"I already have."

"How? Come on, Enrique? By hiding out here? Why do you even care about this place? Because Rachel once came here with you? Did she go and promise to marry you? I remember that was the talk around the office."

"Shut up. Shut the hell up."

Jeremy tried to quiet his breathing.

"The only reason you went along with the drug scheme was because you hoped to make enough money to rebuild your Olympus," Bud said. "For Rachel. Everything you did was always about Rachel, wasn't it? Your grand house on Lotus Island, your impressive office building, and maybe one day, the Olympus."

Enrique stepped toward Bud, his fist raised. Bud didn't move. "She would have been disappointed coming here," Bud said. "Seeing what you had done."

"I didn't kill her," Enrique said.

"I know that. And the police do, too."

Enrique stiffened. "They know who did?"

Jeremy's heart was racing. Where was Bud going with this?

A ray of sun reflected off Bud's short silver-blond hair. There was a film of perspiration on his forehead. "It appears that Rachel's former mentor turned murderer."

"What are you saying? That Irv killed her? Impossible."

"I was shocked when the detectives came to me, trying to understand his motive. They asked if it was true that Rachel wanted him fired because he'd become a drunk."

"He would never have killed her."

Bud wiped his face with a handkerchief. "You never know about people, do you? Irv hasn't been himself these last few years. Once his protégée deserted him, all he had left was the firm. Then she wanted to take that from him too." Bud shook his head. "Irv was a desperate man. You never can tell what a desperate man's going to do."

Was this possible? Could Irv have murdered his mother? Jeremy's head spun. What was going on here?

Enrique was speaking so softly Jeremy couldn't make out his words.

"That's right," Bud said. "He killed her. Irv murdered Rachel. And now he's safe at PCM. He knows I would never ask him to resign, not with what he knows about our little enterprise here.

"Sign the papers, Enrique. Sign the papers so you can be free to do whatever you have to do. Sign them for your son, for Carlos. For the Castillo name." Bud held out the papers and a pen. "For Rachel."

"No," a voice shouted. Irv Luria emerged through the dense foliage. He was panting as sweat ran down his red cheeks. His shirt was soaked through and his black shoes were covered with dirt. Had he climbed up the side of the island as Jeremy had? "Don't sign anything," he was shouting. "This evil dies with you."

Enrique pulled the papers out of Bud's hand and rested them against the stone bench. He signed them with such force the pen could have torn through the paper.

Enrique and Irv stared at each other like a couple of enraged bulls, their eyeballs bulging.

Bud picked up the signed papers and took a step back.

Suddenly, everything made sense. A trick by the chess master. Bud had manipulated Enrique and Irv into believing the other was the murderer.

The two men charged each other, deadweight pressing against deadweight. Enrique was taller, but Irv stout and powerful. For an instant they seemed frozen in their crazed tug-of-war.

Jeremy pushed through the bushes.

"Over here, Jeremy," Bud called.

Jeremy clasped the gun in both hands and aimed, but nothing was holding still. It was as though someone was fast-forwarding a movie clip. Bud darted from column to column, swift as a fox. Enrique and Irv, crushing each other in a bear hug, lurched in front of Jeremy, blocking his shot.

"Murderer," Enrique shouted.

"Murderer," Irv shouted back.

"Stop," Jeremy screamed. "You're making a mistake."

Enrique swung his fist into Irv's face. It sounded like the popping of a champagne cork. Irv covered his nose, falling back a couple of steps. Jeremy tried to get in the middle, trying to stop them before they killed each other.

The sky had darkened and was smudged with orange. Bud's voice came from somewhere behind him. "What are you going to do, Jeremy? Check the king or lose both your bishops?"

Irv shoved Jeremy aside. "Get the fuck out of here." He flung Enrique against a column. Enrique tumbled to the ground. Then he was up, diving for Irv's legs, pulling him down. Punching his face while Irv writhed on the ground, his dusty black shoes flailing helplessly in the air.

Jeremy tried to pull Enrique off Irv, but Enrique flipped Jeremy over his shoulder, knocking the breath out of him. The gun went flying.

Irv was back up, blood spurting from his nose and mouth. He shoved Enrique. Enrique shoved him back. They were getting closer to the edge. They were going to kill each other. Jeremy rushed between them.

"Nice move, Jeremy," Bud called out. "I'll give Robbie your regards."

Enrique's blow fell on Jeremy's cheek.

"Stop," Jeremy shouted. They were at the edge. "Stop. He's lying."

Irv shoved Jeremy with such force that he slid a few feet, hitting his head on the stone bench. Blood ran into his eye. Jeremy got back up, stumbling as he went.

Enrique and Irv were locked in each other's arms near the edge of the mountain. The sun slipped below the horizon, turning the water and sky into spitting flames. The last rays of reddish light fell across their faces. The anger was gone. Only wretchedness remained. And then, as though on cue, the two men, still clutching each other, took several running steps toward the setting sun and dove off the side of the cliff.

Jeremy rushed to the edge. All he could see were the spreading shadows from the last few glints of daylight. And then he heard an airplane's engines. He looked up in time to see a Lear jet lift off from St. Mary's island.

Chapter 53

The plane floated away, a white bird swallowed by the darkness. It took a second for its significance to register on Jeremy. And when it did, he waved his arms wildly, blinded by blood. "Noooo," he shouted. "Noooo."

But it was for nothing. Bud was gone.

Jeremy staggered away from the edge of the mountain. He hadn't even been able to stop them. Two men who had fought to the death believing the other had murdered Rachel Stroeb. Two men who no longer had anything to live for. Would their bodies ever be found? Had they smashed against the rocks, torn to pieces for seagulls to eat? Or had their suicide dive taken them beyond, into the crystal clear Caribbean waters?

Two more deaths. That brought the tally to five: his parents, Marina, Irv, and Enrique.

He picked up his father's gun. The gun he was supposed to use to protect his family. He slipped it into his pants pocket. Against the stillness of the night, he heard a whining sound. He listened closer. It was coming from the airstrip. The other plane. Enrique's plane.

Jeremy's breath caught in his chest; he still had a chance. Jeremy sprinted, going faster than he'd ever run the 100-yard dash. The engine sound grew louder. There was a flash of white in the distance. Jeremy raced in front of the plane, waving. Could the pilot see him? There was still a faint light in the western sky.

"Stop," he shouted, though he knew he couldn't be heard. The pilot signaled to get out of the way. The plane moved forward, turning onto the airstrip.

"Wait," Jeremy screamed. He reached into his shirt pocket and waved a handful of bills.

The plane stopped. Jeremy rushed around to the side and got in.

"Who the hell are you?" asked the pilot.

Jeremy thought quickly. "One of the auditors."

"Then what are you doing here?"

Jeremy knew he looked like a wild man, his head and tee shirt dripping with blood. "I got lost. I fell. McNally probably left to get help."

The pilot wasn't buying it, but he seemed to be assessing the value of the bills in Jeremy's hand. "Sit down," the pilot said, relieving Jeremy of his money. He reached into a compartment and handed Jeremy a towel. "And try not to bleed everywhere."

Jeremy clasped his seatbelt and pressed the towel against his forehead. They were ten, fifteen minutes behind Bud. Maybe they'd catch up to him at the executive airport. But if not, he needed to figure out where Bud was going next.

The plane headed west, following the setting sun. The shades of crimson would have been spectacular under different circumstances, but now Jeremy felt as though they were flying directly into the mouth of hell.

It had all been a game to Bud. Setting up Enrique and Irv to battle each other to the death. A brilliant game. Now neither was alive to accuse Bud of any wrongdoing. Soon Bud would arrange that no one would be left alive to connect him to the drug trade and the murders. Then why hadn't Bud tried to kill Jeremy?

And then he remembered Bud's words. "I'll give Robbie your regards."

"Shit," Jeremy said.

The pilot glanced over at him.

"I need to make a call."

"This isn't your private fucking limo."

"It's an emergency."

The pilot studied the sky in front of him.

Jeremy reached into his pocket and pulled out two more hundreds. It was all he had except for a twenty in his wallet.

"One call," the pilot said, grabbing the money. "Thirty seconds. Give me the number."

Jeremy recited Judy Lieber's number from memory.

The pilot spoke into the phone, his voice so garbled, Jeremy wondered if the person at the other end could understand him. He handed the phone to Jeremy.

"This is Judy Lieber."

"It's Jeremy. I —"

"Sorry I'm not available," her voice mail continued. "Please leave a message and I'll get back to you."

"It's Jeremy Stroeb. Robbie Ivy's in danger. You need to get some protection to her house. Bud McNally will be there in about three hours. He, well, I think you know his plans."

"Time's up," the pilot said, reaching for the phone.

Jeremy held onto it. "Could I make just one more call?"

"Fuck you," the pilot said.

They landed at Opa Locka airport at 9:18 p.m., Miami time. There were several Lear jets parked, any one of which could have been the one Bud had taken, but there was no sign of him.

The customs agent did a perfunctory check of Jeremy's passport, but he studied the wound on Jeremy's head and the blood on his shirt for a minute or so before finally letting him through. Jeremy jogged out to the street and climbed into a waiting taxi. Luckily, the agent hadn't searched him and found the gun.

He gave the driver Robbie's address, then reached into his pocket for his cell phone. It wasn't there. Shit. He'd left it in his backpack, which was lying in some bushes at the summit of St. Mary's.

Jeremy leaned back against the cracked faux leather seat. There was nothing more he could do. Hopefully, Lieber had gotten his message and had arranged a stakeout at Robbie's house. The cab was filled with stale cigarette smoke, which each of Jeremy's long, slow breaths brought deep into his lungs. His head was throbbing, and he couldn't see very well. His eyelid had swollen up. It was a lot like the bruise on Robbie's head. He thought about later tonight, after Bud had been caught. Would he and Robbie laugh about their matching badges of honor? Would they take a hot bath together to soothe their aching muscles?

He'd been so curt with her this morning. So obsessed with rushing off to avenge his parents' murders that he hadn't told her how much she meant to him. Would he ever get the chance again?

The taxi pulled into her Coconut Grove neighborhood, navigating cautiously through the dark, dead-end streets. "Just let me out here," Jeremy said a block away. He handed the driver the twenty and took off down the street, slowing his pace a few houses from Robbie's. What if Lieber had a stakeout in progress and he came barging in? But what if she didn't? Maybe she'd never gotten his message.

He knocked on Robbie's front door, uncertain whether he was doing the right thing. His hand was on the gun in his pocket.

No answer.

Damn. He knocked again.

Through the door, he heard a tapping sound — crutches against tiles.

"Who's there?" Robbie called out.

"Robbie, it's me. Jeremy." She was all right. She was safe.

Robbie opened the door, throwing her arms around him. She balanced on her good leg as her crutches clattered against the floor. "Jeremy. Oh Jeremy."

He didn't want to let go.

Her bangs were over her eye, hiding the bruise on her forehead. "You're hurt," she said. "Do you need to go to the hospital?"

"I'm okay." He locked the door behind them. "Bud said he was coming here. I left a message for Detective Lieber."

"I know. She called me. She's out there. The house is surrounded by cops."

"Good," he said. "Good." He'd gotten to Lieber in time. He collapsed on the white sofa, then glanced down at the blood and dirt on his clothes and started to get up.

"Stay. I can always wash the covers."

She balanced on her crutches and came back a minute later with a liter bottle of water.

He drank it all down. Never in his life had he been so thirsty.

"Tell me what happened." She was barefoot in white velour sweatpants, one pants leg pulled up to the top of her cast. She'd almost persuaded Bud to take her out to St. Mary's with him. Then what would have happened to her?

"Irv and Enrique Castillo are dead."

"No." She flinched as though struck. "How?"

"They killed each other. Bud's little game. He lied to each of them, making them believe the other had murdered my mom. They went after each other like a couple of animals. I think they were both in love with her."

The muscles in Robbie's face relaxed, as though she'd just solved a puzzle. "So Bud's definitely behind everything."

"He has every move planned out, like a major chess game. And he doesn't make mistakes."

"How did you figure out he was coming here?"

"In the middle of the fighting, he said, 'I'll give Robbie your regards.' Then he sneaked away. I didn't realize he was gone until I saw his plane take off."

Robbie was turning her ring around her finger. "I wonder why he hasn't come."

Jeremy looked at the splattered red wax on the coffee table, reminded of the dried blood on Marina's face. "I don't know." He took a deep breath. "I don't know."

Then suddenly, he did.

"What?" Robbie touched his hand. "You look like you've seen a ghost."

The room was spinning. It was a trick. Another trick. He was up, pacing erratically, not knowing where to go, what to do.

"Jeremy." Robbie was alarmed, her face pale. "Talk to me. What is it?"

He threw open the front door. "Lieber," he shouted. "Lieber, are you out there? It was a trick. Lieber, come out."

Judy Lieber appeared from out of the darkness. "What is it? What's happened?"

"He set me up." Could she understand what he was saying? He was breathing so hard. "Bud set me up. He never planned to come here." He put his hand over his eyes. "I let him trick me. I let him."

"Where's he going, Jeremy?"

"To Elise. He's going to kill my sister."

Lieber spoke into a walkie-talkie, giving instructions, directions to his grandfather's house.

Robbie squeezed Jeremy's arm, a gesture to comfort him. But he had no time to be comforted. He'd let Bud trick him.

Take care of your sister.

He had failed them. Failed his parents in the worst possible way.

Cars were pulling out all around them, like a family of cockroaches suddenly awakened.

"I need your car," Jeremy said.

"Sure."

"Call Elise and my grandfather. Warn them."

His grandfather lived only a couple of miles away, on the other side of Coconut Grove, but the cul-de-sacs and the town's barriers made him feel as though he was navigating blindly through a maze.

Don't let me be too late.

Lieber would get there first. She and the rest of her posse. He wished he'd taken Robbie's phone so he could call his sister himself. He couldn't stand the not knowing.

He turned onto 27th Avenue, but was caught at the light. Just another few blocks. The light changed. He floored the accelerator. And then, he hit the brakes, coming to a screeching stop. The car behind him braked and honked.

A sick sensation spread over him. This morning Elise had said she wanted to stay at the house. That she needed to be there to help her remember. And Jeremy had only been half listening. He had wanted her out of there so he could find his father's gun. And he'd told her to come back later.

Had she done that? Had she gone back to Lotus Island? And if she had, would Bud know to find her there?

Jeremy made a sharp U-turn and sped down the street toward Miami Beach. The Grand Master was still one move ahead of him.

Chapter 54

Bud parked his black SUV behind a construction Dumpster on a vacant lot on North Bay Road and unloaded his bicycle. The sky was overcast, the moon hidden behind thick clouds. A lot like that other night, when he had readied their house by unscrewing the bulbs in the sconces on the portico.

He looked out toward the bay. Still and dark. It had been the perfect burial place for the shotgun, his night goggles, gloves, and the Stroebs' laptops along with any inconvenient information they might have contained.

He straddled the bike and took a deep breath, trying to calm the fluttering in his chest. He'd changed into a black shirt and black slacks on the plane, but he was already perspiring. The outer layer of his skin felt tingly, painful, as though all of his nerve endings were exposed. He couldn't understand it; everything was going so well. Every move a classic, straight out of Kasparov.

He guided the bike onto Lotus Island, careful to steer wide, outside the security camera's range. Then he glided over to the park, where he dropped the bike in the bushes, just as he had that other night.

Fools. Most of his opponents were fools. And that took much of the challenge out of the game. Of course, Rachel had never been a fool. And neither had her son.

In the shadow of one of the towering banyan trees, he composed himself. Thinking through his strategy one more time. That's what his mama had taught him. "Be certain of your next move, Bud. Don't let anyone rush you."

He was shaking. The air was thick and steamy, so why was he shaking? It was crazy; there was no reason to be nervous. He had everything under control. The key he'd taken from Rachel's brother-in-law was in his pocket. Did that moron even realize it was missing?

And he'd brought a special weapon. Not a sawed-off shotgun. Not a knife. This time it was more personal. This time her children would understand the pain he'd suffered. He'd make them understand why he couldn't let Rachel, or any of them, fuck up his life. Why he couldn't go back.

He shivered with the memory of the satisfaction he'd felt that night when their daughter had come home unexpectedly. He could have killed her, but it never would have been as gratifying as hearing her screams. A good lesson for that privileged little bitch, but this time he'd really make it stick.

He opened the buckle of his daddy's strap and slid it out of his pants. He held it close to his nose. Sometimes he imagined he could smell his own blood on it.

No, Daddy, no, Daddy. Little Bud huddled behind a chair, but the strap found him, cutting into his back, lashing across his shoulders, his bare buttocks. Snap, woosh, thwump.

You worthless piece of shit, Daddy said. Whap, woosh, thwump.

The sting, the pain. Little Bud screamed. *No, Daddy. No, Daddy*.

And when the whipping stopped, Bud heard only the sound of his broken sobs.

His mama, cooing as she rubbed ice on his wounds, kissed his tears, helped him into bed. Her hair was gray; a button missing from her blouse.

He could only lie on his stomach. He couldn't stop crying. He was just a little tyke. Five or six. And his mama brought out the tattered chessboard, the worn wooden pieces. *This is how the pawns move.* She showed him. *The rooks, the knights, the bishops.*

No, he cried. He didn't want to learn. He hurt too much.

She showed him again. There were scars on her cheeks and her nose leaned to the side where it had been broken. *Use your brains and get out of here. Then never come back, no matter what.*

The lashings continued.

You're a fake, his daddy said. *You might could build up your body and get yourself to a fancy school, but you'll never be more than a stinkin' piece of shit.*

And when Bud got word that his mama died while he was away at college, he didn't go back for her funeral.

Never come back, she had said.

She knew, he knew, if he went back, he'd kill his daddy, and that wasn't what she'd intended for him.

He threaded the strap back through the belt loops. The street was deserted. A couple of streetlights were out. But he stayed close to the hedges, just in case.

He'd risen to the top of one of the most successful firms in the country. He was quoted in business articles and had been featured on the cover of a national magazine.

And he knew his daddy had seen the success Bud Martin McNally had become.

You'll never be more than a stinkin' piece of shit.

No. No one would ever send him back.

He stood in the shadows of the tall hedges across from the Stroeb house, just as he had that other night.

The light in her daughter's bedroom was on.

Chapter 55

Elise pulled the towel off her head, then opened her bathroom door a few inches to let the steam out. Her damp hair hung against her bare shoulders and back. The speakers of her iPod were blaring a song from *Rent*. She wondered if Jeremy had come home yet. It was already after ten, and she hadn't seen or spoken with him since early this morning when she'd come by here with her grandfather. Jeremy had seemed annoyed with her, but maybe he was just preoccupied. She knew Jeremy had been involved with the girl who'd been murdered. That he must have cared about her.

"Marina." She said the name aloud. She'd always liked the sound of it. But now she was dead.

Elise shivered. Maybe it had been a stupid idea coming here. She'd double-checked all the doors and windows to make certain everything was locked, but she still felt jumpy. The house was too strange without Geezer. She wished Jeremy would come home soon.

She ran a wide-tooth comb through her hair, and water dripped from the ends onto the bath mat. She felt badly about lying to her grandfather. She had called him from school to tell him not to pick her up. She'd be staying on Lotus Island tonight, she'd told him. Carlos was giving her a ride. "Please don't worry about me, Grandpa. Jeremy's home."

But he was still worried. He'd argued with her, insisted that it wasn't safe. But Jeremy's here, she'd lied. He'll take care of me.

She couldn't have told her grandfather the truth. He never would have understood. How could he? It hardly made sense to her. For the last few weeks, she'd existed in a state of terror whenever she was alone in the house. But now that her memory had started coming back, she knew she needed to be here to remember. It frightened her, but it was the only way to make the nightmares stop.

Her mother would have understood.

She tightened the bath towel around her and stepped into her bedroom. One of her favorite songs was on — "Another Day."

She was almost there. Another day.

She dug through a drawer and pulled out her mother's tee shirt. Flora had washed it, but the outline of her mother's splattered blood was still visible. She kissed the three teardrops. Then she let the towel drop to the floor, slipped on a pair of panties, and pulled the tee shirt over her head.

A noise. Coming from downstairs. She froze, waiting. If it was Jeremy, he'd call up to her. He'd know she was home because he'd see the lights on.

She left the volume on her iPod turned up, but went to stand at her bedroom door. She opened it a crack and listened. The house was perfectly quiet.

It was her imagination. If someone had come in, she couldn't have heard anything with the music blasting and her door closed. She was overreacting because Dwight had spooked her. Then why was her heart racing?

She stepped barefoot into the hallway, moving along the wall. At the banister, she stopped, her back against the far wall so she couldn't be seen from downstairs. And then she heard it. The softest clink of metal, like a belt buckle. And then she felt it. A presence that sucked up the air around her. She became chilled and sweaty and light-headed. Don't pass out. Don't pass out.

She ducked as she darted past the landing and ran into her parents' room, closing the door behind her as quietly as she could.

The murderer was back. Just as she'd always known he would be. What to do? Where to hide? Had he heard her come in here?

Someone was climbing the stairs — slow, heavy. She was breathing too loudly. Could he hear her through the door? She covered her mouth.

The footsteps stopped. Please, please go away.

It seemed like forever. She was shaking so hard, she had to clench her jaws to keep her teeth from chattering.

Then she heard movement. He was going away, down the hall, toward her bedroom.

Her parents' bedroom was almost pitch-black. She darted under the oversized skirted chair in the corner, curled up in a little ball, and squeezed her eyes shut. If she couldn't see him, he couldn't see her.

Her nest smelled dusty, stale, a bit like Geezer. But she could smell something else.

A paralyzing fear crept over her. She was remembering.

The foyer, it was dark. So dark. And it smelled metallic, smoky.

Carlos was shouting at her. "Come on, Elise. Let's go. I'm leaving."

A shadow moved. A shadow without a face — no nose, no mouth, no hair, just bulging eyes. Bug eyes. Staring at her. But she couldn't move.

Your mama's calling you.

And now she remembered running up the stairs shouting. *Mommy, Daddy. Mommy, Daddy.*

Their bedroom door was open. The footsteps were closer. Now? Then? It was all mixed up in her head.

Don't turn on the light. Don't turn on the light.

But suddenly brightness flooded the room. Elise screamed. *Mommy, Daddy.*

Where were they? Why was everything splattered with red paint? Red paint and strewn garbage. All over the bed, on the walls, the floor. Everything such a mess. Their pretty, neat bedroom such a mess.

Mommy, Daddy?

Her mother's hand. Her mother's hand was reaching for her.

I promise I'll never leave you.

"Mommmeeeee," she screamed.

Someone was pulling her. Pulling her out of her nest.

She stared at their bed. The mess was gone. The blood was gone. Her mother's hand was gone.

The light went out. Someone gripped her, wrapping his arms around her, whispering in her ear, his breath foul. "Your mama's not calling you anymore."

Chapter 56

Jeremy saw the light on in Elise's bedroom. He jumped out of Robbie's car before it had come to a full stop and raced to the front door. Unlocked. He pushed it open, hesitating for a split second before running up the stairs, his father's gun in his hand.

"Elise," he shouted.

In the distance, he could hear music — the soundtrack from *Rent*.

The door to his parents' bedroom was open, the room dark. Jeremy braked, realizing he was backlighted to the murderer. He ducked down, pulling the door shut behind him, closing himself and his parents' murderer into a tomb of darkness.

Please, Ellie. Be safe.

His heart was pounding wildly in his chest.

A movement gave away Bud's location; near the window by the head of the bed. What had he done with Elise? What was he planning?

Jeremy could hear two sets of breathing, one rough and labored, the other rapid, light. Elise. She was alive.

Jeremy crept along the edge of the room and felt the wall just above the baseboard. His hand touched the emergency flashlight that his father kept in each of the bedrooms. He pulled it out of its outlet, pointing it toward a vague shadow, the gun in his other hand.

He flicked on the switch. A beam of light fell across his parents' bed. Across his sister.

She was lying on her stomach wearing only panties and a tee shirt. Her feet and hands were tied, a gag in her mouth. Her eyes were terrified.

Bud stood over her, a gun pressed against her head, a worn leather strap in his other hand.

"Jeremy, my boy. Glad you were able to make it." Bud flicked the strap in the air, causing the gun to press harder against Elise.

Jeremy felt an uncontrollable rage toward this monster. This monster who had killed his parents, Marina, and now, what had he done to his sister?

Jeremy aimed the gun, still holding the flashlight in his other hand. He had a clean shot, but if he fired, Bud would pull the trigger of his own gun and kill Elise.

The monster was grinning. "Game ain't much fun without the queen, is it, boy?" Perspiration was running down Bud's cheeks, into his eyes, but he didn't wipe it away. He cracked the belt in the air like a whip. Whap, woosh, clank. The buckle swung at the free end.

"I don't reckon you kids ever felt the sting of a strap on your sweet, tender, rich little asses? No, not you. Not in your world. You have no idea what it's like growing up in shit. Comin' from nothin'. Just your daddy's beatings to get you going. You and your sister and your mama — y'all think the world's a tough place when your cable TV's broke or you can't get an Internet connection." Bud's eye was twitching, his accent growing thicker. "Y'all don't know, don't understand. When ya pull yourself up out of a shit pile and make somethin' of your life, you ain't gonna let nobody take it 'way from you. Ya hear me? Ya hear what I'm saying?" He snapped the strap; it came down across Elise's butt with a thwump and she let out a muffled cry.

"Damn you, Bud," Jeremy shouted, stepping closer. "You want to hit someone, hit me. Or do you feel powerful like your daddy when he whipped you? Come on, Bud. Hit me. What kind of chess game is it — all queens against all pawns?"

Bud threw his head back and laughed. His movement changed the angle of his gun so it pointed away from Elise.

Jeremy fired. The sound reverberated in the room.

"What the fuck?" Blood spurted from Bud's shoulder. He seemed momentarily stunned by the sight, as though the blood couldn't possibly be his.

Pain. Jeremy wanted this monster to feel pain. He fired again, catching the top of Bud's ear, spraying blood as if from a broken sprinkler head over Elise.

The second shot reawakened the stunned ogre. "Fuck," he bellowed as he raised his gun toward Jeremy. "You fuck with me, boy?"

Jeremy flicked off the flashlight and dove over his sister, firing into the space where Bud stood. The echo settled into silence. Had he missed?

And then, Jeremy saw a flash followed by another deafening bang. Jeremy's gun flew out of his hand. It felt like someone had driven a stake through his palm as warm liquid pulsed out.

The monster was just above him. A thick moving shadow.

Elise shifted beneath him, her body trembling uncontrollably.

Take care of your sister.

Whap, woosh, clank. The strap stung Jeremy's back and a searing pain cut into his neck. The belt buckle clanked.

Jeremy reached his bleeding hand toward the sound. He caught the belt buckle, holding tight as he jerked it out of the monster's hands. Jeremy thrashed the strap wildly at the shadow just above him. Whap, woosh. Whap, woosh. Whap, woosh, thwump. Bud yelped like an injured dog. "Mother fucker."

Something hard smashed into Jeremy's head. He felt himself falling, falling into darkness. *Hold on*, a voice in his head said. *You can do it.*

His father was shouting from the sidelines, jumping up and down. *Come on, Jeremy. Faster, faster. Beat 'em. You can do it. You can do it!*

Jeremy ran, faster, faster. His heart pounding through his chest, his breath coming in short gasps. And when he broke through the finish line, gagging and dizzy and ready to collapse, his dad was there, hugging him tight. So tight.

I'm proud of you, son.

Running feet. Running feet getting closer as he floated away.

"Dad," he called, as he felt the weightlessness. "Dad, I'm sorry."

"Freeze. Police."

As he floated into brightness. Movement, blurs. Everything in motion.

"Freeze. Police."

Something hard and cold against Jeremy's forehead.

"Drop the gun, McNally."

Ellie trembled beneath him.

Take care of your sister.

Jeremy stared into the brightness. The shadow took form. Blood covered McNally's face, skin hanging in flaps, rage in his eyes. And pain. The monster was in pain.

He pressed the barrel harder into Jeremy's head.

Jeremy had caused the monster pain.

"Drop the gun, McNally," someone shouted.

"Fuck you all," Bud McNally said, blood spilling out of him. His hand was shaking, as though engaged in an intense arm wrestle. Slowly, slowly, the gun turned away from Jeremy. Bud fought it, fought the movement as the barrel of his gun turned toward his own face, into his mouth.

His mother's breath was warm against Jeremy's cheek, her voice a whisper in his ear. *I promise I'll never leave you.*

A single shot rang out.

McNally's brains splattered on the clean white wall.

They formed a curious image.

Like that of a falling chess king.

Epilogue

Geezer was covered with shampoo. He looked from Jeremy to Elise with a distressed expression. Then he shook his body, and water and suds went flying everywhere in their grandfather's kitchen.

"I thought you knew how to give him a bath," Elise said, laughing.

Jeremy marveled at that. Elise laughing. The bruise on her cheek where Dwight had hit her was gone. How much longer would the scars of the last few months take to fade? Elise had been going to therapy regularly since the trauma in their parents' house, but Jeremy doubted she would ever completely get over the memory of seeing her parents' mutilated bodies that night and the horror of almost being killed herself.

"I suppose I should cut you some slack." Her stutter was miraculously gone. "You do only have one useable hand."

"Thank you." Jeremy glanced down at his bandaged hand. The bullet had punctured an artery, broken a bone, and torn up a ligament, but the doctor assured him he'd be good as new in a few weeks. Though taking up the violin wouldn't be a smart idea.

Elise pulled the hose attachment out and ran warm water over Geezer's back, careful to keep the soapsuds out of the dog's eyes and ears. She lifted Geezer's loose skin and washed away all of the shampoo.

Elise had moved in with their grandfather in Coconut Grove.

Their parents' house on Lotus Island was on the market, but as the real estate agent pointed out, it would likely be a while before it was sold, and then probably to a foreign investor who didn't know, or care, about the house's history.

After Dwight's disbarment, Jeremy and his grandfather had successfully petitioned the court for joint guardianship of Elise. Judy Lieber called from time to time to keep them informed of the case. The SEC had taken over, and Liliam Castillo, CEO and majority shareholder of Castillo Enterprises, had been indicted for stock fraud and her involvement in an extensive money laundering scheme. "Imagine," Lieber had said one day. "Liliam Castillo continues to vehemently deny any knowledge of the drug operations. She says she was tricked."

"Does anyone believe her?" Jeremy had asked.

"Are you kidding?" Lieber had said.

There were voices on the porch. Robbie and their grandfather had returned.

"Okay, Geezer." Jeremy towel dried the dog, then placed him gently on the floor. Geezer gave another shake.

Elise pushed her sleek dark hair behind her ear. She'd recently cut it, and the resemblance to their mother was more pronounced than ever. "What about his next bath?" she said.

"You don't really want to rely on me for Geezer's next bath, do you? He gets pretty damn stinky."

She wasn't smiling. "I'll miss you."

"I know, Ellie." He kissed the top of his sister's head. "I'll miss you, too."

The old Corvair sparkled in the sunlight. Robbie was wearing shorts and a tee shirt, no makeup, but she was as beautiful as ever. She had gotten her cast off recently and her right leg hadn't yet regained all its muscle and definition. Jeremy hoisted her suitcase into the trunk and slammed it closed. With the imminent collapse of Piedmont, Coleridge, and Miller — once the twentieth largest CPA firm in the country — Robbie had decided to take a break from the business world.

Jeremy's grandfather was rubbing his cheek. He had on a clean shirt, and the thick lenses of his eyeglasses shone with clarity. Jeremy extended his hand, but his grandfather pulled Jeremy against him. "You and Robbie come back to us safe."

Jeremy was reluctant to let go of the man who once carried him high on his shoulders so he could see the world from a fresh perspective. "We will, Grandpa."

Elise's eyes were bright with tears. His little sister.

He ran his fingers through her hair, missing the weight of her long thick braid. He imagined she felt freer without it. The umbilical cord finally cut.

Always take care of your sister, his mother had said.

Well, he'd done the best he could. Now it was time to take care of himself.

He and Robbie climbed into the car and pulled away. He could see his sister and grandfather in the rearview mirror, waving good-bye.

The silence felt heavy and awkward as he fumbled for a tape.

"What's that?" Robbie asked.

"Something my dad used to play." Jeremy popped the old tape into the cassette deck. "He loved classical music."

The car filled with the measured, stately entrance of the clarinets. And although he knew what was coming next, Jeremy was still startled by the attack of the brass, then soothed by the blending of the choral voices.

"It's beautiful," Robbie said.

"Mozart's *Requiem*. A Mass in honor of the dead. I never appreciated it before, but my father said someday I'd find comfort in it."

"And do you?"

"Over the last few months, I've learned how little I know about life. About my parents. Who I really am. I was always running from them. I believed they were so different from me that we couldn't possibly understand each other."

"And now?" She took his hand.

"I've learned we're the same. Their blood runs in me, and that's a bond that can never be broken."

He drove the car over the Julia Tuttle Causeway and came to the crest. The bay spread out before them. Jeremy had no specific mission, no tangible goal. But he knew his parents would always be with him. That they had never left him.

The woodwinds were sweet, pulling him in, reassuring him.

His hands settled into the grooves of the steering wheel.

He hoped his parents could rest in peace now, even as he knew his own journey was just beginning.

Dona eis requiem, sang the chorus.

Yes, Jeremy thought. Rest now, Mom and Dad.